# Wisdom of the Ages

Robert Bernardo

 Bernardo Entertainment Company LLC

Bernardo Entertainment Company LLC-Grapevine, TX
Paperback ISBN: 978-0-578-60141-0
Title: *Wisdom of the Ages*
Author: Robert Bernardo
Available formats: Paperback
eBook Distribution

This is for Lisa, Adam, David & Emily.

# Preface

It is with great trepidation that I share my story with you because ignorance is bliss in this case—although I feel you have every right to know what is going on behind the scenes in our troubled world. The truth is, we've been at war with a hidden enemy for centuries, and yet there is no mention of this struggle in any book, until now. So, proceed with caution. Some of the passages in this novel are shocking, but accurate down to the last drop of blood, sweat, and the myriad of tears it took to complete this journey of nine lifetimes.

# Chapter One
### *Rude Awakening*

I'm a helpless passenger stuck behind the wheel of a runaway car. Around and around I go up a steep mountain. Spiraling toward a hazy peak. I seem to know this bumpy road that I drive upon. Almost like the back of my sweaty hand. I'm suddenly forced to put the pedal to the metal and I'm now speeding past every turn when I desperately want to hit the brakes! Around and around I go, until the trees become a blur of green and I can now add dizzy to my delirious state. "Help!" I wail for the hell of it because I know there is no helping me at this point. If only I could stop this blasted car! If only I could turn around. If only…

I finally reach the sunny summit, high above the clouded sky, where my car streaks past the gates of hell and stops in front of a quaint colonial structure that I recall being referred to as the Big House, which still looks as hauntingly inviting as ever. I see that the front door is ajar and that it is dark inside. I'd give anything to leave before anyone spots me, except that my body has other plans.

Yes… save for my swiveling head, the rest of me is out of my control. I've got no choice but to leave the relative safety of my rented Chevy, where I catch a whiff of honeysuckle amid the cool pine that suddenly fills my lungs. The incredibly fresh air is soothing to inhale. Even invigorating. I soon feel rejuvenated like I'm a teenager again! Although, there is also something horribly draining about this mystical place that leaves me feeling worn to the bone.

But if my eyes are to tell the story, the flowers still seem surreal here at the Kilborne Academy because every plant is always in perfect bloom during normal business hours. I see purple butterflies dancing in a garden of bright orange tulips, while songbirds croon away in a forest of majestic oaks. There is also a sparkling hint of the enormous Great Lake that is nestled in the rocky canyon behind the Big House, which itself sits upon an acre of freshly cut bluegrass.

Paradise comes to mind when I look around and yet I still want to, "Turn around!" I demand of myself. "Turn around!"

Instead, I can't help but walk with a purpose toward the front door of the haunted abode, like I'm coming home for the holidays. "Turn around, you fool! Turn around before it's too late!"

Powerless to heed my own warnings, I'm soon through the entrance, where I come to a stop after the door shuts behind me. "Hello?" I whisper in the dark. My eyes have to adjust to the flickering candlelight; then I find that the empty entry hall is just like I remember it from forty years ago—now that my memory of being at this strange and mysterious reform school was restored on the long drive I was forced to take here this morning. "Hello?" I query a little louder this time. "Is anyone here?"

All things considered, I'm somewhat relieved to get no response. I then take the opportunity to turn my head toward the painting hanging on the wall to my right. Bushy black hair dominates the canvas. It's a far cry from the neatly cropped salt and pepper I have nowadays. And a few wrinkles have replaced pimples, but otherwise, it's almost like looking in an old mirror. I want to move in for a closer look at the dusty oil portrait, although my feet take me in the direction of the staircase on the opposite wall. I know better than to scream for help for fear of waking the dead. But I then think of all the pain and suffering I experienced here, and it causes me to yelp, then softly cry: "Help!" To which there is no reply.

At the top of the stairs is a narrow catwalk that I recall seeing from my prior visit. It leads to a set of double doors that are closed. I'm forced to work my way up the stairs and stop in front of those doors and I gasp when they fly open. Much to my relief, it's nothing more than an empty cedar closet. It's then that I hear the pitter-patter of little feet running the rafters above. Rats! My head is on a swivel, but I still can't see them—although I hear the little critters closing in all around me. I desperately want to run. Yet here I stand. Frozen in place. Helpless to do anything other than count each terrifying second with my hammering heart. I once again succumb to my fears and cry out for help—only louder this time. "Help!" But with the exception of the pitter-patter of little rat feet, I still get no response.

With my stomach in knots, I'm anything but hungry, until I catch that first whiff of the buffet and it's like I haven't eaten in several days—maybe even weeks! I savor a myriad of mesmerizing flavors wafting up from the dining hall, before slowly exhaling. I hunger for my next breath… and the one after that. I'm soon lightheaded, yet willing to swallow my last breath at this point. I'll do anything to have that taste in my mouth. Anything! I rub my growling belly and realize I've regained control of my body for the first time since the day began. I jump for joy just to make sure I can, then say to myself: *To hell with the freaky food, I'm getting out of here while I still can!* That said, I race down the stairs, looking to make my departure before ghostly Fitzhugh and his three little bitches show up and have their way with me. But by the time I reach the front door, I've somehow convinced myself to put my departure on hold just long enough to hit that killer buffet one last time before I go.

As if in a hypnotic trance, I do an about-face at the exit and move toward the dangers that await me inside the dark opening under the catwalk. I avoid the drool coming down from the buffalo head above the opening and then I'm in the black hallway, which is still blacker than black, if not for a layer of Green Fog that illuminates the ground with its green glow. And I'm quickly reminded that with the Green Fog comes the constant hissing of what sounds like a thousand snakes accompanied by the sweet smell of honeysuckle that is as intoxicating as ever.

To top it off, a loud chorus of eerie voices can now be heard above the hissing. There are barking boys to the east, where I smell the dining hall waiting at that end of the long and narrow hallway. And giggling girls to the west, where I remember the hallway leading to a room that sleeps the twenty teenage victims who are forced here to this horrible, godforsaken place every summer. Victims like the thousands of lost souls who never made it back home. Victims like the ones calling out to me now…

"You still look like you're in great shape, Johnny Boy!" bark the boys. "Come this way and join the brotherhood!"

"We've missed seeing your pretty blue eyes, Johnny," giggle the girls. "Come our way and let us taste you again!"

I'm reasonably sure I'm blushing. But instead of seeing red, I'm aglow in green from the waist down with my feet lost in the fog. The rest of me is in the dark, although I can feel my ears ringing. I'm being hammered as we speak. It doesn't take long for the constant rants of the boys and girls to take a toll on me. I begin to quiver. Honeysuckle perfumes the air with every word the girls groan. I can feel their soft lips. And their many hands and fingers teasing my tingly flesh. My mind ablaze, it seems like only yesterday I stood conflicted in this very spot with these two powerful forces vying mightily for my attention. Except that I now know the giggling girls will try and suck the life out of me if I wander west, so I stay the course and head east toward the feast, knowing it'll be a sausage fest all the way to the dining hall. But the girls do not go down without a fight. They coo and boo this happily married man who is thrice their age, then tease and taunt the heck out of me as I leave them behind in favor of the growing cheers and jeers of the barking boys.

"That's right, Johnny Boy… keep walking this way!"

Each step brings tantalizing new flavors to my nose, but I'm also confronted with enough testosterone to fill a thousand locker rooms.

"Don't leave, Johnny," plead the fading girls. "Come back this way and you can sleep with all seven hundred of us!"

Rather than retreat in favor of those incredibly sexy, albeit shamefully young voices, I cover my ringing ears until the last temptress is out of earshot. Meanwhile, the boys grow louder to where I can feel their ghoulish presence resonating all around me. My skin crawls even faster than I can run, yet run I do, finally coming to a stop at the entrance to the dining hall. My eyes need a moment to adjust to the candlelight, as the fog disappears behind me and the boys go silent now that I'm out of the hallway. All is quite except for one harrowing voice that I know all too well. "Welcome back, Johnny," Marty says, impishly. "I see you've put on a few years since we last met."

My eyes lock in on the grungy looking hipster standing in the middle of the otherwise empty dining hall. "And you're still just like I remember you," I say, noticing he's even still wearing that same old black Led Zeppelin tee shirt draped over his lean frame with the faded blue jeans covering his long legs. His cowboy boots are looking none-the-worse-for-wear—still broken down just like the day I met him.

"Grab a plate," he insists. "We've got some catching up to do."

I meet Marty by a stack of plates and a chill runs down my spine after looking deep into his evil brown eyes, but the buffet owns me to where not even standing next to this demonic teenager is enough to send me packing.

"So, you've really been here all this time?" I ask, gingerly… not wanting to offend.

"Been stuck here on sweet sixteen for forty years," he answers, curtly. "And quite frankly, I've grown a little tired of it."

I nod, sympathetically. "I hope you don't blame me for that?"

"The past is the past," he replies. "Let's eat!"

His words of wisdom cut through the growing tension like a hot knife slashing through warm butter. Without saying another word, I grab a plate and begin nibbling my way through a world of incredible edibles, until my plate is full and so is my belly. And even though I know I'm playing with fire it still doesn't keep me from wanting more and more of the fatally attractive food. Chewing away, I cautiously follow Marty to a round table and sit opposite him, noticing he hardly has anything on his plate.

I burp. "Excuse me."

"No problem, man."

"I see you're not eating much."

"I've learned to pace myself over the decades."

I glance down at fried chicken that's clucking my name. "Easier said than done."

"Yeah… but if ya swallow too much of that killer stuff, it'll be the last thing ya ever do."

I tremble mightily knowing he's right. I'll never see family and friends again, if I can't somehow find the inner strength to stop feeding the ravenous monster that lies within. Still, it's a bitch to lose the fork to the table and nudge the plate away—though I do. "So, why am I here?" I ask, wanting to take my mind off the surreal feast by cutting to the chase. "Why now after all this time?"

"You're here cause ya never finished your hundred-day sentence when you were a punk kid," he answers. "Did ya honestly think you could escape Kilborne and Fitzhugh would just let ya go the rest of your life without ever jacking with ya again?"

"Look… I didn't know you or Fitzhugh or this evil place even existed, until a few hours ago when this knowledge just popped into my head after I lost control of my body and couldn't avoid coming back here no matter how hard I tried to turn my car around."

"That's cause Fitz used his black magic to keep ya in the dark all these years, until now that you're back under his control."

The pieces of this horrific puzzle begin to take shape in my once clueless mind and it all suddenly makes sense to me, and it's like I've just been hit with a ton of bricks knowing that I'm in some serious trouble. The kind of trouble I can't talk or buy my way out of. The kind of trouble a team of hotshot lawyers can't save me from. The kind of trouble that could last an eternity if I'm not careful. "So, what happens next?" I ask with bated breath, because it's the only breath I've got left.

He smiles, smugly. "Honestly, I don't know what kind of cruel punishment Fitz has in store for you, but I'm sure it's gonna set ya back a few years at the very least."

Overwhelmed with grief, I become teary-eyed. "But I have a wife and kids now and a business to run!"

"You got no one to blame but yourself for trying to escape this haunted dump, when we were both told it couldn't be done."

My head hurts and my stomach is singing the blues. "I don't feel so good."

He snickers. "I guess the food here is even too rich for a wealthy man like you."

"I can't keep my eyes open."

"Then maybe you won't mind if I steal your ride."

"What?" I stiffen to where it feels like rigor mortise has set in and watch helplessly as Marty comes around the table and robs me of my car keys and wallet. The next thing I know it's like I died and went to heaven. But instead of heaven, it turns out that I'm lost in the fog somewhere at the Kilborne Academy, where I find myself bouncing around from one century to another, like I'm on an amusement ride for the ages. The seconds pass like hours and the hours like seconds, until time becomes a timeless thing without beginning nor end. My travels continue unabated, until I eventually land back in the present, feeling like I should be exhausted after all that I just experienced, except that I wake incredibly refreshed and alert. Scanning the table, I notice the food on my plate is still warm, so I know I haven't been out near as long as it had seemed, although long enough for Marty to be gone.

"Marty!"

I quickly jump up and race after him. Down the hallway I go to a cacophony of barks and giggles, stopping at the halfway point where my picture is hanging large in the entry hall. I run for the now open front door and much to my relief; save for a thin layer of greenish dust, there's my white rental car just as I had left it—although there is no sign of Marty that I can see. I check the car and I'm pleasantly surprised to find my keys sitting in the front seat, but my wallet is still missing along with all of my credit cards and about five hundred dollars in cash.

"Marty! I know you're hiding out here somewhere. Come out! I won't hurt ya. I just want my credit cards back and you can keep the cash." Although extremely anxious to leave the reform school from hell while I still can, I allow fifteen seconds to pass without getting a response. "Hello, Marty… are you out here?"

Just to be sure, I check the trunk and find it empty. It then occurs to me that I should cancel the credit cards, but my phone is dead. Still, no worries though… because I feel like I'm on Cloud Nine when I see the Kilborne Academy in the rearview mirror. So much so that I'm oblivious to everything around me on my return to civilization, until I finally arrive back at my sister's house where this bizarre odyssey began early this morning.

All is good though, until Emily opens her front door and screams at the sight of me, before falling to the ground in a heap. I immediately scoop her off the tile floor and deposit my fainted sister on her living room couch. Adding to the confusion, I just now notice that she has more gray than blonde streaming from her head and more wrinkles than she had yesterday when I flew into town.

"Emily, wake up! It's me, Johnny."

She begins to stir. Mutters something, then pops up and gives me a wide-eyed once over like she's looking at a ghost. "Johnny!" she shrieks. "Johnny!" She then plops back down and is out cold again, as if seeing me was too much for her to handle.

I stand in disbelief. "Emily, wake up. Emily!"

# Chapter Two
### *Heart of Gold*

I'm parched to the point of feeling like there's a big wad of cotton stuck in my throat after shouting Emily's name to no avail, so I leave my snoring sister behind on the couch and head for something cold and refreshing in her kitchen. But I'm floored after seeing that it's been completely renovated during the few hours I've been gone.

I check the rest of the house and find it full of change, then reflect on my strange morning with Marty and realize that there really is no escaping the Kilborne Academy. Even here the creepy reform school seems to be very much in play, but to what extent? I grow even more parched thinking of the dreadful possibilities, yet I decide to put my thirst on hold and run back to the living room and shake Emily repeatedly, until she gasps when our eyes meet again.

"Johnny?" she says, dreamily. "Where've ya been?" she adds with a playful smile, like she's all in on some gag.

"Well… I've had a crazy morning if that's what you mean?"

"A crazy morning?" she questions, hysterically.

I immediately stiffen. "How long have I been gone?" I nervously inquire after first glancing at her grayish hair.

She shrugs, mindlessly. "At least a decade."

"Be serious!"

"Yep," she is quick to return. "At least ten years have passed since you flew in from Texas for the weekend to help move mother to a nursing home, but then you spent the night here at my house and disappeared early Saturday morning without so much as a goodbye."

I swallow hard seeing that my sister is not trying to be funny anymore. "How's Mom doing?"

"She's dead, Johnny!"

I'm taken aback. "What?"

"She died four years ago. The whole family was gathered at her funeral… except you."

"Hmmm… I don't know whether to believe you or not."

"Oh really?" she returns, as if offended. "Everyone was looking for you as that Saturday wore on after you went missing. Finally, the police were called in that evening and then it became a full-fledged manhunt. They even investigated *us* after nothing turned up in the weeks that followed. But in the end… you and your rental car where never found. So, it was like for reasons unknown, you just decided to vanish off the face of the earth."

Now I'm the one who is offended. "C'mon, Emily… you know I wouldn't do a thing like that!"

She suddenly gasps, then has a curious look on her face as she reaches out to touch me. "At first, I was just playing along with you cause I thought I was having some really strange dream where I finally got to blow off some steam at you for disappearing on us like you did, but I'm not dreaming this… am I?"

I sigh, forlornly. "If you are, it's one hell of a nightmare."

Wide-eyed, she jumps up to give me a hug. "Johnny! Johnny! It's so good to see you again! Oh my gosh… where've you been all this time and how come you haven't aged a day in all these years?"

Knowing the truth will only lead to more questions, I offer a clueless shrug. "Look, Emily… I don't know what's going on here, but I should call Leslie."

"Johnny… there's something you should know."

I brace for bad news—because it's written all over her suddenly pale face. "What? What is it, Emily?"

She clears the frog from her throat and it almost takes my breath away. "Ah… well, Johnny… you were officially presumed dead a few years back and so Leslie remarried."

"What? Are you serious?"

She nods in a way that feels like death is coming. "Yes… I'm afraid so."

I'm beyond stunned. "And what about my kids?"

"Adam and Liz are both doing fine, but they're grown up now."

"Surely you're joking about all this?" I croak. "Surely you are?"

"No, Johnny… I'm afraid not. A lot has changed since you've been gone."

I shake my wary head and plop down on the couch. "This hurts so bad it feels like I've just been sucker-punched in the gut. I can't believe all these sudden changes. That what you say is really true. I can't! I can't! Oh, my... I feel like I'm going to be sick. I really do!"

She dabs at her forming tears. "It was the not knowing and all the finger-pointing that killed us. In the end, I just hoped someone would find your remains to bring closure to this horrible mess, but there wasn't even that." She takes a deep breath and whines. "You could've at least called someone to let us know you were still alive!"

"Look, Emily... I went out to get a coffee at Starbuck's early this morning and a few hours later this is the world I've come back to!"

She smirks while rolling her glassy eyes. "Do you really expect me to believe that?"

"Would you rather I make something up?"

"So, you're telling me you've been hiding out at Starbuck's all these years?" she probes with an exaggerated snicker. "And you really expect me to believe that?"

Again, I think of Kilborne. "If I tell you where I've really been, you'll think I've gone plum crazy."

She giggles. "Look, Johnny... this whole thing is crazy, so maybe if you tell me the truth, maybe then I can make some sense of it all."

"Okay, fine. I'll tell you everything I know about the incredibly strange morning I've had. But I'm warning you, Emily... I'm not so sure you or anyone can handle the truth in this case."

"Try me."

"First catch me up on the rest of the family."

"Deal!"

We head for the kitchen where I quench my thirst with spring water, then spend a shocking hour hearing stories of all the changes while seeing the startling family pictures on her fancy phone. It's terribly gut-wrenching to see what I've missed, good times and bad. But Emily can't wait to hear my story, so I gather myself and give it to her as best I can, which makes her laugh and cry when not looking at me like I've gone completely mad, and I haven't even gotten to the really weird stuff yet. "I warned you this was crazy."

I'm relieved when I notice she's no longer taking me seriously, as it affords me the opportunity to change the subject to something more palatable. But then her husband comes home from work and we start the process all over again once he recovers from his fainting spell. I can tell Mark has put on a few pounds. I know this because I have to help lift him off the ground and put him in a seat at the table, with Emily sitting on one side of him and me on the other.

"Hello, Mark. Are you all right?"

"Johnny?" he replies. "Is that really you?"

"Yeah, Mark… it's me."

"What happened to you?"

I can't help but frown at my pending response. "Apparently, I've been gone a while."

"But you haven't aged a day."

"Johnny has some really interesting stories to tell," Emily chimes in. "You'll never believe this haunted house he's been telling me about."

Mark suddenly looks at me suspiciously. "I hope it's not true what's been said about you, Johnny."

"What's that?" I inquire, defensively.

"That you were on the run from *something big* and were hiding out somewhere off the grid."

"No, Mark. Nothing could be further from the truth."

"Well, that's what many in the media speculated."

I perk in surreal fashion—because everything seems surreal at this point. "I made the news?"

"You had national coverage!" he informs. "People were searching the world for you and that rental car, when they weren't busy camping out in our front yard waiting for your return. But the only trace of you turned out to be the small suitcase you left behind in our basement along with an old-time silver coin."

I gasp. "Where are those things now?"

"The police took them as evidence," Emily offers. "But they were eventually turned over to Leslie."

"I should warn her about that coin!"

Mark snickers, loudly. "I'm sure she's hocked that thing by now along with just about everything else you ever owned, now that her new husband has run your business empire into the ground."

"Yeah, Emily told me all about the husband," I say, ruefully. "I wonder what they're doing for money these days?"

He shrugs, haplessly. "Last I heard they were still living large off the millions of dollars in insurance money they got from your death settlement." He hew-haws. "I guess the insurance company is going to want their money back now."

"Hmmm… I don't know… this just doesn't sound like the Leslie I know and love."

"She changed after you did your vanishing act," he states. "And so did your kids! It was like the silver spoon was suddenly yanked from their surprised mouths, with you going from being 'Mr. Amazing' in everyone's eyes to becoming the guy who abandoned his family and employees… leaving them to fend for themselves, until all was lost."

Frustrated beyond words, I'm about ready to cry when Emily's fancy phone distracts me by playing a catchy tune. "It's David!" she smiles. "Won't he be surprised to hear the news!" She quickly answers the call from our brother. "David," she shouts into the sleek device, while looking my way. "You'll never guess who's here!" Her smile is suddenly replaced by a look of shock followed by bewilderment. "You know? How could you know?" She hands me the phone. "Here, he wants to talk to you."

David starts speaking the second I put the phone to my ear. "Hello, Johnny! We've got a lot of catching up to do now that you've risen from the dead, so why don't you come out to California and stay with us for a while? We've got plenty of room."

"Sounds great, David. I guess I will have to start thinking about a place to crash now that Leslie has a new man in her life. Did you know about that?"

"Yeah, Johnny… she remarried a few years ago."

"Seems like only yesterday she was dropping me off at the airport." I groan in silence while thinking of our last goodbye. "I really need to go see her and the kids, David… but from what Emily and Mark have told me, I no longer have a penny to my name!"

"I know. It must be a real shocker for a rich guy like you to come back to this, Johnny… but fear not. It just so happens my boss is in New York on business and he's willing to fly you back to Texas in his private jet, if you like?"

"Wow! That's mighty generous of him."

"Yeah, well… apparently you two have some history together."

"Oh, really? What's his name?"

"Marty."

"Marty?" I query, wide-eyed. "The only Marty I know is a creepy reform school kid."

"He didn't mention anything about a reform school, just that I should welcome you back with open arms and save the questions for later."

"David, I don't know if you realize this, but you're talking about the guy who stole my wallet this morning."

He laughs. "I highly doubt that. Maybe if you look around Emily's house you might find a current picture of him on the cover of some money magazine. After all, he's well on his way to becoming the richest man in the world. Or better yet… come out to the limo in front of her house and see Marty in person."

"Limo? What limo?"

"The one that's pulling up now."

I run to the living room window and see a shiny black stretch pulling up in front of my dusty white rental car out by the street. "Are you in that thing?"

"No, just Marty and the driver. He wants to talk to you in private."

"What about?"

"Believe it or not, he wants to offer you a job."

"A job?" I snicker under my breath. "What kind of job?"

"He claims you're the smartest man on the planet next to him."

I laugh, incredulously. "Do you really believe nonsense like that?"

"Look, Johnny… if someone like Marty says it, I believe it! Although, if you ask me the honest truth about it, I always thought you were more lucky than smart, until you disappeared."

"Well… I'm not feeling lucky at the moment."

"Bullshit! Everyone on the planet would kill to crack Marty's inner circle, and here you are being invited in on your first day back amongst the living."

"I guess maybe I should be flattered, David… but I still have good reason to be leery of your boss."

"Be leery all you want, but to know him like I do is to truly admire the guy for what he brings to the table, and to love him for how generous he is with his time and money. Honestly, if you ask me… he's been sent here by God to save us from ourselves."

"Ha, I've never heard you praise anyone like that before."

"That's because I've never met anyone like Marty before."

"Yeah, he's a different kind of cat alright."

"Look… all I know is that he's been an absolute pleasure to work for over the last five years and he wants to fly you out to California this afternoon and give you a personal tour of our corporate office and manufacturing facility because he thinks you guys can make beautiful music together. But if you'd rather not take him up on the offer of a lifetime, he's more than willing to drop you off in Texas on his way home."

"Well… I'm sure there has to be some sort of catch to all of this, but since I've got no other way back home at the moment, this will have to do. Although, I'm only interested in going as far as Texas, because my whole life is there… or what's left of it."

"Suit yourself, Johnny… but you're going to need a job and a place to live now that you're broke and homeless."

I take a deep breath and sigh, forlornly. "I know, David. I know. But first I've got to go see Leslie and my kids and try and make things right with them, if that's even possible at this point."

"I understand, Johnny. Just start with Marty and go from there."

"Okay, David. It was good talking to you. Tell Sophie and the boys I said hello and I hope to see you all soon."

"I will, Johnny. See ya soon!"

I end the call and notice Emily and Mark are standing close behind me. I turn and give her a hug. "Thanks for having me," I say, while returning her phone.

"Are ya leaving us so soon?" she asks with a pout, although I think she's ready for me to go—like whatever we once had together is now long gone, perhaps never to return again.

"Yes, Emily… I'm leaving if everything's right with that guy in the limo. Otherwise, I'll have to figure another way to get home."

"What should I tell everyone now that you're back?"

"I don't know. I guess I've got a lot of explaining to do. But I don't want to shock anyone, until I get over the shock myself."

We take a few pictures together. I give Emily one last hug and shake Mark's hand and then I'm out the door. My heart pounds with every step I take towards the limo. Not even the midday sun can penetrate the dark glass as I approach the shiny beast. I gasp when the rear window begins to motor down, but then I see a handsome man in his mid-twenties smiling up at me with sparkling white teeth. "Marty, is that you?"

"Good to see you again, Johnny."

His dark hair is shoulder length, blending nicely with his tailored black suit and silky red tie. "Looks like you've cleaned up quite a bit since this morning. And aged a few years too!"

"I'm actually sixty-six now, but who's counting when you feel like a teenager and look like a guy coming into his prime!"

"How'd you know I'd be here at my sister's house?"

"It's a long story," he replies, while opening the door. "Get in and I'll explain everything."

Throwing caution to the wind, I take a seat opposite Marty, with the limo driver walled-off by glass behind me. "So, what's really going on here?"

"Fitzhugh kept you imprisoned for eleven years after I was released, but now you're a free man."

"But it seems like I've lost everything I have in the course of a single morning!"

"That's just Fitzhugh's black magic at work. Besides, you know time is relative at Kilborne. Anyhow… as a stipulation to my release, Fitzhugh insisted that I offer to help you get back on your feet once you were let out. So here I am, right where and when he told me to be, ready and willing to make you a rich man again by having you come work for me."

"David told me about the job offer, but as I recall… you stole my wallet and keys the last time we were together."

He grins, sheepishly. "If it's any consolation to you, I've turned your five hundred dollars into fifty billion so far, with the best yet to come!"

"That's very impressive, Marty… but what'd you do with my credit cards?"

"For what it's worth, Johnny… I'm sure your expired cards are still collecting dust in the glove box of your car where Fitzhugh told me to leave your wallet."

I glance out the rear window at the parked rental, as the limo begins to pull away. "Oh, I didn't check there."

"He also told me to leave your keys on your front seat and then go find another way back to civilization, which I did. And then I finally started to age again once I was away from his reform school, just like everyone else, one day at a time."

"And now you're somehow sitting on top of the world?"

"That's because I have the Wisdom of the Ages. I know everything worth knowing about life, because I've been through the centuries many times while stuck at Kilborne, until all the key events yet to come have been ingrained in my head. So now I plan for the future well before it happens, always one step ahead of the crowd, always mindful that the world around me remains clueless and that I must handle mankind with kid gloves, so as not to overwhelm everyone with too much too soon."

I muse. "That must give you quite a business advantage."

"Yes! And I'm proud to say that Marty Enterprises is leading the way with one technological breakthrough after another, so not only am I having a blast while making a fortune, I'm making the planet a much better place to live."

"You certainly don't seem like the Marty of old," I say, as I peer into the windows of his soul, feeling relieved that I see no evil. "Wait a minute… I thought your eyes were brown?"

His wink is followed by a sly smile. "I wear blue contacts now. I think it enhances my look." He laughs. "But more importantly, you're right… I'm not the same guy I once was, and neither are you." He removes his tie and unbuttons his black shirt midway, revealing a hairless, tan chest with a shiny gold heart tattooed above his left nipple. He points to the golf ball sized object. "You see this… I've got a heart of gold." He then points to my chest. "And so do you!"

I immediately pull my sweatshirt down from the neck and see the same type of gold heart emblazoned above my heart. "What's this?"

"It's a special tattoo that comes from the future."

"Are you serious?"

"Your memory of such things will slowly fall into place over the next few days, weeks, months and even years, until you have totally recalled your many time travels and what you've learned over the centuries while at Kilborne, making you wise beyond your age. And to go with your powerful new mind, you now have an equally powerful new heart that will help you last forever."

"That's crazy! Surely you're pulling my leg?"

"No, Johnny… I'm not. You didn't put in the forty years needed to acquire the Wisdom of the Ages, but you were at Kilborne long enough to make you —."

"—The smartest person on the planet next to you?"

He nods, approvingly. "You are correct, sir."

Rather than celebrate, I sit back in the plush leather and want to cry about the freak I've become. "I'd give anything for my old life back," I snap. "Anything!"

"Stick with me and this new life will be ten times better."

"Nothing can replace what I had, Marty. Nothing!"

"Look... I'm sure this is an extremely difficult situation for a devote family man with deep roots..."

"—Impossible, if you ask me!"

"Well, Johnny... I can't turn back the clock and return you to the life you once had, but I can drop you off in Texas, if that's what you really want? But just know that I'd like nothing more than to have you join me out in California where we can make beautiful music together for generations to come!"

"Thanks, Marty. I appreciate the offer. I really do."

"Like it or not, Johnny... we're birds of a feather now. A special breed of human that can fly higher than anyone ever has before. High enough to change the world many times over. High enough to advance the human race in every way imaginable. And this is reason enough why we owe it to mankind to pool our enormous mental resources together and become all that we can be. After all, there is strength in numbers."

I mull Marty's words of wisdom over drinks as we drive to JFK Airport. His wealth of knowledge and information quickly catches me up to modern times. I can see why David spoke so highly of him. In addition to his genius, I find him so incredibly dynamic and charming that I'd consider buying stock in his company, if only I had a pot to piss in. I might even vote for him if he should run for office. But in lieu of all that, he has me seriously thinking about going to work for him by the time we pull up to a private hanger. Although, my beating heart still wants nothing more than to return to Texas, while the tattooed one is urging me to go strike gold in California while the iron is hot. Yes, I'm now torn in ways I've never been torn before. My head spins. My hearts beat. I'm definitely not the man I was yesterday. Not even close!

# Chapter Three
*Fly the Friendly Skies*

I exit the car and follow Marty inside the well-lit hanger where we run into a shiny black 737 with a red M painted on the tail. We board the jet and I'm further impressed with the inside of the craft, which smells like a new car, but looks like a yacht with wings. Blond leather trimmed in burled walnut sums up the rich decor. We pass a well-stocked bar and enter a lounge area that can handle a party of twenty or more. Beyond that are ten rows of plush seating followed by a series of open doors, where I can see a dimly lit bedroom at the very back of the plane.

Marty points to a nearby couch. "Have a seat. I've got to go pilot this thing."

"Are you serious?"

He laughs. "No, but I love pulling that on first-time passengers."

The fun continues when a busty blonde flight attendant serves us cleavage and drinks. Meanwhile, the plane is pushed out of the hanger and then with the engines humming ever so softly, it begins to taxi a short distance and then it's full throttle, as the plane quickly gathers speed down the runway.

Marty holds out his glass once we're airborne. "Here's to making beautiful music!"

We clink and drink as the plane heads west. "I can't wait to tell everyone back home about this incredible day!"

"You can't mention anything about Kilborne at the moment. Besides the fact they probably wouldn't believe you, it remains the best kept secret on the planet. So, unless you want to earn the wrath of Fitzhugh, I implore you to keep that between us for now until I can figure a way to put an end to that evil spirit."

"You're trying to get rid of Fitzhugh?"

"It's either that or he'll eventually take over the world."

"Well, we certainly don't want that. But if I can't tell people the truth about where I've been, what do I tell them?"

"Tell them you've been hidden away at a remote location, while spearheading a top secret project for Marty Enterprises for the past eleven years in an effort to develop an incredibly powerful battery that will last forever, without ever needing to recharge!"

"Sounds impressive, but I sold real estate for a living. No one's going to believe I had anything to do with the making of a battery. Especially not my family and friends."

"Tell a small lie, and you may be right. But tell this big lie with someone credible like me to back you up, and it becomes the *gospel truth*, even for them."

"A forever battery," I question. "Is that even possible?"

"It's being tested as we speak," he replies. "In fact, this plane is running on two of our batteries right now."

"Really? Is it safe?"

"Let's put it this way… the plane will give out long before those batteries ever do. But let's not stop there… can you imagine electric cars that never need to charge up no matter how many miles they travel? Or how about a house running on a battery small enough to fit inside a shoebox? Or electronic devices and appliances that run a lifetime without ever having to plug into an outlet? How about an entire big city like New York running on a battery the size of one compact refrigerator that is guaranteed to last forever? And best of all, power outages and brownouts are about to be a thing of the past no matter how much the usage! Yes, how the world fuels itself is soon to be changed when our batteries are introduced into the marketplace, and then the entire planet will have endless energy."

"I imagine this is going to wreak havoc on the oil industry."

"Maybe so, but my environmentally friendly batteries will give unlimited power to the people for untold generations to come!"

"That's fantastic!"

"Yes," he readily agrees, "and I'm willing to let you steal my thunder when this all goes public, just to help with the cause."

"Wow… I really appreciate the offer, Marty. But I'd hate to take credit for something I didn't do. Especially considering this is going to be such a huge deal and I don't know the first thing about your batteries, other than they last forever."

"Lucky for you, this project has been hush-hush up through now. So, it's safe to say that 'ignorance is still bliss' at the moment. That should buy you enough time to learn the basics of what you need to know, and then you can figure out the rest as you go, until you finally become an expert in the field."

"Sounds great, but Leslie can see right through me. She's going to know I'm lying about all this stuff."

"Your ex-wife will jump on the bandwagon once we put the word out about the new battery and she sees everyone on the planet clamoring for your autograph."

"What… you're making me out to be famous?"

"It's better than being infamous."

"True."

"Then we're in agreement that you'll take credit for spearheading the battery project and that not a word about Fitzhugh or anything to do with Kilborne is to be mentioned to anyone, including members of your family, until I say it's alright to do so?"

"I suppose I can go along with that, although… I did mention a little about Kilborne to my sister and her husband before I left."

"Oh, really?" he frowns. "Hopefully, nothing will come of that."

"It's not like they believed me."

"Yeah, reality is a harder sell than telling a lie in our case."

"Not when it comes to the huge lie I'm about to tell."

"Look… if you're worried about the battery thing, I suggest you practice your presentation on Beth before we visit Texas."

"Who?"

He presses a button and the busty flight attendant returns with two more drinks. "Beth, we need your help. Can you take Johnny to the back of the plane and work with him on his battery presentation, while I take care of other business up here?"

"Sure thing, Marty," she responds with a reassuring smile.

Beth takes me by the hand and off we go. We pass down the center aisle through the rows of seats and past bathrooms and a galley, before ending up in the bedroom. "Oh, so we're practicing here?" I ask, both startled and confused.

She closes the door. "The bedroom is where I do my best work."

I feel myself turning shades of pink. "But I'm a married man."

"No, Johnny… you *were* a married man."

I gulp, still clinging to my past. "I've never cheated before."

"And you're not cheating now."

I'm nervous as can be, but that said, the second drink has me feeling a little giddy as well, like I haven't had a drink or sex in many a year. "You make a mean margarita."

She purrs. "That's not all I do well."

Wide-eyed, I take a step back. "We shouldn't be doing this."

She moves in for the kill. "Relax, honey. You'll be ready to conquer the world by the time we land."

"Do you really think so?" I ask, weak-kneed.

She answers me with a kiss, which takes my breath away, before pushing me down on the bed. She then unbuttons the last of her white blouse and allows it to slip to the floor with her bra soon to follow. Her tan breasts are perfect by most standards, just like the rest of her body and I'm thinking I'm lost in some movie that's too far-fetched to be real.

"Tell me about your ex-wife," she inquires, seductively.

"What do you want to know?"

"Everything!"

I describe Leslie from head to toe, while Beth continues to undress her shapely frame. "Actually… she looks a lot like you, except that she's older now."

"I'm sure she's still beautiful."

"Yep," I say, recalling the photos Emily had shown me. "She is!"

"What else can you tell me about her?"

"Well… I remember her as the woman who took care of our two wonderful teenagers before they grew up. She also volunteered at school and church when she wasn't working her part-time job at a flower shop. And when she wasn't doing any of those things, she used to love to shop for others and travel the world."

"Wow! Sounds like quite the woman."

Instead of eagerly agreeing, I respond with a pout. "Which reminds me that she was supposed to pick me up at the airport tomorrow, but that was eleven years ago."

"And therein lies the problem."

"Yes! So much has changed since then." I groan out of frustration. "But besides all that, I don't even know if I can look her or my kids in the eye at this point, let alone get them to believe I've been alive and working on this battery thing all this time and never bothered to call them even once."

Before I know it, my shoes are off and shockingly, Beth is lying nude by my side. "Don't worry, honey... I promise to have you ready for them when the time comes."

"But Leslie knows me like a book!"

"Then I better double my efforts. Let me help you with your clothes."

"I don't know if I'm ready for this. Can we at least get to know each other first?"

"There's no time for that, sweetie."

"But..." Beth plugs my mouth with hers and then her tongue goes to work, and I close my eyes and think of Leslie while we kiss. In spite of my protests, one thing leads to another, then another, and then another, until I'm shocked to find myself actually having sex with a beautiful stranger. Not only that, but a stranger I just met minutes ago! Still, I think of Leslie time and again while I engage in this surreal mile-high stuff—even thinking of her with each thrust of my hips—as if she were the one writhing underneath me now. The pace quickens, then slows to a crawl. Quickens then slows.

"I see you've got a tattoo just like Marty."

"I feel it beating inside me now."

"Marty says it makes him invincible."

"Then how come I feel like I'm dead to the world?"

She grabs hold of my ears and looks deeply into my watery eyes. "You've got a heart of gold, Johnny... you just have to learn how to use it and you'll be just fine."

With Beth leading the way, we change positions on the fly, as our muffled moans are thankfully lost in the jet wash. Before long, I'm fearful Beth is going to wear me out, although, it seems like I too am on steroids. In fact, I'm on fire! But that said, I think of batteries when I'm not thinking about Leslie. The pace quickens, then slows to a crawl. Back and forth it goes, until the point of no return has finally been reached. We explode together with such force, I'm thinking the tail is going to tear right off the plane and Beth and I are going to be hurled to the ground only to land safely on the mattress with Leslie angrily standing over us with furled lips and hands on hips, and I long to hear her yell at me like she's never yelled before.

"I'd light a cigarette," Beth says, dreamily, "but I don't smoke."

"Me neither," I say, although I too can use one at the moment.

She kisses me on the cheek before getting out of bed. "Stay and rest. I've got work to do in the cabin, but I'll let you know when we're getting ready to land."

"Shouldn't I get back with Marty?"

"As busy as that man stays, he won't even know you're gone."

Beth is dressed before I know it and waving goodbye. "Sweet dreams, lover boy," she says, before shutting the door on her way out, and I'm thinking there's a part of me that still feels like I've just cheated on Leslie. I want to get out of bed and leave the scene of the crime, but it's all I can do to keep my eyes open.

Alone with my thoughts, I reflect on the strangest day of my life and conclude that I've been in a *green* fog ever since morning's first light, until now that my real heart is heavy with regret, while the gold one is thinking I just scored.

I cry myself to sleep. Darkness fades to black, until I visit a collage of unfamiliar people, places and things that are new to me, although I do recognize Thomas Edison and Abraham Lincoln in the mix. The shocking images come and go in snippets, but I see Edison rejoice after flipping the switch on his incandescent lightbulb, and then I go from that historic event to sitting a few seats away from Lincoln when he gets shot in a theatre. I'm there just long enough to be startled by the loud, blinding flash and smell the gunpowder after being sprayed with warm blood, then I'm gone.

The snippets continue as if I have a front row seat to the best and worst mankind has to offer. I'm then thrust into a futuristic classroom where yellow holograms containing facts and figures jump off a glass blackboard and circle my head like buzzing bees. Round and round the neon critters go, until they penetrate my skull, thus allowing me to spit out the answers on call—first time, every time, without fail!

It's a really easy way to learn. And it sure beats endless hours of study. But what really blows me away is when the teacher tells me that all the neon critters are really doing is stimulating my brain to unlock information I already know. He claims we're born with all the essential knowledge we need to survive. It's imbedded deep within our DNA like hidden treasure designed by our creator to advance the species. So, there's actually more to animal instincts, gut feelings, brilliant ideas and random thoughts than you might think. He then declares that science has proven evolution to be nothing more than a theory—because we are all born with the Wisdom of the Ages and have been since God created the first man.

"Whether you're a believer or not," he professes, "God believes in us. And he's blessed us with the tools necessary to stand the test of time. Now it's up to each and every one of us to try and make good use of what we've been given, because we're only as strong as our weakest link and it would be a shame not to learn as much as we can about the things we already know! Although, to learn everything that is contained in our DNA is impossible to achieve in one lifetime, unless you've been to the Kilborne Academy."

I want to stay and hear more of what the teacher has to say, but I find myself leaving the future and returning to the present, as if I've been daydreaming all this time, because we've apparently landed at DFW airport and another limo is busy chauffeuring us towards the suburbs of Ft. Worth. Although feeling guilty about Beth, I can't wait to see Leslie and the kids in their current state. The stretch finally turns on my street and I'm ready to run for the front door, until I see hordes of people waiting in front of my house. I look over at Marty and he's grinning from ear to ear.

"Welcome to your new life, Johnny."

"But there are a bunch of reporters out there," I whine. "What do I tell them?"

"The same story you tell everyone else."

"Which is?"

"That you were off making the world a much better place to live."

"What if they start grilling me with a bunch of battery questions I can't answer?"

"You're a hero now," he replies. "It's time you start acting like one."

"But what if the truth slips out?"

"Then you put me at risk of being sent back to the Kilborne Academy to suffer for all eternity. And not only that, it gives that crazy Fitzhugh yet another reason to kill everyone off and start the world anew."

"Wow... I feel like I'm between a rock and a hard place."

"No. It's more like you're on a big stage where the rewards are great for people like us, but so are the consequences."

"Well, I guess that's one way to look at it."

"Anyhow, here's a chance to practice your presentation before you hit the bright lights of Hollywood," he says. "Don't keep your fans waiting any longer. I'll just make myself at home here until you're ready to make that beautiful music I was talking about."

"Sounds great, Marty." I then grab the door handle with a sweaty hand. "Hope I'm ready for this."

I'm mobbed the moment I leave the limo. I force a smile for the camera, time and again, until my cheeks grow numb. There are so many flashes going off in my face that I feel like a celebrity. Amid it all, I see two young adults perched by the front door. We make eye contact and they wave. I know they're my kids, or what's become of them. I wave back and want to get to them immediately, if not sooner, but first I must wade through the many reporters and autograph seekers that stand in my way. Slowly but surely, I shuffle along. Slowly, but surely.

I'm finally close enough to where I can almost talk to them above the chatter that engulfs me. I can see that Adam is now taller than me and Liz is even more beautiful than Emily's pictures had revealed. And like the mighty oak trees that have doubled in size since I last saw them yesterday morning, it's just as shocking to see what eleven years can do to budding teenagers. By the time I reach them, my battery story is complete. I have it down to where I can tell the big lie like it's the… *gospel truth.*

I give Liz a bear hug. "You look just like your mother did when I first met her."

Her smile is as bright as ever. "It's so good to see you again, Daddy. I always felt you were alive."

I desperately want to tell her the truth. "Guess I should've called."

I pull away from Liz and shake Adam's hand, then follow with another bear hug. "I hope you're not mad at me for being gone so long."

He laughs. "How can I be mad at the man who just solved the world's energy problems? You're a hero, Dad!"

I blush but say nothing.

"Can you tell us more about your amazing battery?" he asks.

I smile meekly to cover the shame I'm feeling. "The battery is still being tested, so I can't divulge any details at the moment. But you'll be the first to know when I can."

Liz giggles. "It's so exciting having a famous father!"

Adam cheers. "It's just exciting to have Dad back!"

I hug them both. "I never want to leave you two again."

She grunts, loudly. "I suppose you know Mom remarried."

I grimace at the thought. "I heard."

Adam also grunts. "They're both waiting for you inside."

I'm almost afraid to turn towards the ornate bronze door, knowing it's going to be awkward as hell to see Leslie with another man. Then again, I want to punch her new hubby's lights out for taking my wife and ruining my business, but I'm supposedly a hero now and need to start acting like one—if that's even possible for a troubled guy like me. I take in a mouthful of air and sigh on the exhale… then ring the doorbell, which sends a chill racing down my tingly spine, almost taking the last of my breath away.

Within seconds I see a shapely figure walking towards the beveled glass in the door. I'm sure it's Leslie. I can see that she's alone and I'm excited at the opportunity to speak with her without hubby standing over her shoulder. My real heart is pounding. There's so much I want to say to her, although someone's pulling my leg. Literally! I look down and I'm shocked to see that it's the busty flight attendant by the foot of the bed.

"Beth! What are you doing here?"

"It's time to wake up, lover boy," she says. "We'll be landing in ten minutes."

"What?" It takes me a moment to realize I'm still on the plane. "Oh, thanks," I manage, while pulling the satin sheets up around my neck.

"You must've been in a really deep sleep."

"I've never dreamt like that before," I say. "It was so real."

"Marty wants to see you."

"Okay. I'll be right there."

Beth leaves the bedroom and I quickly dress. I stop off at the bathroom and check my look in the mirror. It hurts to see lipstick on my face that didn't come from Leslie. I clean up as best I can before rejoining Marty in the lounge, although I can still smell hints of Beth lingering on me—following me around wherever I go.

"There's been a change of plans," he says, abruptly.

"Oh?"

"Your sister posted stuff about Kilborne that could go viral, so now you'll have a lot more explaining to do than I originally anticipated."

"Damn!"

"Damn is right. There's no way I can have you associated with me now that this has gone public. Fitzhugh is going to be furious if he finds out about this! Therefore, I think it best if we go our separate ways, until the dust settles on your return."

My jaw drops to my knees. "Wow… what a mess."

"I'd offer to help, but you know your family better than I do, so this is one problem you're going to have to fix on your own."

"Is that even possible at this point?"

He shrugs. "I don't really know because I've never dealt with a situation like this before. But I'm hoping the second smartest person on the planet will figure something out before all hell breaks loose."

I scratch my head like it might help me to think. "But if I can't tell anyone about Kilborne and I can't tell them I've been working for you for the past eleven years, what do I tell them?"

"Just start thinking about your options and I'm sure something good will come to that soon-to-be-brilliant mind of yours."

"Speaking of which, I had a dream earlier where I was learning all kinds of things after time-traveling into the future."

"Yes… the more you sleep, the more you'll learn like that."

"But it doesn't seem like information I can use at the moment."

"You'll reach a tipping point where it all starts making sense to you and then you'll be able to invent incredible things that change the world!" He hands me an envelope. "Here's the five hundred dollars I took from you eleven years ago. I'm sorry, but it's the best I can do under the circumstances."

"No problem. I appreciate you paying me back," I say, as the plane begins its descent. I now sit in silence while Marty focuses on one text message after another. I'm free to contemplate my future, or lack thereof, until distracted by the number of lights twinkling in the dusk down below. Adding to my uncertainty, I can see that Dallas has more than doubled in the last twenty-four hours and I'm soon to be a stranger in town thanks to all the sudden changes. The flaps begin to lower. The wheels come down next. The plane turns and is now on a collision course with the glowing runway. We land ever so quietly at Love Field, then whisper over to a dark hanger.

"I secured an Uber ride for you, Johnny."

"Uber?"

"It's like a taxi."

"Thanks, Marty. Thanks for everything."

"Hopefully, we'll get a chance to make beautiful music someday," he says. "But until then… it's like we never met."

"I understand."

I shake his hand and head for the exit, thinking the cash I just received may have to last a good while considering my seemingly hopeless situation. A few more steps and I see that Beth is waiting for me at the doorway with a pleasant smile on her heavily painted face. It's awkward, but we air hug; then I'm off the plane and I walk up to a compact car being driven by a college kid.

"Are you my ride?"

"Where to, Mister?" mumbles the masked man. *I can only assume the kid is suffering from some highly contagious disease with the way my day is going, yet that doesn't stop me from getting in the car.*

"Probably the nearest cheap hotel," I reply with a sigh. "I need to rest my head and hopefully I'll wake up refreshed tomorrow and find that everything is back to normal again."

"I've got some weed, if you'd like to buy a joint?"

"No thanks. But how about stopping for a moment at that liquor store across the street?"

"Sure thing, Mister."

I'm not much of a drinker by most standards, so going to a liquor store when there is not a pending party is a strange occurrence for me. Although, that doesn't stop me from buying the biggest bottle of booze I can afford before returning to the car—except now I'm feeling the need to lift my spirits even higher after seeing more masked people milling about like there is some sort of pandemic going on. "Hey, kid… on second thought… I'll take that joint now."

"Sure thing, Mister."

# Chapter Four
*Memory Lane*

I take refuge at the Hotel California of all places. It's a dive in the heart of Irving, Texas—the only place I could find that would take cash and didn't require a valid ID. The room is small and hasn't been renovated since back in the day when things were much simpler. Speaking of simple, I'm sure my dinosaur of a phone has long since been disconnected, so it doesn't even matter that the battery is dead. Perhaps soon to be one of the last dead batteries on the planet! That said, I'm busting at the seams to call my wife and kids right now, but what would I tell them? What incredible lie do I make up to earn back their trust? Even more daunting of a task, how do I make things right with the world before all hell breaks loose? I take a swig of scotch and swallow hard. A puff of weed comes next. I feel so lonely and helpless I could die! Another swig and puff does little to ease my pain. I finally plop my weary head down on the stale pillow and notice roaches on the ceiling. I'm sure this creaky bed has lice. And to think… just yesterday I had everything I could possibly want and today I'm down to the wrinkled sweatshirt on my back and the crinkled money in my pocket. "How could this be?" I cry. "How can this possibly be my fate?"

My search for an answer takes me all the way back to when I was a sixteen-year-old problem child, growing up in the suburbs of New Jersey. And I recall that it was like taking a trip down memory lane when someone suggested we have a water balloon fight. "Fire when ready!" became the battle cry, as a dozen pimple-faced combatants poured in from blocks away to join the fray. Balloons soon filled the blue sky with a rainbow of color, as splash after splash left many soaked down to their Fruit of the Looms. "Bombs away!" The rubber hit the road, time and again, leaving behind a myriad of tiny puddles on my tree-lined street, while lawns and gardens began to glisten like the dampness had come from the morning dew. The fighting continued unabated for hours, until the ammo ran low and a truce had to be called. I thought the exhausting conflict was over when everyone went home, but no… the real battle was about to begin…

"Hey," clamored Rudy, who was peering out my second-floor bedroom window. "Here's a chance to welcome that new kid into the neighborhood. Check it out… he's coming our way!"

I shuffled over to the open window and caught a second wind after seeing a lone rider peddling down the sidewalk. Awash in the late afternoon sun, young Tom Ramsey had a yellow and black striped shirt on that made the chunky twelve-year-old look like a wingless bumblebee sitting proudly atop his shiny purple bike.

Just to confirm, I looked Rudy's way and saw him glancing down at what remained of our once mighty arsenal, which now consisted of two green water balloons sitting in a pail on the floor. "Are you serious?" I inquired of my battle-hardened friend.

Sure enough, he answered me with an affirmative nod and before I knew it, we each had a bloated monster in hand and were staying low while waiting for the new kid to saunter into range.

"Hope he hurries up," I said. "I suddenly gotta take a piss."

"Fear not," Rudy snickered. "The little guy is almost here."

But the seconds passed like hours and I got to where I was thinking this pending act of cruelty was way too easy to be fun—and besides that, there was always a chance the kid might get hurt. Needless to say, I was having second thoughts when I heard Rudy mutter: "FIRE!"

Not wanting to be a party-pooper, I aimed well over Tom's head before letting loose. But my arm was worn from the day's events and much to my dismay, the water balloon fluttered from my hand looking like a wounded duck on a collision course with an unsuspecting bumblebee.

Tom's radar eventually detected the two objects that were wobbling down from the sky. He looked bug-eyed as he turned to face the danger, then quickly swerved and barely avoided one green balloon by the skin of his metal-clad teeth, only to be hit in the head by the other.

"Oh shit!" I said, as the watery explosion sent his bike reeling out of control. With one shaky hand Tom grasped the handlebar, holding on for dear life, while the other hand flailed up in the air like a bull rider about to be tossed from the saddle.

Unfortunate as it was, the wingless bumblebee flew off the back of his purple machine and landed face down in that dog-friendly area of grass that resides between the sidewalk and curb, before tumbling to a stop by the fire hydrant near my driveway.

"I think I nailed him!" Rudy was quick to boast.

Rather than argue the point, I stared out the window for what seemed an eternity, while Tom lay motionless next to his dirty mangled bike. I then turned to my partner in crime. "I don't know about you, but I'm worried."

"Hmmm… what should we do?"

I shrugged, clueless. "I don't know… but if he doesn't come around soon, we're gonna have to call for help." Checking for witnesses, I looked up and down what was normally a busy block with parents planting and children playing, but all was quiet. "Must be dinnertime," I surmised. "Nobody's out." I returned my gaze to Tom. "We should go check on him while the coast is clear," I suggested, growing antsier by the moment.

"Let's give him another minute before we get carried away," Rudy responded, flippantly.

Thankfully, another minute was all it took. Tom fluttered back to life on his own, albeit looking a little dazed and confused, and he even managed to sit up before facing the street with his head tucked between his legs. Perhaps it was wishful thinking on our part, but Rudy and I agreed that he appeared to be recovering nicely and should soon be able to return from whence he came. Relieved by this optimistic notion, I quietly shut the window, ready to put the incident to bed. "I don't think he saw us," I murmured. "Let's get out of here, before he realizes we're up here."

After relieving myself in the hall bathroom, we headed downstairs to the main floor and grabbed a bag of potato chips and two cold sodas from the kitchen, then sailed down more stairs, until we were snug as two bugs on the cozy basement couch.

"Too bad about that kid," Rudy muttered.

I sighed, ruefully. "We should've never done that."

"But wasn't it your idea to blast the little guy?"

"No, I think it was yours."

He shrugged. "Oh, well… hopefully nothing will come of it."

I crossed my fingers. "Hopefully."

Baseball was on TV. All was good after watching the Yanks take an early lead. I was just starting to lose myself in the game when I heard the pitter-patter of little feet racing down the stairs, as if the bell had just sounded on a three-alarm fire and all that came to mind was Tom!

"What's the problem?" I quizzed my eight-year-old siblings.

"Johnny! Johnny!" David squealed excitedly to where his big brown eyes looked like they were about to pop out of his little head. "There's people in front of our house!"

"Yeah, some kid got hurt on a bike," Emily announced with controlled excitement, as if yet another perky blonde was anchoring the breaking news of the day. "I saw blood everywhere!"

Rudy gasped, meeting my wide-eyed stare. I then turned back to the twittering twins. "Did ya see any grown-ups out there?"

Emily batted her brilliant blues. "There was a bunch!"

"Yeah," David added, "maybe fifty or a hundred of 'em!"

"No frickin' way," hissed Rudy. "You guys are making shit up!"

"Does Mom or Dad know about this yet?" I gingerly inquired.

"I don't know," Emily replied with a shrug. "But I heard somebody called the police."

"An ambulance too!" interjected David.

After groaning, Rudy whispered in my ear, "I think it's time I slip out the side door."

"No way, man." I loudly whispered back. "You're not bailing on me now."

"We need ta go find Mom and tell her about this," beamed Emily.

"Yeah," David agreed. "We should go tell her!"

I jumped to my feet. "Hold on you two." I then pointed to the couch. "Have a seat until I get back. Then you can go tell Mom. Okay?"

Emily clasped her hands together, as if begging. "But, but, but..."

"But nothing," I snapped. "Just do as I say!"

"Bully!" she pouted, before parking herself next to David.

I could feel Rudy's hot breath against the back of my tingly neck as we made our way up the stairs and out the side door by the kitchen, where dusk was setting in, turning the blue sky a silvery gray. We stayed close to the tall hedges on the side of the house. Then inched our way toward the chain-link fence to sneak a peek out front.

I heard chatter and my heart raced, then skipped a beat when I saw a handful of adults surrounding Tom, who was still on the ground. Curious kids circling on bike and those hovering on foot completed the scene. And there was blood! A red-streaked towel clung to Tom's nose. To make matters worse, I saw my mother run out the front door closely followed by a skipping Emily and a bouncing David. "Darn busybodies," I muttered under my breath at the gleeful twins.

"Well shit," Rudy said after seeing his mother emerge from her house across the street. "This is turning into a fricken block party."

I mused. "It's almost like last summer when we started that campfire and almost burned down the woods."

He frowned at the memory. "Yeah… and this is looking like it could be just as bad."

Sirens filled the air off in the distance. And there was the buzz of a lawnmower in my backyard, which reminded me that I forgot to mow yesterday. "Shit!" I was thinking Dad was about to come around the corner of the house pushing that whiny red machine, pissed that he was doing my job. "This could get ugly in a hurry," I stated the obvious.

Rudy fidgeted. "Got any suggestions?"

I quickly mulled our options and concluded they were not good. Since it was probably too late to sneak back into the house, we could either face my teddy bear of a father who could get grizzly when provoked or take a chance with the block party in my front yard. "Let's try and fit in with the crowd," I responded.

I was about to push open the gate in the fence when a police cruiser pulled up across the street. Startled, even though we knew it was coming, the sight of the black and white made us retreat, until half-buried in the tall hedges. A loud monotone female voice did little to ease my nerves when she belted out an address over the loudspeaker of the police radio. "Ten-four," came an equally loud male response that sent a chill racing down my spine. And then I realized the sirens had gone silent and so had the lawnmower.

"What's all this?"

"Dad!" I shrieked. Rudy and I quickly pulled away from the hedges like we had ants in our pants.

"How come you didn't mow the lawn yesterday?" he growled.

I squirmed, but felt I had this somewhat in the bag. "I had baseball practice in the morning, and then I went with Mom to visit Nana in the afternoon. We didn't get home until dark."

Dad grunted. "What about today?"

The squirming continued in earnest. "Ah… I didn't remember until I heard the mower out back a second ago… but I would've done it after school tomorrow at the very latest."

He smirked. "Likely story." He then gave the party a glance. "What's going on out front?"

I faked a shrug. "I don't know. Rudy and I were about to check it out ourselves."

"Really?" he rolled his eyes while lumbering through the gate. "Looks more like you two were hiding out." Without saying another word, Dad disappeared into the gathering on the front lawn.

"That went well," Rudy snickered.

"Let's go mingle before he comes back."

He nodded. "Sounds like a plan."

The ambulance arrived, turning the block party into a circus. There were red and blue lights that flashed and reflected off everyone and everything. Tom was lifted onto a stretcher. He waved to the crowd, looking happy as everyone cheered him on. I was both pleased and relieved to see him in good spirits and enjoying what appeared to be his fifteen minutes of fame, before disappearing into the ambulance. But then again there was his teary-eyed mother and angry father following close behind, which caused me to cower.

The ambulance pulled away, but much to my chagrin, the police car remained behind. "Good evening!" A tall officer with a shiny skinhead began to address the crowd. "I'm Officer Rose." In spite of an intimidating appearance, Officer Rose had a friendly public servant voice that resonated like he was using a megaphone. "Did anyone see what happened to the boy?" I held my breath, until I saw nothing but shrugging and headshaking coming from the gathering. "I'm sure it was just an accident," the officer concluded. "Happens all the time."

Rudy elbowed me in the rib cage. "Looks like we dodged a bullet."

"Yeah," I nodded in the affirmative. "Looks that way."

It was getting dark, but I could still see two neighborhood buds tossing a football up the street. Eager to leave the scene of the crime,

I grabbed Rudy and off we went, as the officer returned to his vehicle.

We arrived just as Mitch lofted a deep, wobbly pass toward a running Billy. The football landed just out of his reach and bounced off the asphalt a couple of times before almost hitting the still parked police car, as the party began to thin out. "How come you didn't invite us to that shindig in front of your house?" asked Mitch.

"It was kind of a spur-of-the-moment thing," I replied.

He smiled like he was trying to be cute. "Looks like the new kid crashed and burned."

"Probably had a little too much to drink," Rudy quipped.

"Naaaaa!" Mitch pointed fifty yards downfield to where my bedroom window hung above the front-entry garage of my house. "Seems more like he took a direct hit from that hornet's nest you had up there."

I played dumb. "What hornet's nest?"

"You know what I'm talking about," he jabbed. "You and Rudy were raining water balloons down all day long from your bedroom window."

Mitch and I went back and forth. He wouldn't let it rest. I continued to play dumb, until I had no choice but to stare down my bombastic buddy. We stood toe to toe and eye to eye. Neither of us flinched. Even my bushy hair remained in place. I was truly hanging tough, trying to be the last one standing, although the pressure mounted with each tick of the clock.

"All right, already!" Rudy intervened. "Johnny nailed him."

"I knew it!" Mitch laughed. "I knew it had to be you, Johnny," he added, as Billy returned with the football.

"Wait a minute now," I insisted. "Rudy's the one who nailed him. He even admitted it to me after the kid went down."

"Bullshit!" Rudy said with a sheepish grin. "We all know your aim's a lot better than mine, hotshot."

Aim? What aim? If he only knew I had tried to miss the kid by a country mile. But rather than throw that into the equation, I thought the logical choice was to make peace and move on. "All right... let's just say we don't know whose balloon nailed him for sure and leave it at that. Okay?"

Rudy kicked the idea around and nodded. "Fair enough."

"So—so—so… it—it's o-o-official then," Billy said. "N-neither of you are t-t-t-taking c-credit for that k-k-killer h-h-hit."

"Call it an accident, Billy," I said, impishly. "Not a hit."

"An accident my ass," hooted Mitch. "You two could end up in jail for picking on a little kid like that!"

"No way," Rudy snapped. "I'm not going down over this!" he added, petulantly, while I cringed at the thought of jailtime.

"Okay, w-w-whatever," Billy said. "Let's just p-p-play before it gets t-t-too dark to s-see the b-b-ball."

"Hike!" I rolled to my right, looking to hit Mitch with a better pass than my last balloon throw, when I saw the police cruiser heading our way. It took no time at all for the car to roll the fifty yards to where we had become a rag-tag team of worried faces. I did however notice two little busybodies standing back where the vehicle had been. They watched expectantly as the cruiser came to a stop alongside our makeshift huddle. Officer Rose stuck his head out the window. "Did you gentlemen see what happened to that young man on the bike?" he stated more than asked.

I was speechless, but I was not alone. You could hear a pin drop. After an awkward delay, Rudy finally broke the ice. "We were playing football," he offered, "and didn't see a thing." And with that the floodgates opened. A rally had begun! Our team fed off Rudy's lead and with Billy stammering away, we all had something to say.

The amused officer nodded; seemingly satisfied with the performance of our songbird quartet. But then he dangled a wet piece of green balloon out his window that took my breath away. "Can anyone tell me who this belongs to?" he interrogated.

I knew it could be mine… the dripping evidence that would send me down the river. And even though I was big for my age, there was no way I was man enough to spend time in jail. So, with my freedom hanging in the balance, I somehow managed to find the balls to step forward on shaky knees. "All I know is there were a bunch of kids running around with water balloons earlier in the day," I truthfully admitted, before attempting to lead the officer astray. "Maybe he lost control on a wet spot they left behind," I suggested with a pleasant smile that I strained to maintain. "It was like a flood out here earlier!" I added for good measure.

The officer nodded favorably. "And your name is?"

"Johnny Bishop, sir."

"And these are your friends?"

"Yes, sir."

The officer took some notes but appeared to have a satisfied look on his face. "It's getting dark. You gentlemen might want to think about calling it a night," he said, before rolling up his window and slowly driving away, as I breathed a major sigh of relief.

"Nice job!" Rudy said. "I didn't think you had it in ya to bullshit a cop like that."

"Me neither," I admitted with knees that were still shaky.

"Yeah, that was a good sales job, man," Mitch said. "Ya had me fooled."

"No s-s-shit," Billy agreed. "I c-c-couldn't have d-done it b-b-better m-m-myself."

After a little more boy-talk, the team separated, thus bringing an end to the weekend. I returned home to find the family in the kitchen with spaghetti and meatballs on their plates. I washed my hands in the sink and took my customary seat next to my dad and across from my mother with the busybody twins capping off the other end of the rectangular table.

"Too bad about that boy," my mother said. "Hopefully, he didn't break anything."

"He was probably going too fast and lost control," Dad assumed, and I happily concurred.

"I'm thinkin' he got hit with a water balloon," Emily spouted, causing me to choke on the meatball I had just put in my mouth.

"A water balloon?" my mother questioned my dear little busybody sister, as I quietly tried to recover after swallowing hard. "What makes you say that?"

"I saw a bunch of big kids with 'em earlier," David chimed in before Emily could respond, bringing me to the edge of my seat. "I almost got hit in the head with a yellow one when I came home for lunch today," he added, like he was lucky to still be alive.

"Hey, Dad," I blurted, "catch any of that Yankee game?"

"Yeah," he smiled like a fuzzy teddy bear. "That was pretty good."

Thankfully, the conversation moved on from Tom and I made it through dinner unscathed, although days later I got a SUMMONS TO APPEAR in court. It was shocking at first. Especially since Tom had made a full recovery and all was forgiven. I checked with Rudy to see if he had been served, but I was the only one. My mother called the courthouse to see what was going on, and they told her my case was slated to be dismissed, although we still needed to show up in court to make it official. Otherwise, all was good in my life; save for having to meet with the pissy principal tomorrow about my pending suspension from school. Dreaded school!

# Chapter Five
*Day in Court*

I was having a sleepless night, until dreams of water balloons crept into my head. The glowing green orbs fell from a stormy sky and splashed down on my street to where puddles soon became a raging green river that ran from one end of the empty block to the other. Strange as that was, cardboard snowflakes began to flutter to the ground with dreadful D's and frightful F's reported on one side. The manila monsters even had my mother's signature forged on the back. I was busy picking up the shameful sheets of paper in a frantic effort to cover my tracks when the alarm clock came to my rescue, taking me from guilt trip to the mornings first light.

Weird dreams aside, I began that fateful Friday with a Coke and Twinkie in my hand. It's how I started many a day when pancakes were not in the offing. I ate in relative silence after Emily and David left for school, because Mom was busy checking her look in the mirror, while Dad paced the kitchen more worried about seeing my pissy principal than standing before some friendly judge. After all, we knew the charges were to be dropped. Dad even joked about it on the drive to the courthouse; saying it would be a cakewalk that would last a half-hour at the most, then it would be on to dreaded school.

With my parents by my side, we walked the crowded halls of justice looking for Courtroom B6 and finally found it down a dark hallway that was off the beat and path. My mother turned to face me in front of the closed double doors. "Now you be on your best behavior, Johnny."

"I will, Mom," I replied, feeling confident of the outcome.

We entered a large, windowless room with a tall ceiling that rained florescent light down on twenty rows of empty wood benches. The mass of wood was parted in the middle by a marbled runway. The courtroom was indeed empty with the exception of a tiny old man dressed in black. He was perched high on a wooden throne on the opposite end of the shiny runway. From afar, the frail looking judge seemed less than intimidating, but then he raised a shaky arm and hammered his gavel once, and the sound reverberated off the oak-paneled walls, making my spine tingle.

"Good Morning!" he said with a scratchy voice that sounded like an old recording. "I'm Judge Reinhold, and I pray that you come forward." He beckoned repeatedly with his other arm, while giggling like a tickled child. "I want you to come closer, until you can see the blue in my eyes." He giggled again and hammered twice, and I could smell something sweet in the air that was intoxicating. "Hurry up and move forward please," he giggled yet again.

"Is this guy for real?" I whispered to my father.

"Just shut up and do as he says," Dad whispered back.

I did as told and walked between my parents down the center aisle, until we lost our forward momentum at the halfway point. From thirty feet away, I could see that the judge hardly had any skin on the top of his head and what remained was opaque. His frosty hair ran sparsely around the sides of his bumpy skull in white clumps. He had one bushy eyebrow to speak of; its twin had vanished along with the skin on the opposite side of his narrow face. But it was his eyes that scared me the most. I could see the part that was supposed to be blue was mostly white too! And his pupils were the size of tiny black pinholes through which he was busy checking me out from head to toe. Shocked, I turned to my left and my father's jaw had dropped, and he was looking wide-eyed at the judge. To my right my mother was doing much the same.

Alarmed, I was ready to grab my parents and bail when the judge bellowed, "It's 10 a.m. on this twenty-second day of May in the year nineteen-sixty-nine and court is now in session." He hammered and a strange green mist billowed out from behind his perch and quickly filled the entire courtroom from floor to ceiling. In an instant I was blanketed in a forest of green cotton candy that was sticky sweet. There was also a hissing sound that reminded me of snakes. Thousands and thousands of snakes! I was scared to death. Afraid to move! I called out to my parents, but they did not, or could not respond. Besides the constant hissing, I now heard the judge giggling away in the background like he was enjoying himself at our expense.

"Mom! Dad!" I cried. "Where are you? Where are you?"

"Fear not." I heard the judge say, before hammering once again. And with that the green quickly faded from the courtroom, although I was still lightheaded to the point of feeling like I was drunk or stoned, if not hallucinating on something much stronger than whiskey or weed.

"What was that stuff?" my mother inquired. "It smelled like honeysuckle in here."

"Yeah… it was so sweet," my father said, "I feel like I'm still on a sugar high."

"Hey… I'm stuck in place!" I wailed. Even though my foggy head was on a swivel, I noticed that I couldn't seem to budge the rest of my body even one inch in any direction. "I'm stuck! I'm stuck!"

"What the hell's going on here?" demanded Dad. "I can't move either!"

"Oh my," cried Mom, "I can't either!"

"The Green Fog has you in a hypnotic state," the judge informed to our mutual vexation. "Your heads are free to move about and converse as best you can manage under the circumstances, but the rest of your bodies will remain under the control of this court until we are adjourned. Now move forward please," he ordered, after hammering again, which was then followed by more giggles.

"I feel like fainting," my mother whined as the three of us marched along like puppets on an invisible string. "But I can't seem to crumble to the ground no matter how hard I try."

"I wish we could run for it!" I slobbered, looking for the nearest exit with every step I was forced to take.

"I must be dreaming this," Dad grumbled. "I must! I must!"

We were only ten feet away from his perch when the judge hammered again, causing us to come to an abrupt stop where we remained frozen in place. "I see you haven't changed a bit," he said, smiling down at me with a mouth half-full of rotting teeth—the others missing.

I shook my clueless head. "Do I know you?"

"What do you want with us?" my mother soughed.

Dad growled. "What's this all about?"

The judge hammered. "Quiet please while I address destiny's child." He turned his whites on me and I would've stiffened from fear had I not already been stiff as a board. "Johnny Bishop… any last words before you're formally sentenced?"

"Sentenced?" I shrieked. "Sentenced for what? I thought I was supposed to go free?"

The judge giggled yet again. "No one in this world goes free. We're all prisoners of one sort or another."

My dad had fire in his eyes. "Is this some kind of sick joke?" he snarled at the judge. "We demand to know what this is all about!" He then gritted his teeth to express the anger and frustration we were all feeling.

In mocking fashion, the judge gritted his few remaining teeth at my father and lost one to the floor. "In spite of my various attempts at humor here this morning," he said, "this is no laughing matter." He waved a dusty manila folder in the air. "In fact, Johnny's file goes back centuries and reads like a horror story in the making!"

"Centuries my ass," Dad scoffed on my behalf, while Mom shook her head in disbelief.

The judge rolled his pupils. "Need I remind you that your son is here today because he attacked a defenseless child with a water balloon?"

I was able to blush, although kicking myself for that stupid act was still out of the question.

"But apparently that's not the only crime he's been dealing with of late," the judge continued to my dismay. "Not that it's any of my concern, but it has come to my attention that you are scheduled to meet with Johnny's principal later today to beg forgiveness for the stolen report card he's been using to forge his way through his sophomore year of high school."

My mother grimaced, while I continued to blush. "Look… I know Johnny's no angel, but I was told on the phone yesterday that this water balloon matter was to be dismissed."

"Dismissed?" the judge cackled. "You didn't hear that from me."

Dad barked. "Sounds like we need a lawyer."

"Yeah," I chimed in, "we want a lawyer!"

Another giggle ensued. "I'm afraid a lawyer would only complicate matters in a case that was decided long ago." The judge looked my way and hammered twice, and my knees would've surely buckled if they could only move. "Johnny Bishop… it is by the authority vested in me that I hereby sentence you to one hundred days at the Kilborne Academy."

"What?" I screamed above my parent's howls, the three of us were like bobbleheads clamoring away. "You've got to be kidding me!"

"If you manage to survive your sentence," the judge said, as my parents and I gasped in unison, "which is easier said than done," he continued to more gasps, "you'll be allowed to return home and resume your life, as if your sentence had never happened. But if you fail to survive the treacherous journey that awaits you, your soul will remain in our custody forevermore, and your place in history will be stricken from the record books, as if you'd never been born."

"You can't do this," Mom protested. "You can't!"

Dad looked like a crazed bear mounted to the floor. "Let us go! Let us go now!"

The judge hammered again, and I saw myself running out the courtroom doors. I just kept running, assuming my parents were following along. I looked over to my left and then my right and was shocked to see Mom and Dad standing right where I had left them. "Hey… what are ya still doing in that courtroom?"

My mother peered up at me with a puzzled look on her wary face. "This is no time for fun and games, Johnny. What are you doing?"

"I'm running for my life, Mom!"

Dad also appeared puzzled when I looked his way. "What are you talking about?" he spat. "You're still standing right between us in the courtroom."

"Johnny has been specially targeted by the Green Fog," the judge indicated, which took me by surprise. "For the next hundred days, fact and fiction will mingle like old friends inside his troubled mind to form a magical roller coaster ride for the ages. At times he'll think and see things more clearly than ever before—and other times not so much, if at all."

"You're crazy," my mother snapped. "We want to go home!"

The judge giggled. "The Green Fog will take you home when the time is right."

"What's the story with this Green Fog you keep mentioning anyway?" my dad inquired.

The judge cleared his heavily wrinkled throat and a puff of green flew from his rotting mouth. "The Green Fog is a hydrogen-based gas that has been around since the beginning of time. It can only be found here on earth at the illustrious Kilborne Academy, where it seeps from the depths of a great lake. But it travels well. In fact, it has been well-documented by NASA to be working its magic deep in outer space by creating planets out of thin air, light years away from the human race. It is my belief that this is how God spreads his vast empire throughout the ever-growing universe. And I know for a fact that he who controls the Green Fog here on planet earth, has many of the same powers as God, himself!"

"Sounds like bullshit to me," my dad muttered. "But whatever."

We watched helplessly as the tiny judge climbed down from his tall perch. "I'll be taking Johnny in a school bus," he informed my parents. "I suggest you follow us to the Kilborne Academy when you are free to do so. Otherwise, should he remain amongst the living, you'll have no idea where to find him at the conclusion of his sentence."

"Wait a minute," my mother pleaded. "Please! Johnny didn't do anything to deserve a punishment like this. It's just not fair!"

"Life is often times not fair, Mrs. Bishop," the judge giggled. "But it still goes on with reckless abandon just the same."

"This is kidnapping!" growled my dad. "I'm going to call the police and have you arrested!"

"Have me arrested?" the judge gave a haughty laugh. "I answer to a much higher authority than what governs the masses, Mr. Bishop. I answer to the man who controls the Green Fog! And in him I do trust." The judge waved to me. "Now come along, Johnny. Your treacherous fate awaits you."

Suddenly, I could move. For real this time! But all I could do was walk when I wanted to run. I had no choice but to follow the judge like a dog following his master. I looked back at my stuck-in-place parents, and screamed, "Mom! Dad! Help! Help me!"

"I'm calling the FBI the first chance I get!" roared my father.

"Run, Johnny! Run!" shouted my mother.

I tried to take her advice, but all I could do was walk. To make matters worse, I saw green smoke filling the courtroom as we left out the side door. "What's happening to my parents?"

"They looked like they could use another hit of Green Fog to set their minds at ease," the judge replied. "They need to have smiles on their worried faces and tunnel vision for the long drive up to Kilborne."

I noticed the judge looked even older in the light of day. Much older! Befitting, I saw that his black robe was moth-eaten and dusty like something from the grave. He waddled when he walked. His faded black leather shoes squeaked with every step he took. And his bones creaked along like his skeleton was hanging by a thread inside his decaying body.

I wanted to yell for help, but it was futile since we were on a deserted sidewalk at the rear of the courthouse—on a collision course with a yellow school bus. Desperation set in and I began gnashing my teeth to where I was afraid they might chip or start falling out. "I wanna run so bad!"

"Of course you do," he snickered. "But go ahead and board the bus instead, and we'll get the show on the road. You'll soon be experiencing wondrous things that'll blow your mind."

# Chapter Six
*Road Trip*

The smell of honeysuckle hit me hard when I boarded the near-empty bus, and I became even more lightheaded than I was before. I saw that the bus driver reminded me of an old Santa Claus, except that he was wearing blue jeans with a white tee shirt and red suspenders instead of the usual Santa garb. His eyes were faded like the judge's—only with a hint of brown instead of blue, and his clammy skin was similar in that it was also opaque to the bone.

He pointed with his thumb. "Take a seat across from that sleeping hippie a few rows behind me," he said in surprisingly cheerful fashion, even sounding like an old recording of Santa, "and chain yourself in just like he is."

As if in a trance, I slowly turned and walked down an aisle that was a shag carpet of Green Fog. In the first row of seats to my left looked to be a snoring Boy Scout, although he appeared to be in his early twenties with thinning blond hair that was cut short. His khaki pants were bloodstained and there was a red bandana tied around the right epaulet of his yellowed button-down shirt. A few rows beyond him on the right side was that sleeping hippie in chains. Otherwise, the bus was empty. I took a seat across the aisle from the hippie and without so much as blinking an eye; I belted and cuffed myself in just as the driver had instructed.

All chained up, I sat quietly and reflected. Sensibility came to me in waves. Crashing waves! I knew I was in trouble. Fighting for my life in fact! *And yet I went and obeyed Santa like it was the night before Christmas?* Surely there was cause for concern. Especially when I noticed black metal screens on the side and back windows like a prison bus. Seeing my smiling parents holding hands as they walked out of the courthouse brought a smile to my face. Save for the teary-eyes, they looked like they didn't have a care in the world—so why should I?

The judge pointed to my parents after boarding the bus. "Honk at those two, Chester," he said, before taking a seat behind the driver. Chester honked and waved. My parents waved back as they headed for their car in the parking lot. "They'll be following us back to the academy," the judge continued, "so don't try and lose them."

"Wouldn't dream of it," replied Chester. He turned the key and the engine cranked to life. He slowly drove toward the parking lot exit with my parents following in my mother's white station wagon and off we went—rumbling down the road.

I looked out the screened windows, until everything near and dear had faded from sight. Tears filled my eyes, but strangely, there remained a smile on my face. The judge's head began to bob like he was fighting sleep. The Boy Scout was still snoring away, and the hippie was out cold. I didn't exactly feel secure with Chester behind the wheel. He did a lot of weaving and had more than a few near misses with just about every vehicle within range of the bus. I figured he was either drunk or he couldn't see worth a darn with those funky eyes of his. Even so, I eventually got used to the near misses and was rocked to sleep. It was restless at first, but I was heading for what appeared to be a deep and peaceful state, when I suddenly sensed evil eyes upon me. Alarmed, I awoke to the nightmare where I was sitting all chained-up on a swerving school bus, and it was then that reality hit me like a punch to the gut! Adding to my woes, I still felt those evil eyes upon me. I slowly turned to my left and found the hippie looking my way.

"Marty's the name," he said, smiling warm and friendly, although his big brown eyes were dark and vacant like the blackness of space, and yet there was a twinkle about them that could suck you in deep. He jingled his cuffs. "I'd reach across the aisle and shake your hand, but I'm a little tied up at the moment."

"Yeah, me too." I jingled back. "I'm Johnny."

"So, what brings ya to paradise, Johnny?"

I shrugged, mindlessly. "Bad luck, I guess."

He laughed. "I didn't know there was any other kind."

Evil eyes aside, my first impression of Marty was that he needed a hug. Otherwise, he had long sideburns and scraggly black hair that ran halfway down his faded black Led Zeppelin tee shirt. I had figured he was in his late teens back then, but it was hard to tell for sure. He had a rugged baby face that seemed old and worn like his blue jeans and scuffed like his black cowboy boots. "So, how long have you been on this bus?"

"Seems like forever," he replied, before giving me the once over. "Is it Sunday, man? You look like ya just got out of church."

I was in a blue button-down shirt with black slacks and a pair of shiny black loafers that my mother had bought me for a wedding I was forced to attend a few months back. "It's Friday," I answered. "I was all dressed up for my day in court and it's like I've been stuck in the Twilight Zone ever since."

"Well… if it's any consolation to ya, I hear there's a killer buffet waiting for us on the other end of this joy ride." He winked and almost sucked me into his brown depths. "At least you're dressed nice for that."

"I can't imagine eating at a time like this."

Marty nodded toward the Boy Scout. "For what it's worth, that snoring dude got drunk last night and spilled the beans about the Kilborne Academy. Calls himself Sergeant Stevens. He, the judge, and that bus driver are 'The Three Little Bitches.' That's what he called them. He said they're all long dead, but the Green Fog brings 'em back from the grave every spring so they can go out and collect victims like us for their boss-man's reform school from hell."

"I can't believe this is really happening."

"It ain't all bad, man. I hear we get reformed by taking acid trips through time at this school." He grinned. "I can hardly wait ta see what that shit's all about!"

"I feel like I'm tripping already."

"Far out, man," he said. "So, what'd they nab ya for, partner?"

"I got busted for hitting a kid with a lousy water balloon." I shook my befuddled head. "What about you?"

"I got busted for hitting my old man with a baseball bat," he admitted with an impish grin.

"Seriously?" I questioned, hoping he was just trying to impress me with his gritty, tough guy act. "You hit your dad with a bat?"

He shrugged like it was no big deal and because of his chains, it sounded like spare change hitting the floor. "It was an accident, man."

Skeptical, I raised a doubting eyebrow. "For real?"

His evil eyes became weak and shifty. "Okay… maybe the first couple of times was my fault, but that last shot to the head was definitely an accident."

Hardly amused, I was thinking Marty was the best actor in the world, or he was telling me the truth. Either way, I was not getting the warm and fuzzies from hanging with the guy. "Did ya kill him?"

He shrugged again and after his chains had settled down, he calmly said, "Your guess is as good as mine."

Looking to change the subject or at least my view, I diverted my eyes out the windshield where I noticed we were on a two-lane highway with rolling hills and scant houses and towns dotting the lush greenery up ahead. I could tell that picking a lane was not Chester's claim to fame. He continued to be all over the road. Luckily, the traffic was light. I looked over my shoulder to check on my parents, but the screened window at the back of the bus was too high to see them from my seat. I tried to stand, but I was firmly belted in place. Frustrated, I yanked on my chains to where I lost a button on my shirt. "I can't believe I locked myself up like this."

"Yes sir," Marty guffawed, "I'm thinking you can be made to do anything while under the influence of the Green Fog… maybe even screw your own sister!"

I was not too far gone to be taken aback. "Wow! You must have quite a home life to say something like that."

"You wouldn't believe the half of it." He laughed and it sounded more like a cry for help. His evil browns turned glassy before shifting downward. "Maybe we'll save the storytelling for another time," he said, before turning his head away and going silent.

The ride continued uneventfully, until Chester hit the brakes. The tires screeched. The bus swerved. We exited the highway onto a road that looked to be far removed from civilization. I half-expected to see dinosaurs come out from behind the many tall trees or see them roaming the patches of open field that dotted the wooded hills. I saw that the wooded hills rose up to become small mountains. There were even larger mountains beyond that and more beyond that. The mountain range looked like it was posing for a family picture with the tall ones in the back, and the thought made me homesick. Again, I tried to check on my parents, and again I was held in place.

There was nary a sign of life, until the judge's head stopped bobbing aimlessly, then snapped to attention—losing another tooth to the floor. The sergeant managed one last snore before opening his eyelids. He came out of his slumber and startled me by immediately jerking his head around in my direction. I was suddenly in a staring contest with a man with milky blue eyes. But what distinguished the sergeant from the other two bitches was that he otherwise looked alive. He even sported a healthy tan. His teeth were all there, as white as his eyes.

"Well, well, well," he said with a voice that sounded young, but scratchy like the judge and Chester, "if it ain't Johnny Paradise in the flesh."

"Ah, sorry… you must have me confused with someone else."

"Not likely," he returned. "You're the spitting image of the portrait hanging in our entry hall. –And you get to remember a face after seeing it for a hundred and ninety-nine years!"

Nonplussed, I shook my befuddled head yet again. "Excuse me?"

"That's right, Johnny Boy," he sniggered. "You have a lot more history than you thought. In fact…"

"—That's enough, Sergeant," the judge intervened. "No need to let the cat out of the bag just yet."

I stiffened to where my chains rattled. "What's going on here?" I probed. "What's this really all about?"

"All of your questions and concerns will be addressed in due time," answered the judge. "We're almost to Kilborne now, so enjoy what's left of this peaceful ride, because the real fun is about to begin in earnest."

"But I've got rights," I clamored. "I wanna know what's going on before we go any further!"

The judge sneered. "Your rights have been taken away from you, now it's up to you to earn them back… or die trying."

I gulped, but said nothing, wondering if I was up to the task. The bus passed a closed gas station on the corner of a dead-end street where five gutted houses sat nearly burned to the ground. Three of the houses formed a crooked line on one side of the street; the two others were a short way down from the gas station on the opposite side. A weathered plaque on a broken light pole read: FITZHUGH FALLS. POPULATION ZERO.

"I called a place like this home once," Marty snorted.

I sighed, forlornly. "I'd give anything to be home now."

We reached the end of the short street and motored past a big sign that read: PRIVATE DRIVE—NO TRESPASSING, before disappearing through hanging branches and onto a narrow rocky road that cut into the approaching mountain like a garland wrapped around a Christmas tree. I tried to brace myself for anything and everything as the bus followed the tree-lined road up to the summit. There was a clearing at the peak that led to a thorny old gate with metal signage high above that read: KIL. The rest of the letters had been ravaged by time to where only rusted nubs remained of: BORNE ACADEMY.

"Welcome to the illustrious Kilborne Academy," the judge trumpeted. "Home sweet home to troubled youth of all ages!"

Marty grumbled. "This place looks like death warmed over."

"Seems more like hell to me," I said, while gazing out the windshield. To the left and right of the old gate was a crumbled wall of gray stone that extended fifty feet before disappearing into a woody thicket on either side of the clearing. The wall was five feet tall in some places, three in others, and like the gate it was overrun with thorny briar. Beyond the wall on a small rolling hill of weeds was a half-toppled brick chimney that was charred. It stood like a tombstone lording over the burned-out remains of a large building that was near to being swallowed by the surrounding woods. The place seemed lifeless, save for hornets that repeatedly buzzed the bus and statuesque-like vultures that clung to dead branches on nearby rotting trees. Dreary, gray clouds hung low and blanketed the horizon in all directions.

The sergeant chuckled. "This is the one place on earth that can scare the crap out of a dead man."

I winced. "There's no way we can stay here."

"Oh, but of course we can," the judge insisted. "You're about to behold the magical power of God's secret formula at work here on this most sacred of all mountaintops."

I heard a rumble and saw a huge wave of Green Fog come rolling our way from behind the rubble of the building. It blanketed everything in its path as it rolled down the hill and billowed over the stone wall and between the rusted bars of the old gate. The windows of the bus were soon covered in fog, illuminating the cabin with its green glow. The air was thick with honeysuckle. It coated my lungs, making everything sticky sweet. The bus began to shake from the powerful fog that had swallowed us whole. "Help!" I screamed above the hissing of thousands of snakes. "I can't believe this is happening! I can't! I can't!"

"What... going crazy already?" The judge giggled. "But your sentence hasn't even begun yet."

The Green Fog faded away leaving clear blue skies and brilliant sunshine above. But strangely, a thick layer of gray still covered the land below, making it seem like the mountaintop was floating peacefully in the heavens. Furthermore, when I looked out the windshield again, I was surprised to see that the once crumbled stone wall was now ten-feet tall. Even more surprised was I that the old gate looked pristine and was opened to a cobblestone driveway that led up to a large red brick house with a tall chimney. The miraculously restored building was adorned with black shutters on the windows and it had two stately white columns that supported an overhang. The quaint structure was surrounded by colorful gardens and the woods were kept at bay by lush green lawns that were manicured to perfection. The trees were full of life. The vultures had been replaced by singing birds, while butterflies filled the air instead of hornets. "I surely must be dreaming this," I concluded. "There's no other way to explain what's going on here."

"Must be the acid, man," Marty said. "We're jacked up!"

# Chapter Seven
*Food for Thought*

"The Kilborne Academy is now officially open for the season," announced Chester, before hitting the gas. "Paradise awaits!"

The bus motored up the bumpy cobblestone driveway and veered left before stopping in front of the red brick building where there was a big, black front door to my right. We were parked parallel to the front gate, which I noticed was now closed when I looked out the screened windows across from me on the left side. I got excited when I saw my mother's white station wagon pull up and stop in front of the gate. Dream or not, it was reassuring to know my parents were only fifty yards away.

The sergeant caught my eye when all five feet of him stood facing us in the aisle. He pulled a silver key out of the leather pouch strapped to his waist. "You two shitheads won't be needing your chains anymore," he snickered. He then marched our way with a confident, if not cocky strut.

"Works for me." Marty raised his cuffs. "Can't wait to hit that buffet," he added excitedly. "I'm starving, man!"

"Just follow your nose once inside the front door," the sergeant instructed after setting him free, "and you'll have the feast of a lifetime!" He then turned towards me. "You're next, Johnny Boy."

Free at last, I made a beeline for the front gate. To hell with paradise, I was thinking. And to hell with the buffet! And most of all, to hell with my hundred-day sentence! Down the cobblestone driveway I went, frantically waving my arms in the air. "Mom! Dad! I'm coming! I'm coming!" I got down to the tall gate and it was locked. I yanked on the thick metal bars but couldn't get them to budge. Teasingly, I saw the station wagon parked not more than ten feet away. But all I could see through the glare of the windshield was Green Fog swirling around inside the cabin. "Mom! Dad! Are you all right in there? Mom! Dad!"

"They're fine," came a raspy voice from behind.

Startled, I quickly turned around and saw the smirking sergeant standing halfway up the driveway with his head cocked to one side and his hands on his hips. The cloudless sky almost brought out the blue in his eyes. "They don't seem fine to me," I snapped. "They're not responding to a word I say."

"They're taking a little fog bath to prepare for the long journey home and can't hear you at the moment," he informed. "They'll leave here with no memory of this place or the child they left behind, and the world will suddenly be clueless of your existence for the next hundred days. Forever, if you don't survive."

I shuddered with fear and anger. "None of this makes any sense. I just wanna go home and forget this day ever happened!"

"Tell me something I haven't heard a million times before," he razzed. "It don't matter what century it is… you recruits are all the same."

"Recruits?" I said, incredulously. "I'm no recruit! I didn't volunteer for this. I'm a prisoner!"

"I get twenty losers like you every season coming from all over the planet and not a one has ever volunteered yet. So yeah… I guess you can say you're a prisoner. We all are! Handpicked by the boss. But because you and your boyfriend in the dining hall are so special, there's only gonna be the two of you suffering along with us this year."

"Special?" I questioned. "What makes us so special?"

"You'll find out soon enough."

"Can't you just tell me now?"

"What and spoil all the fun?" he chuckled. "All I know is that I just celebrated my 214$^{th}$ birthday thanks to you. And there's no end in sight."

"Thanks to me?" I scoffed. "That's ridiculous!"

The sergeant rolled what was left of his eyes. "You've gotta lot to learn, but your formal education won't begin until you walk in the front door of the Big House," he said, before pointing to the building on the hill. "Once inside… you're officially on the clock and will start learning things about yourself that'll shock the shit out of you." He paused for effect, leaving me to wonder what if anything there was to know about myself that I didn't already know. "If you somehow manage to make it out of here alive after serving your sentence," he continued, "you'll have one hell of an amazing story to tell the world, if the Green Fog wears off your head before you're too old and senile to remember your name."

Dream or no dream, I had heard enough. I quickly turned back around and tried to shake open the unyielding bars of a gate that was too tall and pointy at the top to climb over. I then looked to either side of the gate, noticing that the stone walls were so smooth they could not be breached without the help of another. I sighed wistfully, then gazed at the green that filled the windshield of my parent's car. "Mom… Dad… please say something!"

"In case you're wondering," I heard the sergeant say, "the survival rate here at the academy is around five percent." He divulged to my horror. "Many years all twenty recruits bite the dust," he added to my further dismay. "So, I wouldn't go making any long-term plans if I were you. But then again… you are Johnny Paradise."

Aggrieved out of my mind, I swiveled around to face the cocky sergeant. "You've got the wrong guy!" I clamored, as tears flew from my eyes. "My name's Johnny Bishop! I don't know any Johnny Paradise!"

"If you think I'm just blowing smoke up your foggy ass," he chuckled, "then I suggest you come inside and meet Mr. Paradise for yourself. I think you'll be more than a little surprised at how much ya have in common. Shocked in fact!" he sniggered. "And besides that… the longer we dick around out here, the longer your parents get to stay in the fog, far away from their two remaining children."

Thoughts of Emily and David popped into my head. I knew the twins could never take care of themselves for too terribly long without adult supervision. "I feel so helpless," I pined. "I can't believe this is happening. I can't!" I began to tremble. "Please tell me this is a bad dream. Please!"

"If you think you're having difficulties now, just wait 'til ya get inside." He chuckled yet again, chuckling as often as the judge had giggled. "It's not all bad though," he added smarmy, "cause the food's ta die for."

"Eating's the last thing on my mind right now."

"That's what they all say," he returned. "But in any event, I suggest we get a move-on before your siblings come home to an empty house."

Thoroughly vexed and out of options, I looked out the gate one last time at my Green Fog encased parents. "Mom! Dad! Honk if you can hear me!" The silence was broken when the engine started, and the station wagon slowly backed up, then turned around and drove away without a honk. "Mom! Dad!" After crying a few more tears, I felt I had no choice but to join the sergeant. I was in the middle of dreading every step we took toward the Big House, when a gaggle of butterfly suddenly swooped in out of nowhere and buzzed my head. One playfully landed on my ear. It glowed of gold and purple with a black head that was trying to look me in the eye. The butterflies seemed to accept me as a friend and yet I could tell they were trying to herd me along. "As beautiful as this place seems, I'd still give anything to leave as fast as I can."

"We all would," he admitted. "But there's no way out of this hell hole for us dead folk. At least you recruits still got a fighting chance."

"Huh... not much of a chance from what you say."

"At least it's better than what I got to look forward to. To hell with eternal life! I'd just like to rest in peace for a decade or two without seeing the light of day. But no... like it or not... I have ta come back from the grave every year and escort a bunch of shithead losers like you around."

Rather than take offense, I saw opportunity knocking. "Just help me over the stone wall, and I'll be out of your hair before ya know it!"

"Look... I don't care if you're Johnny Paradise or not, there's no escaping the Kilborne Academy."

My hopes dashed, I let my watery eyes wander. Besides butterflies, I saw birds frolicking up in the many trees, while deer dominated the grassy plains down below in a meadow. I heard small animals and even insects going about their business in the neighboring brush. Surprisingly, nature was more abundant and vibrant inside the walls of this prison than outside in the freedom. We reached the porch of the Big House and I noticed that the black door was half opened to the shadows inside. I peered into the darkness. "What's waiting for me inside?"

"A whole lot of wicked pleasures and a million ways to suffer an extremely painful death," he replied, while I cringed. "But as I said before... the food's ta die for."

My knees were shaking, as my stomach churned in knots. "There's no way I can eat at a time like this. No way!"

He chuckled. "We'll soon see about that."

"And what's this about wicked pleasures?"

He chuckled yet again. "Just wait, Johnny Boy. Your mind isn't the only thing about to be blown away."

If nothing else, the Big House at least looked nice and homey on the outside, even bordering on whimsical with the way the cream-filled red brick walls bowed and bulged. The building had clearly shifted one way and then another over time. I saw paint chips peeling away on the white trim. And the black shutters also looked like they could use a fresh coat of paint, while the dark shingles on the pitched roof were faded in spots and torn in others. Although the place was weather beaten, an abundance of vibrant red, white and blue flowers lined the porch, giving way to the violets, pinks and yellows that encroached from the surrounding gardens, thus bringing the Big House to life and making it seem almost like new again. "What happened to Chester and the judge?" I asked, having just noticed the bus was gone.

"I'm sure you'll be running into those two bitches again before long," he foretold. Chilled to the bone, I cautiously followed the sergeant up a short flight of red brick stairs before settling on the wood surface of the porch. The butterflies began to leave me as I creaked along, until I was without wings inside the front door that the sergeant then closed and locked with a twist of his silver key. "You're officially on the clock," he said. "Now all ya gotta do is survive the next hundred days."

I stood rigid… ready for anything and everything as my eyes adjusted to the dimness. The first thing I noticed was the place smelled like an old cedar closet, but with a hint of honeysuckle. I began to see that the entry was an unfurnished tall, boxy room with a planked wood floor. And well above my head was a large circular wrought iron chandelier whose many candles bounced yellow light off the white textured walls. All that remained of the sunlight could be seen peeking through the shuddered windows on either side of the door behind me. To my left was that wood staircase that led up to the double doors in the middle of that small catwalk that ran across the far end of the entry. I then heard the pitter-patter of little feet running the large rafters that were near the high ceiling, as the rats made their presence known.

I was feeling nauseous at best when I caught that first whiff of something out of this world. "Whoa… that smells great!" I said. "Is that the buffet?" I asked, with nostrils flaring.

The sergeant nodded, sporting an impish grin. "That's correct."

I began savoring every breath I took to where I was soon high on flavor. My mouth watered with anticipation, as I imagined the incredible edibles that were hiding out somewhere inside the Big House. "Any chance I can go check it out?" I begged more than asked.

"I thought you weren't hungry?" he snickered.

I shrugged with a sheepish grin. "Food's all I can think about all of a sudden."

The sergeant tilted his head toward a large gold-framed image hanging on the wall that was almost lost in the shadows to my right. "Don't ya wanna meet Johnny Paradise first?"

I was thinking it could wait, but then my eyes traveled past the sergeant onto the flickering image on the wall, where I saw a pair of brilliant blues staring at me with black bushy hair jumping off the canvas and a glaring pimple painted on the chin. "Hey… that's me!" Stunned, I put the buffet on hold and took a step closer to the oil painting. "It's like looking in a mirror. Even my clothes are the same as what I have on now!"

The sergeant pointed to a small plaque on the bottom of the frame. "As you can see, this was painted in 1780 when Kilborne first opened its doors… and it's been hanging here in the entry hall ever since."

Doubting his every word, I moved in for a closer look. The gold plaque read: Johnny Paradise. Painted in 1780 by Nathaniel Fitzhugh. "How can this be?" I interrogated. "I wasn't even born yet and besides that… these clothes are only a few months old."

The sergeant smirked. "Well if that's the case, then obviously the artist must be a true visionary. A man born before his time!"

I touched the canvas and the paint was bone dry with a layer of dust that looked like it had been there for ages. "No. This is impossible. This has to be some kind of joke," I insisted. "This painting even shows that I've got a missing button on my shirt."

He shrugged, mindlessly. "So what?"

"I lost that button about an hour ago on the bus ride over here."

"I told you the artist was a visionary," he said. "Or maybe it's because your present has just met up with your once hidden past."

I couldn't help but laugh. "My once hidden past? What hidden past?"

"Believe it or not, you really do have more history than ya think."

"You can't fool me."

"Then have it your way, Johnny Boy." He chuckled. "Or maybe I should call you, Mr. Paradise?"

My building frustration with the sergeant was suddenly trumped by a heavenly whiff of goodness that rose up above the other aromas and could not be ignored. "I'd give anything to check out that buffet now."

"Then follow your nose to the dining hall," he replied, "and you'll eat like ya never ate before."

I left Johnny Paradise behind, letting my nose guide me the short distance it took to the end of the entry hall where there was an opening the size of the front door. It was dark inside, save for the narrow carpet of luminous Green Fog that hissed within. Above the center of the dark opening and below the shadows of the catwalk was that big, wooly buffalo head that was mounted on the wall. Its lifeless glass eyes stared down at me, although it was snorting and chewing its cud like it was somehow still alive. Long strands of drool dripped down from its busy mouth and splattered in a slimy puddle on the floor. Undeterred, I moved past the puddle, thinking the buffalo head was as anxious as I was about the buffet, because I was drooling too.

I stepped inside the opening and was on firm ground, although I was ankle deep in the glowing Green Fog that was the width of a sidewalk. It covered the ground, running east to west as I faced north toward the blackness of the far wall, which flickered a dingy yellow courtesy of the chandelier hanging high behind me. Whether I looked left or right, the neon green sidewalk was straight and narrow and appeared to run forever in either direction. Besides that unsettling observation, I began to hear ghostly teenage voices calling out to me from afar—boys eerily from the east and girls wantonly from the west. They were a chorus of desperate whispers meeting me in the middle. *Come play with us, Johnny. Come play. We've been waiting for you, lover boy... we wanna be with you now and always.*

My head was clamoring for me to run for my life, but my stomach demanded that I follow my nose. And so, against my better judgement, I turned right and headed east toward the feast, following my nose down a hallway that had me aglow in green from the waist down. Otherwise, I was as black as the walls that hemmed me in.

I remember being pleased that the footing remained solid, although it bothered me that I couldn't see below my ankles in the thick soup that continued to hiss. And it didn't help that the voices had gone from whispering to barking. *That's right, Johnny... be a man and come this way! Be a man like us and join the brotherhood!* And the girls were cooing loudly behind me. *Come back, Johnny. We love you! We love you!*

The trek was arduous, but the distance much shorter than it had appeared. Still, my ears were ringing by the time the voices went silent at the end of the hallway, which fed directly into the dining hall. I found myself standing in a large, rectangular-shaped room. The place was without windows, but the lighting was warm and cozy by way of several wrought iron chandeliers that hung from a ten-foot wood-beamed ceiling. There was also a crackling fire burning in a stone fireplace that warmed the room, giving yellow life to the white textured walls.

I saw Marty sitting at one of five otherwise empty round tables that were cloaked in white, each with four chairs parked in front of elegant place settings and a flaming red candle in the center. I cautiously approached the dude with the evil eyes. He had a red linen napkin draped over his shoulder and several sparkling white china plates filled with steak and lobster positioned in a neat row like they were lined up on a runway, waiting to take off into his mouth.

"How's the food?" I asked, figuring I already knew the answer to that question.

"I feel like I'm on an all-time high eating this shit," he slobbered. "Go check out the buffet, man... and when you dig in, you'll feel like ya died and went ta heaven!"

Of course, Marty didn't have to twist my arm. I grabbed an empty plate and followed my nose past the tables to the back wall where there was a long row of large cast iron skillets that were filled with simmering meats. I picked up a rib, but it quickly fell off the bone. I tried another and this time the rib made it into my mouth where it melted before I could chew, but the incredible flavor was mind-blowing.

I eagerly surveyed the riches, seeing chicken that was cooked twenty different ways along with roasted turkey, glazed ham, stuffed pork chops, thick bacon, and juicy fillets that were all piled high like smoldering pyramids of protein. And there was salmon and giant shrimp to go with lobster that was a foot long. The lasagna looked like seven layers of cheesy madness. The pepperoni pizza seemed by the endless slice. There were mounds of fruits and vegetables that tasted fresh out of the garden. The cakes were delightful to behold and seemingly just baked. Thick chocolate pudding was available by the bucket. Ice cream too! By the time my plate was full, I was starting to get that way as well, having sampled everything as I went. "I've never tasted anything like this stuff before," I said, after returning to the table. I took a seat across from Marty, fearful of nothing save for a bloated belly.

"No doubt," he said. "I could easily spend the rest of my life here."

I bit into a crunchy fried chicken breast that sent me into another world. The savory juices overran my mouth and dripped down onto the red napkin in my lap. I wiped my chin with the back of my hand and licked, not wanting to miss a precious drop of the tremendous flavor. "Wow… this is amazing!" I twinkled, before taking another bite. With a crunch, my teeth penetrated the crispy exterior of the breast, cutting through the juicy white meat like a hot knife through warm butter, until hitting chicken bone. I quivered with delight after swallowing. "Every bite's better than the last," I exclaimed, trying to find room in my stomach for the next perfect bite and the next after that.

"That's just the acid doing its thing, man."

Reluctantly, I lowered the succulent chicken breast from my lips, before swallowing the joy in my mouth. "For real?" I asked, skeptically. "I know I'm pretty high right now, but no one else has mentioned anything about acid."

"Trust me," he said, "I've tripped enough to know when I'm high on acid, and this is some pretty outrageous shit we're on right now."

I shrugged, halfheartedly. "If you say so."

"I'm serious, man… I'm hallucinating that one of these roasted lobsters is crawling off my plate as we speak."

"Then ya better eat it before it gets away."

"Nah… I'd rather save room for dessert."

"Dessert?" I smiled knowingly, thinking of the cakes and pastries I had sampled during my travels around the buffet. "I've got a long way ta go before I get back around to the sweets again."

"I hear ya, man. I don't want this meal ta ever end."

I returned to the chicken breast and nibbled away. A little of this. A lot of that! I became a ravenous zombie with eyes far bigger than my bulging stomach could handle. "I'm gonna eat 'til I explode."

"You know, partner… they're gonna have ta tear my sorry ass away from this bitchin' place, cause I'm not leaving without a fight."

"I'm going back for more." I staggered to my feet and stumbled over to the buffet where I grabbed a bucket of steamy mashed potatoes drenched in thick brown gravy, later returning to the table with a plate full of turkey, corn stuffing and candied yams capped with marshmallow. There was also a jiggling mound of cranberry sauce in the mix. "I'm feeling homesick," I said, after taking my seat. "So, I was thinking a thanksgiving dinner might help to cheer me up a little."

"You have all that for thanksgiving?" he asked, looking shocked. "Shit… I'm lucky to get a TV dinner. You must be rich!"

"Nope… not even close. But we still manage to have a big family dinner every thanksgiving. The thing is… there's no way my mother can cook like this. No one can!"

"Heck, my old lady hardly knew her way around a kitchen, but I hear she was pretty good in the bedroom!"

"Speaking of kitchens," I said, "have ya seen one in this place?"

"Nope," he replied. "But the food stays piled high, no matter how much we eat."

"Yeah… I was noticing that." Besides no kitchen, there were no cooks or waiters either, just two guys eating themselves to death from a bottomless pit. "I'm parched," I said. "Anything ta drink around here?"

He quickly scanned the room and shrugged. "Not that I can see, but I'm getting thirsty myself."

I panned the cornucopia of good eats against the back wall, looking for a solution to our problem. "We could always squeeze some oranges and make juice," I proposed.

"Sounds like a plan, man."

The orange juice was like liquid candy. More food was then consumed, and liquid candy gulped. We just couldn't stop ourselves. I had my eye on a bucket of chocolate pudding, but my stomach said no. I took a spoonful anyway. It didn't hurt that whipped cream was piled high on top. The pudding was creamy smooth on the way down, but my stomach still said no. I defied my aching belly and took another spoonful. *Take the pain*, I demanded of myself. *Take the pain!* I saw across the table that Marty had finally succumbed and was passed out in his chair. His head was slumped to one side, but he was still chewing away.

Like a junkie in need of a fix, I forced yet another spoonful of pudding into my mouth and choked it down. A sharp pain took me by surprise when it hit bottom. My stomach convulsed. My chest burned like fire. My heart shockingly stopped, and my intestines blew. I was in full panic mode, desperately trying to catch my last breath, when I felt myself slipping away to a place I had never been before. A dark place without boundaries… and yet the limitations were endless. And then everything that mattered to me suddenly mattered no more.

# Chapter Eight
### *Playing with the Dead*

**D**ead to the world, I wallowed in eternal darkness. If there was a bright side to my situation, it was that I felt no pain. But time continued unabated to where even family and friends became a distant memory.

The monotony went on uninterrupted for what seemed like centuries. Bored to tears, I was hoping to see heaven before losing what was left of my mind. I searched and searched but found nothing except the blackness of space. There wasn't even a star to light my way.

I was deaf, until I heard hissing. And breathless, until I inhaled the sweetness of honeysuckle. I then noticed a small patch of Green Fog in the distance. It glowed and became the center of my universe. I was drawn to it because there was nothing else in my vanishing life. Nothing!

A shrill sound suddenly blared that could wake the dead and I slowly began to feel again. But my awakening soul became troubled when my memory returned in a hideous flood. Shocked by my perilous plight, I opened eyes that I thought were already open and saw Sergeant Stevens standing nearby with a whistle in his hand.

"Whoa… what happened?" I muttered, last remembering a bucket of chocolate pudding before the lights went out. I then saw Marty sleeping in his chair and my heart skipped a beat after recalling my painful last breath. "Seems like I've been gone a lifetime."

"You have," the sergeant said. "But ya get eight more lives before you're officially dead for good."

That brought a smirk to my face. "So, you're saying I really died?" I twittered, thinking more like I'd probably been knocked-out all that time and only thought I was dead.

"Among other ailments, you had a massive heart attack from eating food that was ta die for," he informed, jolting a dreadful memory that went virile inside my body. "But fear not," he continued, "just like a cat has nine lives, you get nine chances to make it through your hundred-day sentence. Otherwise, not a single recruit would last a day here."

I began to muse and noticed that I seemed older and wiser than my previous life. Wise enough to want to put an immediate end to this nightmare. "I just want to go home," I shrieked. "I've had enough of this creepy place and don't wanna spend another moment here!" I was about to shed a few tears, when heavenly aromas once again found my nose and surprisingly, I was soon toying with the idea of picking up an empty plate. "I'm still stuffed from my last meal, but that buffet's calling my name again in a very big way."

"You wouldn't be the first recruit to eat yourself to death... nine times!"

I savored another tasty breath like I was sipping fine wine and it was delightful. "I can think of worse ways to die," I said, dreamily.

"Die eight more times and you'll join the roughly thirty-five hundred losers in the hallway for all eternity. Faceless spirits who had a past that only they can remember. I call 'em 'The Unborn' cause the Green Fog has left behind no trace that they ever made it out of their mother's vagina."

Shocked, my appetite suddenly escaped me as I glanced across the room at the dark opening with the glowing green trail, thinking back on the myriad of ghostly voices I'd heard clamoring away in there.

He chuckled, mournfully this time. "Last I checked... there were about three thousand male souls from the ages of twelve to eighteen stuck in there, the rest are female. Some of the chicks used to be babes too," he hooted. "Now they're just sexy voices calling out in the dark."

"I'd hate to end up like that."

"Just so ya know... there's no getting ta rest in peace when ya die here at the Kilborne Academy. No sir! That'd be way too easy! So, I suggest ya fight the urge to hit the killer buffet again and be ready to get down ta business, cause the only way out of this death camp is ta find a way to survive your sentence."

"So, what happens next?" I inquired, expecting him to tell me I had to swim in a tank full of sharks or run through fire or jump off some tall building—or even worse!

"Your treacherous journey begins by playing baseball."

I fought the urge to laugh. "Baseball?" I said, thinking he was surely pulling my leg. "There's baseball here?"

"There's everything here… and then some," he responded. "But we'll start off with America's pastime and go from there."

Although skeptical, I nodded approvingly. "Okay. I think I can handle that. I play baseball all the time."

"Except that today you'll be playing for your life."

I should've expected him to say as much. "Seriously?"

"Much like the buffet," he began to lecture, "Kilborne has treats that can bring extreme delight, but more than anything, there's a shitload of pain and suffering and challenges that'll test your will to live. Before all is said and done, you'll experience highs and lows like never before and just about every unimaginable thing in between. Your mind and body will be messed with time and again for a hundred days straight. But if you survive your sentence, you'll leave this place wise beyond your sixteen years, having experienced things no man alive could ever top."

"How many have survived so far?" I asked, hoping to join their ranks.

"There've been nearly two hundred who've graduated from the Kilborne Academy since we opened in 1780," he replied. "And about a dozen or so of those survivors are still alive and kicking, but that's more than enough to take over the world, if need be."

"Is that what this is all about," I probed, "taking over the world?"

"Fear not," he replied. "The graduates have no clue of each other's identity or whereabouts. For most, their knowledge of all things Kilborne remains dormant inside their heads, save for the occasional nightmare or stroke of genius. They're scattered all over the globe and would never think to join forces unless the boss wanted it that way. Otherwise, the boss only calls on them as needed to further his evil cause from one generation to the next."

"Wow… someone should warn the world about this place!"

"Easier said than done," he snickered. "As it is, Kilborne remains the best kept secret on this planet. —But enough talk, it's time I go wake your friend so we can get the show on the road."

A lot to digest in one sitting, I was left to contemplate my fate and that of the world's while the sergeant went over to Marty, who looked as lifeless as I felt inside. The sergeant took a deep breath and put the whistle to his lips. I didn't hear a sound, but Marty jumped to life and said: "What the heck happened?"

The sergeant settled him down and brought him up to speed before leading us single file into the hissing dark hallway. The honeysuckle was stronger than ever. The boys were barking. *We can use a man like you, Johnny! Stick around and join the brotherhood! Be a man, Johnny! Be a real man like us! Don't go, Johnny! Don't run off! Pussy! Don't be a pussy, Johnny! Stay here and be a man!*

"Sounds like a sausage-fest in here," Marty said, while hot on my heels. "I think one of 'em's trying ta get in my pants."

"No kidding?" I hew-hawed. "I thought that was you grabbing me from behind."

"You two shitheads breathe in much more of this green fairy dust," the sergeant heckled, "and you'll both be too messed up ta make it out of the hallway alive."

"Don't blame us," Marty said. "It's the acid, man."

"I'm thinking it's the green fairy dust," I giggled like the judge. "The stuff is great!"

The sergeant chuckled. "It's the nectar of the gods!"

Without another word said, save for the three thousand boys having their way with us, we continued our march west towards the cooing girls, moving quickly past the entry hall where my big-as-life painting was hanging on the wall for all to see. "So, what's it like ta be famous, Johnny?" Marty razzed.

"So far it sucks," I replied, drunkenly. "But the good news is I've only got a hundred days left to go."

"Yeah, man… it's hard ta believe we're just getting started."

We continued down the other end of the hallway and were quickly overwhelmed by an orgy of beautiful sounding girls. I heard all five hundred of them cooing my name. *Oh, Johnny… oh, Johnny! You're my hero, Johnny! So big and strong… handsome too! You're the perfect man for me, Johnny! You don't know how much I love you! How long I've waited to be with you! Oh, Johnny, my, Johnny! Wait, Johnny! Stop walking away! Spend more time with me! Spend more time with me, Johnny! Just say the word lover boy and I'll be yours forevermore! Stop now and you can have my girlfriends too!* Their perfume was honeysuckle sweet and I was drawn to each and every one of them. "Hey, Sergeant Stevens," I said, while slowing to a crawl, "if you don't mind, I'm gonna hang out here for a while."

"Yeah… to hell with the baseball," Marty said. "I sure dig the way theses bitches call out my name. Where're they hiding out?"

"They're calling your name too?" I asked, trying to act more surprised than hurt.

"That's all I'm hearing, man."

"If you two don't move along," the sergeant said, "these invisible ladies of the night will make ya die of heartache time and again, until they've sucked the eight remaining lives right out of ya. Then you'll wake and find yourself down at the other end of the hallway, swimming forevermore in a dark fishbowl of lost souls with the rest of the barking boys. –And then your only break from that eternal monotony will come every spring when ya get to scare the crap out of the twenty new recruits who enter this hallway for the first time. So, if that's the kind of future ya want, we can stop right now."

"Have I told ya I swing a mean bat?" Marty proclaimed. "If ya don't believe me, just ask my old man."

"Yeah," I nodded, "I'd rather take my chances playing ball."

There was an opening at the other end of the hallway. It was a room resembling the dining hall in every way, except that instead of tables there were beds. Two rows. Ten per side. They were facing each other with a wide birth running down the middle. All twenty beds had pressed white sheets with gray flannel covers.

"Pick a bed," the sergeant instructed.

"Wait a minute," I said. "I thought we were gonna play ball?"

"First ya gotta take a little nappy-pooh ta get yourselves ripe for time travel. Once that's been accomplished, we'll head for the Tall Grass out back where there awaits an historic field of dreams."

"The Tall Grass?" Marty twinkled. "I hope you're not talking about marijuana, man. Cause if ya are… you can count me in. Wow! First the kickass acid… then we get ta smoke some weed! What next… a case of ice-cold Miller?"

The sergeant responded by putting his whistle to his lips. His cheeks puffed when he blew, and all the chandeliers dimmed to where the candlelight resembled a myriad of tiny flickering stars. A crackling fire in a corner hearth suddenly took centerstage. It illuminated the textured walls and beamed ceiling and kept the pulsating shadows at bay. "Now lay your heads down ta rest," he said, "and I'll be back for ya when the time is right."

Marty and I faced each other after the sergeant disappeared back into the hallway. "Well, partner," he yawned, "I don't know 'bout you, but I'm ready ta hit the sack." He plopped down on a bed and by the time his head hit the pillow, he was snoring.

I wanted to fight sleep, but my knees began to wobble so I parked myself on a nearby bed. The pillow was not fluffy like the one at home, but it still did the trick. I was soon out cold, until I heard thunder. I opened my eyes and saw green water balloons raining down from my bedroom window, which I knew couldn't be real. Still, it was good to be back home again, if only in my dreams. Meanwhile, lightning struck as balloons fell in buckets from a gunmetal sky. They exploded on the ground just like in a previous dream, leaving behind puddle after puddle on my street. It got so the land couldn't hold the water and the road became a raging river with a green glow that lit the darkening ground and sky above.

I looked down from my window and saw an unsuspecting soul riding his shiny purple bike in front of my house. He was that new kid on the block that Rudy and I had ambushed. Aglow in green, Tom shed his bike and did the backstroke down the middle of the block. Mom was next in line. Her blonde hair reflected the water to where there appeared to be a green halo surrounding her head. My angelic mother waved up to me and I eagerly waved back as she floated by. Dad came next. He looked like a grizzly bear in search of wild salmon as he rumbled down the river. My busybody brother and sister were moving like twin torpedoes with their little heads barely above water. Rudy, Billy and Mitch were neck and neck as they raced downstream after them. Miss Willows, my incredibly hot high school teacher, picked a bad day to wear a miniskirt. It had crept up around her hips, revealing white panties that looked neon green as she swam past my window, followed by a parade of family and friends that paddled by in seconds, and then the water was empty. It was like my entire life had just splashed in front of my eyes.

The house was deathly quiet now that everyone was gone. No busybody twins to contend with. No parents to order me around. No school to bring me down. But there were no friends, either. Try as I may, I couldn't even escape my own bedroom at the moment. In short, there was really nothing left to do in this dream but wait and wait… until I was bored silly.

*Oh, Johnny... oh, Johnny! You're my hero, Johnny! So big and strong... handsome too! You're the perfect man for me, Johnny! You don't know how much I love you! How long I've waited to be with you! How much I want you, Johnny! Come be with me while we have the chance to be alone. I want you now, lover!!!*

I heard sexy voices cooing in my head that finally had me reading through some of my favorite magazines, and I couldn't decide which month I liked better—Miss April or Miss May. They both looked like they were ready for a roll in the hay. There was also a lot to like about Miss March. I blew my paper playmates kisses—one and all. And they smiled back in ways that you could only imagine.

*Oh, Johnny... oh, Johnny! You're the perfect man for me!*

I got in bed and went back and forth from month to month, trying to decide who was going to be my candid lady of the moment. The competition was tight. Ever so tight! But in the end, April fooled me the most. I was so completely lost in her hypnotic grip that I failed to notice my mother standing a few feet away. "Mom!" I scrambled to cover myself from further embarrassment, while the pages of my girlfriend flew in the air. "How long have you been there?" I asked, feeling myself turning shades of ever darkening pink.

"Long enough," she replied with a motherly scowl. "So, where'd ya get the Playboy magazines?"

"Rudy gave 'em to me," I admitted with a sheepish grin. "He said he didn't need 'em anymore now that he's got a steady girlfriend."

She raised a curious eyebrow. "Do you masturbate often?"

"Only when I get the chance," I quipped—trying to put a smile on her wary face.

Caught red-handed, I was glad the dream finally came to an end when a shrill sound jolted me out of my slumber. The candles were again burning bright in the sleeping quarters. I saw that Marty was out of bed and the sergeant was standing near the entrance to the hallway with his whistle in his hand. "How long have I been out?" I asked, feeling groggy and stiff. "Seems a long time," I added while stretching. "But on the other hand... it could've only been seconds."

"As you will soon find out," the sergeant replied, "time is relative here at the Kilborne Academy. Now let's go play ball!"

Like a sleepwalker coming to life, I got out of bed and followed Marty and the sergeant. The hallway was speechless. The Green Fog was gone. Instead of a green path, the narrow black walls were aglow with sconces positioned at eye-level about every ten feet. The white candlelight painted the picture of a long, black tunnel that went on for as far as the eye could see. I assumed the distance was shorter than it looked because that's the way it was when the Green Fog carpeted the hallway. "What happened to the girls?" I asked, missing them a bit while shuffling along.

"They're cooing away as we speak," the sergeant answered. "And the boys are barking on the other end. But without the aid of the Green Fog, they can't communicate with those still in the flesh."

Marty grunted. "Dang, man… this hallway looks like a fricken' mine shaft."

"Then keep walking and you might find gold!" the sergeant snickered, perhaps prospecting for a laugh that didn't come his way.

"I feel like I've completely lost my buzz," I whined.

"Yeah, I can use another hit of acid," Marty pined. "Or at least some weed, man. Didn't someone say something about weed?"

"You two shitheads sound ripe for the picking," the sergeant chuckled. "This should be fun."

We stopped at the halfway point after walking what seemed to be a mile. To my right was the opening to the entry hall. To my left was the back wall in the hallway where there was a big, black door. "I didn't notice this door the other times I passed through the hallway," I said. "Has it been here all along?"

"The backdoor only shows itself when it's time to travel," the sergeant informed. "Otherwise, it remains invisible to the naked eye. Now I suggest you two get ready for the ride of your eight remaining lives, cause what doesn't kill ya a total of nine times will surely make ya stronger." He chuckled again. "That's what Kilborne is all about… making you stronger! Against impossible odds the hope is that you'll both have what it takes to graduate from this horrible place, cause a mind is a terrible thing ta waste and we'd hate ta have yours end up as a permanent fixture here in this hallway." And with that said, the sergeant opened the backdoor.

In came a rush of refreshing pine scented cool air that did little to ease my jittery nerves, but I was astonished to see that the Big House had an even bigger backyard. "Whoa! This mountaintop goes on forever!"

"Forever and a day," the sergeant crooned. "Forever and a day."

# Chapter Nine
### *Game On*

I stood between Marty and the sergeant on a shaky wood balcony behind the sturdy Big House, which itself rested near the edge of a shallow but rocky cliff that formed a huge watery basin that jutted out as far as the eye could see.

We were gazing out at a magnificent sunset where the sun hovered above a perfectly still body of endless water that was brilliantly reflecting the orange globe's image on its glassy surface, as if two suns were slowly merging into one big sun that set the distant horizon on fire, before sinking below the surface.

"As you can see," said the sergeant, "this millpond is big enough to be called an ocean, but it's to be referred to as the 'Great Lake' moving forward. Failure to do so will result in a painful death."

"How's the fishing?" quizzed Marty.

"Fine, if ya like sharks."

I needed to be funny for my own peace of mind. "So, I guess swimming's out of the question?"

The sergeant chuckled. "There are much worse ways ta die here than to be fish food."

My attempt at humor had backfired in my face. "Why are you trying to scare the crap out of us?" I snapped. "Why?"

"Look... kid, I just work here. If ya got a problem, take it up with the boss."

"Can we talk to him now?" I was quick to inquire.

"Yeah, man," added Marty, "we need ta talk to that dude before this shit gets out of hand."

"Trust me," replied the sergeant, "he's the last person on the planet you wanna run into. But that said, your visit with him will come soon enough. But first it's time to play a little ball."

"And where are we supposed to do that?" I asked, seeing nothing but an ocean of blue surrounded by patches of sandy shoreline.

The sergeant put his whistle to his lips and blew. I didn't hear a thing until the Great Lake went from millpond to Jacuzzi, as water began bubbling up from the depths. Then wave after wave gathered steam and rushed ashore with a frothy rumble that spanked the rocks below and made the balcony quiver. I took a shaky step back like that was going to help, but with the back door now closed and locked, the only way off the balcony was to descend a long wood ladder that led down to a boat dock a hundred feet below. The boat dock jutted out a relatively small but respectable ways into the Great Lake, where weeds began to sprout out of the water. Golden brown stalks with sparkling black heads quickly reached ten feet above the turbulent sea.

The weeds came in waves—sprouting tall and straight—soon overtaking the Great Lake until just ponds remained, then puddles, and finally there was nothing but feathery black heads filling the basin like a vast city of twinkling lights. Their white sparkle even lit up the dusk.

No sooner had the sun lost its influence on the day, when a starry night took its place like none I'd ever seen before, followed by a full moon that seemed almost as big and bright as was the sun. "If I didn't know better," I said, "I'd swear we're on a different planet."

"Might as well be," snickered the sergeant. "But this is only the beginning of strange things ta come."

"I don't know about you two," Marty muttered, "but I'm ready ta get off this fricken balcony."

The sergeant chuckled. "Ask and ye shall receive." He again put his whistle to his lips. This time Green Fog came out from under the boat dock and began to cut a neon green path straight out into the heart of the city of lights, before branching out like a big tree. Some branches seemed to reach the ends of the earth before drifting off into the blackness of space in luminous green wisps. "Now let's go down into the Tall Grass and play some ball."

The sergeant ordered us down the long, wobbly ladder, telling us not to worry… the distance was a lot shorter than it looked, and he was right. A mere five rungs later we were standing on the wood surface of the boat dock. I looked up the ladder and saw that it took at least ten times as many rungs to reach back up to the balcony. "Nothing's what it seems around here," I observed. "Nothing!"

"Ain't that the truth," Marty grumbled.

I turned from the rocky cliff and faced out noticing that the dock appeared to be longer in length at eye level than it did from above. I also saw that we were boxed-in by the Tall Grass. The ten-foot wall of grass extended along the sides of the dock, where it was capped off at the end by the entrance to the neon green path.

Marty grunted. "I feel like a rat trapped in a maze down here."

"There are paths deep inside these wacky weeds that can take you all the way back to the beginning of time," the sergeant informed, "and all the way in the other direction to the end of days."

"I hope we don't have time for any of that," I spouted, not feeling particularly adventurous at that moment.

"Nope," the sergeant replied to my relief. "Not unless you plan on sticking around for forty years. That's how long it takes to hit the entire campus from A to Z. But then you'll have earned an advanced degree that'll make you all-knowing."

"Forty fricken years?" Marty howled. "I'm out, man."

I nodded in agreement. "Me too… I'm out."

The sergeant pointed to the opening at the end of the dock. "Okay you two… let's stop messing around and get started on the course."

"But what about the sharks?" I asked. "Isn't there still water under the weeds?"

"There's nothing but Tall Grass right now," he responded. "Now stop with the questions and lead the way."

"What if I refuse?" I queried, defiantly holding my ground.

The sergeant swaggered over and looked up at me with his tiny pupils bouncing between my eyes—his faded blues looking gray in the moonlight. "If ya don't wanna play along," he snarled, "you can always stay behind and wait for the man-eating rats to get ya. They come out at midnight and sweep the grounds looking for stray recruits to feast on." He then raised his whistle. "Even worse… if I blow this thing again, all hell will break loose. So, I suggest you stop complaining and move forward!"

I reluctantly and with the utmost consternation slowly began to walk the plank, so-to-speak. I creaked along with the sergeant on my heels and Marty behind him. The feathery black heads to my sides were sparkling above me like a runway. They led me to where the dock ended, and the narrow path began. I gulped. "I'm afraid to go in there."

The sergeant chuckled. "You should be. But it's either that or end up barking in the hallway for all eternity. At least this way you've got a fighting chance."

I took a second to pray for guidance before entering, hoping God would grant me a safe return—or better yet, get me the hell out of there! I inched forward onto dry, solid ground that was covered in a glowing green mist that concealed everything below my ankles. I took one tentative step after another into the Green Fog swirling at my feet. Its hissing sound reverberated off the Tall Grass and filled every nook and cranny of my being. Although I was by no means high, there was however plenty of soothing honeysuckle in the air to help ease a mind so troubled that I was flirting with insanity, only to be spanked back to reality now and then.

It was a tight fit around the shoulders and I often rubbed elbows with thick blades of Tall Grass, but I eventually got to where I was moving okay. We steadily walked the glowing green trail, as the feathery heads danced and sparkled to a silent beat overhead, always herding us along. I saw the moon once it reached high enough to join the stars that hovered above the sparkle of the feathery heads. The straightaway finally ran its course and there was a fork in the road, forcing me to come to a stop. "Which way," I asked. "Left or right?"

"You can't go wrong either way," the sergeant replied. "What does your gut tell ya?"

"It wants me ta run for my life!"

"Then pick a path and run like there's no tomorrow," he chuckled. "Maybe you'll even get lucky and find your way home."

I knew the sergeant was jacking with me. Still, the thought of going home was exciting, even if it was just a pipe dream. Being a lefty, I took the path to the left. And even though my dress shoes were made for walking, I ran like the wind. I wanted to get lucky. I wanted to keep running, until I was home in my mother's arms.

I soon felt lost and alone, having left Marty and the sergeant in the green dust. All I heard was hissing as I moved along. Constant hissing! Otherwise, it was quiet. Deathly quiet! I was busy running from my own shadow, when I saw a white glow filling the night sky. I ran even faster toward the brilliant light, hoping to find some semblance of life. The long narrow path suddenly widened to form a huge circle that was big enough to house a baseball stadium for the ages. Huffing and puffing, I came to a stop near the main entrance.

"Dang, man," Marty said, "what kept ya?"

My mouth agape, I had to catch my breath before responding. "How'd you two get here so fast?" I asked him, while the sergeant was laughing his head off nearby.

"The sergeant told me to take the shortcut ta the right," he replied. "It only took a few steps and we were here."

I saw that the sergeant was clearly enjoying himself at my expense. I wanted to give him a piece of what was left of my mind, but I was startled when I heard the roar of a crowd, and my focus returned to the ballpark. "This has ta be fake," I concluded. "There's no way a stadium this big can be filled with a bunch of people out in the middle of an empty field like this. No way!"

"Fake?" the sergeant chuckled. "Then ya should have no problem having the balls ta play in front of the twenty thousand rabid fans who're waiting for the game to start inside this fake ballpark."

"Twenty thousand?" my eyes bulged. "The most I ever played in front of was a few hundred people and that seemed a lot."

"Shit… except for the time I was taking swings at my old man," Marty whined, "I've never even played fricken baseball before."

The sergeant laughed. "Good luck with that. Now let's go!"

We passed under an awning at the front of the massive brick and terra-cotta complex that read: EBBETS FIELD. I peered into the ornate rotunda. It allowed me a glimpse of the lush green infield that was tucked inside the concrete and steel structure. Fake or not, there was a big game feel coming from inside and it made the butterflies in my stomach churn like never before. "I was thinking a small backstop in an open field when ya said we'd be playing ball," I admitted to the sergeant. "Not a bigtime stadium like this!"

"Yeah, man," Marty soughed, "I might need to sit this one out."

"The worst that can happen is ya get stabbed and beaten if ya mess up even once," the sergeant divulged to our horror. "It'll hurt like hell until your dead, then ya get ta move on to your next adventure. But that'll mean ya have just seven lives remaining and you're hardly into your first day."

"Shit!" Marty bristled.

"I wouldn't mind a beer right now," I quivered. "Or some more of that Green Fog."

"You've got ta be kidding me," the sergeant razzed. "Don't ya wanna be sharp for the game?"

"Hey, I'm just looking for something to calm my nerves," I replied. "And that's what came to mind."

"Great minds think alike!" Marty gave me an evil wink. "How 'bout it, sarge?"

"Hell no!" The sergeant replied. "Now let's move along before I lose my patience with you two shitheads."

We continued our journey through a side door that was marked: PLAYERS ONLY. Once inside we went through the dank concrete catacombs of the grand old ballpark. We turned this way and that and arrived at the home locker room, which had a sign on the door that read: ROBINS. The sergeant opened the door and the smell of sweaty socks was the first thing I noticed about the empty room, as it was enough to make me gag. He pointed toward the vacant red lockers that lined the back wall. "You'll find your baseball uniforms over there in the last two stalls," he said, before taking a seat by the door. "Now hurry up and get dressed for the game!"

There was hazy light raining down from an overhead lamp on the metal lockers in question. Marty sauntered over to the stall that had number 13 and I shuffled over to the one that had number 20.

"Thirteen used to be my lucky number," he said. "Until now."

"Yeah, I don't suppose it's a coincidence that twenty has been my favorite number since my little league days," I speculated.

"Can ya imagine that?" the sergeant intervened. "And now ya get ta wear that number in a World Series game!"

"A World Series game?" I returned. "Are you serious?"

The sergeant nodded affirmatively. "As the storyline goes, you two shitheads have been called up from the minor leagues to play in game three of the 1916 World Series."

"We're tripping in 1916?" Marty snickered. "Far out, man!"

"I hope that means we're playing against old timers," I probed.

"Not exactly," the sergeant replied. "These professional athletes are in the prime of their once-upon-a-time lives."

"Then we won't stand a chance," I pined. "We can't be expected to compete against big leaguers without messing up."

Marty pouted. "Yeah, man… we're as good as dead!"

"Sounds like a personal problem," the sergeant said, flippantly. "Now get your sorry asses into your uniforms, so we can get up to the dugout and you can meet the coach before the game starts."

Resigned to my fate, I was busy doing as told when a roach the size of a mouse caught my eye as it lumbered across the cold concrete floor. Not a big fan of the species, it further soured my dourly mood. But then the crowd roared overhead, and it shook the building causing the roach to scamper off under a locker. I was relieved that the critter was gone, yet envious of the simple bug life it was leading… getting to run from trouble at the drop of a hat.

I finished getting ready; putting on a uniform made of a heavy wool material that was white with blue trim sewn in checkered pinstripes. The shirt and pants were baggy, but the shoes and blue cap fit okay. The baseball glove was stiff and tight though. "I'll never be able to catch anything with this prehistoric thing," I whined. "I'm as good as dead if the ball comes my way."

"At least you'll look good at your funeral," the sergeant chuckled. "But I'm not so sure about lover boy over there."

I saw that Marty had put his cowboy boots back on. They were covering most of the blue leggings that were pulled up to his knees, where his baseball pants were bunched up like a pair of britches.

"Marty, that's not gonna work," I said. "You need to put your baseball cleats on like me."

"Nah… those shoes cramp my style, man."

"But they're made for baseball."

"Maybe so, but if I'm gonna die in front of twenty thousand people tonight, I wanna look good doing it."

"But the boots don't go with the uniform," I said, primly. "And besides that, you won't be able ta run in those things."

He shrugged, haplessly. "I'm not planning on doing much running when I'm probably gonna bite the dust anyway."

I shrugged haplessly, as well. "Okay, whatever… but don't say I didn't warn ya."

"Let's go!" demanded the sergeant.

We went through a maze of tunnels. Arrows pointed the way to the home dugout. The crowd got louder with every cleat-grinding step I took. There was a constant buzz in the air by the time we reached the bright lights. We were standing just inside the far end of a long dugout that was an empty concrete shell, although we were just three steps below the action, where the entire team was lined up on the playing field between home plate and third base—all standing tall rather than taking a knee—while a band in center field played the

Star-Spangled Banner. What could be seen of the large crowd was also on their feet. Everyone had hats over their hearts, while facing the flag and singing along.

The crowd cheered thunderously when the song was over, then again when rockets went off like it was the fourth of July. I was feeling neither brave nor free at that moment, but rather trapped inside a giant fishbowl of a stadium that seemed anything but fake. I quivered in terrified silence, but truth be told… I had often dreamt of playing major league baseball someday and now it appeared my dreams were about to come true in the strangest of ways.

# Chapter Ten
*Baseball Blues*

**"L**ADIES AND GENTLEMEN," a godlike voice echoed from the press box. "WELCOME TO EBBETS FIELD AND GAME THREE OF THE 1916 WORLD SERIES BETWEEN THE BOSTON RED SOX AND YOUR BROOKLYN ROBINS!"

The players were introduced. One by one they stepped forward and tipped their caps to the crowd. I heard names that were unfamiliar to me, with the exception of Casey Stengel. I knew him as an old manager, not a young baseball player. When the Red Sox were introduced, I was amazed to see they had a guy named, George Herman Ruth. Even from across the field I could tell he was a younger version of the guy I had seen in old newsreels. I elbowed Marty, then pointed. "That's Babe Ruth over there!"

"Who the heck's that?"

"He's only the most famous baseball player of all time!"

Marty shrugged, apathetically. "Looks fat ta me."

"Maybe so, but he can hit the ball a mile."

"Actually, he's the pitcher who won game two of the series for the Red Sox," informed the sergeant. "He won't become famous for hitting homeruns until after he gets traded to the Yankees in 1920."

"1920?" Marty nodded, seemingly impressed. "You must be some kind of sports buff or something for knowing shit like that."

"Not really," the sergeant replied. "It's just that ya get to learn a lot of trivia when you've gone back and forth in time as much as I have over the centuries."

After the introductions were over, Babe Ruth and the Red Sox retreated to their dugout on the first base side, while the starting nine for the Robins took their positions on the field and began to warm up for the start of the game.

The rest of the team returned to our dugout and congregated at the other end, which was closest to home plate, seemingly avoiding us until a heavyset man waddled over. "Welcome to the team," he said. "I'm Coach Robinson, but everyone around here calls me Robbie."

"Wait a minute," I said, after looking into his faded eyes. "Aren't you Chester, the bus driver?"

Robbie snarled at me before turning to the sergeant. "At least there's only two of 'em this year. Should be a piece of cake."

"You'd think so," the sergeant agreed, "but the boss wants 'em each playing for two full innings this game instead of the usual brief appearance in the field."

"No problem. I've had to manage up ta ten boys and girls in a game before. So, this should be a piece of cake."

The sergeant chuckled. "The boss wants 'em to play the infield."

Robbie stiffened. "That's ridiculous! I only sneak recruits into the outfield when I gotta put one in for a pitch, but the infield?"

"And get this," the sergeant snickered, "he even wants 'em ta each have one at bat before the game's over."

Robbie almost came out of his cleats. "That's like committing suicide! I've never had to bat recruits before! Never!" He kicked dirt. "No wonder the real Robinson doesn't wanna come back from the dead and coach his team anymore."

"I thought you *were* Coach Robinson?" I interjected.

"Shut up, kid! I don't care if you're Johnny Paradise or not." Robbie glared at me before turning back to the sergeant. "How 'bout filling in for me tonight, old buddy?"

The sergeant waved Robbie off. "Not a chance. I'm no coach. And besides that… the last thing I want is ta put my dick on the chopping block down here, when I can give it to the hot mamma I've got waiting for me in the upper deck."

Robbie pouted. "Must be nice having a perk like that."

"I met her a few years ago during one of these games," the sergeant recalled. "It's about the only thing I look forward to when I come back from the grave every year." He then turned his attention to us, bouncing his faded blues back and forth between Marty and I. "Dead or alive, I'll meet up with you two shitheads after the game is over and we'll move on to your next adventure."

"I hope it's not more sports," Marty muttered.

The sergeant laughed. "Just think of all the things that scare the crap out of you and then add the unimaginable into the mix and that will at least give you some idea of what to expect for the next hundred days. It only gets harder from here, gentlemen… so good luck with the baseball." The sergeant did an about-face, then disappeared back into the catacombs of the old ballpark.

"Have either of ya played much ball?" Robbie inquired, gingerly.

I raised my hand like it weighed a ton. "I'm on the high school team," I admitted with trepidation, hoping not to impress.

Robbie nodded approvingly, then turned toward Marty and frowned. "Ya still look like a hippie ta me."

"Actually, man… I'm a rock 'n' roller. So, ya might wanna go easy on me when it comes ta putting me in the game."

Robbie groaned. He took a seat across from us on the concrete steps leading up to the field. "I don't know what the sergeant told ya, but just know that as far as the baseball world is concerned, I'm Coach Robinson tonight, faded eyes and all, and you are two rookies that our players would rather not see participating in a game of this magnitude. Ya see as far as they're concerned, this really is game three of the 1916 World Series and they're oblivious to the fact that we bring 'em back from the dead to relive this game on an annual basis. I'm just trying ta spare them the agony of defeat before they return to the grave after the game."

"Then keep us on the bench," I suggested. "We won't mind."

Robbie snorted. "I wish it were that simple, kid… but I have ta play you as ordered by the boss and still find a way ta win the game. But just know that as rookies, the fans will cut ya no slack. Commit an error in the field or strike out at the plate and a dozen or so rabid fans will come out of the grandstands, rush the field and kill ya on the spot. Then the game will stop like there's been a rain delay. The ground crew will come out and clean up your bloody mess. Then the game will resume as if nothing happened."

Marty grunted. "Wow… baseball's more gnarly than I thought."

"It is here," Robbie said. "I can't tell ya how many times I've seen recruits crying for their mammas as fans began cutting them ta shreds before beating their heads in with wooden clubs for good measure. And if we lose this game that history claims we won by a score of four to three, the entire crowd will rush the field and murder everyone on our team before they know what hit 'em. And let me tell ya something… you haven't felt pain until you've had a blade or two or three twisted deep inside your gut and your insides have turned into chop meat before the mob turns your head into roadkill!"

"What if we refuse to play?" I asked, more curious than defiant.

"I like your balls, kid," Robbie replied. "But if ya refuse to play, the boss will most likely strip you of your remaining lives and give ya a one-way ticket to the black hallway in the Big House for all eternity, if he doesn't send ya ta hell first."

"I thought this was hell," I grumbled.

Robbie rolled his faded browns. "Pretty darn close, kid… but not quite." He cleared his throat and a wisp of green seeped out of his mouth and disappeared into the air. "Now this night can go either one of two ways. It could end horrifically with a gruesome blood bath at the hands of an angry mob bearing knives, clubs and fists." He paused to let that soak in before continuing. "Or the game could end in victory with you signing autographs for a throng of adoring fans, along with kisses from some of the pretty girls in the crowd, before you get to walk away a proud winner."

Marty and I were in total agreement. "We wanna win!"

Robbie smiled. "Great! That's what I want ta hear!" He pointed toward the bench. "Now take a seat here and don't say a word to the other players. The less they know about the truth of the matter, the better it'll be for all concerned. So, sit tight while I try and figure out the safest way ta pencil you two into the lineup without getting us all brutally murdered." He then waddled back to the other end of the dugout where he joined the rest of his team on the bench.

The adrenaline was flowing in the dugout and the crowd was buzzing with anticipation. If nothing else, Marty and I had great seats for the game. The players looked our way from time to time, but they kept their distance and no words were exchanged. We were just spectators like the thousands in the grandstands who were a blur of shadowy figures from where I sat. But their knives reflected the stadium lights like a sea of flashbulbs popping off in the dark.

The first pitch of the game came and went in uneventful fashion. The crowd became relatively quiet over the next couple of innings, until George Cutshaw hit a single to drive in the first run of the game. "That a boy, George!" came shouts of encouragement from the other end of the dugout, as rabid fans thundered their approval. The place was rocking, and you could feel the intensity in the air. Robins one—Red Sox nothing in the third restless inning.

"At least we have the lead," I said. "But hanging with these guys is gonna be even harder than I thought."

Marty groaned. "So, we really don't stand a chance?"

"I don't know. I've played a lot of ball in my day, but never against talent like this."

Jack Coombs, the Robins pitcher, continued to throw strikes, keeping the Red Sox off the scoreboard, even helping himself to a single in the fourth inning; scoring shortstop Ivy Olson from third base to give our team a little breathing room. Robins two—Red Sox nothing at the end of four nail-biting innings.

Marty grunted, working up a sweat as time passed. "I wonder when the coach is gonna put us out ta slaughter?"

I shrugged nervously, sweating as well. "I'm hoping he forgets all about us until the game's over."

Jack Coombs pitched perfectly in the top half of the fearful fifth and the Robins had the meat of the lineup coming up in the bottom half of the inning, hoping to send Carl Mays, the Boston pitcher, back into the history books where he belonged.

Even with a lead, Robbie nervously paced his side of the dugout, constantly checking the scoreboard while shouting words of encouragement to his players. I was just mindlessly watching him do his thing when our pupils met. I locked onto his faded browns and gasped. My heart began to race when he started to waddle over. "Brace yourself, Marty… here comes trouble."

"Well, shit… I was almost starting ta get warm and cozy sitting here."

Robbie arrived with a concerned look on his opaque face. "I plan on putting you two in when we take the field again," he said businesslike, before pointing to me. "Besides going by Johnny Paradise, what's your real name, kid?"

I cleared the angst from my throat, but I still croaked. "Johnny Bishop."

"Well, Bishop… you'll be at second base next inning."

He pointed to Marty. "And what's your name, ya hippie freak?"

"Marty McCoy's the name… and I'm no freak, man."

"Well, McCoy… hopefully ya won't freak-out at third."

"No problem, man. Just point me in the right direction."

"You don't know where third base is?" Robbie became wide-eyed, showing more of his whites than I cared to see, but I looked on in amazement anyway.

Marty scanned the infield. "I'm sure it's one of those three white pillows scattered around out there." He pointed toward third base. "I think it's the one closest to us."

Robbie winced. "I can only hope you're messing with me, or we're in deep shit!" He sighed. "Now you two rookies hang tight. I'll come over and get ya when we're ready to take the field again."

Casey Stengal hit a pop foul to third base for an easy out. Zack Wheat walked and moved to second on a groundout by George Cutshaw. Mike Mowrey also walked, bringing Ivy Olson to the plate with runners on first and second and two out.

The crowd was clamoring for a hit and Ivy came through with a deep shot that allowed Wheat and Mowrey to score easily, as Ivy raced around the bases for a triple. Otto Miller grounded out to end the inning. Robins four—Red Sox nothing after five gut-wrenching innings.

I held my breath when Robbie again waddled our way. "Okay," he said, "this is the moment of truth." He pointed to the bag closest to the dugout. "Marty, you go take…"

Before Robbie could finish, George Cutshaw ran over and angrily barked at the coach. "Are you pulling me out of the game?"

Robbie groaned. "Well, Cutty… I'm afraid so."

Mike Mowrey ran over as well. "Are you thinking of putting these two rookies in for us?" he asked. "Surely not with the Series on the line!"

Robbie cringed. "Well, Mike… I'm afraid I've got no choice in the matter."

"What's that supposed to mean?" asked Mowrey. "You're the coach!"

"Let's just say that I've got people ta answer to as well," Robbie offered, defensively.

"Yeah, I know what's going on here," Cutshaw snapped. "First Mr. Ebbets bumps ticket prices for the big game, and now this!"

"No, Cutty," Robbie said. "The owner has nothing to do with this move."

"Then what gives, Robbie?" Mowrey was fuming. "This is the World Series we're talking about here!"

"I know, Mike. I know. But… if not for these two rookies sitting here, this game wouldn't even be going on right now."

"What… have ya been drinking or something?" grilled Cutshaw.

Robbie snorted. "I wish it were that simple, Cutty."

"Really, Robbie… what's this all about?" pleaded Mowrey.

"I've already told you more than I should, Mike," Robbie replied. "Now I suggest you guys take a seat down with the rest of the fellows on the team and support these young rookies with everything you got!"

Mowrey and Cutshaw kicked dirt, then began muttering their way back down to the other end of the bench, as the umpire showed up at the edge of the dugout steps. "Robbie," the ump shouted, "it's time to start the inning and you're short two infielders."

Robbie waved the umpire off. "I've got it covered." He turned to face us. "Okay you two… the good news is Boston has the bottom of their lineup coming up this inning. I'm hoping our pitching can shut them down. But if not, I've got two of my best and most experienced players around you. Ivy at short and Jake at first. Listen to them and maybe you can make it through this game alive!"

# Chapter Eleven
*Between the Lines*

After taking a deep breath, I grabbed my prehistoric glove with a sweaty hand and managed to climb three concrete steps on shaky legs, and then I was standing firmly on a field of dreams that sent goose bumps coursing through my body. And even though I was racked with fear, it was still awesome to be on that big stage and feel the incredible energy of the crowd.

Marty had a glazed look in his evil eyes. "Holy shit! It's like we're headlining a fricken rock concert!" He pointed to the stands. "Look… there's even sexy bitches sitting in the first row!"

Marty was right. We couldn't see them from within the confines of our concrete shell, but there was a row of nothing but Dream Girls sitting directly behind our dugout. Otherwise, I saw mostly men in drab business suits in the good seats down low. The shadowy masses occupied the nosebleed seats in the upper deck, where the flash bulbs were going off everywhere. "I wouldn't mind kissing those girls after winning the game," I said, trying to think positive.

"Yeah, man… that'd be the thing ta do."

"Good luck," I said. "I've gotta run over to second."

"Good luck, man."

I reached second base and turned toward home plate and panned the massive grandstands that surrounded me. I felt tingly in the spotlight with the way those powerful lights were shining down from up high, seemingly following my every move.

I checked in on Marty across the way at third base. He was shaking his hips and playing the air-guitar while facing the Dream Girls in the stands. His long hair flowed wildly from under his cap. His boots were kicking up a storm. He was putting on quite a show and it would've been fun to watch except that he was about to miss the first pitch of the inning.

"Marty!" I yelled to cut through the crowd noise, as I pounded my glove and got down into position. "Get ready, Marty!"

The pitcher made his pitch and the batter swung. With the crack of the bat, the baseball skidded on the ground toward Ivy at short. He scooped it up like it was something he'd done since birth and fired it to Jake at first in time to nip the Boston runner. It happened so fast I never fully got up from my ready position and the play was over.

I did however get to warm up when the ball was thrown around the infield after the first Boston out with Ivy getting it back from Jake and then zipping it over to me. Luckily, I caught the ball with my old-time glove, which gave me a little boost of confidence. I was supposed to throw it to third, but Marty still had his back to me while playing to the Dream Girls. I moved in closer and finally got his attention. "What the heck are ya doing?"

"Just entertaining the ladies, man."

"But you're gonna get yourself killed!"

"I can't play this game worth a shit, so I might as well have some fun on the way out."

"But you'll be stabbed and beaten to death!"

He shrugged. "I'll get over it."

"Okay, but don't take the rest of the team down with you," I said, before lobbing the ball over to the rock 'n' roller, who almost made an awkward-looking catch. The ball ended up on the ground in front of him, so he kicked it back to the pitcher before returning to his one-man show.

The fans near third base were reacting to his performance. The Dream Girls were affectionately cooing, but the businessmen were vigorously booing. The rest of the crowd grew restless when Jack Coombs walked the next Boston batter. A light show of flash bulbs ensued when the batter after that tripled to score a run.

The shrill sound of knives being sharpened and the moans and groans from the shadowy masses eerily filled the stadium. It was haunting to hear. I was chilled to the bone, and so I guess was Marty. His guitar had vanished into thin air and he was standing guard over the unwelcomed visitor from Boston, who occupied third base.

Our lead had been cut to three with still only one out and Boston had the top of its lineup set to come up. You could cut the suffocating tension with a knife. Many knives! I saw that even the Dream Girls were waving shiny daggers.

"Get ready, kid," Jake at first base shouted above the deafening noise of the crowd. "This guy may try and slap the ball our way to score that runner from third."

"Okay," I shouted back. I burped hoping to set some of my butterflies free, but no such luck. They were content to stay put in my belly, stirring up the buffet that I was trying to keep down. Burp!

"If the ball is hit to you on the ground," Jake added to my misery, "check and see if you've got a play at home plate if that runner on third base should try and score. If not, play it safe and throw the ball here to me at first base, and we'll get the sure out."

"Okay." Burp!

"If the ball's hit to you in the air," Jake continued to my dismay, "catch it and make sure the Boston runner stays put on third base. You don't want him to tag up and then try and score on ya."

I had played enough baseball to know what I was supposed to do in that situation. Been there, done that many times before. But knowing it and pulling it off were two separate things—especially when playing against seasoned professionals who were good enough to make it all the way to the World Series!

The more I thought about it, the more I found it difficult to breathe, thinking I might even choke should the ball come my way. I held what little air I had in my lungs when the next Boston hitter swung. I burped when he made contact. The ball hit off his bat and rocketed into the air like it had been shot out of a canon.

"Second base! Second base!" Jake said, as I gasped my last breath. "That's your play, kid! That's your play!"

I could feel my heart pounding, as I searched the night sky. "I got it! I got it!" I watched intently as the ball continued to ascend, climbing well past the stadium lights to where it looked like a ghostly speck that was so high up; I even had time to pray. *Please, God... you take this one. It's a lot closer to you.* I blinked and lost the ball in the stars. Burp! I searched skyward, distracted by the crowd. I could hear heckling above the roar, and knives being sharpened at a feverish pace. Burp!

"It's all yours, kid," Jake shouted. "It's all yours!"

My life was busy passing before my eyes when I caught sight of a small object drifting in space. Much to my relief, it was the baseball. I began to track it, backpedaling, moving this way and that. The ball finally reached its agonizing peak and teasingly hovered in place before finally beginning a slow descent. By then I had drifted over to where I stood trembling near the right field line. From there I could hear the fans up close and personal. "Miss that thing and I'll cut your heart out, rookie!" Other people were shouting similar threats. My ears were ringing. I was unpopular at best. I knew many in the crowd were just itching to pounce on me if I didn't make the catch.

"Stay with it, kid," Jake hollered. "Stay with it!"

The ball looked like a snowball from heaven when the stadium lights picked it back up on the way down—a snowball that was coming fast and furious and beginning to spiral out of control. I became disoriented but dared not take my eyes off the prize for even a split second, or blink again for that matter.

"Throw it to me when you make the catch," Jake assumed, "and we'll hold that runner at third!"

The ball approached like a little white meteor. I was thinking I was either at ground zero or about to be murdered. I made small adjustments—a step here and a step there. The ball was nearly on top of me when I realized I was not where I needed to be to remain alive. Burp! In a last-ditch effort, I allowed my baseball instincts to take over. My cleats dug firmly into the grass and my body thrust forward in a dive with my glove hand stretched out as far as it could reach. It was like going off a cliff into the unknown.

I was still airborne. Hanging by a thread. Eyes now closed. Teeth clenched. I was bracing for a brutal death when I heard a whack. Felt it too! I hit the ground with the ball stuck at the end of my prehistoric glove to where it looked more like a snow cone than a snowball, but still I had somehow made the catch. The umpire raised his thumb to signal that the Boston batter was out. Aided by a flood of adrenaline, I quickly got to my feet and fired the ball over to Jake, as the Red Sox runner retreated back to third base, where Marty continued to stand guard.

The crowd roared its approval. In an instant I had gone from unpopular at best to a fan favorite. What a rush! "Way ta go ya worthless rookie!" I took a moment to bask in the glory. Soaking up the love like a sponge. I wanted to jump into the stands and begin signing autographs, or at the very least take a bow, but instead I pranced back to my position at second base feeling like an all-star.

The Red Sox scored another run, but Marty and I were safe. No balls came our way for the rest of the inning. Robins four—Red Sox two in the scintillating sixth.

I was hoping for a high-five or two from my teammates, but they ignored me as we trotted off the field. I did however catch up with Marty, who was walking alone in foul territory on the way to the dugout. "One down," I said, referring to the innings we had left to play, "one ta go!"

"If it wasn't for the fricken baseball," he said, "I could hang out here under the big lights and play music all night long."

Marty and I stopped just short of the dugout and faced the Dream Girls, who were grinning impishly at us with daggers in hand. They could've been sisters. They all had long blonde hair and big blue eyes, and they wore velvety red dresses and had big white hats adorned with lots of roses and ostrich feathers.

Marty strummed a note. "How'd ya like the show, ladies?"

Before the cooing Dream Girls could answer, the home plate umpire yelled for us to get in the dugout, or he'd have us killed for delaying the game. Fearful of a brutal death, we quickly parked ourselves on our side of the bench.

"Those are some mighty fine bitches sitting out there," Marty slobbered, rakishly.

"Tell me about it," I said, dreamily. "I hope we can meet up with them after the game," I added, trying to remain positive about our future, although it was still very much in doubt.

Robbie waddled over and my mind returned to baseball. "Nice catch, kid!" He winked at me. "I thought you were a goner there for a moment."

"I've never caught a ball hit that high before. Not even close."

"Well ya did good." Robbie then turned to Marty. "What the hell were ya doing out there at the beginning of the inning?"

Marty grinned, sheepishly. "I was playing 'Whole Lotta Love' ta the crowd. It's by Led Zeppelin. Ever hear of 'em, man?"

"Can't say that I have," answered Robbie. "I just know you better keep your head in the game before you lose it!"

Marty and I both kept our heads in the game and survived the next inning in the field without a ball being hit our way. But Boston had closed the gap. Robins four—Red Sox three in the scary seventh.

Robbie waddled over to our side of the dugout with a bat in his hand. "Congratulations on surviving the infield, gentlemen. Now let's see if ya have what it takes to survive at the plate." He sighed sullenly like he didn't think we had a snowballs chance in hell. "First off… you'll live if you're lucky enough to hit the ball somewhere, even if ya make an out. Or you can walk. The one and only thing you can't do is strike out, cause that's the kiss of death."

I'd been observing the new Boston pitcher warming up on the mound. He looked intimidating from afar. His pitches were a white streak that spanked the dust right out of the catcher's mitt. "Maybe we should try and bunt," I suggested. "It might be our best chance."

Robbie laughed. "Get real, kid! That's Rube Foster pitching for Boston. He's tricky and throws hard. There's no way you're gonna get a bat on the ball… bunting or otherwise. The way I see it… your only chance is ta try and draw a walk, but even that's easier said than done cause Rube strikes out a whole lot more people than he walks and for you to get a hit off the guy will be next to impossible."

Thankfully, I was at least still riding what was left of my high from the one catch I had made. I kept replaying that play in my mind, hoping the mojo would carry over to my looming plate appearance, although fielding and hitting have about as much in common as night and day.

Casey Stengel didn't waste any time flying out to right field to begin the last half of the scary seventh inning. I moved from the confines of the dugout to the on-deck circle, where I felt thousands of eyes upon me. I took practice swings to ease my nerves with Zack Wheat at the plate.

"I hope ya know how ta use that bat, big boy," cooed one of the Dream Girls. Glancing her way, I blushed while continuing to practice my swing. Otherwise, I was busy watching the pitcher do his thing when Wheat energized the crowd by singling to right field. I should've been happy for him and the team, but it meant it was my turn at the plate. Gulp!

"YOUR ATTENTION PLEASE," the public address announcer bellowed, "NOW BATTING FOR THE ROBINS, NUMBER TWENTY, JOHNNY BISHOP, NUMBER TWENTY." My butterflies were back in force. Burp! They must've been on steroids with the way they were moving about inside my belly. Burp!

My testicles shrank to the size of chickpeas while walking up to the plate. It didn't help that I was being greeted with a chorus of boos and cat calls from the hostile crowd. "Ya better not strike out ya worthless rookie, or yur dead meat!" Apparently my one and only catch was already yesterday's news in the minds of the many and I was no longer a fan favorite.

I took a deep breath and gingerly stepped into the batter's box like it was a minefield. I exhaled, but it was more like a wistful sigh. I took a half swing, trying to imagine my bat making contact with the ball, although I was hoping for a walk.

I held my breath when Rube Foster went into his windup. I tried not to get too caught up with the fact he looked even more intimidating up close and personal, standing tall on a mound of clay, only sixty feet away.

I had planned on watching Foster's first pitch without attempting a swing. Just to see what it was like. He spun the ball toward home plate. It was clearly a curveball that was low from the start and never really flirted with the strike zone before ending up in the dirt. The catcher managed to block the ball, but it was enough for Wheat to move over to second base.

With a runner now in scoring position, the crowd suddenly was on their feet, clamoring for me to come through in the clutch. I felt the weight of the world on my shoulders. Sure… I wanted to be a hero for the fickle fans, but more than anything… I wanted to avoid their wrath. I glanced over at the Dream Girls, and it was like the tale of two cities. They had warm, encouraging smiles on their pretty faces, but they were also waving their shiny daggers in the air, slashing this way and that like they were practicing their swings. Burp!

Ahead in the count, I planned on taking the next pitch… trying to make Rube Foster throw strikes before having to swing the bat. Foster checked the runner at second before winding up and firing to home plate. Unlike his first pitch, this ball came in smoking hot, cutting through the air like a runaway freight train, leaving a white vapor trail in its wake. His blazing fastball began to tail away from me before smacking the catcher's glove. "STRIKE ONE," shouted the home plate umpire.

I groaned, thinking the pitch looked a little outside. Still, I dared not inch closer to the plate, but rather I took a step back. I wanted to get deeper in the batter's box to buy a fraction of a second more time to observe his fastball—if he should throw it again.

His next pitch was coming in way too high to be a strike. Relieved, I began to ease my grip on the bat when the spinning ball reached the midway point, thinking he had misfired. But a split second later the ball began to slow, then drop like my jaw. Stunned, I might as well have been frozen in place because it was already too late to attempt a swing by the time his amazing curveball landed in the catcher's glove. "STRIKE TWO!"

I was beginning to feel like a spectator at my own funeral. Rube Foster wasn't giving me anything good to hit, and I was down to my last strike. The restless crowd gave me grief when I briefly stepped out of the batter's box to catch my breath. I took yet another practice swing; but all I really needed was a moment to gather myself before the next pitch. "Come on, Johnny," I muttered. "Hang in there!"

I cautiously stepped back into the batter's box. With two strikes and only one ball, I had to be ready for anything and everything. I was thinking blazing fastball when Foster began his windup; but then again, he might throw me another amazing curve. Or maybe something he hadn't thrown yet. In truth, my back was against the wall and I needed to stop thinking and just play! "Relax and focus," I whispered, trying to coach myself up. "Watch the ball all the way in. Don't be overanxious and swing at a bad pitch. Just try and make contact and put the ball in play. You can do this! You can do this!"

I saw what appeared to be a fastball. What shocked me was that it was heading for my rib cage. I braced myself, ready and willing to take a free pass, but expecting to not only get the wind knocked out of me, but to break a rib or two in the process. I was fighting the natural urge to get out of the way when I noticed the ball begin to tail over the inside part of the plate, suddenly on a collision course with the edge of the strike zone. I quickly stuck my bat out in a desperate attempt to make contact and just grazed the ball as it sped by, but it was enough to change its trajectory to where it bounced off the catcher's glove before falling harmlessly to the ground. "Foul Ball!" the umpire said. I was lucky to be alive. I again stepped out of the batter's box to catch my breath, only to have the ump order me back into harm's way. "Play Ball!"

Overmatched, I was anything but confidant as I waited for the next pitch. Rube Foster owned me and I'm sure he knew it. He grinned ever so slyly before going into his windup. He released what looked to be a fastball heading for the heart of the plate. My eyes got big and I cocked my bat and was ready to swing when the ball began to slow down, as if it had brakes. It was then that I realized it was his changeup pitch. The ball slowed to a speed I could relate to, although it was running out of steam, barely able to make it to the plate. I eagerly waited and waited, then almost waited too long before taking a golf swing at the ankle-high baseball.

Heard a whack. Felt it too! I looked up and had no trouble spotting my ball. It was drifting harmlessly in the air. Heading toward the first baseman's glove. It didn't even hover long enough to get a rise out of the crowd before it was caught for an easy out.

But that didn't stop me from jumping for joy like I had just hit a homerun. "I did it! I did it!" The Dream Girls were not impressed with my performance, although they were kind enough to put their daggers down, if only for the moment. I passed Marty as he casually strolled up to the plate.

"It's pretty scary up there," I warned. "Good luck!"

"Thanks, man," he said. "Watch me put on a show for the ages!"

Marty was holding his bat like a guitar and he had swag in his step as he approached the plate. He turned his back on the pitcher and began strumming the barrel of his bat and fingering the handle up top, playing to the fans behind home plate. Rube Foster looked taken aback on the mound. Like everyone else in the ballpark, he didn't quite know what to make of the rock 'n' roller. Marty still had his back to Foster when the first pitch smacked the catcher's glove.

"Ball One," shouted the umpire.

Marty was busy pirouetting when Ball Two came whistling in. He was playing his guitar high above his head for Ball Three. Foster looked flustered, and the crowd was beginning to cheer and jeer trying to get under his skin to force Ball Four. Marty decided to face the Boston pitcher head-on while continuing to jam away. He moved to the very front of the batter's box. If anything, Foster was the one who looked intimidated by that move, while Marty had a big smile on his face like he didn't have a care in the world.

The place was rocking when Foster delivered his next pitch. Apparently, he was looking to make a little music of his own, sending a blazing fastball heading for Marty's chin. Luckily, the ball hit his guitar instead, causing the bat to shatter into many pieces. The ball bounced back to the pitcher during the explosion of wood, who then picked it up and threw it to first base for the final out of the inning. Unscathed, Marty walked back to the dugout to a standing ovation from the twenty thousand strong.

I greeted him at the steps with a high-five. "Way ta go!"

"I should have no problem getting laid tonight!" he twinkled.

Robbie was all smiles when he waddled over from his side of the bench. "Congratulations, you two have managed to survive playing in the game! Now take a seat and hopefully the Robins can hold Boston off for the next two innings, and then we can all sign a few autographs and go our merry way."

Marty pointed above the dugout. "Any chance we can hang with those sexy bitches after the game?"

Robbie snorted. "What ya do after the game is your business. All I care about is winning this historic battle once again and getting out of here with my balls intact!"

"Fair enough, man."

Robbie brought Jeff Pfeffer in to pitch what turned out to be an easy eighth inning for the Robins. He continued to pitch into the ninth, and with the cheering crowd on their feet, Casey Stengel caught a lazy fly ball in right field to record the last Boston out of the game. Final score, Robins four—Red Sox three. Thankfully, history had repeated itself once again.

Happy fans were storming the field waving paper and pen, as Marty and I ran out of the dugout and quickly turned toward the Dream Girls, but those seats were now empty, save for Sergeant Stevens, who was relaxing with a content look on his face. "I see you two shitheads are still alive," he chuckled.

Marty grunted. "What happened ta the sexy bitches?"

"Left before the final out," the sergeant replied to two frowning faces. "I guess they wanted ta beat the crowd back to the grave."

# Chapter Twelve
*Paoli*

The Star-Spangled Banner seemed a distant memory now that I was back in my street clothes, marching through a narrow path in the Tall Grass between Marty and the sergeant. The rock 'n' roller strummed his air-guitar. "Still missin' them *sexy* bitches!" he sang. "Baseball 'n' bitches, man. Ya gotta love it!"

I nodded in agreement. "I could almost do that again sometime."

"Yeah, man… it makes me wonder if all that talk about a painful death was just bullshit to try and scare the crap out of us."

"Shut up and pick up the pace!" demanded the sergeant.

Forced to be alone with my thoughts, I recalled the fans mobbing us after the game. Besides making nice with the ladies, I must've signed my name a thousand times. Men young and old were clamoring for my autograph. They were dressed more for a funeral than a ball game, but that didn't stop me from signing away. I also saw old-fashioned baseball moms in the mix. Much like the Dream Girls, they were parading around in long dresses with fancy hats. Their daughters were dressed in similar fashion, while their sons wore knickers and had leather kickers on their feet. There wasn't a sneaker in the house—or a knife once victory had been achieved, just a bunch of happy people enjoying the moment. Just for grins, I was hoping to track down Babe Ruth and get his autograph before we were done. Casey Stengal, too! Although by the time the crowd had thinned out, the players were all gone—vanished into the air. I can't speak for Marty, but I left that stadium physically and mentally drained like no baseball game I'd ever played before. In fact, I was running on fumes when the Tall Grass parted like the sea.

We found ourselves atop a small cliff overlooking a vast city of tents nestled snugly in a large meadow that was surrounded by thick woods. Blazing campfires dotted one end of the campsite to the other. Ghostly plumes of hickory rose into the chilly night before fading away, although the smell lingered to where I was feeling warm and cozy. "Looks like we'll be camping out here tonight," I assumed with a yawn.

"I hope that's not a Boy Scout convention down there," Marty muttered, "cause I'm not in the mood for another sausage-fest."

"Shut up," the sergeant hissed. "There's a surprise party going on here tonight and we don't want to spoil the fun." He checked the red bandana tied to his right epaulet and seemed satisfied with how it looked. "Now you two shitheads stick close to me and don't make a sound." He navigated us down a steep wooded hill by the side of the cliff. We reached the edge of the meadow where three men in buckskin were waiting for us with raised muskets. They smelled like the great outdoors and had missing teeth. "Do ya know the password?" one of them whispered.

"HERE WE ARE AND THERE THEY GO," the sergeant whispered back with aplomb, to which the three musketeers immediately lowered their guns and allowed us to pass.

Along with the occasional campfire, the moon helped see us down a dark and muddy road that was cut through the middle of what was a shantytown of tents. Everyone was asleep, with the exception of a few Daniel Boone types that we passed along the way. They looked at us like we were the ones dressed funny. "Are we still supposed to be in 1916?" I asked the sergeant.

"That's part of the surprise," he whispered his reply. "Now shut up and follow along."

All was quiet, until what sounded like a firecracker popping off in the distance. And then another firecracker went off. I was thinking party, but then I heard a deathly scream. It was far away, although it sounded gruesome enough to make me stop dead in my tracks. "What was that?" I questioned wide-eyed.

"Surprise!" the sergeant chuckled. "Let the party begin!"

I looked off from the sergeant when I heard a bomb burst in mid-air and I even caught a glimpse of a rocket's red glare shooting off into the night. More bombs soon burst in the air and the pops and screams escalated, until they were nonstop. "This doesn't seem like a party to me," I said, before turning back toward the sergeant, only to find him gone. And there was no sign of Marty, either. "Sergeant! Marty! Where are you guys?" I looked every which way, but they were both missing in all that action. "Sergeant? Marty?"

A firestorm erupted on the outer fringes of the camp. It continued to spread, until it had formed a huge ring of fire around the entire perimeter, with flames shooting twenty feet into the air. I was still too far off to feel the heat, although the ring-of-fire was steadily creeping in toward the center of the camp where I was in perfect position to pass for the bullseye.

I wanted to run for my life, but there was no place safe that I could see, so I huddled in the mud on the edge of the road. "Sergeant Stevens! Marty! Where are you?" Adding to the misery, an icy mist began to fall, putting a slick shine on everything it touched.

I first felt, then saw several shadowy figures approaching on thundering horseback. The ground rumbled louder and louder as they grew near. From up close, I could see that these men were decked out in fancy blue uniforms. The man in the front of the pack began to wield his sword high in the air, shouting: "TURN OUT MY BOYS—THE LADS ARE COMING! THE LADS ARE COMING! TURN OUT MY BOYS! TURN OUT!"

Men by the hundreds filtered out from their tents with muskets in hand. They too had blue uniforms on, although theirs were wrinkled and worn. With the impressive looking men on horseback leading the way, I was shocked to see the men in blue charge out toward the ring-of-fire. They sparkled red, white and blue once they penetrated the yellow flames. Their battle cry quickly became a deathly wail that was sickening. Hearing the young ones gasp their last breath hurt the most, although a piece of me died with each and every one of them. "Help!" I cried. "Help me!"

Scanning the flaming perimeter, I saw men in buckskin emerge from their tents. With muskets in hand, they organized into small groups, then scattered in all directions while shooting away. They too kept going, until they ran into the ring-of-fire. Little fireballs ensued that went pop. I gasped at their blood curdling squeals.

"Huzza! Huzza!" Out of the distant inferno now came men in red uniform. They marched in through the flames of the ring-of-fire with swords raised. One carried a smoldering head on the tip of his blade. It was the head of a buckskin man. I could tell this because he still had his raccoon hat on. His long, scraggly hair dripped blood and what remained of his tears. But the men in red were all smiles, although their eyes were filled with fury and rage. They continued shouting: "Huzza! Huzza!" as they began burning tents ahead of the closing ring-of-fire.

There were desperate screams coming from the poor souls inhabiting those burning tents, while the smiling men in red waited with torches and swords just outside. When men in blue uniform and those in buckskin dared venture out, they were immediately hacked to pieces. Even those attempting to surrender were being slaughtered. I couldn't believe my eyes. Blood squirted and heads rolled. Flaming pieces of arm and leg flew everywhere. Torsos were methodically piled like logs and set ablaze.

The mayhem was a hundred feet away and closing fast when I decided to dig myself deep into the mud. I was not six feet under, although it felt like a grave to me. I lay in bone-chilling darkness, fearing the horrible death that was just seconds away.

The war came at me like a tornado. Yells and frightful screams rang out from above. I was underneath a thunderous orgy of pain and suffering. I could feel the desperation all around me. The cries and wails went on and on and on, until they were finally replaced with laughter and cheers. I then heard an army of feet marching off into the distance. I was thinking I was either in the eye of a great storm or the war had suddenly passed me by.

I was starting to feel safe in my hiding spot when I heard what sounded like a freight train coming my way. The ground rumbled and shook, and squeaky wheels and galloping horses could be heard. Curious, I raised my head out of the mud and saw a long line of horse-driven wagons racing in my direction. The wagons were large and filled to the brim with supplies. They took the entire width of road. I had no choice but to surrender my hiding spot or soon be crushed to death.

I crawled away from the road and stopped in a clump of weeds. I was relieved to see that the ring-of-fire was gone. It had apparently burned itself out and darkness was now solely being flamed by hundreds of torched tents and the roasting dead. Men in red were chasing those in buckskin and blue around the outskirts of the camp. It was a turkey shoot; save for the fact the men in red were relying on quiet swords instead of loud guns to inflict damage. I got to my knees and was getting ready to go find a new hiding spot when a powerful blast caused my ears to ring.

Dazed, I looked up and saw a large grandfatherly man hovering over me with a sword held high above his head. His eyes had a look of terror and surprise that I'm sure rivaled mine. Draped in red with white trim, he could've passed for a shopping mall Santa, although I could tell he was just about to put me out of my misery with that raised sword, but something had frozen him in place to where he looked like a mannequin.

It was then that warm blood hit me in the face. I saw that it was squirting from a tiny, smoldering hole in his large belly. A dark red circle quickly expanded over his white shirt. He began to choke and cough blood. His sword suddenly dangled from his hand, as he began to teeter back and forth. He groaned the kind of groan that is your last groan, and it was like his soul took the opportunity to escape from his parted lips. Lifeless, he fell backward into the muddy road with a hefty splat.

The first horse-drawn wagon rushed by and bounced over him like he was a speed bump. The second wagon flattened the man so that his bloody nose was all that remained. It stuck out of the ground like a sore thumb, until the third wagon sped by and buried it deep. In an instant, the man had been reduced to crimson colored mud.

"'Tis yur lucky day, lad."

Surprised by the scratchy voice, I quickly jerked my head around and saw a teenager in buckskin. He was crouched ten feet behind me with the barrel of his smoking musket resting on a muddy knee.

"Did you shoot that guy?" I asked the stranger.

"Yep!" he nodded. "That Redcoat 'twas 'bout ta cut yur head clean off, so I plugged him in the gut for ya. Now you'd better grab his sword 'n' defend yurself before his buddies swing back 'round this way again!"

I scampered over by the road and reached down to grab the sword and was greeted with a face full of crimson mud that came off the wheels of a passing wagon. I managed to pick the sword up before the next wagon passed and joined the stranger, who had moved and was now crouching down behind a dead horse. I was nearly out of breath after lugging that sword around. It was made of heavy steel, sharp like a razor and stained with blood. "I've never held one of these things before," I admitted.

"'Tis no time fur jokin' around, lad… we're bein' massacred out here tonight!"

"Massacred… massacred by who? What's going on here?"

"The British are launchin' a surprise attack against us as we speak," he replied with big brown eyes that looked like he hadn't slept in days. "I was standin' guard by an outpost when I heard shots. I ran into camp 'n' was lookin' fur the rest of my unit when I saw that stray Redcoat standin' over ya like he was ready ta send ya ta the hereafter."

If not dazed, I was definitely confused. "Where are we? And what happened to the two guys I was with?"

"I don't know what two guys yur talkin' 'bout, but we're sittin' smack dab in the middle of hell right now," he replied, while scanning the bloody horizon. "Our best bet is ta follow those retreatin' wagons out before we get hacked ta pieces when the Redcoat return in force."

"I'm ready when you are," I was quick to say. Much like the sergeant, the buckskin dude was not tall. He was maybe five feet at best when we stood, yet I clung to him like he was my big brother. We latched on to the side of a splintered old wagon and made like rotting wood. Our wagon, like the others in front of us, began to slow, although it was still going fast enough to shower us with the mud that came off the front wheels.

"It looks like more Redcoat are pourin' in!" he observed.

"There must be a thousand of 'em!" I shrieked. The Redcoat had joined forces with a band of men in kilts. With bagpipes blaring, they marched across one half of the camp, destroying everything in their path. Then came an army of Redcoat on horseback. They thundered across the other half of the camp by the hundreds. Their swords hacked away at anything that dared move. Both groups quickly made their rounds and were now on a collision course with the wagons in the middle. I felt like a bullseye again. "We're running out of time!" I stated the obvious. The knotty situation went from bad to worse when the wagons came to a sudden stop, causing me to lose control of my bladder. I was so scared it didn't even bother me that warm pee was running down my legs only to settle in my shoes.

"We must be bottlenecked up ahead!" he said. "We're gonna have ta make a run for it!" I followed the buckskin dude and we moved like the wind to a small wooded area, where we took cover behind some trees. "We should be safe here for the night," he whispered. "Just make yurself comfortable, lad."

It was still cold and wet, although I almost felt warm and cozy in the damp thicket after what I'd just been through out there in the open. I reached out to offer the stranger my quivering hand. "I'm Johnny… thanks for saving my life!"

"I'm Willie." He shook firmly with a hand that could've easily passed for sandpaper. "But I'm afraid yur life is far from saved, Johnny Boy."

I took a deep breath and sighed, forlornly. We remained in huddled silence while the massacre continued in earnest all around us, until the men in blue and those in buckskin were nowhere to be found. Music and laughter then replaced the frightful wails and screams. It soon looked like there was a Santa Claus convention being held at the wagons. But it wasn't anything like Christmas. Instead of giving, the Redcoat were busy pilfering the supplies.

A victory celebration ensued that was made even more surreal by the smoldering body parts that were glowing around the camp. Some were like candles. A lump of coal was all that remained of many tents, while the others had burned completely to the ground. Like the party, the smell of hickory and burning flesh ran well into the night.

Willie smiled, revealing a mouthful of yellowish, crooked teeth. "Looks like the marauders are finally pulling out," he said. "Now maybe we can get some shuteye before dawn comes."

"I just wanna go home," I muttered, as the threat marched away. The icy mist had long since become a steady rain that chilled me to the bone. "I wanna take a hot shower and sleep in my warm bed," I said with a whimper. "Then wake up to a big family breakfast before going out to hang with friends like I do every Saturday morning."

"Ahh, home is indeed where the heart is," he said. "I wouldn't mind bein' back on the farm myself."

I shivered, relentlessly. "Heck, I'd even settle for being at school right now, just to have a roof over my head."

"Ya seem a bit like a city slicker, Johnny boy… where ya from?"

"New Jersey. But I'm no city slicker, Willie."

"Well ya ain't no country boy neither."

"Maybe not," I agreed. "I'm from the suburbs."

"The suburbs?" Willie scratched his raccoon hat with a puzzled look on his weathered face. "I don't know nothin' 'bout no suburbs, but what unit do ya hail from? –I'm with General Smallwood's Dragoons… or what's left of 'em. How 'bout you?"

"I'm not from any unit. I'm stuck at the Kilborne Academy, or at least I was, until all hell broke loose. Me and the two guys I mentioned earlier had just come here after playing baseball."

"Baseball?" Willie again scratched his raccoon hat and again looked puzzled. "What's that?"

"You've never heard of baseball?" I asked, incredulously. "What year is this supposed to be?"

Willie chuckled. "It's 1777, lad. What year did ya think it twas?"

I rolled my eyes in disbelief. "Are you jacking with me?"

"Ya must've taken a blow ta the head that knocked ya silly before I came along," he assumed. "Not ta worry... just hang tight here with me 'n' we'll make our way out after sunrise."

Desperate for answers, I wanted to continue the conversation with Willie to learn what I could about this strange place I found myself in, but the cold rain began pounding the ground to where we'd have to shout. So instead I balled up, trying to keep from crying like a baby with this brave soul lying by my side. Although during a moment of reflection, I realized this marked the first time that I had ever spent the night away from family or friends in my life, and it brought a tear to my eye to think that I might never see any of them again. "I just wanna go home," I murmured. "I wanna go home." Quietly, I cried myself to sleep.

# Chapter Thirteen
*Home on the Range*

The rising sun began to warm the chilly morning, as the fog lifted to reveal a football field of smoldering body parts that looked even more gruesome in the light of day. Dead horses and broken wagons littered the muddy road. There was nothing but death and destruction that I could see, no matter which way I turned. "I was hoping this was just a really bad dream I was having, but I guess not."

"From the looks of things," Willie said, "we're lucky ta be alive."

I nodded in agreement. "It sure seems that way."

With Willie leading the way, we searched for survivors, but found nothing that could pass for a complete human. And there was no trace of anything resembling Marty or Sergeant Stevens in the gore, although they could've been there amongst the guts. I became nauseous from the sight and smell of charred flesh to where I felt the need to throw up, and so I did. "Blaaaa!" There went the killer buffet. Vomit flew out of my mouth and nose and added to the crimson mud and pee that stained my clothes. "Blaaaa!" I was a mess from head to toe… smelling as bad as I looked.

"'Tis just a skirmish compared ta what I saw at Brandywine a couple a weeks ago," he said. "In one day, we lost over a thousand men."

I grimaced from the horror of it all. "Seems like there's more than that here."

He shook his head in the negative, and said, "Naaa… if we piece 'em all together, I bet we don't come up with more than a few hundred men at the most."

"Still sounds like way too many to me," I blurted. "And for what? What was this fighting all about anyway?"

"Freedom, lad! We're fightin' fur our freedom! The only way the British are gonna govern our thirteen colonies is over our dead bodies!"

Although I found Willie's words hard to believe, he said them with such conviction that I felt I had to give him the benefit of the doubt and at least play along, until I had evidence to the contrary. "Well anyway, Willie… thanks for saving my life last night."

He blushed. "Maybe ya can return the favor someday."

I shrugged. "I don't see how. And besides… I'm just passing through."

"Ya sure 'bout that, lad?"

I had what amounted to a pensive moment. "Hmmm… without the guys I came with, I've got no idea where I'm supposed to be or what I'm supposed to do next." I panned the tree-lined cliff looking for a way out but saw no sign of anything resembling the Tall Grass, or anything that looked even remotely familiar. "Where are we?"

"We're near the Paoli Tavern," he replied. "Just outside of Philadelphia."

"Philadelphia?" I begged. "Wow… I'm even further from home than I thought."

"Speakin' of home," he said. "I wouldn't mind visiting the farm."

"Is it nearby?"

"'Tis only a long day by horse."

"A long day?" I groaned, before scanning the battlefield. "But there's nothing but dead horses around here."

"I like ta be prepared fur the worst." He winked. "I stashed my horse away fur safe keepin' up on the ridge before comin' down into this valley of death last night. Now we better get while the gettin's good!"

"Sounds like a plan," I assumed, before following Willie into the woods and up a steep hill. We stopped after reaching level ground and looked down at the massacre in the meadow. "It looks like an atom bomb went off down there," I observed.

"An atom bomb?" he scratched his hat. "What the heck's that?"

At first, I thought he was trying to be funny. Although I could see that he was all ears while waiting for my response, so I continued to play along. "Ah, it's a big bomb dropped from a plane."

He nodded like that was a no-brainer. "Okay… I get the bomb part, but what's a plane?"

I couldn't help but let out a slight snicker, but then I looked up and all I saw were birds in the bright blue sky. "Wow... it's really strange not seeing any planes flying around up there. It's like something's missing."

Willie glanced skyward, then shook his head in awkward fashion, sending the dusty tail of his raccoon hat flying this way and that. "I'm figurin' ya either gone plum crazy from too much battle, or ya took a bigger blow ta the head last night than I suspected. But don't ya worry none… I'll take good care of ya either way."

I smiled warmly at my little partner. "I've gone plum crazy if you wanna know the truth. But thanks, Willie… you've been a great friend. I don't know what I'd do without you."

"Just doin' my part, lad. Just doin' my part."

I turned from the valley of death and gazed at the endless pastures and rolling hills that dominated the landscape. The peace and quiet seemed to go on forever. And the air was fresh and invigoratingly clean to where I was enjoying each and every breath inhaled. "The earth seems like new again!" I said. "This is definitely land worth fighting for."

"Now yur talking, lad!" Willie put two fingers to his mouth and whistled like a bird. Suddenly, out of a patch of woods came a dark chocolate horse with a white spot on its snout. "Come, Samson," he ordered, and the perky-eared horse responded by trotting over. Willie rubbed the horse's sturdy neck before putting his foot in a stirrup and hoisting himself up onto the tall saddle with ease. He then reached down to give me a hand. "Hop on up behind me, Johnny Boy."

A chill ran down my spine and I stepped back. "Ah, maybe I should wait around just in case those other two guys show up."

"But we've searched everywhere for yur friends, lad. Now we better get a move on just in case the Redcoat come back."

I gulped. Afraid to leave—afraid to stay—just plain afraid! "I've never been on a horse before," I admitted.

"And ya say yur no city-slicker?" he razzed.

Throwing caution to the wind, I managed to get on the bony back of Samson and off we went, bouncing up and down, until I was hurting inside and out. My rump was battered and bruised, and my legs were completely numb, but I hung on to the back of Willie, even as my testicles were taking a serious beating. "I won't be able to have kids after this ride."

"Ya wouldn't wanna bring little ones into this world right now anyway," he said. "Ther's too much fightin' 'n' political unrest."

"Some things never change, but I still wanna keep my balls."

"'Tis yur scalp ya gotta worry 'bout now, lad! The Indians will leave yur balls for the vultures, but they'll take yur scalp clean off while yur still alive 'n' sell it ta the British fur ten bucks."

After gasping, I searched the hilly horizon. "Really? There are Indians out here?"

"Between the Redcoat 'n' the Indians, ther's plenty of ways ta die between here 'n' home, if the loyalists don't get us first."

"The loyalists?" I questioned warily, wondering how it could get any worse. "Who are they?"

"Ther traitors amongst us who still support British rule. They'll shake yur hand real friendly like, then go behind yur back 'n' turn ya in ta the Redcoat fur execution."

"Wow… I can't see how anyone makes it to old age around here."

"These are tough times, lad. Tough times indeed!"

My bobbing head was on a swivel looking for Indians and Redcoat—Sergeant Stevens and Marty—the Tall Grass—or anything that reminded me of home. But all I saw were scattered farmhouses and the occasional small town popping up out of nowhere. There wasn't a skyscraper or big city or factory in sight—nothing to remind me of the life I had yesterday, or all the days before that.

Willie confidently steered Samson along like he'd been down those many dirt roads before. Meanwhile, living in constant fear with nothing but uncertainty looming in my future was taking a serious toll on me. I felt weak and fragile every time I took stock of my seemingly hopeless situation. I was looking for something positive to hang my hat on, to give me a shred of hope, but all I found was gritty dust in the wind as we passed from one small town to another.

"We've been ridin' fur hours now, lad… let's take a break by that tree line over ther by the edge of that creek."

"Sounds great!" I was quick to reply. "I could use a break."

"We'll just stop long enough ta stretch our legs 'n' get somethin' in our bellies ta hold us over 'til we can get some home cookin'."

We came to a stop and I could hear my aching bones rattle when I got off the horse. "How much longer before we get to your farm?"

"We still got a way's ta go, but we're makin' good time. With any luck at all, we should be ther by dusk. Care fur some dried beef?"

I rubbed my belly. "No thanks. I'm somehow still full, even after throwing up all that food this morning."

"Wow… yur last meal must a been quite a feast ta still be full."

"Yeah… it was all you can eat."

"Really?" he quizzed. "Ya should consider yourself lucky, cause I haven't had a good meal since I joined the Militia a month ago."

"So, what'd ya do before that?"

"I was in school."

"Yeah, me too," I said. "I really hate school, although I wish I was there now."

"Me too," he said. "But duty calls."

Again, we rode like the wind. I kept my eyes peeled for anything and everything—especially Indians, because the thought of being scalped alive weighed heavily on my troubled mind. It ranked near the top of the list of things I didn't want to experience in my life, next to drowning or being burned alive, not to mention my fear of heights. Eventually, fatigue added to my many woes, as the day grew long and the scenery even more sparse.

"Home-Sweet-Home!" Willie finally said. He pulled the reins and Samson came to a stop on a ridge. A lone farmhouse sat minutes away down below in the middle of a large pasture. "'Tis where I was born," he continued, "'n' 'tis where I hope ta die someday."

"I hope that someday isn't today," I deadpanned, nearly delirious by now, and exhausted and drained and hurting from head to toe.

"Hopefully, my mother and sister are in the kitchen," he said, while nudging Samson slowly down the ridge. "Cause I'm starvin'!"

"I'm still not hungry."

"'Tis hard ta believe after the day we've had."

"I know," I said. "I'm probably too worn out to eat."

"Maybe you'll change yur mind after ya try Ma's cookin'."

Willie guided Samson toward the small farmhouse, which reminded me of a log cabin. Smoke rose from a stone chimney. And there was enough dark in the looming dusk to notice flickers of yellow light coming from under the door.

We dismounted, and as expected, I was wobbly on my feet. Willie walked ahead of me while I slowly shuffled along as best I could.

"Hold it right there you two!" barked a husky female voice that caused me to stiffen to the breaking point, the sound coming from the right corner of the farmhouse.

"Ma!" said Willie.

"Willie!" said the female voice. A heavyset woman in a blue dress emerged from around the corner with a musket in her hand. She lumbered toward Willie with her arms opened wide. Willie reached out to receive the woman. And then a statuesque figure in a flowing white dress came from the opposite corner of the farmhouse and glided toward Willie with a buck knife in one hand. The three merged as one by the front door, offering hugs and kisses. I watched, wishing I could join in on the fun, although not wanting to intrude.

Willie broke the happy huddle and pointed my way. "'Tis me new friend, Johnny Boy."

"Any friend of Willie's 'tis a friend of mine!" The heavyset woman smiled big enough to where I could see that yellow crooked teeth ran in the family. "Welcome ta our home, Johnny Boy!"

"Ah, thanks, ah…"

"Just call me, Ma."

"Okay. Thank you, Ma." I moved in to shake her hand, but she brushed that aside on her way to grabbing me by the waist and giving me a bear hug for the ages. She was a big, powerful woman and I was putty in her rough hands.

"And this here's me sister, Martha."

Out from Ma's big shadow came the most beautiful girl I'd ever seen, and it took my breath away. I stood in stunned silence with my heart racing like a wild stallion. Adrenaline shot through my tired and aching body like I'd just been injected with a gallon of caffeine. I was so mesmerized by her awesome beauty that my troubles suddenly and miraculously took a backseat. I felt myself being drawn to her like she was a powerful magnet, and I was made of steel. "Hello, Martha." I managed to say, before stepping forward and losing myself in her emerald greens. Her skin was fair and without blemish. Her nose was slightly upturned. Her lips full. She wore little or no makeup, and yet she looked too perfect to be anything but a porcelain doll… or a figment of my imagination.

"Hello, Johnny Boy," she said. "Welcome ta our home." She held out her slender arms and I gladly moved in for a hug. Her alluring flowery scent drove me crazy. It was every bit as intoxicating as the powerful Green Fog. My hands suddenly had a mind of their own and began to roam. I felt her supple curves. I ran my fingers through her silky brown hair. It was thick with curls that reached down to where her waist tapered thin. "Don't stop," she whispered into my ear, before surprising me there with her tongue, which again took my breath away. Speechless, our hug became a lasting embrace with her perky breasts planted firmly against my heaving chest.

I was lost in my own little world, thinking Martha was the sum of all the women in my Playboy magazines rolled into one steamy Dream Girl, and then some! Besides hearing wedding bells, music was playing in my head and I wanted to dance the night away! The celebration was put on hold when I heard Ma and Willie conversing behind us. It served to remind me that there were still others in the world, if only I'd open my eyes and take notice. But no, I preferred to have them shut while Martha probed my ear with her wet tongue. And then her hands began to roam until they met mine and our fingers locked. "I love ya, Johnny Boy," she purred. "I really do!"

"I love you too," I murmured dreamily, and then our lips met and our tongues danced away. I wanted to explore more than just her sweet mouth, although I was willing to settle for a kiss and hope it never ended.

"That didn't take long," Willie chuckled, and it reminded me of Sergeant Stevens' constant chuckling, and it was like they both had a chuckle for every conceivable occasion.

But then I heard Ma chuckle, too. Although her chuckle rumbled big and robust, whereas Willie's chuckle was comparatively frail and shallow. "Johnny Boy looks big 'n' strong," she said. "Hopefully, we can get a few good days work out of him, before Martha guts him with her knife."

# Chapter Fourteen
### *Hard Times*

They say love is blind, although it's certainly not deaf. I heard what Ma said and an alarm should've gone off in my head, but I was still hearing wedding bells—ready to walk down the aisle and spend an eternity with the stranger in my arms. I was breathing hard, taking in Martha's flowery scent to where I was feeling giddy drunk, if not on an all-time high!

Adding to that surreal moment was the wildfire that was burning out of control between my trembling legs. I still couldn't feel my testicles after the long ride, but I could feel the throbbing erection that suddenly stood between us like a sizzling hotdog imbedded between two toasted buns.

I was both shocked and embarrassed by the pulsating intruder, although Martha didn't seem to mind. She rubbed her lithe body against mine; slowly gyrating her hips from side to side, while delicately exploring with her fingertips. I was completely lost in her magnetic grip, until I heard Ma and Willie chuckle yet again.

"Willie," Ma said, "ya haven't been gone but a month and ya already look as skinny as a rail."

"That's what war will do ta ya," he sighed. "Speakin' of which, I could sure use a hot meal. 'Tis been a long day."

"Come now, Martha," Ma said. "Let's get ta cookin' fur these men."

Martha removed her lips from mine and loosened her grip on my waist, which was a reality I didn't want to face. I could feel her nails teasingly scrape against my sides as she pulled away. Reluctantly, I yielded and let go myself and watched her step back, until she was a foot away and then two. I remained awestruck by her amazing beauty, as though I was a throbbing statue that refused to blink for fear of losing sight of her for even a precious half-second.

"Snap out of it, Johnny Boy," she giggled. "Ya act like ya never seen a girl before."

I somehow found the blood to rush to my head. "I'm sorry, Martha... I-I-I didn't mean to stare," I responded by gawking instead.

Ma waddled toward the door. "You two men should try 'n' get yourselves cleaned up before sittin' down ta the table," she said, before disappearing into the house. Martha smiled at me with perfect teeth to go with her perfect everything else and I shuddered from the power of her gaze. She studied me from head to toe and nodded her approval before turning to follow Ma inside the house. It pained me to see her go. My heart began to ache, but at least my gnarly erection went away. I finally blinked, then turned to face Willie. "Your sister's amazing," I exclaimed. "Does she have a boyfriend?"

"Not at the moment."

Relieved, I jumped for joy like Christmas had come early, although the landing jogged my memory. "What was Ma saying about a knife?"

"Stay on Martha's good side 'n' ya got nothin' ta worry 'bout."

"Are you kidding? I could spend the rest of my life with that girl!"

"So, I guess yur no longer homesick?"

"I can't believe I'm saying this, Willie... but home can wait."

"Stay as long as ya like, lad."

"I don't wanna intrude."

"No problem... we can always use help on the farm," he replied. "Now let's go 'round back ta the barn 'n' get Samson put away 'n' warsh up fur dinner. I can almost taste the beef stew now."

"Sounds good," I said, although I only hungered for one thing at that moment. Martha! "I wish I could shower before dinner."

"Shower?" he scratched his raccoon hat. "What the heck's that?"

"Ah, it's kind of like when rainwater falls into a bathtub," I referenced. "You do know about bathtubs, don't ya?"

"Sure, lad... I've heard of 'em, but never used one before."

"Really... then how do ya get clean?"

"Either with a bucket of water, or by goin' out back to the creek."

"Okay, I guess that'll do in a pinch."

"And ya still say ya ain't no city-slicker?"

"Huh... after meeting your sister, I don't care if I ever see the city again."

We parked Samson in the barn. It was dark, although I could still see chickens running around. There were several pigs, too. I heard cows mooing out in the pasture. The creek babbled like a brook. The crickets chirped away. Raccoons and skunk scurried about. Wolves howled in the distance, sounding like they could be Indians. We washed our hands and face from a bucket of cold water by the barn.

"Let's go eat, partner!" he licked his chops.

"Sounds great," I said, anxious to feast on Martha's incredible beauty once again.

Willie led me to a shack behind the farmhouse, which served as the kitchen. He opened the door and I saw a rustic table parked on a dirt floor. A flaming stone hearth was beyond that where Ma stirred a kettle and Martha was busy adding sugar and spice and everything nice to whatever she touched. I was getting ready to say "Hello" when my erection returned in earnest and began to throb uncontrollably. Embarrassed, I quickly took a seat, wondering what was going on between my legs. Willie grabbed the chair next to me and we greeted the ladies, then watched them shuffle about with iron pots and pans clanging away. I took in a whiff of the hearty smelling stew and it caused me to burp, which everyone took notice of and laughed. "Excuse me." I offered.

"I like yur manners, Johnny Boy," Ma beamed. "Hopefully, some of that'll rub off on my children during yur stay with us."

"Give us a double portion," Willie said. "We're both starvin'!"

Ma brought us two large bowls of simmering stew. Martha followed with two smaller bowls and the ladies took seats opposite us with Martha sitting across from me. Our eyes met and an exhilarating chill ran down my tingly spine. She glowed like a porcelain angel in the candlelight. I found her beauty to be intimidating, if not downright overwhelming, yet there was no place on earth I'd rather look. It even hurt to think about something else, and it was enough to send me in orbit when I caught whiffs of her flowery scent wafting across the table, cutting through all that sugar and spice in the air.

"You men still look like death," Ma chuckled. "Smell like it too!"

"Yes sir… that's what war will do ta ya," Willie said. "Ain't that right, Johnny Boy?"

"War is hell," I said, knowingly. "There's nothing worse!"

Ma soughed. "We'll save the prayer talk for another time since ya both need ta eat before ya starve ta death. Then ya can go out ta the creek 'n' warsh up proper 'n' get ready for a good night's sleep."

"Amen ta that!" Willie said, before shoveling stew into his mouth.

Ma shoveled too, while Martha began taking dainty bites. She smiled while she chewed. Everyone seemed to be enjoying the meal, so I turned my attention to the bowl in front of me and put a spoonful in my mouth. I chewed and chewed, then swallowed the hearty stew and it tasted great, although that didn't keep me from almost throwing it back up. "I can't eat," I groaned. "There must be something wrong with me."

"Ya just need a bath and a good night's rest is all," Ma said. "You'll be good as new in the mornin'."

"I can't wait ta see ya all cleaned up, Johnny Boy," Martha purred. "I'll bet yur a handsome devil under all that mud 'n' blood."

I blushed like a little schoolboy, while throbbing away under the table. "Thanks, Martha… I can't wait to get cleaned up myself."

"So, where ya from, Johnny Boy?" Ma asked.

"I'm from a small town in New Jersey."

"New Jersey?" she swallowed hard. "I lost my other son, Nicolas, ther last winter at a place called Trenton. I hear it was a horrible battle fought in the bitter cold."

"Oh, I'm sorry for your loss, Ma."

"Have ya lost much kin ta this war?" she asked gingerly, like she was expecting to hear bad news.

"I don't think so," I answered. "At least not anyone I know."

"Well then ya should just consider yurself lucky," she said, "cause this war has torn many a fine family ta shreds."

"Do ya have many girlfriends back home, Johnny Boy?" Martha asked. "I'll bet ya have 'em waitin' in line ta be with ya."

I thought of my Playboy magazines for a second and turned a little red. "No, Martha… I don't have a girlfriend."

"Good thing!" Willie chuckled. "I hear the women folk are all cows ther 'n' Jersey."

"Not really," I was quick to respond. "They're fine." I glanced Martha's way. "But not as fine as the ones here in Pennsylvania."

Martha cooed. "Keep talkin' like that, Johnny Boy… and I'll take ya ta the barn right now!"

Willie shook his head in apparent disgust. "Johnny Boy just got here 'n' yur already actin' like a bitch 'n' heat."

"Shut up, Willie." Martha snapped. She made an ugly face at him that was still beautiful in my eyes. "At least I'm no freak like you."

"I'm no freak." Willie snarled with a truly ugly face that would've curbed my appetite, had it not been lost already. "Yur the freak, Martha!"

"Oh really?" she snickered. "Anyone who likes ta fondle sheep 'tis a freak in my book."

Ma nearly jumped out of her seat as my jaw dropped. "Martha McCoy," she said, "how could ya say such a thing?"

"It's true, Ma," Martha insisted. "That's why Pa got rid of all the sheep before goin' off ta war 'n' gettin' himself killed fur nothin'."

"He didn't die fur nothin'," Willie wailed while slamming the table with his fist. "Twas fur a just cause. 'N' we'll need many more good men like him ta join the fight fur freedom before all's said 'n' done."

"We've got needs here too," Martha said, smartly. "And besides that, what good is freedom if we send all our young men off ta die?"

"Martha does have a point," said Ma with a nod that made her double chin jiggle like jello. She then looked me in the eye with her rustic browns. "We can sure use a big, strong man around here ta help with the chores now that Pa and Nicolas are gone. Yur welcome ta stay as long as ya like, Johnny Boy."

I smiled appreciatively, before once again glancing Martha's way. "Thanks, Ma... this feels like home already."

"That's good ta hear," Ma said, as Martha cheered and Willie clapped, which really did make me feel at home. "Sorry ya had ta hear our family squabbles though," Ma added with a frown, "but these two children of mine always fight like cats 'n' dogs when they're together. Do ya have any brothers 'n' sisters of yur own?"

Shockingly, I had to give that a little thought because it seemed a lifetime had passed since I last saw my siblings, when in fact it was just yesterday morning. "Ah, yeah, Ma... I've got little twins named, Emily 'n' David," I responded, still not feeling the least bit homesick with Martha dominating my every thought.

"'Tis nice ta have younger ones ta help with the chores," Willie said. "Bein' the youngest, I've had ta do all the grunt work 'round here since I can remember."

"Who ya tryin' ta fool, Willie?" Martha laughed. "Ya know as well as I do that Nicolas 'n' Pa did the lion share of work while they were still alive, cause ya were always too busy chasin' after the sheep."

"Bitch!" Willie slobbered. "At least I'm no whore."

Martha was the first to be taken aback by Willie's comment. She took in a howling breath and I thought she was going to reach across the table and scratch his eyes out, but instead she only gritted her teeth and glared at her angry brother. "Yur lucky we have company, Willie… or I might've taken offense ta that last remark." She then turned from Willie to me and I melted like warm butter. "Sorry 'bout my retarded brother, Johnny Boy… but he's a little off in the head from all the sheep he's fondled over the years."

Willie again slammed the table with his fist and grunted as he rose from his seat, amid a cloud of dust. "Let's go get cleaned up, Johnny Boy, before I say somethin' I'll regret later." He then quickly exited out the door, leaving it open for me to follow as a chill began to fill the room.

It was an awkward moment in more ways than one. "Ah, thanks for dinner, ladies," I said, having noticed that my gnarly erection was still throbbing away under the table. Feh!

"Yur welcome, Johnny Boy," Ma bellowed, while Martha said nothing, but smiled ever so brightly to where she sent shock waves coursing through my quivering body.

I eased myself out of the chair and quickly turned my back on the two women and exited out the open door. The chilly night helped take my mind off lovely Martha enough so that I thankfully went limp. Although, my recurring stiffy remained a complete mystery in that I was able to maintain an erection without ever thinking about sex. It was like my penis had a mind of its own and was in fierce competition with my aching heart for Martha's love and attention. My penis wanted her luscious body and my heart wanted her unwavering affection, but together they wanted her everything!

# Chapter Fifteen
## *Buckskin Blues*

I caught up with Willie and could tell he was still stewing over the argument he just had with his incredible sister. "This place could pass for the dark side of the moon," I commented on the night, looking to take his mind off lovely Martha, which was something impossible for me to do. "So… what do ya do for fun around here?"

"Accordin' ta me sister," he grumbled, "it's fondlin' sheep!"

"If you'd rather not talk about it?" I was hoping.

"Hell no! I got nothin' ta hide. 'Tis been nearly six months since Pa got rid of the sheep 'n' I haven't fondled a one since."

I nodded like that was a good thing because Willie seemed proud of himself. But otherwise, he had me more than a little worried. We passed the moonlit barn on the way to the creek. "What was Martha saying about taking me to the barn?" I recalled her dinnertime coo.

"'Tis where she goes ta have sex."

I stopped dead in my tracks. "Are you serious?"

"Did I mention she was a whore?"

"Yeah, Willie… you did. But you shouldn't go saying nasty things like that about your sister."

"Just wait… she's gonna take ya to the barn soon enough."

At first, that brought a smile to my face, but then reality set in and I got nervous. "I've never been with a real woman before."

He chuckled. "Ther's a first time fur everythin', lad."

"I was thinking my first time would come in the backseat of a car or something like that."

"A car?" he scrunched his crooked nose. "What the heck's a car?"

"Ah, I guess you could say it's a little like a horse and wagon."

"Okay," he said. Although I could tell he let it go over his head like the other future stuff I'd been throwing his way. We resumed walking and were soon at the water's edge. The creek seemed more like a raging river that was twenty feet wide in places, ten in others, and it looked dangerously deep.

"Last one in 'tis a rotten egg!" he said, after removing his dirty clothes.

Taking a more cautious approach, I let Willie win that race, preferring to ease into dark water that was seriously cold. But I soon manned up and was walking chest deep in the brisk current, while Willie waded along up to his neck. "I guess I'm the rotten egg."

He sprayed water out of his mouth and laughed. "I think we both are after the day we've had."

Ma approached the shoreline with a bundle of clothing. "Hopefully, Nicolas' old clothes will fit ya, Johnny Boy," she said, "cause I know Pa's will be way too small on ya. I'll take yur dirty things 'n' get 'em warshed as best I can first thing in the mornin'."

"Thanks, Ma," I exclaimed. "Thanks for everything!"

"Not a problem. Just don't forget ta watch fur snakes," she warned, before turning and waddling back toward the house.

Willie howled. "I'm startin' ta freeze me balls off in this creek."

"I'm just glad I can finally feel mine again." I shivered. "I don't suppose Ma was kidding about the snakes?"

"Nope. Ther's all kinds of critters in these waters," he replied. "I'm ready ta get out 'n' dry off now."

"I'm right behind you!"

I followed Willie out of the freezing water and dried off with several cloth rags, then squeezed into Nicolas' buckskin britches. Next came a white ruffled shirt that was frilly and baggy, followed by white leggings that rose up below my knees. I completed the ensemble with a return to my dress shoes, which Ma must've wiped clean before leaving. I turned toward Willie, who was dressed in fresh buckskin. "How do I look?" I asked, expecting him to laugh or at least chuckle once again.

He nodded his approval instead. "At least ya don't look like a city-slicker no more."

"Don't feel like one neither. But these pants are a tight fit."

"Fear not. Ma should have yur clothes cleaned tomorrow."

Willie and I left the creek. We moved past the barn and then the kitchen on our way through the back door of the house. We entered the cozy single-room structure. It was illuminated by candlelight and had a crackling fire that reflected light off the wood walls and beamed ceiling. Directly ahead of me were six homemade chairs parked by a rectangular table. The front door, which was bolted closed, was beyond that, with a shuttered window on either side. "Where's Ma and Martha?" I asked, after panning the empty room.

Willie thumbed the back door. "Probably still out cleanin' up in the kitchen," he replied, before pointing to a cluster of game pieces on the far end of the table. "Wanna play a game of draughts while we wait?"

"Sure," I responded. "How do ya play?"

He looked surprised. "Ya never played draughts before?"

"I guess it hasn't caught on in Jersey yet."

Willie shook his head to where the tail of his raccoon hat bounced from side to side. "That Jersey sure seems like a godfursaken place."

"I know I'm not in any hurry to get back there."

"Come have a seat 'n' I'll show ya how ta play."

I took the end seat, with Willie taking the seat to my left. I was facing the back door and could see the entire room from where I sat, which included two rocking chairs that were parked in front of the flickering hearth that was centered against the back wall, with a bunk bed to the right of that. I came to find that draughts was a lot like checkers. I quickly caught on and the game went back and forth, until Willie finally beat me.

"That was fun," I said. "But I can't stop thinking about Martha no matter how hard I try."

"Sounds like she's already got ya by the balls."

I grinned, mischievously. "She can have 'em."

"Ya should watch what ya ask fur, lad… cause she's liable ta take them off too when she adds yur dick ta her collection in the barn."

I dropped my checkers. "What's this?"

The back door opened before Willie could respond. Ma waddled inside. She came to a stop near the other end of the table, then Martha glided in by her side, causing my heart to go pitter-patter as my erection returned in earnest, both organs once again competing feverishly for her love and attention.

"My, my," Martha cooed, "don't ya look pretty sittin' there all cleaned up! Stand 'n' let me have a good look at ya."

There was a part of me that wanted to show Martha just how much she meant to me, but with Ma and Willie nearby, I opted to sink in my seat, rather than risk showing my jewels to the entire family. "Ah, Nicolas' pants are a bit tight," I disclosed.

Martha giggled. "Let me be the judge of that, lover boy."

"Fear not, Johnny Boy," Ma intervened. "Martha 'n' I will knit ya somethin' comfortable ya can move 'round in, just in case I can't bring yur dirty clothes back from the dead."

"Thanks, Ma," I said, relieved. "I really appreciate you and Martha doing that for me."

"Not a problem," she replied. "Now come, Martha."

"But, Ma," she whined, "can't it wait? I wanna get ta know Johnny Boy a little better."

"I'll bet ya do!" Willie hooted.

"Shut up, Willie," Martha snapped.

"Martha, that's enough," Ma said. "Can't ya see these men are all beaten up from battle? Now leave 'em alone 'n' let's get ta work."

Martha pouted. "Okay, Ma… have it yur way. But Johnny Boy is all mine when we're done."

The ladies retreated. They grabbed needle and thread from a basket on the floor by the hearth and took to the rocking chairs. Martha's hands were a blur. She knitted fast and furious and a crème colored shirt began to take shape, while Ma knitted a pair of pants.

My heart went pitter-patter, and I throbbed uncontrollably every time Martha glanced my way, as she sized me up for the shirt she was making. Mesmerized by her beauty, I eagerly waited for the next time our eyes would meet… and the next… and the next time after that. I couldn't get enough of her no matter how hard I tried to think of something else, because all of my roads led back to Martha.

Willie whispered. "Hey… maybe another game of draughts will help take yur mind off me sister for a bit?"

I turned to Willie and whispered back. "Doubt it." I then pointed to the bulge in my britches. "I love your sister so much… I stay hard every time I'm near her."

He chuckled, knowingly. "'Tis the curse of Martha McCoy."

I nodded in agreement. "Yeah, I feel cursed all right… cursed with a boner that won't go away."

"If it's any consolation to ya, all three hundred of her past boyfriends had the same problem."

"Three hundred boyfriends?" I said, incredulously. "Now I know you're pulling my leg." I lovingly glanced her way. "Honestly, the more I look at her, the more she seems like Snow White to me."

"I don't know who this Snow White tis, but besides bein' a whore, she's also a witch!"

I shook my head in the negative. "You're crazy, Willie."

"She not only has ya by the balls ta where yur dick will stay hard in her presence… she's got ya completely under her evil spell ta where she can do no wrong in yur eyes."

"Sounds like love to me."

"It 'tis until the knife comes out. Then she'll bleed ya dry."

Again, I shook my head in the negative, before admiring my little angel from afar. "Martha would never do a thing like that."

"I know, lad… I know. 'Tis what all of her ex-boyfriends thought before they were put out ta pasture. But if ya should come ta yur senses before it's too late, just know that ya should try 'n' run fur the distant plains if ya get the chance, cause she's afraid ta step one foot off the farm. Claims she'll turn ta dust if she does."

I snorted trying to stifle a laugh. "That's good ta know, but I can't imagine leaving this place as long as Martha is still here. I just want this darn boner to go away so I can be normal around her and the rest of the family, without feeling embarrassed every time I stand up."

"Not ta worry, lad. Your boner will be hangin' on the wall of shame inside the barn in about a week, along with the three hundred or so dicks that came before ya, while the rest of yur body becomes fertilizer out in the field where the corn grows the tallest."

I frowned. "Why are you trying ta scare me, Willie? Why?"

"Cause I've grown ta like ya now that I've gotten ta know ya 'n' I'd hate ta see ya end up like all the others. —Ya see, Nicolas 'n' Pa used ta go hunt fresh meat fur Martha ta devour in the barn. But now that their dead 'n' buried, 'tis up ta me ta carry on the family tradition 'n' keep feedin' the beast as best I can."

"And what does Ma have to say about all this?" I questioned, halfheartedly.

He shrugged, apathetically. "She just loves havin' men around ta help with the chores. Otherwise, she really don't care what happens ta 'em after they're gone from her sight."

Just for grins, I decided to amuse myself. "So, that would make me your latest catch, right?"

"I'm afraid so, lad," he sheepishly admitted. "Ther's no way I could return home empty handed 'n' face Martha's wrath. I'd rather take me chances out on the battlefield 'n' ya know what that's like."

"So, Willie… I guess I should be mad at you for bringing me here, but I'm liable to give you a big hug instead!"

"Before ya thank me too much… just know that Martha's gonna wanna take ya ta the barn often. Yur gonna have ta try 'n' satisfy her as best ya can each and every time. But when she finally wears you out or just grows tired of having sex with ya, she'll whip out her trusty knife 'n' do the deed when ya least expect it."

Rather than run for the distant plains, I glanced Martha's way and my heart went pitter-patter and my penis throbbed. "I hope she never tires of me, Willie… because I can't imagine ever tiring of her."

He chuckled. "All I know is relationships can be a bitch, especially with a witch who is in constant need of fresh meat. As it 'tis… even normal women will break yur heart or pick yur pocket of coin. Sometimes both! 'Tis why I prefer the company of sheep."

I grimaced. "I could never do anything like that."

"Ya never know, lad. Ya might be ready fur a walk on the wild side after ya been in the barn with Martha one too many times."

"Johnny Boy," Ma blared above our whispers, "yur gonna have ta come hither so I can measure ya fur a good fit in the britches."

Modest me, I gulped after glancing down at my bulge. Speechless, I looked to Willie for support and he once again came to my rescue. "Ma," he interjected, "we're dead tired. Can't it wait 'til mornin'?"

She yawned. "I wouldn't mind a little shuteye myself. Johnny Boy, I hope ya don't mind sleepin' up in the top bunk with Willie?"

"Not at all, Ma. I'm just glad to have a roof over my head."

She smiled. "Well, we feel blessed ta have ya."

Willie yawned with arms stretched wide. "'Tis always good ta have a warm body ta share the bunk with."

"If Willie gets fresh with ya, Johnny Boy," Martha purred, "ya can always come down 'n' sleep with us."

"Witch!" Willie said. "Ya should go sit on yur broomstick."

Martha hissed. "I think I'll make you sit on it instead."

"Hush!" Ma said. "I don't want no funny business from either of ya until Johnny Boy's had a chance ta sleep 'n' eat a big breakfast, so he can have the strength ta help with the chores tomorrow. Now let's all take our shoes off 'n' get ta bed, cause we got the usual early start ta the day."

Ma squeezed herself out of the rocking chair and slowly rose with boots in hand, while Martha floated out of her chair, until standing tall and graceful with her little booties held by her delicate fingers. She seductively blew out candles on her way to the bedding, and it hurt my heart to lose sight of her in the growing darkness.

Willie blew out the candle on our table and now just the flickering glow from the hearth lit the room. "We're good ta go now, partner," he whispered before rising to his feet.

"Thanks, Willie." I got up and walked behind him on our way to the bedding where Ma and Martha were now two shadowy figures under fluffy white covers.

"Good night, Ma. Goodnight, Martha," I said, as we approached.

"Good night, Johnny Boy," Ma bellowed. "Don't let the bed bugs bite."

"Good night, lover boy," Martha cooed. "Sweet dreams."

I desperately wanted to cuddle with Martha, although there was no way with Ma in the same bed. Wistfully, I followed Willie up the ladder to the top bunk thinking I was going to have sweet dreams for sure with Martha down below. But the bed bugs were going to bite. I could feel them already. Still, all things considered, I thought I was doing pretty darn good for a homeless kid from the future, who was incredibly lost and hopelessly in love with a woman from the past. "Good night, Willie. Thanks for everything."

"Good night, Johnny Boy," he said. "I'll try not ta get too close."

"There seems to be plenty of room up here," I noticed. "It shouldn't be a problem."

He chuckled, wildly. "Not unless ya want it ta be!"

My body stiffened to match my relentless stiffy. "Say what?"

"Just kiddin', lad. Just kiddin'."

# Chapter Sixteen
*Moonshine Madness*

In spite of his assurances, I lay a safe distance away from Willie, near the edge of the bunk to where I could almost reach down and touch Martha—had my arm been long enough. Ma began to snore, and it sounded like a runaway freight train and Willie the caboose. But Martha was as quiet as a church mouse. I could smell her flowery scent wafting up from down below, which was a wonderful relief from the musty gaminess that otherwise permeated the bedding.

The hearth crackled and I saw flashes of yellow flicker against the rustic walls and beamed ceiling. I meant only to blink, although my tired eyes stayed shut and I was soon out like a light. The darkness that ensued gave way to a repeat dream where I found myself once again looking out my bedroom window, and I thought… if only Martha could join me here in my world instead of me being lost in hers, my life would be so incredibly complete.

As before, green water balloons rained down from a gunmetal sky. My street became a raging river with a green glow. Tom dropped his purple bike and paddled down the block. My angelic mother came next. Dad still looked like a grizzly bear in search of wild salmon. The busybody twins were spying on Rudy, Billy and Mitch as they backstroked down the street. And I could see that Miss Willows still had neon green panties. She floated by my window, followed by a parade of family and friends that passed in seconds. It was good to see all the familiar faces again, although it was like a dream come true when Martha swam by. My heart went pitter-patter, and I desperately wanted to chase after her as she slowly paddled away, but I was stuck in place. "Martha! Wait for me, Martha!"

Then, in the blink of an eye, I was back on the farm. I saw myself standing on tipi-toes, peering through a quarter-sized hole in the barn. I was on the outside looking in, when my heart again went pitter-patter at the sight of lovely Martha. She was standing on a bale of hay in the middle of the empty building. Beams of sunlight filtered down through cracks and crevices in the tall ceiling and illuminated her like spotlights trained on a stage. She looked like an angel in her flowing white dress. I heard what sounded like a violin play and then an invisible orchestra filled the air with music as she began to dance, leaping from one bale of hay to another. It was a joy to watch her twist and turn like a majestic ballerina. She twirled; then spun so fast her dress flew off and floated to the ground. It took my breath away to watch her dance in the nude. Her body was flawless. She was so picture-perfect that she even put Miss April and the rest of my sexy paper playmates to shame. I wanted to take off my clothes and join her, but I was again stuck in place. All I could do was look through the peephole and watch. Frustrated, I shouted out to her time and again, but she tormented me by not responding, save for the occasional glance that sent me throbbing.

Hopelessness gave way to horniness and a hand worked its way down my pants. I assumed it was mine, until I realized my hands were stuck in my pockets. Shocked, I wanted to drop my eyes and survey the situation, although I had no choice but to look straight ahead and admire Martha as she danced up a hay storm. Meanwhile, after years of flying solo, I couldn't help but notice that my co-pilot was doing a fine job at the controls. I was joining the mile-high club on tipi-toes and began to see stars. An explosion of stars! The light show ended when I opened my eyes and saw that I was still in bed with Willie hovering over me. "Whoa… what are ya doing?"

He smiled. "'Tis time ta start the day, partner."

"What?" Willie moved out of the way and I looked past the foot of the bunk and saw the morning's first light peeking under the front door. I then reeled in my view and was relieved to see that my pants were still on and my erection was thankfully gone. "Wow… I was having a really strange dream."

"Did Martha take ya to the barn last night?"

"Ah, not exactly."

"Trust me, lad… you'd know it if she did."

I reached for my crotch. "I felt someone tugging on me though."

"Really?" he chuckled. "Do ya know who?"

I shrugged, clueless. "I guess it was just part of that strange dream."

"Ma 'n' Martha are makin' breakfast, so let's go join 'em in the kitchen, before we start on the chores. I don't know 'bout you, but I'm ready fur some grub!"

"Sounds good, but what if Ma wants to measure me for britches with Martha around?"

"Don't worry none 'bout Ma, lad. We can hold her off 'til she's had her fill of moonshine after lunch. Then let her take yur measurements while she's too drunk ta notice if yur hard or not. Just tell her ya like yur britches a little baggy."

"She gets drunk after lunch?"

"Every darn day since I can remember."

"Okay," I nodded with a shrug. "I guess that'll work."

"Speakin' of work, we got plenty of chickens 'n' cows that need ta be tended to after breakfast."

"I was never much for chores," I admitted, "but this could be interesting."

"I was never much fur chores either," he said. "That's why I joined the militia. But war is hell as ya say. So here I am, back on the farm, 'bout ta teach ya the ropes when yur only good fur a week's worth of chores at best, before yur dick's hangin' in the barn on the wall of shame, and I gotta go find yur replacement."

"Sorry, Willie… but I find that crazy talk hard to believe," I said, before adding, "And even if it was all true, I still think things are different between Martha and me. We've got something really special together that only comes around once in a lifetime, if ever!"

"Now yur really dreamin', lad."

"Sometimes dreams come true."

He chuckled. "'Tis why I like ta count sheep before I sleep."

I grinned, sheepishly. "You just need to spend some time with a Playboy magazine."

He smirked. "Is that another of those Jersey things?"

I hew-hawed. "It *twas* for me."

Willie and I went out the backdoor and followed the smell of bacon grease to the kitchen. The women were facing the hearth, busy clanging away with pots and pans and didn't notice us walk in. Martha glowed in the morning light that filtered in from the murky window facing out to the barn. She was candy to my eyes and my heart went pitter-patter once again.

And before I could even say *morning ladies*, I felt that familiar stirring in my loins and my erection returned in force. Frustrated, wanting to shrivel and hide, I quickly took my seat at the table with Willie taking his seat as well.

Ma continued to clang away in earnest, although Martha turned and looked at us both suspiciously, before focusing solely on me with a surprised and somewhat curious look on her face. "Ya didn't have ta sneak in with yur little sidekick taggin' along, Johnny Boy."

"You seemed preoccupied, Martha. Willie and I didn't wanna bother you while you and Ma were in the middle of cooking."

"Preoccupied?" Martha's dourly look turned dreamy and she began to purr like a kitten. "I just love when men use big words on me," she said in a husky voice.

"'Tis not the only thing she likes big," razzed Willie.

Martha glared at Willie as Ma turned around to face us. "Mornin', gentlemen," she said with a crooked smile. "Did the bed bugs get ya last night, Johnny Boy?"

"No, Ma," I lied. "The bed was fine."

Willie grunted. "Never mind the bugs, how 'bout serving us some breakfast!"

"Comin' right up," Ma beamed. She then turned back toward the hearth and took to stirring a steaming kettle.

Martha giggled. "How'd ya sleep last night, lover boy?"

Her sudden look of anticipation suggested to me that she already knew the answer to her question. "Ah, just fine," I replied. "How 'bout you?"

"I danced the night away!" she twinkled, before twirling around to help Ma plate up the food, as I inhaled the flowery bouquet that was left behind in her wake and it made my heart throb, and my penis was now going pitter-patter, if that was even humanly possible. But then again, I knew I was caught up in something terribly bizarre and all I could do was go with the flow and hope for the best.

"Johnnycakes hot off the griddle," Ma said. She brought a platter of steaming pancake-looking discs to the table, where there was already butter and jam. She put the food down and sat across from Willie. Martha then glided to the table with a plate full of bacon in one hand and a bowl of scrambled eggs in the other. She sat across from me, just like the night before. Martha served me a mountain of eggs. She then added a tall stack of johnnycakes and a pile of thick bacon to the plate she put in front of me. "Ther ya go, lover boy," she mothered. "Now eat up cause I know ya got a long day ahead of ya… 'n' hopefully an even longer night."

Wanting to please the woman of my dreams in every way imaginable, I bit the end of a strip of bacon, swallowed after chewing, and it felt like I just ate an entire pig. "Whoa… I don't know what's going on here," I groaned, while rubbing my suddenly bloated belly, "but I can't seem to eat worth a darn anymore."

"Now, Johnny Boy," Ma scolded, "I'm not opposed ta warshin' yur mouth out with tallow now 'n' then too, if ya should start cussin' up a storm like Martha does when she gets mad."

"Oh, sorry about that, Ma," I offered. "I'll try and watch what I say next time."

Ma nodded appreciatively before turning to Martha. "Why can't ya be more respectful like Johnny Boy?"

"If I was like Johnny Boy," Martha giggled, "I'd be out lookin' fur a hot woman ta fondle."

Ma squealed like a pig while my jaw was busy dropping. "Martha," she said, "maybe ya wouldn't go through so many doggone men if ya wasn't so crude all the time!"

Martha looked my way and smiled dreamily, before facing her mother. "Frankly, Ma… I don't care if I ever have another boyfriend again, cause I've finally found the man of my dreams!"

"Really?" Ma seemed delighted with the news, as I throbbed away on Cloud Nine. Ma faced me with her big, rosy cheeks jiggling away. "And how do ya feel 'bout Martha, Johnny Boy?"

I took a blissful moment to admire Martha, before answering Ma, and it was like going from beauty to beast. "I love her so much, Ma… that she's all I think about anymore."

Ma jumped from her seat with joy, as Martha cheered, and Willie chuckled. "This is cause fur celebration!" she said, before waddling over to a cupboard and pulling out a large clay jug.

"Ain't it a little early fur moonshine?" Martha snickered. "We're not even done with breakfast yet."

"'Tis a special day," replied Ma, as she waddled back to the table and then uncorked the jug. "I say we start it off right!"

"Even though I can't eat," I said, "maybe I can drink?"

"Ther's only one way ta find out," Ma said. She held up the jug and poured the cloudy liquid into four wooden cups. "If this doesn't cure what ails ya, Johnny Boy... I don't know what will."

Willie chuckled. "Maybe if ya went out back 'n' took a dump it might help ta free up room fur grub?"

I shook my head in the negative. "I'm good. I don't need to go to the bathroom right now."

"The bathroom?" Martha's eyes lit up. "What's that?"

"Johnny Boy 'tis full of fancy words," Willie chimed in.

Martha closed her eyes and moaned. "I love smart men!"

Ma raised her cup. "I can't wait 'til Johnny Boy fills yur belly with offspring, Martha... so we can become one big, happy family again 'n' have plenty of children ta work the farm fur generations ta come. Let's drink!"

It smelled like rubbing alcohol, but at least I could handle the bitter tasting moonshine better than I could the bacon. "Wow... my head's spinning already."

"That's cause yur drinkin' on an empty stomach," Ma said.

Martha tried to force a piece of johnnycake in my mouth. "Here ya go, lover boy."

I cautiously nibbled. "Wow... that taste's great." I wanted to eat the whole thing, but I dared not. I chewed thoroughly, then swallowed what little I had in my mouth and it felt like I just ate an entire bakery. "Whoa... I need another drink to hold it down."

Ma gladly refilled my cup with moonshine, and I guzzled away. The johnnycake stayed put, along with the bacon that had preceded it. There was now plenty of good conversation and laughter at the table. Even Martha and Willie were getting along. "We already seem like one big, happy family," I said, to which all agreed.

Suddenly, I felt Martha's bare foot under the table. I saw that she was looking at me with glazed eyes, as her foot slowly traveled up my leg, before settling in my crotch. She blew me a kiss, purred seductively, then further shocked me when she said, "I don't know 'bout you, lover boy... but this moonshine is makin' me horny."

"Now, Martha," Ma hissed. "Don't be so crude!"

"Ya do wanna big family, don't ya, Ma?" she grilled.

"Sure do," Ma was quick to respond. "The more, the merrier!"

"Then ya need ta step aside 'n' let me do my thing, cause Johnny Boy 'n' I are meant fur each other. I can feel it in my foot."

"In yur foot?" Willie sniggered. "Don't ya mean yur heart?"

Martha grinned, mischievously. "There too!"

Martha continued to massage me with her toes, while the four of us drank the morning away. Thanks to the moonshine, I was able to maintain my composure under her expert touch without exploding on the scene. It was our little secret. I felt so grown up. I was drinking booze and playing sex games that I knew could soon lead to the real thing, because Ma and Willie had just passed out at the table.

"That feels good, Martha."

"We're just gettin' started, lover boy. Ther's much more where that came from."

Martha certainly had my imagination running wild. *What could be better than to make crazy love to the woman of my dreams?* Although on the flip side, first time fears suddenly crept into my head. Other than my throbbing heart and the bizarre pitter-patter of my penis, both fighting maddingly for her attention like never before, I had to wonder if virgin me was really man enough for what was about to happen next. I sighed, pensively. "I may need another drink to calm my nerves."

"Sure thing, lover boy… sure thing."

# Chapter Seventeen
### *The Barn*

I awoke naked in a barn stall. I was on my back, half-buried in hay. My annoying erection was thankfully gone, but so was Martha. I knew hours had passed. Even though the barn door was closed and there were no windows to see out of, I could tell it was around high noon because hazy beams of sunlight were shooting straight down from the many cracks in the tall ceiling. "Hello? Is anyone here?" Even the animals were gone. Probably out to pasture. I was alone, save for the myriad of flies that were buzzing all those dick skins that were hanging from chicken wire along the far wall.

Much to my chagrin, Willie had been telling me the truth about Martha. It looked like she had a museum full of manhoods on exhibit. The colorful skins came in all sizes and dangled freely while twisting and turning in the breeze that came whistling in between narrow gaps in the timbered walls. And they sparkled when touched by the sunlight, reflecting murky shades of yellow, hazy brown, brilliant blue and fiery red throughout the barn. It was a cathedral of color, until the door swung open and the light show was overpowered by the sunshine that poured in from outside.

"Willie!" I said, while covering up with hay. "I'm over here!"

He chuckled after coming upon me. "Ya missed lunch."

"I hardly remember breakfast." I shook my woozy head. "What happened?"

"Apparently, Martha took ya ta the barn when Ma 'n' I was out cold," he replied. "'Twas time ta eat 'n' drink again when I woke up."

"I guess you weren't kidding about her ex-boyfriends," I pined after glancing at their remains.

"No, sir. I'm just glad yur not already amongst 'em."

I gasped, but then my heart throbbed when I saw Martha standing by the door—and my penis went pitter-patter again. She approached with what appeared to be garments draped over her arm. And in spite of the army of dick skins twisting ominously on the wall, my erection was bold enough to return as she drew near.

"I've got yur new outfit, lover boy." She smiled, seductively. "I took the liberty of measurin' ya fur britches when ya was sleepin'." She dropped the clothing near my exposed feet. "I finished knittin' 'em while Ma was busy fixin' lunch."

"Ah… thanks, Martha." I warily returned her smile. "What happened to the clothes I had on?"

"Got torn ta shreds in the heat of the moment," she replied. "They ended up way over ther." She belatedly pointed to the far side of the barn, where the skins dangled freely. She then turned to face Willie. "Get out of here so Johnny Boy can try on his new britches without ya droolin' over him like a crazed fool."

Willie sneered at Martha and kicked hay at her feet. "Haven't ya had enough of him fur now?"

Martha glared at Willie. "Get out or you'll end up on the wall of shame with all the others!"

Willie's sneer turned into a pout and he sadly looked my way. "I'll be out in the pasture if ya need me, partner." He then did an about-face and left for the great outdoors with his tail tucked firmly between his legs.

"I really should go help Willie with the chores."

"You'll have plenty of time ta help my idiot brother later," she replied. "Right now yur all mine." I held my bated breath when Martha shut the barn door, causing the cathedral of lights to return. She then pirouetted back over to me. I shuddered when her flowing white dress fell to the ground. My heart began to race when she slid down into the hay next to me. Her heavenly body was soft and warm up against mine, and her flowery scent dominated even the lingering smell left behind by the farm animals. "Now that yur not a virgin anymore," she purred, "are ya ready fur sloppy seconds?"

"I don't even remember the first time."

"That's cause ya were so drunk, ya slept through all of it," she giggled. "I had ta put ya on yur back 'n' do the dirty work myself."

I blushed but said nothing.

"Hopefully, you'll do better this time," she snorted, "cause I'm a hard woman ta please."

I glanced at the dick skins. "You're making me nervous."

"Relax," she said, before sticking her tongue in my mouth. We kissed. Her hand slipped down between us and I was soon lost in her magnetic grip to where the mounting pleasure had washed away my many fears. Except inexperienced me had quickly gone from one extreme to the other, as I was now thinking I just might explode prematurely. *Hold on Johnny!* I muttered to myself. But then my heart and penis suddenly joined forces and began throbbing away to a rhythmic beat that went pitter-patter in my overwhelmed mind. *Hold on Johnny!* I was coming upon the point of no return. *Hold on before you embarrass yourself and end up dead!*

I thought of baseball to try and cool my jets, but then Martha had me round first base and head for second, where I ran into her firm breasts. I felt safe there and wanted to linger all day long, although Martha was now waving me on to third. Not wanting to disappoint my new coach, I made a beeline past her navel and slid between her parted legs. Martha cheered me on with moans and groans before instructing me to get on top of her. I did as told and proceeded to slide home for an easy score. I was more than a little surprised at how it felt. Fooled again was I, as the real thing was far different than what I'd imagined while toying with my dirty magazines.

We made fast and furious love, then shifted gears and went slow and easy. I began to feel like a big leaguer after a while. Even more than when I played in the 1916 World Series! My confidence grew and grew with every thrust of my hips, until I reached a point where I didn't need to think about baseball anymore.

Martha and I changed positions on the fly. We became tangled time and again as we maneuvered about. We even got up from the stall and moved from one bale of hay to another as we began to build toward a powerful climax.

It started with a violin, but then I heard an orchestra begin to play just like in my dream. I closed my eyes and saw stars. I opened them and saw a crescendo of color reflecting off the dangling dick skins on the wall. It was magical, if not surreal. Martha and I continued our torrid pace and eventually collapsed into each other's arms.

"Oh, Johnny Boy!" she moaned. "The second time's the charm!"

"Wow… that was fantastic, Martha! I can't wait to try that again!"

"Now yur talkin', lover boy," she cooed. "We'll try again tonight after Ma and Willie have gone ta bed."

"I love you, Martha!"

"Love ya too, Johnny Boy!"

We picked the hay from our sweaty bodies and dressed. My new pants were a perfect fit. We kissed again and again, then Martha danced back to the house and I strutted out of the barn feeling proud of myself, like I'd just earned the right to be called a man. A real man that was in love with a real woman! Not some love-starved kid married to his hand.

I then joined Willie out in the pasture where I saw a dozen or so grazing cows. I pointed to a large rectangle of land that held the tallest of the cornfields and gulped. "Is that where Martha's old boyfriends are buried?"

"Yes, sir… 'tis the most fertile acreage we got."

Although remorseful, I let out a sigh of relief. "I'm sure glad I won't be joining them anytime soon."

He chuckled. "I wouldn't count yur chickens before they hatch."

"Naaa… Martha and I are better than ever, Willie."

"I wouldn't be too sure 'bout that if I was you, lad… but at least she did a nice job with yur new britches."

"Yeah… I'm comfortable now." I gleefully gave myself the once over. "I'm even ready to do some chores."

"Then ya came ta the right place, partner."

I was soon eating my words, as we plowed endless fields with Samson strapped to a heavy wood plow that Willie and I struggled to keep from tipping over or getting stuck. It was backbreaking work that was testing my manhood bigtime! "We do this every day?" I asked, while straining to keep pace.

He grunted. "Since the ladies haven't plowed while I was gone, we'll be doin' this 'n' a whole lot more in the days ta come."

The sky was a cloudless blue where only birds flew. The air was refreshing, although the hot sun made its presence felt. Sweat dripped like salty rain. Only thoughts of Martha helped ease my pain. The arduous day became the longest in memory. I got to where I was more sore and tired than I'd ever been in my life.

"'Tis near dinnertime, lad. Let's go roundup the cows," Willie said, and off we went. Even that was harder than it looked. The cows were like statues jand didn't listen worth a darn. Willie and I tried to get them to move toward a pen by the barn, but had no luck, until the dinner bell rang from the kitchen and the cows started heading in on their own. "The ladies must a trained 'em while I was off fightin' fur our freedom."

"Good thing," I said, wearily. "Or we'd be out here all night."

Chickens and pigs followed the cows in organized fashion. We watched as the animals corralled themselves, then Willie and I washed up and headed into the kitchen. Ma was clanging away, and my heart and penis sprang to life when I saw Martha by her side. "Beef stew!" I licked my lips. "My favorite!"

We took our usual seats and with Ma leading the way, we prayed for an end to the war and a large family to work land that was fertile and filled with livestock. We said *Amen* and dug in.

"I'm stuffed!" I whined after one bite of the hearty stew. "This is impossible! I've never gone this long without eating before. Never!"

"Ya may have ta go see a doctor before ya die of starvation," Ma said.

"But that's just it, Ma… I'm not starving… I'm full!"

"Ya didn't eat dinner last night," she recounted. "Ya hardly touched yur breakfast. Ya missed lunch. Ya been out doin' chores all day 'n' now after one bite of dinner ya say yur full?" She shook her head in the negative and her double chin wobbled freely. "'Tis not normal."

I shrugged, haplessly. "I don't know what to tell ya."

Ma shrugged, too. "Well, Johnny Boy… as long as ya can still do plenty of chores, I guess it don't matter none if we have one less mouth ta feed 'round here."

"Well, lover boy," Martha purred, "as long as ya can still make love ta me, I guess it don't matter none if ya can't eat." She reached across the table and took hold of my hand, while her foot traveled up my leg. "But I still can't help but worry that if ya go without food ya might not be able ta last the night."

Willie snickered. "Whore! Sex is all ya care 'bout."

"Shut up, Willie," Martha snapped. "Ya just need ta mind yur own business fur a change."

Willie grunted. "Maybe I should leave 'n' never come back."

Martha smiled. "Wouldn't that be nice!"

Willie smirked. "Then who would do yur fetchin' fur ya when ya need more men folk?"

Before answering, Martha looked me in the eye like only she could, while magically working her foot between my trembling legs.

"They say a bird in hand is worth two in the bush," she cooed with curled toes. "Besides… ya know how I feel 'bout Johnny Boy."

Willie chuckled. "I know you've had two in the bush before!"

Martha hissed like a rattlesnake. "Shut up, Willie… or I'll say somethin' in front of everyone that'll cut ya ta the bone!"

Willie turned white as a ghost leaving me to wonder what could be worse than fondling sheep? He muttered something under his breath and then quietly went back to eating. Dead tired, I murmured a groan due to Martha's touch before falling asleep at the table. I awoke after dinner and Willie and I thanked the ladies for the meal before heading to the house. We entered and took our usual seats, with me facing the back door and Willie to my left. "You look like you could use a shot of moonshine," I said, noticing he was still downcast. "Are ya alright?"

He sighed. "It's just that Martha always has her way with me."

"Maybe a game of draughts will cheer you up," I suggested.

"Sure thing, partner," he forced a smile. "I guess yur startin' ta like that game?"

"It kind of grows on ya after a while," I replied. "Besides… what else is there to do around here?"

"I've got another game or two I could show ya."

Willie reached into his pocket and proudly pulled out several clay marbles. I acted impressed with his dull brown orbs, although my little brother had pretty glass ones somewhere at home that sparkled in the light. Speaking of home, I noticed my dress clothes. They were neatly folded over a chair. I got up and quickly went over to them. "Look… Ma was able to get these things clean!" I picked up my shirt. "Except for that missing button, it almost looks new." I put the shirt down and picked up my pants and a crinkled dollar bill fell from the pocket. "I love when I find money," I said, as I retrieved the green wad from the floor. My fingers tingled while smoothing out the paper. "It's still in mint condition," I observed, while making my way back to my seat. "Here… check it out!"

He looked the bill over. "Ther's a lot of fake currency circulatin' these days, but I haven't seen nothin' like this before. Where'd ya get it?"

"Probably from my mother," I assumed. "Must've been left in my pocket from the last time I wore those clothes."

"'Tis it worth anythin'?"

"Not much where I come from," I replied. "But it might be worth a small fortune here!"

"A small fortune ya say?"

I pointed to the date. "Look… this bill was printed in 1969."

He chuckled. "Like I said, lad… ther's plenty of funny money floatin' 'round these days sayin' anythin' 'n' everythin'."

"Did any of that funny money come from the future?"

"No sir."

"Of course not," I agreed. "This bill's one-of-a-kind!"

He ran his finger over George Washington. "Why would people of the future bother ta put a picture of the general on ther money?"

"Because he was the first president of the United States."

He scratched his raccoon hat. "The United States… wher's that?"

"Right here!" I answered. "Pennsylvania is one of fifty states."

"Fifty states?" he smirked. "Heck, we've got enough trouble holdin' on ta thirteen colonies, let alone fifty states."

"I don't know what to tell ya, Willie. I was never one to study history, but I do know that George Washington became the first president and there will be fifty states, and America will become the most powerful country in the world someday."

He handed the dollar back to me like it was a worthless piece of paper. "If ya say so, partner."

I soughed out of frustration. "If I could just show this money to someone like a banker or teacher or someone like that, I'll bet they would know its true value… or at least know someone who would."

"I don't know no banker," he said, "but I do know a teacher."

I perked. "Really? Can you take me to them?"

He laughed. "I'd love ta, lad. But Martha's not gonna let ya leave the farm with yur dick intact. 'N' she's liable ta chop mine plum off too if I help ya ta escape."

"We'll come right back," I was quick to say, but then I began to reflect while looking at my dollar bill. Thoughts of family and friends began to filter back into my head like pieces of a puzzle that had been long lost, and now suddenly found. My heart ached, although not for Martha this time, but rather I became anxious and excited at the prospect of returning to the life I once had. "On second thought," I admitted, "this dollar is making me homesick again."

"If ya really are from the future," he chuckled, "then how do ya plan ta get back ther?"

I shrugged, clueless. "I don't know. I'm grasping at straws here, but maybe this bill can somehow buy me a ticket home."

He smiled, dreamily. "Do ya think ther might be any change left over fur a fella like me?"

"I have no idea, Willie. But you're welcome to it if there is."

"That's good enough fur me, partner," he nodded. "My teacher's schoolhouse 'tis but an hour or so ride in ta Allen's Town. We could leave after gettin' the ladies good 'n' drunk after lunch tomorrow ta where ther passed out until we're long gone."

I shook Willie's hand. "Sounds like a plan."

The back door squeaked open, Ma waddled in and my heart and penis did not react when Martha glided in by her side. She was still the most beautiful girl I'd ever seen, although it appeared that I was no longer blinded by her love.

"I was goin' ta surprise ya," Ma said, "but I see ya already found yur fancy clothes."

"Thanks, Ma. I really appreciate you cleaning them for me."

"'Twas my pleasure," she said. "Martha 'n' I will take our seats by the hearth 'n' let ya men play yur games."

Ma retreated to her rocker, but Martha held her ground and there was a concerned look on her beautiful face. "Ya seem a little distant, Johnny Boy… is everythin' all right?"

I held back a gasp, although I may have temporarily lost a little color in my face. "Ah, I'm just a little tired, Martha," I replied with a wistful sigh. "It's been a long day."

"Well the night's still young, lover boy," she said, before gliding over to her rocking chair.

I turned to Willie and whispered. "I must be over your sister. I don't even have a boner anymore!"

Willie whispered back. "Ya must've somehow broken her evil spell. Only problem is she's gonna wanna take ya ta the barn tonight and have her way with ya 'til sunrise."

I swallowed hard, wondering if I could stay awake, let alone make it through a night of nonstop sex. "I hope I can do this."

"If ya can't, she's liable ta chop yur dick off while ya sleep."

I shuddered at the thought. Willie put his marbles away and we played a game of draught to pass the time, although my focus was on surviving the night with Martha, then finding my way home, if that was even possible. I had nearly worried myself to death by the time the candles were blown out for the evening. Ma was first in bed. She was snoring within seconds. Willie wished me luck before climbing up the bunk. I was hoping to slip in behind him when Martha reached out and grabbed me by the wrist. "Let's go ta the barn, lover boy," she purred. "I can't wait ta have ya inside me once again."

"I'm awful tired, Martha. Any chance we can skip tonight?"

She giggled. "I love funny men."

Willie chuckled from above. "Ya love anyone with a dick."

"Shut up, Willie… or I'll cut yur's off tonight!"

As expected, Willie went silent. I swallowed hard when Martha took me by the hand. We headed for the barn. It was a cold, star-filled night. I thought of running for it, but where would I go? With my luck, I'd probably run into Indians and be scalped before dawn.

We entered the barn and Martha began lighting candles. She instructed me to let Samson and the three little pigs out and then shut and bolt the door. After reluctantly doing as told, I turned and saw her lying nude on a large bed of hay. I began to sweat nervous bullets. I was not ready for her, not even close. I tried thinking of my paper playmates to get aroused, but all the sexy women in the world couldn't get a rise out of me with those dick skins glowing in the candlelight. Reds, yellows, browns and blues illuminated the walls and ceiling and flickered off the hay. It was like being at a rock concert without sound.

"Come take yur clothes off 'n' join me, lover boy."

I shriveled. "But I'm cold."

"I'll keep ya warm."

With my clammy hands tucked inside my pockets, I took baby steps over to her and she quickly reached up and yanked on my britches and they became undone. "What's this?" she grabbed my limp penis in her hand and pulled on it like it was made of rubber. "Is this some sort of joke," she frowned, "cause I'm not laughin'."

"I told you I was cold," I offered meekly. "I just need some time to warm up."

"I hope that's all it 'tis," she hissed, "cause otherwise this dick is no damn good ta me, dead or alive!"

I looked over at the dick skins on the wall and shriveled even more. "I'm scared, Martha… I don't wanna end up like them."

Her frown suddenly became a warm and inviting smile, and she held out her arms. "Come my love. I promise ta go easy on ya."

Throwing caution to the wind, I hit-the-hay. And in spite of my eagerness to bail, I did appreciate her flowery scent. We embraced and her warmth began to melt the frost from my body. We kissed. She stuck her tongue in my mouth but didn't stop there. She slowly and seductively worked her way down my torso with a series of wet kisses that soon had my full attention.

"Now that's more like it, lover boy," she giggled. "Still cold?"

Before I could respond, Martha had me in her warm mouth and I was rendered speechless—save for a sudden gasp. I closed my eyes and moaned repeatedly. I even crowed like a rooster. I was holding on for dear life. Even thinking of baseball. But she kept reminding me that I was completely at her mercy.

She continued her fabulous assault, until I squealed louder than the three little pigs combined. An explosion of color blurred my vision. Trumpets blared in my ringing ears. It was a clenched teeth, white knuckled ride that I eagerly rode out to its delightful conclusion. My trembling body then settled down to where I only tingled from head to toe, before everything faded to black. I thought I was dead. But then realized I was dreaming, because I was the guest of honor at a welcome home party…

All of my family and friends were there. Even my hot teacher and schoolmates were in attendance. Shedding tears of joy, I did the meet and greet, not wanting to miss a soul. There were people inside the house and out in the backyard. There were even people gathered in the street. It was a block party for the ages! I even saw Sergeant Stevens and Marty milling about. Willie and Ma were there too. Everyone I ever knew was there except for Martha. I guess in spite of her best efforts, she was no longer the woman of my dreams.

I awoke to the sound of the barn door creaking open and saw the morning's first light. Martha was gone. I checked between my legs and was relieved to find myself still intact. I was about to get dressed when Willie approached. "Looks like I somehow made it through the night!" I beamed.

"Ya must a put on quite a show last night, partner… cause Martha's waltzin' 'round the kitchen with a big smile on her face."

"Really?" I questioned. "I don't know why… I don't remember doing anything to her."

"Ya must a pleasured her somehow, lad."

"No, Willie… I'm thinking she was the one who pleasured me."

He shrugged. "I've never seen her happier."

"I'm pretty happy myself right now."

He seemed disappointed. "Have ya had a change of heart 'bout leavin' her?"

"Hell no!" I responded emphatically. "Are we still on for today?"

"We leave after lunch." He winked. "Now let's get us some breakfast. Can ya handle a little grub in yur belly?"

"I'm craving a Coke and Twinkie right now."

He scratched his raccoon hat. "What's that?"

"Ah, another of those Jersey things," I replied. "Come on… let's go to the kitchen. We wanna start the day just like normal, so Martha doesn't get suspicious."

"I'm with ya on that, partner."

We entered the kitchen. "Morning, ladies," we said in unison, and as expected, my heart and penis remained calm, although I was jumping at the bit to make my great escape. Willie and I took our usual seats, while Ma was getting ready to serve us a platter of johnnycakes and jam. Martha seemed to be floating on greasy air while bringing the bacon and eggs to the table.

"You're in a good mood," I stated, curiously.

Martha looked skyward. "I tasted true love last night." She then purred like a little kitten before giving me a dreamy stare like I was the greatest thing since sliced bread. "And it 'twas ta die fur!"

Meanwhile, Ma passed the johnnycakes around and everyone began to eat. As a courtesy, they left a plate in front of me, although it remained empty. "Smells great," I said, wishing I could dig in.

"Yur welcome ta try some, Johnny Boy," Ma said. "I'm sure a little won't hurt ya none."

I licked the yolk off the spoon Martha had put in front of my face. I swallowed and it was like eating a dozen eggs. I was ready for a nap, but Willie and I had chores to do, so off we went after a quick breakfast.

"I love ya, Johnny Boy," Martha cooed, as I was on my way out the door.

"Love ya too!" I lied, although there was still a hint of truth to that, even without her black magic to cloud my judgement. But there was also much about her that I now found repulsive as well, if not downright scary.

"Looks like ya got Martha eatin' out of the palm of yur hand," Willie said. "Sure ya wanna leave now that ya tamed the beast?"

"I gotta try and get home, Willie… even if it's the last thing I do!"

"Hopefully, yur money 'tis worth plenty of coin."

"Hopefully. But I guess we'll find out soon enough."

"If my old teacher can't help, I'm sure ther's someone ther in Allen's Town that can point us in the right direction."

"I hope so, Willie. Cause I don't know where else to turn."

"Yur always welcome ta carve out a new life with me, partner."

"I appreciate that. You've been a great friend."

"Ya know once we leave the farm ther be no turnin' back, cause Martha will be waitin' fur us with a knife in her hand, if we should return. Plus, ther's always the chance we could run in ta Indians along the way ta Allen's Town 'n' get scalped."

I looked Willie in the eye. "Are you sure you wanna go through with this?"

He nodded, affirmatively. "I'm ready ta leave now."

"Me too," I said. "But let's stick to the plan."

We spent the morning doing chores in the field, then went and cleaned out the barn. I gazed at the army of dick skins dangling away, and it made me sick to my stomach. "I can't wait to be gone from this horrible place."

Willie nodded. "Me too!"

We had leftovers for lunch. My plate remained empty as the food was passed around the table. It still smelled good enough to eat, although the only thing I hungered for was home! "I'm thirsty," I said. "What should we celebrate today?"

Martha twinkled. "We can celebrate that ther's gonna be a new addition ta the family." She rubbed her flat belly. "I can feel it kickin' away as we speak."

"What?" I blurted. "How can that be? We just went to the barn yesterday and you're pregnant already?"

Martha giggled. "Who said it's yurs, lover boy?"

"Let the celebration begin!" Willie announced. He got up from the table and went for the moonshine, while Ma and I sat in stunned silence.

"I don't know why ya look so surprised," Martha said to me. "Yur not the first man I've ever taken to the barn."

I winced, thinking of all those colorful dick skins. "I know, but I didn't realize you were already pregnant."

"No harm done, lover boy," she purred. "We can still make love without doin' damage ta the little fella."

"Now, Martha," Ma smacked her lips, "when ya said 'little fella' 'twas it cause ya got a boy in yur belly?"

Martha smiled, dreamily. "I think I'll call him Nathan."

Ma cheered. "Ya can't have enough men on the farm!"

"I'll drink ta that!" Willie said. After taking a swig of moonshine, he handed me the jug. I then took in a mouthful and passed the jug over to Martha. She cocked her head back and began to guzzle, while I discreetly spit mine out into an empty cup.

"Ahhh, that hit's the spot," she said. "Nothin' like a little moonshine ta help make it through the day!"

"Take another swallow, Martha," Willie said. "After all... ya don't get pregnant every day."

"Don't mind if I do, Willie." She raised the jug to her lips, arched her back and swallowed another mouthful. "Ahhh," she fidgeted in her seat, "I can already tell Nathan likes ta drink."

"Let me have some," Ma said. "I wanna celebrate too!"

Ma and Martha passed the jug back and forth to each other, leaving Willie and I as cheerleaders on the sidelines. We faked an occasional swig, before passing the jug back to the women again. Ma finally passed out, but Martha hung on, rambling away. "It's too quiet 'round h-here," she slurred. "I hope Nathan learns ta p-p-play the g-g-guitar like his daddy."

"The guitar?" Willie scratched his raccoon hat. "What's that?"

"'Tis some kinda n-n-new-fangled instrument from the future," she replied. "Nathan's d-d-daddy told me all about it. He was p-p-playin' the air-guitar fur me after we made beautiful m-m-music in the b-b-barn."

My curiosity was suddenly piqued. "Who was playing the air-guitar?" Martha didn't respond. Instead, she bobbed and weaved in her chair like she was hanging on by a thread. "Hello, Martha," I raised my voice to get her attention. "Tell me about this guy!"

"H-h-he was t-t-tall, dark 'n' h-handsome," she burped.

"What was his name?" I probed.

"H-his n-n-name was... his n-name w-was M-M-M-Marty."

I jumped out of my seat. "Marty's been here?"

"H-h-he came ta s-s-see me the night before ya showed up with Willie," she replied. "Why… d-d-do ya k-know him?"

"Hell yeah I know him!" I answered. "Where's he now?"

Martha shook her wobbly head in the negative. "I d-d-don't know. I w-w-woke up to an empty b-b-barn 'n' haven't s-s-seen him since." She smiled, affectionately. "He w-was the l-l-love of my life, 'til you c-c-came along the next d-d-day."

Willie snarled. "Take another swallow ya lousy whore 'n' we'll be done with ya fur good."

Martha strained mightily to raise the jug to her lips. Moonshine dribbled out of the corner of her mouth. She then put the jug down and moved her plate out of the way before resting her head on her folded arms. Within seconds she was out cold. Mother and daughter were snoring away.

Willie cheered. "Looks like we're good ta go, partner!"

"Ready when you are!"

I quickly followed Willie out the kitchen door. I was anxious to leave the past behind, but before escaping the farm, I first went into the house and changed back into my regular clothes. I wanted to be ready for the future… just in case it should come my way.

# Chapter Eighteen
### *Allen's Town*

**B**ack in the saddle again, I clung to Willie with a sense of hope knowing that Marty was still alive. *But where could he possibly be?* It was just one of many questions I could not answer, as we rode like the wind, blazing a trail of dust on the open prairie that could be seen for miles. My head bobbed from side to side while searching for Indians and Redcoat. Thankfully, we seemed to have the world to ourselves, until the wilderness finally gave way to civilization.

"Welcome ta Allen's Town," Willie said. We approached a cluster of small brick buildings that were surrounded by quaint churches and rustic houses to form a bustling town. "Mind if we stop off before goin' ta see me teacher?" he continued. "I could sure use somethin' ta drink."

"Sounds good," I managed with gritty teeth. "I'm parched."

Willie snapped the reins and Samson trotted into town where I saw many a horse trekking through roads that were caked with dung, while people milled about in what looked to be their Sunday best. Some folks were standing around talking. Still others roamed from shop to shop. We parked in front of McBride's Tavern, which was a brick building with double doors. "Being in this town is like watching an old-time movie come to life," I said, amazed at the sights, sounds and smells of the past.

"What the heck's a movie?" he snorted. "And don't tell me it's another of those Jersey things."

I grinned, impishly. "Nope. This one's a Hollywood thing."

He scratched his raccoon hat. "Hollywood?"

"It's a famous town in California," I informed. "Which is one of those fifty states I was telling you about."

Willie rolled his eyes like he had heard enough. "Now follow me," he said, and so I did. Murky windows and candlelight aside, the tavern was on the dark side and reeked of stale cigars, cheap perfume and soured whiskey. But there was lively chatter throughout. Fiddles and flutes played in one corner. Dancing girls were alive and kicking in another. Cheering men gathered around the stage to see them raise their frilly pink skirts, while other patrons played cards at the round tables that were scattered around the large room. I saw smiling ladies showing off their cleavage by leaning over the railing up on the second floor, as men young and old made the journey up and down the creaking stairs. Willie waved toward the bar, and said, "Let's get us a beer."

"Are we old enough?"

"They'll serve anyone who can pay, lad."

"But all I have is that dollar bill."

"Fear not," he smiled, assuredly. "I've got a pocket full of coin 'n' two dozen furs stored in the saddle outside. 'Tis me life savin's!"

"Really… how long will that last?"

Willie looked like he was doing the math in his head. "'Bout a day if we stay the night here at McBride's," he replied, "two at the most. After that, we'd be livin' off the land."

I gulped, before patting my pants. "Then this bill in my pocket better be worth something, or we're screwed."

"Let's drink ta better times," he said.

The beer wasn't cold. But at least it was wet. Although, it reminded me of bath water with suds. I considered drowning my sorrows in the large mug, except that Willie and I weren't the only ones with problems…

The news circulating around the tavern wasn't good. According to rumor, the British had just taken control of Philadelphia and General Washington and his Continental Army were in full retreat. It was even rumored that the general had moved the Liberty Bell to a church in Allen's Town for safekeeping.

Willie looked at me cockeyed. "Are ya still stickin' with that far-fetched story 'bout fifty states?"

I nodded, confidently. "I've known fifty states since I could remember."

"But it sounds like the British army may be here in a few days, lad! Then what are we gonna do?"

I shrugged, clueless. "I don't know. I just know we're going to somehow win this war, and Washington will become our first president. But when that's gonna happen, or what we're supposed to do in the meantime… your guess is as good as mine."

"Well… I sure hope yur right fur everyone's sake."

"I'm no Einstein, Willie… but that much I know for sure."

Willie scratched his raccoon hat. "Einstein? Who the hell's that?"

"He's a really smart guy from the future."

"Well if all that's really true," he twinkled, "then maybe we should stay fur another drink 'n' celebrate our victory ta come!"

"I'd love to stay and celebrate with you, Willie… but I'd really like to try and find my way home, if that's even possible. Do you mind if we go see your teacher now?"

"Okay, but let's try the bank across the street first," he suggested. "Maybe we can get a feel fur what that dollar bill of yur's is worth."

I agreed and we were getting ready to settle up and leave when I saw a familiar face strutting down the stairs on the other side of the room. "Marty!" I called out to him, but my voice got lost in the crowd. I got off my seat and began moving his way. "Marty!" I waved my arms repeatedly and then others began to do the same, and soon everyone around me was chanting *Marty! Marty! Marty!*

Marty swaggered down the stairs like he owned the joint. In fact, he was all the rage at the tavern—especially with the ladies. They flocked to him like he was a rock star. "Marty!" I hollered, as I made my way through the heavily scented crowd. His evil eyes lit up when he noticed me. He quickly shed the women clinging to him and we shook hands before hugging like old friends.

"Hey, man," he said, "I thought you were dead."

"I thought the same about you, until today," I returned. "What happened to Sergeant Stevens?"

"Hadn't seen him since the bombs started goin' off at that campsite we were at. I got blown away and the next thing I knew… I was in a barn with the hottest chick I'd ever seen in my life! At first, I thought I'd died and gone ta heaven, but that crazy bitch couldn't get enough sex no matter how much I screwed her, so I had ta sneak out before dawn. And then I bummed a ride into town, and I've been here ever since."

"Not to change the subject, but what's up with Kilborne and our hundred-day sentence? Is any of that still going on?"

He shrugged, mindlessly. "Don't have a clue, man. And I don't really care, cause I've found myself a new home right here."

"Not me… I'm trying to find a way back to the future."

"Yeah, well good luck with that, man."

"So, I don't suppose you've seen the Tall Grass?"

"Nope. But why don't you let me buy ya a drink before ya hit the road?" he offered. "It's the least I can do for a friend in need."

"What are ya using for money these days?"

He winked. "I've been able to cash in on my good looks."

I rolled my eyes and smirked. "Okay fine. I'll let ya buy me a drink." I then turned and pointed toward Willie. "But first come meet your future brother-in-law."

"Say what?" he blurted, with a surprised look on his kisser.

"You know that crazy bitch you were just telling me about… well, her name's Martha, and she thinks you're the father of her child."

He went wide-eyed on me. "What? You know the bitch?"

"I was planning on spending the rest of my life with her, until I came to my senses yesterday."

He suddenly began to fidget. "I hope there's no hard feelings, man. It was just a fricken one-night stand. You know how that shit goes."

"Relax… it's cool. I'm on the run from her as we speak."

"So ya say the bitch is pregnant?" he probed.

"That's what she said, but who knows for sure," I replied. "Anyway… come meet Willie."

I did the introductions, noting that they both shared the same last name, which was McCoy, although there appeared to be no family resemblance that I could see. We took seats and Marty ordered us a round of beers and we talked and drank and talked and drank.

"Curiously, Johnny," Marty said, "if there ain't no Sergeant Stevens, and there ain't no Tall Grass, just how do ya plan to get back to the future?"

"I don't know," I replied with a wistful sigh. "But at the very least… I'm hoping to cash in on the 1969-dollar bill I've got in my pocket, until I can figure it out."

Marty came to the edge of his seat. "I'll give ya ten silver coins for that thing right now!"

Willie chuckled. "That won't last long."

Marty sniggered. "All the money in the world can't buy Johnny a ticket home, so what difference does it make?"

A teardrop fell from my eye and got lost in my warm, sudsy beer. "Then hopefully there's a miracle worker in this town, cause otherwise, I guess I'm stuck here for good."

"Personally," Marty quipped, "I think you're stuck here for good. But I'm still willing to give ya ten silver coins for that dollar bill."

I countered with the best poker face I could muster under the circumstances. "I'm thinking we can do better someplace else."

Marty pointed to the row of smiling ladies showing their cleavage up above on the second floor. "I'll even throw in a few fine bitches for the night," he smiled, rakishly. "How 'bout it gents?"

"Let's go try the bank," Willie said. "We can always come back here if all else fails."

"I can't promise ya the same deal if ya come crawling back on your hands and knees at the end of the day," Marty hissed. "Sorry, but I've got a business to run."

"I can't believe you're calling this place home," I snapped. "And besides that… I hear the British are coming!"

Marty cackled. "Ya sound like fricken Paul Revere."

I frowned. "Don't say I didn't warn ya."

"Fair enough, man. Fair enough."

Marty and I politely shook hands, before parting ways. He headed upstairs with a trail of women following behind, and I went out the double doors with Willie by my side. We crossed the muddy street and entered the bank and found it empty, save for a balding, heavyset man sitting behind an antique-looking desk against the far wall. I noticed a large painting of George Washington hanging behind the banker and I took that as a good sign… hoping he was a collector of all things Washington.

Willie approached the banker with a shit-eating grin that had me a little worried. "Have we got a deal fur you, partner!" he was quick to say before I could open my mouth.

"Pardon?" said the stuffy banker, after raising a bushy, gray eyebrow.

"Ah, excuse me sir… I'm Johnny Bishop and he's my friend, Willie McCoy." I reached into my pocket and pulled out the dollar bill. "I have something that may be of some interest to you." I held the bill by my fingertips, just out of the banker's reach. "As you can see… this bill was printed in 1969… and it even has a picture of George Washington on one side!"

Much to my chagrin, the banker seemed unimpressed. "I've been accused of many things, lads… but being a drunken fool isn't one of 'em. So, I suggest you take your funny money elsewhere. Have a good day."

Willie was ready to leave, but with my options at a premium, I stood my ground. "Look, sir… I know what I'm saying is terribly hard to believe, but this money really did come from the future. There won't be another like it for almost two hundred years!"

The banker gave me the twice over, and I was relieved to see a smile creep across his round face. "I'm Mr. Caldwell," he offered his hand and we shook. He then pointed to several scattered chairs in the room. "Pull up seats, gentlemen… and let's see what the fuss is all about."

Willie and I quickly grabbed two chairs and parked them near the desk. I held out the bill for the banker. "Would you like to take a closer look, Mr. Caldwell?"

The banker gingerly took the dollar from my hand and held it up to the light. He opened a draw and pulled a magnifying glass from his desk and virtually put the bill under a microscope, before handing it back to me. "You should be ashamed of yourself for trying to circulate counterfeit money into our war-torn fragile economy," he snarled. "It's like committing an act of treason as far as I'm concerned!"

Willie nearly came out of his seat, as my jaw dropped. "Treason?" he said, wide-eyed. "We're not traitors! We were busy fightin' the British just a few nights ago. We almost lost our lives in that battle!"

The banker blushed. "Oh, sorry, gentlemen… I didn't realize you were out fighting for our freedom."

"Yes sir… I was with General Smallwood's Dragoons," Willie proudly stated, "and me friend here," he cocked his head in my direction, "me friend here really is from the future 'n' so is that money in his hand."

I gave Willie an appreciative nod for finally believing in me, if in fact he did. Now all I had to do was convince the banker. Again, I held out the bill. "Please, Mr. Caldwell… please take another look."

Again, the banker inspected the bill, before returning it to me, only this time with a sly grin. "Curiously, how much would something like that be worth in 1969?"

"Not much," I replied. "Cause there's a whole bunch of 'em in circulation where I come from, but there's just this one here in 1777." I hoisted the bill up again. "I'm hoping to sell it to the highest bidder before the day is out."

The banker rubbed his double chin like he was deep in thought. "As you can see," he snickered, "there are no bidders here, just me. But I'm willing to go out on a limb for you gentlemen and give you five silver coins for that piece of paper."

I groaned after wincing. "Five silver coins?"

Willie chuckled. "Heck, a fellow at McBride's said he'd give us twice that!"

"Then I suggest you go across the street," the banker snorted, "and collect on your money. Good-day, gentlemen."

Ignoring the banker's advice, Willie and I went from shop to shop instead. We even tried the baker and the candlestick maker, but we had no takers for the dollar. Frustration mounted as the day grew long. We stopped off at more taverns on the way to the teacher. There seemed to be one on every street corner and we practically hit them all.

"That'll be three silver coins," said Harry the bartender.

Woozy Willie reached into his pocket and tossed a few coins onto the bar. "Here… k-keep the change."

"What… no tip?" Harry grumbled.

"I h-heard the British are c-coming," I slobbered.

Harry smirked, before saying, "Thanks for the tip, asshole. Hopefully, they'll have more money ta spend than you poor slobs."

My head was spinning in surreal fashion, and I was flirting with becoming an angry drunk. I slammed my not-so-precious dollar bill on the table. "I'd give ya this, but it's the only one I got."

Harry looked at George Washington staring him in the face and laughed. "What's this pretendin' ta be?"

"It's only the m-most v-valuable m-money in the w-world," I proclaimed. "But n-no one will g-give us m-much for it c-c-cause they all t-think we're f-f-full of s-s-shit."

"Hell… I'll give ya a silver coin for it right now," said Harry, before sliding one of Willie's three coins my way.

"N-no thanks." I picked up my bill and slid the coin back over to Harry, who departed for the other side of the bar, as Willie and I got ready to leave. "I g-guess we're d-down to s-seeing your t-teacher," I belched. "Or h-heading b-back to McBride's with our t-tails between our l-legs."

"'Tis a shame." Willie grunted. "I h-had high h-hopes yur money w-would at least f-fetch us a lamb, but n-now I see it w-won't even g-get us out of a j-jam."

I nodded in agreement. "That's c-cause everyone t-thinks we're trying to p-pull a s-scam."

"Oh well," he said. "My t-teacher's only a f-few blocks away. At least he knows I w-wouldn't try 'n' pull the w-wool over his eyes."

"W-what's his name?"

"Mr. Fitzhugh."

"Fitzhugh?" I scratched my spinning head. "W-where've I h-heard that n-name before?"

"I don't k-know, lad. M-maybe in y-yur dreams."

"H-hopefully, Mr. F-Fitzhugh is a m-miracle worker," I dribbled dreamily, "cause I'd love ta be g-grounded by my p-parents for being drunk before this day is out. H-hell... I don't even care if they l-lock me in my r-room and t-throw away the key. Just as l-long as I'm b-back w-where I belong."

We stumbled out of the smoke-filled bar. The fresh air helped to clear the senses, although not enough to where we could get on Samson's back, so we bumbled along on foot. Drunken happiness was soon replaced by staggering anxiety and I was ready to puke my guts out, but there was nothing in my belly, so I dry-heaved instead.

Only a numbing headache remained of my buzz by the time the quaint little schoolhouse was in sight. It was very picturesque... a white building with a steep black rooftop surrounded by mature sycamore trees. My breath became short and my heart began to pound as we neared the front door. "I'm nervous, Willie. If this doesn't work, I'm stuck here for life."

"Fear not, lad. Mr. Fitzhugh's a smart man who always seems ta have an answer fur everythin'. Besides bein' the furthest out, I wanted ta save him fur last, just in case all else failed. But I know he's not a rich man, so we're not gonna be hittin' the jackpot with him. That much I know fur sure."

"I just wanna go home."

To that end, I followed Willie into the schoolhouse. We were in a small entry that led to a larger space, where there were open windows a plenty that offered a pleasant view of the sycamores, while filling the classroom with natural light and fresh air. I saw no books, just the backs of a dozen kids holding paper paddles with numbers and letters on them. Everyone turned around to look our way when Willie shut the door behind us. I saw faces ranging from about five to fifteen sitting on benches. There were seven boys—two had toys, and five girls—three with curls.

The teacher was in a chair behind his desk, which was facing out toward the class from the opposite side of the room. He didn't necessarily look like a miracle worker from afar, although there was a youthful glow about him that radiated from his otherwise old and gray appearance. "Good afternoon, Willie," he bellowed with a reassuring voice. "It's good of you to visit."

"Good afternoon, Mr. Fitzhugh… I don't mean ta bother ya none."

"Not at all," Mr. Fitzhugh replied. "I love when former students come back to see me." He gave me the once over and offered a pleasant smile. "I see you've brought a friend."

Willie nodded. "This here's me friend, Johnny Boy."

"Have ya killed any Redcoat, Willie?" a boy of about ten blurted out from his seat on a bench.

Willie turned to face the boy. "Killed more than I care ta remember," he replied. "But war's hell. Ya need ta stay in school fur as long as ya can 'n' hopefully the fightin' will be over by the time ya graduate."

Mr. Fitzhugh rose from his desk and clapped approvingly. I could see that he was tall and thin and wore layers of morbid black with a frilly white shirt peeking through his vest. "That's excellent advice, Willie. Come, gentlemen!" He waved his hand excitedly. "Come to the front of the classroom. I'm sure everyone would love to hear your stories before we go home for the day."

I looked at Willie and he seemed excited, although I got that same old anxious feeling that happened every time a teacher would single me out. Besides, I didn't want to go in front of the class with my story. It was too bizarre! But the last thing I wanted was to piss the teacher off, so I followed Willie as he made his way between the benches, until we were standing side by side in front of Mr. Fitzhugh's antique desk. From up close I could see that the teacher wore a gray wig with a ponytail to go with curly gray sideburns that ran down his long and wrinkled face. His blue eyes were droopy like a sad dog, although he maintained a smile that I found encouraging.

I listened as Willie told one war story after another. The class was on the edge of their benches, hanging on his every word. Willie was really soaking up the attention and basking in the glory—as well he should—but he finally reached a point where he had come full circle and was telling the same story twice.

"Not to cut you off, Willie," Mr. Fitzhugh chimed in, "but I'm afraid we're running low on time today and Johnny Boy still needs a turn."

The class looked all bright-eyed and bushy-tailed, as they peered my way. "Hello everyone," I croaked. I then coughed the frog from my throat before continuing. "Ah, my name's Johnny Bishop…"

"Have ya killed any Redcoat, Johnny?" that same boy of about ten blurted out from his seat on the bench.

"Ah, no," I admitted to the sudden gloom of the room.

"Wer'd ya get the funny lookin' clothes?" a teenage girl with curls asked from the third row.

"Well, I don't normally wear clothes like these, but my mother bought them for a special occasion."

"Is this a special occasion?" A wise guy shouted from the last row, and I blushed to a chorus of giggles and laughter.

"Class dismissed!" the teacher bellowed before I could respond, and with that said, the class scurried for the door much like what kids still do today. I turned and saw the teacher looking at me curiously, like I was from another planet. "Besides the rather unique attire," he said, "I can tell by the way you converse that you're not from around here."

"I'm not," I responded—glad that he noticed, and then Willie added, "Johnny Boy's from the future!"

As expected, the teacher laughed, although I took the opportunity to press on. "It's true, Mr. Fitzhugh! It's true!" I insisted, before pulling out my dollar bill for support. "And I'm not alone," I added—hoping strength in numbers might wipe the skeptical look from his face. "There's a guy in town who also came with me from the future!"

"'Tis true," Willie chimed in. "I drank with him at McBride's."

"I've always been fascinated by the prospect of time travel," Mr. Fitzhugh divulged, "although, I'm afraid it's a topic better suited to those with a vivid imagination or a belly full of beer."

Down to my last straw, I held out the dollar bill I had been grasping with a trembling hand. "Here… this is my proof. It's money that was printed in 1969! All I ask is that you take a good look at it before deciding to believe us or not."

"Fair enough." Mr. Fitzhugh politely took possession of my dollar bill. He put on wire-framed glasses that stood at the end of his long nose and gave the dollar the once over. He then moved out from behind his desk for the nearest window, where he examined the bill further in the fading light. He studied it carefully front and back. He flipped it time and again. He held it out as far as his arm would go, then reeled it in for a closer look. In and out he went, until his skeptical expression turned to one of astonishment. "I believe you!" he said, as I jumped for joy, while Willie cheered. "I believe you!" Excitedly, he returned to his desk and took his seat. "I've been a collector of currency for as long as I can remember," he added, while gingerly placing my dollar bill down on the surface of his desk, "and never have I seen anything quite like this before!"

I imagined myself soon hugging family and friends, and a wonderful chill ran down my spine. "I'm so glad you believe me. You don't know what this means to me!"

Mr. Fitzhugh was almost breathless as he gazed at my bill. "Do you have any more of these?"

"No," I replied. "That's the only one."

"Then I believe this to be the most valuable bill in the world!" he declared, while hovering over my dollar like it was backed by gold. "A collector's item for the ages!"

Willie chuckled, dreamily. "I see a herd a sheep in me future."

"Not so fast, Willie," warned the teacher. "There's only a small handful of people in the world who would know and appreciate the value of this currency… and are rich enough to pay its true worth."

"I just wanna go home," I said. "You guys can keep the money."

"I appreciate the kind gesture, Johnny," Mr. Fitzhugh said, "although, returning you to the future is something easier said than done."

"But it's possible, right?" I begged a positive response.

I was at first relieved when Mr. Fitzhugh nodded in the affirmative. "Yes!" he said. "You are living proof that time travel will someday be possible!"

"Someday?" I slumped. "I don't see what good that does me now."

"I know it's not the news you want to hear," he said, remorsefully, "but if it's any consolation to you, I'd sure love to hear every detail of your fascinating story from beginning to end. After all... it's not every day I get to meet someone from the future."

With my hopes dashed and my knees ready to buckle, I took a seat on a first-row bench and began to cry like a baby. "I'll never see my mother again!" I sobbed. "Or my father! Or my brother and sister! Or my friends! My entire life has been taken away from me," I wailed. "I can't believe this has happened to me! I can't! I can't!"

My pity party of one finally ran its course and I settled down enough to have an intelligent conversation about planes, trains and automobiles to help take my mind off my woes. I told Mr. Fitzhugh everything he wanted to know. I became the all-knowing teacher and he the eager student. He took notes, lots and lots of notes. He asked a million questions about Kilborne, and I answered what little I knew. It was dark by the time we finished, and I was still no closer to home then when the day began.

"I guess you now know just about everything there is to know about the future," I said, after a melancholy sigh. "But where does that leave me?"

"I don't have much to offer," Mr. Fitzhugh admitted, "although I'll gladly pay you what I have for your precious dollar bill."

"How much do ya have?"

He reached into his pocket and pulled out a large silver coin that was even larger than the silver coins Willie had earlier in the day, before we drank them all away. "Unfortunately, all I have is this 1776 Continental Dollar on me right now."

"But isn't my dollar worth more than that?"

He nodded, affirmatively. "Yes. If this bill of yours was to find the right hands it would fetch much more money than I could ever hope to pay."

"Then I guess I need to find the right hands."

Mr. Fitzhugh looked heartbroken. "It's not like I was going to try and sell it mind you." He pointed to my bill. "This here is a thing of beauty. Something to be cherished and admired! Not passed around from hand to hand like everyday currency."

"Well… you know my situation. What would you do in my case?"

Willie intervened. "I'd take the coin 'n' run!"

Mr. Fitzhugh smiled. "Yes… taking my coin might seem to be the obvious thing to do in a pinch, although that would be giving up the chance to make a fortune later on."

I rubbed my chin like it was helping me to think. "Where would I find someone who would pay me what the dollar is worth?"

"I would've said Philadelphia," Mr. Fitzhugh replied, "but everyone's scattering now that the British have moved in. I sure wish you knew your history better, Johnny," he frowned while raising a bushy, gray eyebrow, "because I'd sure like to know if the Redcoat are really headed towards Allen's Town."

I groaned from the grief of it all. "Now that I'm stuck here in the past… I wish I knew my history better too."

Mr. Fitzhugh glanced at my bill. "You know it's made of paper. And it worries me to death that the most priceless object in the world could easily get damaged in your pocket. Especially considering current events! How about I hold on to it for safekeeping? At least until things settle down with the British. You can always come back anytime you like and claim it. I'll reluctantly return it to you... no questions asked. And I'll even give you my coin as payment, just for the sheer pleasure of being able to visit with your dollar bill a little while longer."

I looked to Willie for guidance. "What do ya think?"

"If I trust anyone in this world, lad… I trust Mr. Fitzhugh. And besides that… we're broke 'n' could use the coin."

Knowing that my future money wasn't doing us any good at that moment, I agreed, and the deal was done. I now had a shiny 1776 Continental Dollar in my possession. "How much will this buy?"

"I imagine a whole lot more than what your dollar bill will buy in the future," Mr. Fitzhugh answered. "But do spend it wisely, lad."

"Thanks… that's good advice," I said, glumly. "I just wish you could advise me on how to get back home."

"I'm terribly sorry, Johnny. I wish I could help in that regard. I really do. But I'm afraid you're here to stay."

My eyes watered, then came the tears yet again. "Hopefully, you're wrong about that." I clasped my hands together and glanced toward the heavens. "Do ya believe in miracles, Mr. Fitzhugh?"

"I normally would've said NO," he replied. "Although now that I've met you… a young man from the future… I now know that anything in this wacky world of ours is truly possible. Anything!"

"That's what I'm counting on," I said, once again glancing toward the heavens. "It was a pleasure meeting you, Mr. Fitzhugh." I gave the teacher a firm handshake. "Take good care of that dollar bill for me until I return. Okay?"

Mr. Fitzhugh nodded, assuredly. "I'll care for it, as if it were my very own."

Willie hugged Mr. Fitzhugh, then he and I headed out the door and into the dark, where the city was aglow in candlelight. I was feeling like a cold homeless person in need of a warm pillow to rest my weary head. "Let's go back to McBride's Tavern," I said. "Maybe Marty's holding out on me and knows more than he's saying about getting back to the future."

"All right," Willie replied. "But we can't stay too long, just in case the British really are comin' this way."

We got on Samson and bounced back into the heart of town. The streets were empty. The shops closed. Only the taverns remained open, crowded as could be. We passed them all this time around, until we reached McBride's.

I gritted my gritty teeth. "I'm not looking for a fight, but I'm desperate enough to where I'll do anything right now to get back home. Anything!"

"Hopefully, it won't come ta blows, lad… but I'll be on yur side if it does."

"Thanks, Willie. I appreciate that. Although, this is probably one battle I should fight alone." I swallowed hard and prepared for the worst, knowing Marty had taken a bat to his father's head and left him for dead. We entered the tavern and were surprised to find the place empty. "That's strange," I said, while scanning the large room. "Where is everyone?"

"The candles are all still lit 'n' ther's food 'n' drink left on the tables," he observed. "Looks like everyone left in a hurry."

"Maybe they got word the British were nearby," I speculated, before scanning the empty room once again. "Marty! Anyone! Hello! Is anyone here?"

"I'll check upstairs," Willie said, and so he did, while I searched through all the nooks and crannies located on the first floor. It was deathly quiet, save for Willie's creaking footsteps overhead.

I came to notice a green mist wafting in the air from under the red curtain that covered the empty stage where the dancing girls had been earlier. I moved in to have a closer look. I got on the stage and smelled their lingering perfume. I was drawn to the sweetness and soon heard hissing coming from behind the curtain and what sounded like a chorus of girls cooing. *Come to us, lover boy. Come to us now and we will show you the way home!*

I quickly parted the red curtain and there was a sea of frothy green waiting for me, and I was washed away in a mighty wave, tumbling head over heel while sinking deep. I was about to drown when the green water began to bubble like club soda. I bounced around on bubbles for what seemed an eternity, and then the bubbles began to burst and burst, until I was finally standing on dry ground. I found myself in the middle of a dark and foreboding desert, although I could see an oasis of Tall Grass up ahead. Their many feathery tips twinkled along with the endless stars that shimmered high above in the night sky. Elated, I ran toward the city of lights and was soon close enough to notice a green glow coming from a narrow path.

I mirthfully entered the green path, eagerly running to regain the life I once had. I was like a bull in a china shop the way I bounced off the narrow walls, although I kept going through every twist and turn as fast as I could. I kept running, until I was gassed to the point of collapse, but still I chugged along in the glowing green, fueled by honeysuckle and hope and prodded by eerie hissing. And there were girls cooing wantonly like cheerleaders in heat. *Run, Johnny, run! Run, Johnny, run!*

There came a time, although not anytime soon, that the Tall Grass grew silent and gave way to woods. Familiar woods! The very same woods I used to play army in by day and look to avoid in the dead of night. The woods were alive with creepy moon shadows, yet I felt warm and cozy to the point of almost getting down on my hands and knees to kiss the weeds under foot.

But instead I ran in the direction of my house like I had wings. Through the woods I went, and soon enough, I saw my street peeking through the trees, and the goose bumps began to fly. I was giddy with excitement. Overwhelmed with joy! I was like a little kid on Christmas morning. With life seemingly about to return to normal, my only wish was for the light of day so everyone could come out and play.

I went through the last of the trees and saw my home-sweet-home sitting among the other houses on the block. And it seemed as though a lifetime had passed since I last saw the place, although everything still looked the same from thirty yards away, except for the surprising moonlit FOR SALE sign that was shining bright red in my front yard. Rather than dwell on the unfamiliar sign, I raced for the front door as if I had blinders on.

"Mom! Dad! I'm back! I'm back!" I was all smiles while turning the knob. I pushed the door open and was greeted by a stale, musty smell as if the house hadn't been lived in for years. Still, I excitedly flipped on the light switch hoping to run into a surprise party for the ages, but no, the surprise was on me. So much so that it took my breath away. I dropped to my knees, as if I'd been sucker-punched. "Mom! Dad! Where are you? What's going on here?"

# Chapter Nineteen
*Nana*

I thought I'd finally left strange in the rearview mirror, but no… it had apparently followed me home. Besides the blue carpet that was now beige and the beige walls that were now a light blue, the first thing I noticed besides the musty smell was a large brown packing box in the middle of the living room floor. And the furnishings, what was left of them, were all new to me—except that they appeared faded and worn, save for the flat screen on the wall. I moved in for a closer look at the futuristic TV and was dazzled by the colors and brilliant images, until I remembered the big, boxy console TV that was missing from the floor. "Hello," I shouted above the surround sound. "Is anyone here?"

I was almost glad to get no response, so I could return my attention to the TV, where I saw one late night commercial after another. Cell phones? Home computers? The Internet? I didn't know what those things were, but everything seemed to be traveling at lightning-fast speed. And I'd never seen cars like that before, except maybe in my dreams or when I was a little kid at the World's Fair. My jaw dropped when I saw an ad for a new Star Trek movie that was coming soon. It was lightyears ahead of the Star Trek I knew and loved. "Hello," I again shouted above the surround sound. "Mom! Dad! Is anyone home?"

I pulled away from the TV and headed for the bedrooms. Up the stairs I went and saw that the hall bathroom had been updated and the three bedroom doors down the short hallway were painted white, when they should've been brown. I ran the hallway and opened the door to the master bedroom but hesitated before entering the dark room. "Mom… Dad… please be here. Please!"

Hoping for the best, but preparing for the worst, I braced myself before flipping on the wall switch. Much to my surprise, I saw Nana sleeping in my parent's bed. Relieved to see a familiar face, I ran to her side. "Nana! Wake up! It's me, Johnny! Where's Mom and

Dad?" I had a million questions for my snoring grandma, although first I had to wake her. "Nana!" I shook her arm, but she remained dead to the world. "Nana!"

Besides the bedroom being blue when it should've been green, I noticed the bed was different and upon closer inspection, Nana was too! She looked older than when I last saw her a week ago. But after looking in the mirror on the newish dresser, I saw that I too looked older. There were dark circles under my bloodshot eyes, and it looked like I needed to shave the gray stubble from my pimply face. Gray stubble? At least the hair on my head remained dark, although it was greasy and disheveled to the point of being spiked where not curly. I sat on the edge of the bed. "Nana! Wake-up, Nana!"

Nana finally muttered something resembling a word before the snores took over once again. I shook her body lightly and found her thinner and more brittle to the touch then I remembered. "Nana! It's me, Johnny. Wake-up, Nana!"

Her eyelids began to flutter—then opened wide to reveal a watery sea of blue. I could tell she was surprised to see me. Shocked in fact! I went to hug her, but she jerked away with a horrified look on her pale and wrinkled face. "Who are you and what are you doing in my house?" she snapped, while pulling the covers up around her neck for protection.

"Hey, Nana… take it easy… it's just me."

Nana blinked like she was trying to clear the cobwebs, then she stared intently at me, until a light apparently went off in her head and I was pleased when she seemed happy to see me. "Cody… I wasn't expecting to see you!"

I scratched my head like Willie would. "Cody? Who's Cody?"

Nana blushed like she caught her mistake and was embarrassed. "I'm sorry, Glen. You and your brother look so much alike, I still get the two of you confused sometimes." She relaxed her grip on the covers, and perhaps reality. "I assume Cody and your dad are making themselves at home downstairs?"

It was becoming quite a habit for me, but I shrugged clueless once again. "You must still be dreaming, Nana. I don't know any Cody or Glen, and I haven't seen Dad in days."

Nana rolled her eyes and grinned. "Now stop messing with me, Glen. Your Aunt Emily already thinks I've completely lost my mind. You don't need to try and prove her right." She smirked. "Besides, I knew your father was flying in from California to help move me tomorrow. I just didn't know he was bringing you and your brother along for the ride."

Again, I scratched like Willie. "Flying in from California? Cody? Glen? Aunt Emily? I don't know what you're talking about, Nana. Where's Mom and Dad?"

"Nana?" she chuckled. "That's funny of you, Glen. I just now realized you've been calling me Nana instead of Granny." She smiled, dreamily. "That sure does bring back fond memories though. Emily and David used to call Mother that all the time."

"Yeah… speaking of Emily and David… where are they?"

She sighed, forlornly. "All I know is they're planning on carting me off to some nursing home tomorrow where I'll spend the rest of my life amongst a bunch of strangers." A tear ran down her hollowed cheek. "I'm stuck in this nightmare and there's not a damn thing I can do about it!" she said, before burying her head in her pillow and sobbing.

Rather than join her for a much-needed cry, I made a mad dash for the other two bedrooms to check things out for myself. The next bedroom was the one David and I shared. I opened the door and held my breath while flipping on the light switch, and it felt like my guts had been ripped out when I saw an empty room. The bunk bed was gone. The desk too. The posters of Mantle, the Stones and Pink Floyd were all gone. There was no trace that David nor I had ever set foot in that room. It was very depressing to say the least. Even the skeletons in my closet were gone.

I rushed to Emily's room and found more change. Walls once pink were a faded yellow and the many dolls that had filled her room were now gone. Her little metal oven set… her plastic Barbie house… her numerous stuffed animals… all gone. It was truly heartbreaking to behold. I assumed what remained of my kid sister could be found in the three small packing boxes in the middle of her floor. I got down on my knees and searched. The first box had clothes. The second towels. There were old pictures and a scrapbook in the third. I started rummaging through the box and a photo fell to the floor. At first glance, it looked like an old picture of Mom posing with another guy. I turned the photo over and in blue ink it read: *Emily's senior prom, May 24,1980… Emily & Mark!*

Blown away, I found it difficult to believe my wide eyes. I located the envelope where the picture had originated from and saw more photos of Emily all grown up and posing in her prom dress, and then there were images of David. He looked tall, dark and handsome in a black tux. He was kissing a pretty girl in one of his pictures. According to the note on the back, his prom date was named, Sheila, and from the looks of things, she was definitely cheerleader material. Impressed with his catch, I muttered, "Go David!" to the four empty walls, and of course got no response. I was just trying to humor myself to keep from going off the deep end, assuming I wasn't already there.

I went through every picture envelope in the box. Before long, there were family photos scattered all over the bedroom floor and not a single one of them included an image of me. "I feel like Casper the ghost," I whined to no one in particular. "I was in some of these pictures once," I grumbled to the walls, and they remained deathly silent.

Wanting to save the best for last, I reached for the scrapbook like it was a sure thing. A life preserver filled to the brim with pictures of me. I had seen myself growing up in that book more times than I cared to remember as my mother was quick to show it off every chance she got. She had it strategically placed for viewing on the living room coffee table, before Kilborne came along last week and ruined everything. Now the coffee table was missing, and the scrapbook was old and dusty.

I opened the picture book and slowly turned to the first page and began my chronological journey through time. I saw photo after photo of the twins just as I had remembered, but there was no me. I saw Mom and Dad time and again. Nana was there too, along with a host of other relatives, but no me.

I wanted to pull my hair out. "This is bullshit!" I screamed and the empty walls echoed my scream right back at me. I glared suspiciously at all four of them before turning the next page.

I saw family vacations and reunions. The trips to Washington DC and Florida were just as I fondly recalled, except that I was not in a single shot. My slate had been wiped clean like I'd never been born. "I don't know what's going on here," I whispered so the walls wouldn't hear, "but I can't take much more of this. I really can't."

I turned page after page and was thrust into the future where I saw Emily grow boobs on her way to rocketing through high school. She got married soon thereafter to the same guy in her prom pictures, while David went off to college. I turned more pages and saw that Emily had two girls with blonde curls and that the older she got, the more she looked like Mom, while the older Mom got, the more she looked like Nana, who I saw had long since passed away. Besides hurting my heart, it sent chills down my spine to know that Nana was dead and that the shriveled old lady in my parent's bedroom was what remained of my mother. But was I her son? The family pictures offered no evidence of that. None!

Sadly, I turned another page and was shocked to learn that Dad had passed away. If I was to believe the faded obituary clip that was stapled in place, he succumbed to cancer in 1999. Still, tears flowed when I saw the image of his casket. All the roses in the world couldn't make that picture bright and cheerful, but the flowers tried just the same.

The seasons passed like the wind with every turn of the page. By the time I made it to the end of the scrapbook, Emily had put on a few pounds, although she still looked like Mom. Meanwhile, David had moved to California. He had a wife named, Sophie, and twin teenage boys named Cody and Glen. And as for me, I was left to question my very existence.

I returned to the master bedroom and found Mom sound asleep. I straightened her covers. Kissed her on the bony cheek. Then checked my look in the mirror once again to make sure I was real. I then shut the light and headed downstairs to search the rest of the seemingly haunted house.

I went through the kitchen like I was walking on eggshells after finding it completely renovated. I liked the changes, but it didn't feel like home. From there I headed downstairs into the basement and was crushed to find it a blank canvas. There was no evidence of the many Christmas mornings and family gatherings that were held there. The shelves were void of Emily and David's toys, and Dad's collection of beer mugs was missing from the bar. It was all I could do to venture into the normally cluttered washroom. I flipped on the light and found the room empty as well. Even my old train set was gone.

It was one thing to not play with toy trains anymore; quite another to see them derailed like the rest of my life. Another pity party erupted, and I became overcome with despair to the point I could hardly breath. I dropped to my knees and gasped for air.

Eventually, I was able to catch my breath to where I could scream at the top of my lungs: "Help! Help me, God! You're all I've got left!" I closed my eyes and prayed for the longest time and when I opened them again, nothing had changed. Where was God in my time of need? Where?

Things were so bad… I wanted to kill myself just to finally put an end to the misery. But instead I climbed back to the ground floor and explored the rest of the empty house. I debated running across the street to check on Rudy, Mitch and Billy, but I was afraid of what I might find if I started looking for friends at such a late hour. So instead I shuffled into the living room and plopped down on a faded leather couch, the likes of which I'd never seen before, and resumed watching the amazing flat screen on the wall.

It proved to be a great distraction, as late-night TV was never better once I figured out how to use the remote. I surfed through more channels than I thought possible, and still there were more. It was information overload, although I soon learned enough to know that I was as much a stranger in this new world, as the old one I'd just left behind.

Morning came and I was feeling groggy with a miserable hangover from all the drinking I'd done the day before in historic Allen's Town. I still had the remote in my hand and was flipping through endless channels when Mom came creaking down the stairs in a pink bathrobe. Her old bones rattled, and her thin white hair bounced with every step she took.

"Good morning, Glen," she said. "Did ya sleep well?"

"Not really," I groaned. "I couldn't take my eyes off this TV."

"Watching that darn thing is all I do these days," she said. "How about some breakfast?"

"No thanks." I rubbed my belly. "I can't seem to eat anymore."

Mom looked concerned and came over to the couch, and briefly put her hand on my forehead. "Are you coming down with something?"

"No," I replied. "I'm just tired, I guess."

"I can always call your Aunt Emily and have her bring you something for your stomach on her way over."

"Emily's coming over?" I questioned, wondering how I would explain myself to my once-upon-a-time little sister.

"She'll be here sometime this morning," Mom replied. "I know she's itching to finish packing me up for the big move I'm dreading today. Speaking of which, where's your father and brother hiding out?"

"I'm not who you think I am," I responded. "My name's Johnny."

Mom was taken aback. "Johnny? I don't know any Johnny. What the hell are you doing in my house?"

"This was my home too until just a few days ago," I snapped. "I've lived here since I was a little kid!"

She shook her head. "No. You can't fool me. I've lived in this house for over fifty years." I was thinking Mom was about to throw me out, but she took a seat near me and began to cry. "I can't believe this is my last day here," she sobbed. "I'll be lost without this place."

I gave her a hug and began to weep. "Me too!"

We cried on each other's shoulders, until startled by the squeak of the front door. I looked across the room and cowered when I saw Emily come inside. It was one thing to see the pictures, quite another to see her in the flesh. Our eyes met and she stopped dead in her tracks.

"Who the hell are you?" she demanded. Speechless, I turned to Mom for help, but I could tell by the look on her face that she was still wondering much the same thing. "Well," Emily continued with a raised voice, "who are you, and what are you doing in my mother's house?"

"Thanks to you," Mom yelled at Emily before I could babble a reply, "this house is no longer mine! So who the hell cares if the boy wants to visit here for a while?" She ran a cold hand along my quivering cheek. "I won't be seeing many young faces where I'm going."

Emily grimaced and grunted like a mother frustrated with an unruly child. "Mom... please... there's a stranger in the house. We'll talk about this later."

Seemingly forever grasping at straws, I moved to the edge of the couch to better my sister's view. "Don't I look even a little familiar to you... like maybe a long lost brother or something?"

Emily glared at me suspiciously. "Yeah, you look a little like my nephews at first glance, but they're both out in California. So, tell me what you're doing here!"

"That's not true," Mom chimed in. "David and the boys flew in last night."

Emily put her hands on her hefty hips, before cocking her blonde head to one side. "David's not coming, Mom." She frowned. "I talked to him on the phone last night. He said something came up and he won't be coming to town to help with the move."

Mom snarled at Emily before pointing my way. "You think I'm too old and crazy to know my own grandson when I see him?"

"Mom, please… Cody and Glen were never coming on this trip."

"Say what you like, Emily… but I'm not as crazy as you think."

The back and forth bickering only added fuel to the hopelessness of my situation. I felt like an outsider caught in the middle of a family feud. In some ways, it reminded me of the feuds between Martha and Willie. And then it occurred to me that I didn't belong here in this house any more than I did back on that old farm in Pennsylvania. Feeling nauseous to the point of wanting to puke my guts out, I got off the couch and stood on shaky legs. "Look… I don't want you guys fighting over me. I'll just leave and let you get on with your lives."

"Not so fast, buddy!" Emily growled like a grizzly bear, and it reminded me of Dad. "Empty your pockets. I want to make sure you didn't take anything that doesn't belong to you."

"No problem." I confidently reached into pockets that I thought were empty and pulled out a shiny 1776 Continental Dollar. "Oh, I forgot I had this thing," I said. "Don't worry… I didn't steal it."

"Oh really?" My skeptical sister questioned. "Then tell me where you got it, or I'll call the cops!"

I knew the truth would only complicate matters. "Well, I didn't get it here, if that's what you're thinking."

"I know it's not mine," said Mom. "Is it worth anything?"

I shrugged, mindlessly. "I don't know. But you can have the darn thing if it'll help keep the peace around here." Mom smiled at the gesture, which warmed my aching heart, and cooled Emily's angry jets. I handed her the coin and it was like passing a baton from one lost soul to another. "Believe it or not, you were a great mother to me once." As expected, Mom looked dumbfounded. "And I really do love you in spite of all the terrible changes that have happened since I've been gone," I said, before heading for the exit where Emily stood guard. "And believe it or not… I love you too!" I cried to my wide-eyed sister on the way out the door. And truth be told, it didn't hurt all that much to walk out on two people that were like strangers to me, but it killed me to think that I would never be able to call this place home again.

# Chapter Twenty
## *Stranger in Town*

Besides being homeless and now penniless on this gloomy morning, I also didn't have any friends. I saw two unfamiliar teens come out of Rudy's old house, which was yellow instead of green. I hadn't noticed this in the dark last night, but half the homes on the block were painted a different color and the trees had become twice as big.

Other unfamiliar kids filtered out of homes once occupied by Mitch and Billy, and so it went—nothing but new faces up and down the block. Some of the newbies had backpacks, but everyone had a cell phone in hand. Most looked like zombies with the way they stared into those little devices, hardly giving the world around them a passing glance. It was my guess that these kids of the future were heading off to school.

But rather than join them, I headed for the woods in search of the Tall Grass. I wanted to return to the past. My past! I searched and searched, trying to retrace my footsteps from the night before, but unfortunately, there was no Tall Grass that I could see. So, I climbed a tree. And still I found no place from which to flee. Again, I had to ask myself, was Kilborne back in play, or was I here to stay?

For lack of a better option, I retreated back to the street and followed a few teenage stragglers on their way to school. I kept to myself. After all, I was a stranger in town. It didn't help that everyone was in comfortable looking jeans and shorts, while save for my bedraggled hair and gray stubble… I looked like I was going to church in my Sunday best, although I felt like a guy stuck in the deepest recesses of hell.

My ears seemed to be ringing. I thought I heard a bell. *Or was it a ding going off in my troubled head?* Anyway, it afforded me the opportunity to glance at the palm of my hand. I was of course checking my imaginary cell phone for messages. But as far as I could tell, I was the only person left on the planet that didn't have one… a phone or a message. I'd never felt so alone in my life!

I was shocked by all the changes I saw on the way to school. The big change on Main Street was that the quaint little church on the corner had become a concrete monster with a large cross to show who was boss. It was very impressive, although cold. Especially considering none of my prayers had been answered of late, if ever at all. *Where are you God? Where are you during my time of need? Why don't you spend a little less time making fancy churches and throw me a little bone before it's too late?*

Hallelujah, I saw that the cars were just like advertised on TV, way cool compared to the ones of my day. It was at least comforting to see that some of the Mom and Pop stores were still standing in the middle of town, although the buildings had been renovated and contained new businesses in keeping with the sweeping changes that continued to boggle my mind.

I was relieved to see that Jefferson High still looked much the same from afar, other than a new wing had been added. I felt jittery as I closed in on the main entrance, like it was my first day at a new school. I braced myself as I entered the building, wanting to be ready for all the startling changes that were sure to come my way. I walked amongst a sea of unfamiliar faces in the bright hallway, getting plenty of strange looks as I shuffled along through the crowd. Except for a new coat of red paint, the lockers were the same. The walls too. The posters had changed plenty with the times and of course there seemed to be a computer in every classroom. But other than the endless electronics that had taken over, it still looked, sounded and smelled like school to me. Dreaded school!

Out of habit, I headed for my locker. It was what I knew to do before class. I worked my way through a horde of strangers and stood in front of the locker, staring at the combination lock, wondering if my 24 to the left, 5 to the right, and 18 to the left would still work. Besides being anxious and curious, I was desperately hoping to find some semblance of my past hidden inside. I was ready to reach for the dial when I felt a tap on my shoulder. I quickly turned around and much to my surprise and delight, there stood a girl with a curious look on her pretty face.

She giggled, playfully. "I hope there's a good reason why you're standing in front of my locker?"

I couldn't help but notice that her hair was long and silky brown and that her skin was fair, and her nose upturned. The more I canvased her every feature, the more she reminded me of a modern-day Martha. And much to my amazement, she even sounded like Martha. My heart did a little pitter-patter, although thankfully, I didn't embarrass myself by getting hard down below, but rather I was feeling numb from head to toe.

She waved to get my attention, while I was busy taking in more of her beauty. "You look like you've never seen a girl before."

I snapped out of it and returned to the moment. "Sorry… it's just that you reminded me of someone."

The girl rolled her emerald greens. "Likely story. Is she cute?"

I nodded, affirmatively. "Yeah… she's the most beautiful girl I've ever seen."

She blushed, cherry red. "Wow… I wasn't expecting that!"

I shrugged, mindlessly. "You asked."

She smiled, slyly. "So, lover boy… what are ya doing in front of my locker?"

I cocked my head toward the metal door. "This used to be mine."

"Oh really?" she razzed. "What… are ya coming back for a visit?"

I laughed in order to keep from crying. "Yeah… I'm taking a trip down memory lane."

She took a step closer and I could smell her flowery perfume. "I haven't seen you around before, what's your name?"

"I'm Johnny." I held out my clammy hand, which she eagerly shook. "What's yours?" I asked, wanting to be polite.

"Monica," she replied. "Are you a sophomore?"

Again, I shrugged, but this time haplessly. "I'm supposed to be."

"Supposed to be?" she questioned with a raised eyebrow.

I waved her off. "It's a long story."

"Oh?" she twinkled. "Try me!"

Again, I waved her off. "Maybe some other time."

Monica squinted like she was putting me under a microscope. "You seem different, Johnny. Different from the other guys around here." She began to laugh. "And what's with the clothes?"

Before I could muster a reply, the bell rang, and locker doors furiously opened and shut as everyone began to scamper to their classes. Monica brushed up against me. "Excuse me, Johnny… I've got to get a book out of my locker before the late bell rings."

I stepped aside and let Monica do her thing. She spun the dial this way and that and opened the door. I saw nothing familiar when I peeked inside the opening. Monica quickly got her book out, then shut the door and backed up against the wall of lockers. "I've got to go now, Johnny," she purred. "Maybe we can get together after school sometime?"

I nodded, positively. "Sure thing, Monica. That'd be nice."

"What's your number?" she asked, bright-eyed.

"Ah, sorry… I don't have a phone."

As expected, she looked surprised. "Huh, I don't know whether to believe you or not."

Yet again I shrugged. "You can check my pockets, if you like?"

"Hmmm… you sure are a strange one, Johnny," she said, as the late bell sounded. "Lucky for you I like strange guys." She gave me a wet peck on the cheek. "See ya around, lover boy." She then scurried down the near empty hallway and waved back at me, before disappearing into a classroom.

The hallway cleared and I was alone again. Out of curiosity, I headed to my homeroom class and peeked in through the small window in the closed door. I saw a room full of strange faces and it appeared that a middle-aged male teacher had replaced sexy Miss Willows. It was not a pretty sight. I was able to see a calendar on the near wall. Friday, May 22, 2009 was the latest box circled, but not yet crossed off. I did the math and concluded I should be fifty-six years old. *Fifty-six?* Save for the gray stubble, I certainly didn't look my age, although I sure felt like it inside.

But the kid in me was craving a Coke and Twinkie, and so I went to the empty cafeteria. I knew the large room would be crowded in a few hours, but for the time being, I had the place to myself. I noticed a sleek looking soda machine. I got a plastic cup and hit the button and Coke came gushing out. It tasted great! Then came the Twinkie off the snack tray. I took a bite and began chewing. "Yuck!" It didn't taste anything like the Twinkies I knew and loved. I spit it out, then took a seat and began to sulk; wishing my Coke would miraculously turn into moonshine, so I could drown my sorrows away.

As if I didn't have enough on my plate, a gray-haired lady waddled my way from the kitchen. "Shouldn't you be in class?" she asked with a raspy voice that reminded me of Ma.

I frowned. "I wish I had a class to go to."

She smirked. "Are you trying to be funny?"

"No," I responded, contritely.

She pointed to my Coke and half-eaten Twinkie. "Did you pay for those things?"

"Ah, no… I'm sorry, but I don't have any money."

A concerned look appeared on her wrinkled face. "Seriously now… who do you have for homeroom?"

I began to squirm. "I don't go to school here anymore."

"If you can't give me a better answer than that, then I'm afraid I'm going to have to bring you down to the office."

I wanted to snap at the nosy cafeteria lady for bothering me, but I doubted she knew one teacher from another, so I decided to give her what she wanted. "I have Miss Willows for homeroom," I revealed, hoping that was enough to send her waddling back to the kitchen.

"Miss Willows?" she hee-hawed. "Try again."

I suddenly perked. "You act like you know her."

The cafeteria lady nodded like they were old friends. "Yeah… I know her… but apparently you don't. What's your name, son?"

I jumped to my feet. "Johnny Bishop," I replied, excitedly. "Can you take me to see her?"

"You're looking at her!"

Taken aback, I scoured the hefty cafeteria lady for some hint of the sexy beast I knew and loved—but saw nothing. No pretty face. No curvy body. No perky personality. No miniskirt. No Black boots. No neon green panties. Deflated. At my wits' end, I sighed, forlornly. "If you really are Miss Willows, then you'd know that I was in your class when you were young and beautiful."

Her mouth agape, she grabbed the edge of the table for support while eyeing me warily. "I don't know where you're going with this, young man… but it's gone far enough! Now what are you doing here in the cafeteria when you're supposed to be in class?"

"I'm here cause I don't know where else to go!" I admitted, solemnly. "Everything has passed me by. Even you have passed me by! Heck, it's like I was never born, and I can't take it anymore!"

Her wary look morphed into one of motherly concern. "Are you all right," she quizzed. "Do you need me to contact your parents?"

I fought back the bitter tears. "I don't have parents."

"Oh… is there someone else I can call?"

I lost the battle when a lone drop began to trickle down my cheek. "I'm alone in this world," I pined. "All alone."

She folded her hefty arms across her ample chest like she was chilled to the bone. "Well, Johnny… as principal of this school, I just can't let you stay here in the cafeteria unattended. I'm going to have to take you down to the office so we can figure out what to do with you."

I waved her off. "That's all right. I appreciate your concern, but I'm too far gone to be saved at this point." I then headed for the exit.

"Johnny, wait!" she said, while slowly waddling after me. "Please wait. Let me help you!" I ignored her sympathetic pleas and headed down the empty corridor for the glass doors at the front of the building. "Johnny, wait! Please wait." She gasped for air, as her slow waddle became an even slower walk and my walk a run. "Johnny!"

If nothing else, the fresh air was invigorating when I exited the building. I saw a long concrete sidewalk ahead of me as I stood facing out on a world I knew little about, save for what I had learned from the TV last night. There was a parking lot full of fancy cars I'd like to escape within to my left and another to my right. In front of me, at the very end of the long concrete sidewalk, sat a school bus parked in the street. There were houses beyond that where an open field used to exist. I looked every which way. There was really no place to go that I could see. Not even for a visit. I turned and peered through the glass doors and was relieved to see that I was no longer being followed by what had become of Miss Willows.

Still, I ran the length of sidewalk like I was still being chased and didn't stop until I was at the curb. I took a moment to catch my breath and in so doing I caught a whiff of honeysuckle. Using my nose, I followed the source over to the parked school bus. I then noticed that there were black metal screens on the windows of the big, yellow machine. I immediately thought Kilborne, although that didn't keep me from being startled when the sliding door opened, and I saw Chester sitting behind the wheel.

"What's going on here?" I snapped. "Why are you doing this to me? Why?"

"Don't blame me, kid… I'm just doing my job."

"I can't take anymore!" I insisted. "I'm going crazy!"

"If ya got a problem, then ya need ta talk to the boss."

"Where is he?" I huffed. "I wanna give him a piece of my mind!"

Chester chuckled, mightily. "He's waiting for ya inside."

I swallowed hard. "Okay… I'm coming up." I made my way up the steps and was shocked to see Mr. Fitzhugh sitting in the middle of the empty bus. "You're the boss?" I inquired of the schoolteacher, who was no longer of the flesh, but rather ghostly in appearance.

"Welcome aboard, Johnny Boy." He smiled like a sly dog. "And thanks ever so much for the knowledge you bestowed upon me during your visit to my classroom. That enlightening afternoon we spent together back in 1777 was not only enough to forever change the course of history, but the future as well!"

"Say what?" I thought of Willie while scratching my head, because I didn't make the connection until I realized my mistake. "I should've never told you about Kilborne."

"The little you knew about that haunted paradise was all I needed to get started on my conquest of earth," he snickered. "Because truth be told… the only one who really matters on this godforsaken planet is ME… and everyone else is here for my own personal amusement until I tire of them and move on to something more entertaining."

# Chapter Twenty-One
## *Chicken Express*

The bus door shut, and Chester hit the gas, propelling me back toward Mr. Fitzhugh. The closer I got, the more ghostly he appeared. His blues eyes weren't faded like the Three Little Bitches, but otherwise his skin was pale and opaque and even radiated like he could glow in the dark. He waved a dollar bill as I approached. "I believe this is yours, Johnny Boy."

Taking the seat across from him was made easy, as the bus sent me in that direction while careening from side to side. I then reached across the aisle and plucked my dangling bill from the bony fingers of his milky hand, before putting it in my pocket. "I liked you better when you were alive."

"I don't see why you're upset with me," he chortled. "I not only hand-delivered your precious dollar bill back to you in mint condition, I even arranged for your safe passage home."

"Home?" I bristled. "This isn't home!"

"But this is what home will look like forty years from now, if you fail to graduate from my reform school."

Watching him guffaw at my expense made the short hairs on the back of my neck stand on edge. And even though I was taught to respect my elders, I was mad enough to where I wanted to throw a punch at that ancient coot, although I decided it would be wiser on my part to start by kissing his ghostly ass, and so I did. "Please, Mr. Fitzhugh… I can't take any more of this. Please let me go back to my old life. Please!"

"But this is only the fifth day of your sentence, Mr. Bishop. You still have ninety-five days of misery left to go."

I felt a stabbing pain everywhere, but especially in my head where my brain was drowning in a sea of despair. "I'll never make it to the end."

"Then you'll spend all eternity in darkness," he warned, "roaming the boy's side of my black hallway, forevermore."

"I'd rather kill myself first!"

"I'm sure Judge Reinhold and Sergeant Stevens covered the terms of engagement during that first day of your sentence, so need I remind you that suicide is not a way out of my establishment? You'll still end up in my black hallway once your eight remaining lives have been sufficiently snuffed out by your own doing."

"This really sucks!" I shook my wary head in disgust. "I still can't believe this is happening to me! That a place like this really exists! That this isn't some weird nightmare I'm bound to wake from soon!"

Mr. Fitzhugh appeared unmoved by my outburst. "You have no one but yourself to blame for your troubles, Mr. Bishop."

"That's bullshit!" I snapped. "You're the one doing this to me!" I wanted to point my finger in his smug mug; or even throw that punch I was thinking about, but I found that I couldn't move. Other than my wary head, the rest of my body was frozen in place. Frustrated beyond words, I struggled mightily to regain control of my limbs while sitting like a good boy in my seat, hoping Chester didn't make a sudden stop, because if he did, I was liable to go face-first into the back of the seat in front of me. "What did I do to deserve this?" I wailed Fitzhugh's way. "What?"

"This would've never happened had you not elected to enter my schoolhouse back in 1777, where you then proceeded to flash your impressive 1969 dollar bill in my startled face, before filling my ever-curious mind with your amazing stories of the future."

I struggled in vein to move. "I trusted you with the truth and you used it against me!" I snarled. "What… was Willie in on this too?"

He took in a very deep breath like he was getting ready to tell a long-winded story, although he did not bother to exhale. "Little did I know at the time, but my life was forever changed when you agreed to let me hold onto that dollar bill of yours." He paused in a reflective moment. "In the days, months and two years that followed after you and Willie left me on that fateful day, I saw my wife pass away from illness and my only son die defending this great country of ours. And in all that time, your money never stopped haunting me. Day and night, it demanded that I seek out the future—never letting me rest in peace for even one second. You don't know how many times I cursed you for not returning for your precious dollar bill." He finally exhaled and it was frosty enough to send a chill racing down my spine. "Finally, with nothing left to live for, I packed-up and sought the future. I headed for New Jersey because I knew that's where you were from. But when I didn't find the future there, I headed north. Through the hills and valleys my seventy-year-old bones went. Tired and weak, I pitched my tent by the side of a small mountain. When darkness fell, I saw a mysterious green glow coming from the top of the mountain. I was near death when I reached the peak, but then I saw the Green Fog." He smiled, dreamily. "And with my last breath hanging in the balance, the Fog came to my rescue and has since given me eternal life!" He glanced to the heavens. "You see... I was then spirited by God to build the Kilborne Academy exactly as you had described it to me. With the powerful Green Fog doing the heavy lifting, the Big House was miraculously constructed within seconds during that first magical night. And then with the help of the Fog, I got the calling and began doing the Lord's work while patiently waiting for you to be born in 1953. Then like an angel, I stood watch over you from toddler on up to insure that you would come ripe of age in 1969, so that I could bring you to Kilborne and send you back in time to finish what you started in 1777. Thus, you've now come full circle to where only your future remains in doubt."

"My future has always been in doubt," I said, curtly. "But I hope you don't blame me for coming into your life, when it was you who brought me there in the first place!"

"All I know is that I was getting ready to retire from a lifetime of teaching and rest peacefully under a sycamore tree until my dying day, but then you and Willie walked into my classroom and changed everything!"

I was ready to explode with grief when a whiff of honeysuckle ran through my lungs and immediately soothed my troubled soul. I looked out the windshield and saw that we were on a two-lane highway with rolling hills and scant houses and towns that dotted the lush greenery up ahead. "Where're we going?"

"We're heading back to the Kilborne Academy," he replied. "Perhaps you'd like to play a game to pass the time?"

"No thanks," I snubbed. "I'm not in the mood for fun and games right now."

"What came first," he crooned, "the chicken or the egg?"

"Look... I don't want to play. I just wanna go back to my old life and forget I ever met you!"

Fitz suddenly came on like a pompous gameshow host. "I can't promise that will be your fate, Mr. Bishop... but do play along and if you do happen to answer the question correctly... I'll cut your remaining sentence in half!"

I rolled my eyes after peering into his shifty blues. "Really?"

"Yes!" he was quick to reply. "And the beauty of it is, you already have a fifty percent chance of getting the answer right."

"It's not that I trust you, but I've got nothing to lose."

"So, what came first, Mr. Bishop... the chicken or the egg? And please do elaborate on your answer... so it at least appears to be something more than a guess."

"Okay... I'll say the egg came first, because I know for a fact that chickens come from eggs, not the other way around."

He feigned a pout, although I could tell he was smiling inside. "Nice try, lad... but I'm afraid this is not your lucky day."

"Oh really?" I countered with a smirk. "You've got proof the chicken came first?"

"Besides the fact it is written that God created the animals without any mention of eggs," he clucked, "the race to see who came first between the chicken and the egg was so closely contested, it 'twas a photo finish. But upon further inspection, it became crystal clear to all concerned that the egg had cracked under the enormous pressure, thus allowing the chicken to win by a feather."

My smirk became a frown. "You're just messing with me."

"It's what I do in the afterlife," he twinkled. "It started as a hobby to kill endless time, but I eventually turned it into a full-time occupation. So now there is not a day that goes by that I'm not adding to my resume by manipulating an influential mind somewhere on the planet to further my career. But more than anything, I'm proud to say that I've brought unbridled turmoil and chaos to an unsuspecting world for nearly two hundred years now, and my best work is yet to come!"

"And you say you're doing the Lord's work?" I scoffed at the notion. "Seems more like the devil to me."

"That's because I work in mysterious ways," he replied in highfalutin fashion. "And like God... I too have the power to make your dreams come true or turn them into nightmares. So, I suggest you think of me the next time you take to your knees. After all, I'm more likely to respond to your prayers, because God is always off adding new planets to his vast empire, having all but forgotten about the clueless people he coldly left behind eons ago to fend for themselves. And with my help, they've done nothing but turn His beautiful creation into hell on earth!"

Done with the arrogant ghost, I turned my head and again looked out the window. We were now on a gravel road that was surrounded by wooded hills and distant mountains. Civilization was non-existent. I mused during the bumpy ride, thinking about the chicken and the egg, while wondering if I too would crack under the enormous pressure, when not thinking I already had.

My stomach was in knots to where I felt the need to fart, except that I didn't have the muscle control to push, so I had to settle for a burp. For lack of a better option, I gazed mindlessly at the passing scenery, until I was brought back to dreadful reality when I saw the old sign for Fitzhugh Falls—Population Zero. We passed the closed gas station and the five gutted houses and disappeared through low hanging branches at the end of the short, dead-end street and began our climb to the top of the mountain. "So, what happened to Marty?" I inquired. Besides being curious, I was trying to take my mind off my own knotty situation. "Is he still alive?"

"Marty has also come full circle," Fitz replied. "As you may know, he impregnated Martha, who nine months later gave birth to a boy named, Nathan, in 1778. Well, Nathan grew big and strong and also took to the barn with Martha, and she gave birth to a son named, Jethrow, in 1796. And thanks to Martha, Jethrow fathered Chancy in 1812. And Chancy fathered Markus in 1829. And Markus fathered James in 1845. And James fathered Berton in 1864. And Berton, after running away to Oklahoma to escape Martha's endless advances; married a gal named, Sandy, and fathered Mickey in 1881. And Mickey fathered Ashton in 1900. And Ashton fathered Randy in 1917. And then Randy fathered Keith in 1937. And last, but certainly not least… Keith fathered Marty in 1953."

It took a moment for me to connect Martha's many dots, but then my jaw dropped. "Whoa… that makes Marty his own relative."

"You are correct, Mr. Bishop. He's the fruit of his own loins!" Fitz cackled. "A real one-of-a-kind!"

"That's weird, man. Does he know about this?"

"I'm sure Marty is finding out more about himself right now than he cares to know," Fitz crowed. "But that's just a small part of the education you get at my institution for advanced learning."

I couldn't fart, but I nearly shit when I saw the ominous Kilborne sign at the top of the mountain. The bus rumbled through the open gate and up the bumpy cobblestone drive, before coming to a screeching halt in front of the Big House. As I had feared, the sudden stop propelled me headfirst into the seat in front of me, before bouncing me back like a toy soldier. Dazed, my aching head was temporarily spinning out of control. I saw the ominous Big House during my many spins. Surprisingly, I still found the historic building to be whimsical and charming in spite of what I knew to be going on inside. It didn't hurt that there were colorful flowers everywhere and sunny skies overhead, although thick gray clouds continued to blanket the land below. Round and round I went, until the spinning lost steam and finally stopped. I looked out the windows across from me and saw that the gate was now closed, and I thought of my mother's white station wagon. "What's become of my parents?" I grilled. "Did they make it back home to my brother and sister?"

"Life goes on for them and the rest of the world, as if you didn't exist," he answered. "And as previously explained, if you manage to survive what remains of your sentence, you'll leave here with no recollection of this place and return home, as if you'd never left, until I come calling sometime in your future when the time is right."

I sighed, wistfully. "I'd give anything to be home now."

"Hang tight, Mr. Bishop... there's still much you need to learn and pain you need to suffer, if you're to be of future value to me."

"Oh really... haven't I suffered enough?"

"Let's just say that even when you've been reduced down to rubble, there still exists the opportunity to make a full recovery. So be alert and keep your eyes peeled for anything and everything that can help change your fate. And as always, listen carefully my friend, because you never know when opportunity may knock."

I didn't hear a knock, but that didn't keep me taking the opportunity to reach for the stars. "Any chance I can get off early for good behavior?"

He chuckled and giggled. "No, Mr. Bishop... your behavior hasn't been all that good. In fact, you've been acting like a tortured soul ever since we met."

"That's because you've put me through hell!"

"Speaking of hell," he snickered, "you'll be visiting there next."

Chester opened the sliding bus door with a whoosh. "Welcome ta paradise," he said in cheerful fashion. A rush of mountain fresh air soon reached me, along with a big hit of honeysuckle.

I had no choice but to remain in my seat as Mr. Fitzhugh rose from his, until Green Fog shackled my feet and I could finally move again. Although pleased to have regained some movement, I was locked into following the old schoolteacher off the bus. "I'd run if I could," I declared, while fighting for control of my legs.

"I know you would, Mr. Bishop... but since that's not going to happen today, we'll continue on into the entry hall and have a closer look at that wonderful portrait I painted of you in 1780. I named it *Johnny Paradise* in your honor."

"Why Johnny Paradise?"

"Besides sounding more interesting than, Johnny Bishop," he twittered, "thanks to you, I've found paradise here!" He spread his arms wide and rotated around until he had done a 360 of the Kilborne Academy. "None of this would've been possible, had you not come into my life."

I found something positive in all that negative and perked. "Then you owe me!"

"Yes, but payback's a bitch!"

As if on invisible tracks, I followed Fitzhugh in the front door of the Big House, which he then proceeded to close and lock. I came to a stop in front of my centuries-old portrait. Fitz joined me, and said, "'Twas nearly three years after I met you that the Green Fog gave me the power to paint like a pro, while allowing me to recall every last detail about your appearance from our brief, yet historic encounter. Heck... I even remembered the button you had missing from your shirt, and that ugly pimple you still have on your chin."

I saw that ugly pimple on dusty canvas and then felt it on my chin, and it was like the past and present coming together as one. "This is what happens when I get nervous. I'm surprised my entire face isn't covered with pimples this big."

"At least you still have a face," he said, before pointing to the opening of the black hallway. "Those lost souls in there would give anything to have a face again. Even one with pimples."

"Well they can't have mine," I insisted.

"That's the spirit, Mr. Bishop! It'll take everything you've got to survive your remaining sentence. You'll have no chance if you're of weak mind or body. None! Now I suggest you head to the dining hall and get something to eat before you go to hell."

"How can you expect me to eat at a time like this?"

He nodded like he understood. "Yes… I can surely see how you might lose your appetite under the circumstances, but you should at least get an apple for the road."

I waved Fitz off. "No thanks. The thought of food makes me sick right now." I was then hit with something beyond marvelous that came wafting in from the dining hall. I licked my lips and tasted the incredible flavors in the air and my belly began to growl like I hadn't eaten in days, which was right. "On second thought, I wouldn't mind nibbling on a few things while I still have the chance."

Fitz pointed toward the black hallway as my fog shackles faded away. "Be my guest. Just follow your nose like you did the last time you were here, and I'll meet up with you in the dining hall after I take care of some business upstairs in my office."

"Okay," I responded, like food was the only thing that mattered in my life. I heard Fitz creaking up the stairs, as I ducked around the drool from the buffalo head above the opening that led to the black hallway. I entered and immediately noticed hissing coming from the glowing Green Fog at my feet. The boys began to bark loudly from the east: *Come play with us, Johnny… and be a man!* And the girls cooed wantonly from the west: *No come this way, lover boy… and we'll make crazy love all night long!*

I was suddenly conflicted. The girl's side had beds to rest my troubled soul, plus I could fill my weary head with their caressing coos. *It was mental masturbation at its finest!* But the boy's side had the freakishly incredible food. I began teetering this way and that, even leaning toward the girls, when I took a deep breath and tasted air that was to die for. Decision made, I headed east toward the feast! The trek down the hallway was met with a barrage of barking and wave upon wave of flavor. I covered my ears and followed my nose.

As before, the journey to the dining hall appeared longer than it really was.

The large room was eerily empty, although the buffet was on full display. I knew I was playing with fire when I stuck my finger in a bucket of chocolate pudding and licked it off. Burp! I then took a small bite from a juicy grape. I chewed and chewed, before spitting out the flesh. Fart! It nearly killed me to nibble on a brownie. I had to stop and catch my breath before sucking juice from an orange. It hurt to swallow, although that didn't keep me from licking a sizzling steak. I burped and farted; then almost seized up after popping a strawberry in my mouth. I knew I was on a suicide mission, but I couldn't walk away from the flavor that nature had brought to the table, not to mention the incredible edibles prepared by invisible chefs in a non-existent kitchen. Mindful of my macabre meal, I was ready to throw caution to the wind and lick my way from one end of the buffet to the other, when I began choking on a whiff of fried chicken. I tried frantically to catch my breath, but it was a losing battle, as I felt myself slipping away to a place that I'd once been before.

I wallowed in eternal darkness with endless time to think about anything and everything, until thinking became a chore I could do no more. As best I could figure… years, decades, maybe even centuries had passed by the time I heard a shrill sound that not only broke the interminable silence, it brought light back into my world. Blinding at first, I eventually saw Fitz sitting across from me at the table and it was like only seconds had passed since my last meal.

"Welcome back," he said, while putting a silver whistle in his vest pocket. "You now have seven lives remaining."

"Why can't I eat anymore?" I whined. "I hardly ate anything the last time I was alive, and then I was dead before I knew it."

"Besides offering a sweet and savory death, just one serving of the killer buffet is so rich in essential vitamins and minerals that it will sustain a recruit through all of their remaining lives at the academy," he divulged. "So, anything you eat beyond that first meal is just overkill for the balance of your sentence. But of course, that's not to suggest you won't have food cravings that your digestive system simply can't handle in its current state."

I shrugged, haplessly. "Well, at least I won't starve to death here."

"Yes… hunger is not one of your worries here at Kilborne."

I groaned after thinking about my remaining sentence. "But there's still a million other ways to die around here."

Fitz seemed frustrated with me. "Look… I have the Wisdom of the Ages, Mr. Bishop. I've traveled the Tall Grass all the way to the beginning of time… and then the forty years it took to go the other way… until the end of days. I've personally witnessed every major event that's ever occurred on this planet at least once so far, marveling at mighty dinosaurs as they roamed the plains, or being humbled by the sight of Jesus hanging from a cross. I've spent time in every decade there ever was and every decade yet to come." He smiled, knowingly. "So, believe me when I tell you that I've seen it all because I have. And I know that with a little coaching… perhaps even a poor student like you can rise up from sixteen years of failure and do incredible things with your life."

"Incredible things?" I queried. "Incredible things like what?"

"Perhaps you can become a millionaire if you manage to survive this place, or maybe you might even save the world someday!"

"Save the world?" I scoffed. "I can't even save myself."

"You never know… you might surprise yourself one day," he chortled. "But of course, only time will tell on that, Kitty Cat."

And then it was I who became frustrated with Fitz to where I slammed my fist down on the table. "Look… this life and death stuff is all just fun and games to you… isn't it?"

"Speaking of fun and games, it's time for hell!" He grinned in a devilish way. "Would you like an apple for the road?"

"No thanks," I replied. "There's no point in lugging food around when I won't be needing to eat."

"Have it your way, Mr. Bishop. Have it your way. But when opportunity does happen to knock, don't be too preoccupied with your troubles to answer the door."

Before I could second-guess myself, Fitz rose to his feet, as Green Fog gathered around mine. Fog shackles were controlling me again and I had no choice but to follow him into the black hallway, where the boys began to bark: *Be a man, Johnny… and show 'em what you got!* And the girls cooed from the other end: *Don't go to hell unarmed, lover boy… you'll never come back alive!*

"Hey, I'll take that apple now."

"I'm afraid it's a little too late for that, Mr. Bishop."

# Chapter Twenty-Two
## *Cold Night in Hell*

Fitz opened the backdoor and the Green Fog was sucked out the dark opening, causing a myriad of clamoring voices to go silent in the night. Save for the green glow from my fog shackles, the hallway was suddenly blacker than black, but then the wall sconces came on in a flash and the hallway became an endless mineshaft without beginning nor end.

"Just remember," he warned, "die seven more times and you'll spend all eternity here in my black hallway, where you'll remain alive in mind and spirit, but never again in the flesh. Forever trapped with all the lost souls who have failed before you."

I gulped but said nothing. Instead I glanced over my shoulder into the entry hall, wondering what was to become of that pimple-faced guy hanging on the wall. I didn't want to follow Fitz outside, but the fog shackles took charge and I scuttled along like I was the teacher's pet. We stood shoulder to shoulder on the balcony, looking out on a vast valley lit by the feathery black heads of the Tall Grass. The orange moon was full. It hung low on the horizon with the stars twinkling above. The view was spectacular and since I was in no hurry to go to hell, I made small talk to buy time. "Whatever happened to Sergeant Stevens?" I asked like I cared.

Fitz pointed to a small fenced-in area by the far side of the Big House. Inside the white pickets were three moss-covered mounds adorned with crooked headstones. "He's resting in peace until next season."

"And I guess the other two graves are for Chester and that creepy old judge?"

"That's correct, Mr. Bishop. The Three Little Bitches were my first recruits. They hated Kilborne so much… they burned the place to the ground. And they've been paying for it ever since."

"Yeah, I remember everything being burned and dreary around here, until the Green Fog came along."

"The Green Fog restores the property to pristine condition for the hundred days Kilborne is in operation every year," he informed. "Although, the Tall Grass is always open for business. It's where I spend endless days discovering the secrets of the universe, when I'm not scouting the planet for young recruits worthy of spending a summer at my academy, where they'll get nine chances to graduate."

"Seems like most end up dead in the hallway."

He pouted. "Sad but true… only those extremely lucky and the cream-of-the-crop make it through the course." His pout then switched to a grin. "But either way… those who graduate from my academy can leave their mark on the world as you will soon see!"

I wanted to keep the conversation going, but my fog shackles started moving my feet toward the steep set of stairs that led down to the boat dock. Meanwhile, Green Fog came out from the end of the dock and again cut a brilliant neon path through the middle of the vast city of twinkling lights, before branching out to the ends of the earth. "Wait," I yelped. "I'm not ready to go yet!"

"Paradise awaits you, Mr. Bishop! Good luck and may God find the time to be with you because I won't. You're on your own from this point forward."

I wanted to scratch like Willie. "What's that supposed to mean?"

"By coming full circle you've secured Kilborne's place in history, forevermore! Which while I appreciate the kind gesture, it does however mean I no longer require your services to ensure my future," he twittered. "But I do wish you all the best in your quest to survive the rest of your sentence." And with that said, Fitz went back into the Big House and shut the door.

I screamed as my fog shackles had me taking the plunge down the steep stairs. A mere five rungs later I was standing firmly on the dock, heading for the glowing green path in the Tall Grass. I immediately heard hissing and smelled honeysuckle once inside the narrow opening. Forced to run, my shoulders rubbed repeatedly against the Tall Grass and began to itch and burn. I even ran while out of breath. Gasping for air, the shackles took me past the straightaway and through many forks in the road, until the hissing stopped, and the sweetness of the honeysuckle had been replaced by what smelled like sewer gas.

Save for my shackles, the Green Fog had faded away from the ground and the Tall Grass had thinned to where the feathery black heads were mostly gone from what remained of the weeds. They offered little light. Just a twinkle here and a twinkle there. Otherwise, I had only the green glow surrounding my shackles and that full moon above to light my way through fields of gray desolation. The firm ground became soft. The shackles had me sloshing along in dark muck. Every step sent more sewer gas into the foul air. I was ankle deep when I stumbled upon concrete. It felt good to be on solid ground again, although my next step hit nothing but air, and I was propelled downward into even more darkness.

Shocked that I was in a free fall, I began tumbling head over heel in what seemed to be a bottomless pit. My fog shackles were eventually blown away from my ever-gathering speed. I caught glimpses of their green glow in the blackness behind me, while I spun out of control. Panic stricken, expecting to hit bottom at any moment, my heart was racing to where I was afraid it might explode. I held my breath in anticipation of the deathblow that was sure to come. I shut my eyes. Clenched my teeth. I knew I was a goner. Even if I hit water.

More time passed. I began to think I really was in a bottomless pit. I became lightheaded from holding my breath—falling ever faster, until I was finally stopped cold by a rock-hard surface. There was but a moment of tremendous pain as I literally exploded on the scene. But then the pain escaped me, as did everything else. In spirit only, I saw that a ring of blood was all that remained of me at ground zero, while a thousand bloody body parts had shot out in all directions across a dark concrete floor. I wasn't sad. Along with the rest of my scattered remains, I had become detached to where I was a casual observer of my own demise. My spirit lit the way as I examined the gory pieces of my puzzle, wondering if I could ever be put back together again. I didn't get to think on that subject long, as my light soon faded, and I saw nothing for the longest time.

I didn't have to be told… I knew I was dead. Been there, done that for the third time now. Like before, I floated in eternal darkness for what seemed like forever and a day. If there was a heaven or anything else for that matter, I was yet to see it in my travels. But there did come a time when I spotted a green glow. It was a dot in the distance. It continued to grow as it got closer, until I could see that it was my fog shackles. They were coming to save me! I was eager to return amongst the living because no matter how peaceful it was being dead, I wanted to get back in the game of life and feel something again, even if it was pain.

The shackles overtook me. The first thing I smelled was the sweetness of honeysuckle. It was refreshing. The first sound I heard was hissing. It shook me to my core, although it was invigorating. And the first thing I felt was cold. Freezing cold that chilled me to the bone. It was then that I realized my body was miraculously whole again, except without a stitch of clothing to help keep me warm. The Green Fog then faded away and the smell of sewer gas returned, as I danced in place on a slimy, cold surface that was hard on my feet. I remained in complete darkness, until a light flickered on and I realized I was not alone.

Not more than thirty feet away was a man hunched over the surface of a massive oak table. He was snoring face down. His greasy salt and pepper hair shined from a light bulb that hung well above his head. That bulb, which dangled from a frayed wire attached to the tall ceiling, illuminated the man and his rectangular table in a circle of radiating light. Otherwise, there was black on all sides, including where I shivered in the dark of night.

Although the sleeping man seemed harmless enough from a distance, I elected not to disturb him. Instead, I felt my way around the dark perimeter, feeling for a way out of the cold, as my frozen hand slid along the slimy surface that walled me in. I combed every inch of what felt like a large, square, refrigerated concrete box, but found no exit. I was soon back to my starting point, which was one of the four corners of the room.

Still searching for a way out of the interminable cold, I was ready to go into the light in the center of the room, when the man startled me by clearing his throat. He coughed and a plume of Green Fog escaped his mouth. He smacked his lips a few times like he was preparing to talk from his prone position. "Welcome to hell," he rumbled, and his words echoed all around me. His voice was deep and guttural to where he sounded like a walrus barking in broken English. "Fitzhugh only sends me the recruits he's grooming for greatness or the ones he's trying to get rid of. Which are you?"

"I don't know… but it's sure cold in here."

The man slowly lifted his head off the waist-high table and looked in my general direction as he peered into the darkness. I focused on his tired and wrinkled mug and gasped wide-eyed. From afar, he looked like the spitting image of Adolph Hitler. I took a step back and felt a chill against my frosty spine when I hit the slimy wall behind me.

"It will do you no good to hide in the dark." He struggled to raise his chest off the surface of the table by pushing up with shaky arms. "I am your teacher for the night. And the only way out of this bunker is to pass my class. Then your clothes will be returned to you and you'll be sent on your way to your next lesson, whatever that happens to be." Holding onto the table for support, he finally managed to stand erect. He steadied himself before dusting off his brown coat. I saw that it was decorated with many rusty metals and that it was tattered and worn. "Surely you know who I am." He gave a halfhearted Nazi salute that sent another chill down my spine. "I was once the most powerful man on earth!"

"You can't fool me… Hitler's dead!"

"But as you can see, I'm standing right before you."

"You're either a fake, or a figment of my imagination."

He raised a hand to his heart. "You can believe this, my frozen friend… I'm as real as it gets! And if not for the fact that Fitzhugh has me nailed to the floor," he glanced downward, "I'd come over there right now and show you what being a good Hitler Youth is all about!"

I peered under the table, although from where I stood shaking in the cold, I could only see dark shadows below the surface. "You can't move from that spot?"

"As God is my witness, I've not stepped away from this table since 1945," he replied. "And for those in-the-know, that was the year I tried to commit suicide by shooting myself in the mouth. If you care to come closer… you'll be able to see the exit hole in my head."

"No thanks… I'm good here in the dark."

"Then be prepared to die out there in the cold only to come back to life in that spot every time, until you run out of lives. Then you'll end up a lost soul in Fitzhugh's black hallway, forevermore." He guffawed. "Speaking of lives… how many do you have left?"

I was so cold; I could hardly think. "I guess I'm down to six."

"Lesson Number One," he bellowed. "Blind obedience is required in my class if you hope to pass with lives to spare! Now come into the light and warm yourself before you waste a life out there in the bitter cold."

My teeth were chattering away. "Is it warmer over there?"

He gestured to the lightbulb that hung five feet above his head. "It's like being in the sun. You can practically get a tan!"

Almost frozen in place, it pained me to inch forward. "I can't believe a light bulb can put out much heat."

"You'd be surprised what this one can do."

My legs were like numb logs, but they took me to the edge of the light that was hitting the floor. Much to my dismay, the man still looked like Hitler from ten feet away. And although deathly pale, he was clearly not a figment of my imagination. It was still dark under the table, but I was now close enough to be stunned by two bare legs standing in the shadows, and sure enough, there was a large, rusted metal spike embedded in each of his swollen feet. I winced, but also breathed a frosty sigh of relief. "I guess you were telling me the truth about being nailed to the floor. That looks really painful."

"It only hurts when I click my heels," he cackled. "Now come closer and let me put a face with that young, vulnerable voice I'm hearing in the dark."

I tested the light with my foot and immediately felt warmth. And under the circumstances, that was all I needed to know. With my hands covering my crotch, I threw caution to the frosty wind and stepped into a warm summer day. But then came a chill when I peered across the expanse of thick oak that separated me from the scary looking man who was standing six feet away. He became real from that distance, although he reeked of death. His smell even dominated the sewer gas that permeated the room. And his bedraggled appearance was caked with blood! I could see that it once ran like a red river out the hole that had exploded above his temple. But in spite of his awful condition, his baggy blue eyes were incredibly mesmerizing and powerful to behold. So much so that it took everything I had to stand my ground. "Holly crap," I gulped. "You really are Adolph Hitler!"

"In the rotting flesh," he returned with a grieving grin.

I held my breath while he slowly gave me the once over. I watched intently as his eyes crept over every nook and cranny of my crawling skin. I nearly freaked when he tried to sneak a peek at my penis. But besides my hands being in the way, thankfully the table topped-off just below my navel. Done with his inspection, he looked me in the eye. "If I'm not mistaken," he said, "you're that handsome devil Fitzhugh painted in the entry hall." He smiled and it revealed a mouth full of rotten teeth. But then as if flipping a switch, his blighted smile turned into an angry frown that caused me to tremble. "More importantly," he rumbled, "you're the one responsible for giving that crazy schoolteacher the power of God!"

I was immediately put on the defensive, reeling in mind, if not body. "No… it wasn't like that at all! I was living a perfectly normal life until Fitzhugh's creepy helpers came along the other day and then… and then everything went to hell after that… and things just keep getting worse and worse with no end in sight!"

After piercing and prodding me with his brilliant blues, I was pleased to see him nodding like he believed me. "Perhaps we have more than infamy in common." He happy-faced me. "I'm sure Fitzhugh came into your life much the same way he came into mine. I would've been a priest, if not for his meddling in my affairs."

"A priest?" I questioned.

"Ja! Ja!" he replied, before pointing to the hideous hole in his head. "Lucky for you, my memory is still completely intact so that I can educate you on what really happened during my tumultuous time on earth, instead of what historians have written about me."

"Look… I just wanna get out of here as fast as I can!"

"Well… an apple would've bought you an immediate free pass out of hell, but since you've come here empty-handed, I guess you'll just have to suffer through my entire class. Hopefully, I won't *bore* you to death too many times tonight."

"I'd give anything for an apple right now," I groaned, wanting to kick myself for failing to take Fitz up on his apple offer when the opportunity had knocked.

Hitler cleared his throat of decay. "I'll start the class with a brief history lesson about myself, then we'll get to you." He then fiddled with his jacket, before pulling on his sleeves. He seemed to be taking his sweet time before uttering his next word, like the buildup before one of his patented speeches. "The year was 1900." He then paused again while studying my face. "I was a twelve-year-old choirboy when that creepy old judge threw the book at me for no good reason. As previously stated, I had plans to grow up and become a priest, but the Green Fog rolled in on that fateful day and changed my life forevermore!" He paused again, looking down at the table this time. "The next thing I knew," he again paused, briefly looking off into the darkness, before locking in on me, "I was crying my eyes out in the entry hall of the Big House with Sergeant Stevens chuckling maddeningly by my side. I was scared to death! I didn't know what was happening to me. I just knew I wanted to go home in the worst of ways. The sergeant pointed to that painting of you on the wall and said you were the inspiration for all things Kilborne! He proceeded to curse you with words my young virgin ears had never heard before. They of course shocked me, but it was just the beginning of shocking things to come, and I too was soon cursing you!"

"Look... you got this all wrong," I insisted. "I'm sorry for what happened to you as a kid, but I wasn't even born until 1953, so you can't blame me for what happened before that."

"Bullshit!" He began patting the table repeatedly with a shaky hand, as if it was helping him make his point. "That gold-framed painting of you is all the proof I need that you were around long before me," he said. "It clearly states that it was painted in 1780. And even a poor student like you can figure out that 1780 came long before 1900. A hundred and twenty years to be exact. So, it doesn't take a genius to know which one of us came first." He pointed a bony finger my way. "It was you! The only difference being that much has changed for me in the many years since I first saw you in print during my youth, while you still look remarkably the same now that we're finally meeting in the flesh."

"I don't know what to tell you about that old painting on the wall, other than what I heard from Fitzhugh and Sergeant Stevens. Otherwise, I've been at Kilborne a total of five days so far. That's it! That's as far back as my history with this creepy place goes!"

Hitler reached an arm up and stroked what was left of his little salt and pepper mustache, like it was helping him to think. "Ahh, but of course you know as well as I do that once Fitzhugh sent you back in time, you then became a timeless teen for the ages. So yes... like it or not, Mr. Johnny Paradise... you were walking around long before I ever set foot on the earth... and that's no bullshit!"

Sad but true... I had no comeback for Adolph Hitler. He proudly puffed out his chest as if in victory, before resuming his story. "In spite of overwhelming odds, I persevered and somehow managed to survive my hundred-day sentence here at *your* academy." He beamed. "And the next thing I knew… I was back to my old life, like I had never left home! I had no recollection of my time at Kilborne. Not even a clue!" He paused to take a breath and I heard air whistle out the hole in his head. "I drifted through my teens once my father passed," he admitted solemnly. "And I was often homeless in my twenties." His shoulders drooped. "I tried my hand at painting landscapes for a living, but I wasn't very successful at it. I'd peddle my sketches on the streets of Vienna and barely make enough to eat most days, let alone pay for a place to stay. But then came World War One." He perked. "It was my ticket off the streets!" He shuddered joyfully. "I joined the glorious fight and was having the time of my life, until I was wounded in battle." His shoulders again drooped, and he paused to straighten his moth-eaten tie. It hung in black shreds against a faded white shirt with burn marks and dried bloodstains. "Fitzhugh came to me in a dream one night while I lay in my hospital bed and my memory of Kilborne returned." He looked off into the darkness before returning my gaze. "Although I was shocked at first, Fitzhugh said great things would happen, if I just listened to his every word. But when the war ended, I returned to civilian life and was soon back on the streets. I hardly saw Fitzhugh in my dreams for months at a time. Then one chilly day he led me to a small political gathering that changed everything! I joined the Nazi movement and was soon giving speeches in beer halls. The more I talked the more people listened! Fitzhugh kept me out of harm's way during my slow rise to power. The controlling bastard even had me author a book that was more his words than mine. He guided me along like a puppet on a string. Before long I was standing in front of large crowds. And then opportunity finally knocked, and I became Chancellor of Germany!" He lifted his arm high, as if it was being pulled and gave a triumphant Nazi salute, and then as if the string had snapped, he slammed his hand down on the table, sending powdery gray dust into the foul air. "Fitzhugh would come to me in a dream every night once I was in power. He would keep me up to the wee hours of the morning, telling me what needed to be done from one day to the next. I was always dead tired. Sometimes I didn't wake until noon! He wore me down over time, until he was the one running Germany, not I. In the end, I was nothing more than a pawn in his grand scheme to take over the world. He needed me to do the dirty work for him, because he knew the German people would never follow a ghost into battle."

I rolled my eyes, doubting what had spewed from his foul mouth, the stench of which nearly had me backing out into the cold. "So, I suppose you're blaming Fitzhugh for World War II?"

"No, I'm blame you!" he replied, causing me to shudder at the thought. "But anyhow… I was perfectly content with never setting foot on foreign soil, although Fitzhugh insisted that I take the world by storm! He guided me along from one military success to another, until he had me thinking I was invincible!" he twinkled. "I was at the peak of my career in 1940, having conquered most of Europe, with England hanging on by a thread. All of Germany worshiped me like I was a god back then!" he laughed haughtily. "Even the snobs of Berlin were impressed with my achievements!" His mood suddenly turned somber. "It was Fitzhugh's idea to invade Russia," he stated. "My generals said we weren't ready for such a huge undertaking, but Fitzhugh assured me that it was time to strike!" Hitler shook his head in disgust. "I gave the order to invade Russia in the spring of 1941. We were having great success through the summer months and even got within sight of Moscow, when our troops bogged down in the winter snow." He sighed and his head whistled again. "The Russian army somehow managed to regroup by the time the spring thaw came. They not only stopped our further advances; they had us retreating back toward the Fatherland, one bloody battle at a time. There was nothing we could do to stop them!" He wiped sweat from his brow. "The mighty Americans eventually got into the fight and I was being sandwiched from both sides of the globe." He grimaced. "By 1945 the war was all but lost and Fitzhugh had abandoned me. He was nowhere to be found in my dreams, no matter how much I slept. I was all alone… left to fend for myself with an angry world closing in on my doorstep." Hitler paused and began to fiddle with the rusty metals pinned to the lapel of his coat. He diverted his eyes to the dusty surface of the table, where I noticed a torn map of the world in front of him. Besides the map, there were some initials carved across the lengthy wood surface. Words, too. HELP! SHIT! CLIMB FAST! I WANT MY MOMMA! STAY AFLOAT! HITLER SUCKS! FOLLOW THE RISING SON! "This table holds clues that can help you pass my class," he continued. "You would be wise to study it from time to time, when you get the chance."

Much of what was carved on the table was covered in a thin layer of dust, although I could observe arrows on the shadowy edges that pointed to the four corners of the room. The arrow pointing to the far left of me had an X carved through it; like that corner had been crossed off the list. "What do these arrows mean?"

Seemingly ignoring me, Hitler looked off into the dark, before returning my gaze. "All was lost by the time I pulled the trigger on the gun in my mouth. I floated in darkness for the longest time, but then I ended up at this table without pants or shoes, and like I previously stated, I've been nailed to the floor here ever since 1945." He paused and ran a finger through the dust on the table, creating a crooked trail. "Fitzhugh blamed me for losing the war. He said I was too weak to finish the job." He cleared more decay from his throat and a wisp of green wafted into the air. "And now he has me spending a thousand years down here in this hellish place as punishment for crimes against the people he was trying to have me destroy! My only pleasure comes when there's a new recruit to break the monotony. I learn as much as I can from them before they either die off or move on to their next class. The rest of the year I spend sleeping at this table, when I'm not fighting for my death." He smiled, sadly. "But enough about me and my problems... tell me something about yourself."

Ignoring Hitler's request, I pointed to the table. "What about the arrows... what do they mean?"

"I can tell by your accent that you're an American," he said, while nodding assuredly. "Probably from New York or Boston, I imagine."

"I'm from New Jersey," I snapped. "Now what about the arrows?"

"I see by your hair that you're not a Hippie Youth, like the recruit Fitzhugh sent me last night."

"Are you talking about Marty?"

He winced. "I hope he's not a friend of yours?"

I shook my head. "No... not really. Why do you ask?"

"Marty's a bad seed," he replied. "I can see why Fitzhugh is grooming him to become the anti-Christ."

"Can Fitzhugh really do that?"

Hitler grinned, smugly. "He managed to take a lowly bum off the streets of Vienna and turn him into the most powerful man in the world." He pointed a bony finger at himself. "So, I can see no reason why he can't take a degenerate young punk like Marty and turn him into an absolute world beater. In fact, I'm willing to bet he plans to use his future anti-Christ to pick up where I left off in an effort to achieve the Final Solution. Except knowing Fitzhugh as I now do, he won't just target God's chosen people this time around, but rather anyone with a beating heart!"

Being in survival mode, I somehow saw a ray of hope in Hitler's gloomy forecast. "So, I take it Marty made it out of here alive?"

"I was glad to see the Hippie Youth go."

"Well, if he can make it out," I said with shaky confidence, "then maybe I can too!"

"Only about one percent has what it takes to pass my class, so don't go counting your chickens before they hatch."

I heard what sounded like a drop of water hit the ground and echo in the darkness. Judging by the sound, I thought it originated from the X corner. "What was that?"

"I call it the Fitzhugh Flush," he replied. "Like clockwork, the bunker fills with urine every hour on the hour. It's how I keep time."

"Oh my gosh! Won't we drown?"

"I'm afraid so, Johnny."

"Then tell me how to get out of here!"

"That will be covered in the next lesson when we return from the dead," he replied to my absolute horror.

"What? I don't wanna drown in piss! Surely there's a way out!"

"You have two options currently at your disposal," he informed. "You can elect to stay here at the table with me and drink until you're drowning in warm piss, or you can scurry off into the dark and drown in cold piss. The choice is entirely yours."

"That's it?" I wailed. "Those are my only options?"

"You should've brought an apple for your teacher."

"How much longer do we have?"

"The bunker will flood after the third drop of urine pings on the floor," he replied. "Then the piss will gush in so fast, we'll both be dead within a minute, two at the most if you hold your breath."

Panic stricken, my head was spinning, and my heart was pounding wildly. But somehow, that incredibly insane situation triggered an old memory and I flashed back to when I was seven years old. There I was... wandering away from my pregnant mother at a crowded water park, while my dad was off getting us refreshments. I took to the water and was soon waist deep with my feet running along the sandy bottom. Even though I hardly knew how to swim, my confidence grew, and I headed for the middle of the man-made lake.

Without a care in the world, I happily bounced along chest-deep, until I hit nothing but water and sank down under. I landed in a small crater. To make matters worse, one foot was stuck inside the crater and I couldn't seem to work it free. I reached with an arm for the shimmering surface, but my fingers came up inches short. I started to panic. I cried for my mother, except that all that came out of my mouth were tiny bubbles that got lost at sea. I waved both arms for help, but only small fish took notice. I felt myself slipping away when I was jolted back to life, as a strong hand gripped one of my floating wrists and yanked me out of the water. I coughed and gasped for air like it was my first breath ever. I then wrapped my arms and legs around the teenage girl who had saved me. I cried on her shoulder all the way onto dry land. I never did get her name, although now that I know Martha like I do, she could've been her twin sister. Then ghostly Fitzhugh popped into my head and I was left to wonder if he had sent that fallen angel to my rescue long ago. And where was Martha now that I needed her more than ever? "I can't do this," I screamed Hitler's way. "Please let me out of here!"

"You have nothing to fear," he bellowed in animated fashion, like he was mimicking Winston Churchill, "but fear itself!"

Freaking out, I slammed my hands on the table, while running in place. "Seriously… I can't do this! Drowning is my biggest fear!"

"We all have our fears, Johnny. You will need to conquer yours before this night is over, or you'll never pass my class."

My knees nearly buckled when I heard the second ping echo throughout the bunker. Like Hitler, I held on to the heavy table for support, while adding to the pee on the floor. It trickled down my trembling legs and formed a yellow puddle where I stood. "I can't believe this is happening!" I cried hysterically. "I wanna go home!"

He laughed. "I suggest you get ready to be flushed away, instead."

The third ping came sooner than the second and a loud roar came from the X corner. The smell nearly knocked me over before I was hit with the spray from the sticky waste. I saw it rushing across the floor as it entered the light. I jumped onto the table before more pee got on my feet. I again covered my penis and remained out of Hitler's reach. My screams were constant, although they got lost in the roar of the yellow liquid. It quickly rose while swirling underneath the table. Hitler smiled and waved up at me. He seemed to be enjoying himself, even as the piss reached level with his belly and poured over the surface of the table. His map of the world floated away in the circulating current and in spite of my best efforts, my feet were now swimming in warm piss. As bitterly disgusting as that was, it was quickly up to my knees. Hitler saluted me Nazi style, then took in a mouthful of urine and blew it out the hole in his head before calmly going under.

Surprisingly, I found myself craving his company now that there was no one to share my misery with. "Help! Help me!"

Warm piss soon reached my waist. The strong current was pulling me off the table, so I grabbed hold of the frayed wire that was attached to the scorching-hot lightbulb and held on for dear life. I was dizzily circling around and around when the wire sparked.

Shocked, I let go of the cord and was sent spinning out into the dark waters where the piss was ice cold. More sparks lit up the large bunker as I paddled to stay afloat. I took in every breath of precious foul air I could, until I ran out of breathing room. I had no choice but to go under to keep from scrapping along the concrete ceiling. I opened my eyes in the amber waste and saw Hitler down at the bottom. His half-naked body stood anchored to the floor on his side of the table with one hand in his coat pocket, the other floating along like he was still giving the Nazi salute. The submerged lightbulb was circulating above his head like a ceiling fan, until another spark from the frayed wire ignited the room and the bulb suddenly popped and everything turned pitch black. I strained to hold my breath. Besides not wanting to inhale piss, I held out hope for a miracle in my fading state. *God! Martha! Mom! Dad! Miss Willows! Rudy! Mitch! Billy! I don't care who… I just need someone to save me before I…*

I held out as long as I could, before yielding to a tiny breath that turned into the flood that filled my mouth and lungs with cold piss. It hurt like hell, although the overwhelming pain was for an instant. My glowing spirit then separated from my naked body and I saw my remains float down and come to a rest on the floor by Hitler's swollen feet. I wanted to be repulsed by my horrible fate, but all feelings soon escaped me. My spirit then moved away from earthly things, leaving what was left of me in the dark.

# Chapter Twenty-Three
*Happy Feet*

I didn't have to be told… I knew I was dead. For the fourth time I floated in eternal darkness, until bored to tears with the hereafter. Still, I had mixed feelings when the Green Fog finally came for me again, because there was no way I wanted to return to hell. No way! But like before, the Fog took hold and I was born again, right down to that big pimple on my chin.

I stood naked in the freezing darkness of the bunker and then it was like history repeating itself when I saw Hitler aglow in the middle of the room. As before, he was snoring face down on the table. The good news, if there was any, was that there was no sign of the flood that had taken my previous life. I didn't even smell piss above the other rank smells that filled the air.

Not wanting to wake the dead, I quietly moved out of the cold darkness and into the warm light without alerting the once mighty fuehrer. Avoiding Hitler's remains, I brushed away the dust and studied the oak surface, counting eight sets of initials carved into the wood, along with more words: HAVE SOMETHING SHARP TO WRITE WITH! AN APPLE A DAY WILL KEEP THE TEACHER AWAY. LOOK TO THE HEAVENS AND YOU WILL FIND EARTH. THE DEVIL MADE ME DO IT! TAKE IT LIKE A MAN! ONE FOOT WILL DO! SWIM TO DAYLIGHT! WATCH OUT FOR RATS!

Save for the APPLE, I shrugged as if rendered clueless by the information afforded me. But I was on the lookout for RATS! To be on the safe side, I looked under the table for rodents, before checking on Hitler's feet once again. After moving in for a closer look, I could see that they were swollen to the size of water balloons that were purplish, red. His toes were gray and black and looked like they were about to fall off. Puss oozed out from the holes caused by the two large rusty spikes that held him in place and trickled down to form murky yellow puddles around both of his foul-smelling feet.

Confident that he posed no immediate threat, other than to my nose, I got up and eyed the four arrows on the corners of the table and decided to venture out and give them a second feel. I started with the one where the flood of piss had come from. The one with the X. Wary of rats, I cautiously felt my way around in the dark and came upon nothing but cold, slimy concrete. I looked to the ceiling in search of an opening and saw nothing but the blackness of space. I was freezing by the time I reached the next corner. But then I heard a distant rumble that alarmed me enough to return to the warmth of the light, as Hitler was waking from his slumber. I stood on my side of the table and strangely, it felt like home, save for the monster that was across from me. I watched as he slowly rose to a semi-erect position, with his arms spread out across the oak surface for support. His bobbing head came to a rest between his hunched shoulders. He looked me in the eye and smiled. "Did you enjoy that death?"

"It was the worst experience of my life," I promptly replied. "What was that rumbling I just heard?"

He glanced skyward. "Like clockwork, there is a mighty storm coming that will saturate the earth, causing the concrete ceiling to cave in from the weight of the world above. We'll soon be crushed to death."

Shocked by almost nothing at that point, my jaw still managed to drop. "How often does that happen?"

"It will happen on the half-hour between flushes now that class is in session," he informed to my grief, as more rumblings went off in the distance. "We have just returned from the midnight flush. There will be six more tandem episodes of flush and storm, until the sun rises, and class is dismissed at exactly six in the morning."

"But you're talking about twelve more deaths when I only have five lives left to lose," I pined. "I'll never make it until morning!"

"Lesson Number Two," he bellowed before pausing like he was about to say something profound. "Death is what you make it."

I waited patiently for Hitler to continue with his lesson, but he was apparently done. At first, I wanted to scratch clueless like Willie would, except that my mind seemed more intelligent and mature than I could ever remember it being before, although I remained puzzled by Hitler's rather vague response. "That's it?" I questioned. "That's all there is to Lesson Number Two?"

He looked as puzzled as I was. "Need I say more?"

"I can't do anything with that," I whined. "I thought you said this lesson would explain how to get out of here?"

He nodded affirmatively. "It does."

I held out my hands in bewilderment. "How so?"

"It brings you one step closer to Lesson Number Three!" he bellowed, as the rumblings intensified. "If you embrace a horrible death to my lofty standards, then you will immediately pass my class and be dismissed early!"

"Lofty standards?" I quizzed, incredulously. "I just drowned in a room full of piss! What more do you want from me?"

"Anyone can do that," he cackled. "But if you really want to impress me, then I suggest you nail yourself to the floor after you return from the devastating storm that's about to hit. And then we'll sing together until the next Fitzhugh Flush takes our breath away, as we remain anchored to the floor in a swirling sea of piss!"

"Nail myself to the floor?" I gulped. "You're kidding, right?"

"There are steel rods embedded in the concrete," he indicated. "When the ceiling gives out from the storm, you must find two twelve inch pieces of steel and a chunk of concrete that's large enough to use as a hammer before you die. And when you return to life, the bunker will be fully restored like it is now, and you'll have those items in your possession to finish the task."

My feet were not the least bit happy. "That sounds like a really painful way to go. What else can I do to impress you?"

"Now that you mention it...."

I perked, like maybe opportunity was about to knock.

"Lesson Number Four!" he bellowed. "When all else fails... you can always resort to having sex with the teacher."

My mouth agape, I stepped back into the freezing shadows and was chilled to the bone. "Surely you're kidding... right?"

"Sex is a powerful weapon that can be used time and again, without ever running out of bullets! It has not only saved many a struggling marriage, it has also caused countless political victories to be snatched from the jaws of defeat by those who possessed a silver tongue." He grinned, rakishly. "Now come over to my side of the table and let's see if your oral interpretation skills are up to snuff."

"Yuck! I'd rather die first!" I took another step back that left me colder than the last. Although the thick surface of the table spared me the view of his midsection, it appeared from his frantic movements that Hitler was busy masturbating. "I can't believe you're doing that."

"I've got it ready for you, Johnny." He moaned. "All I need now is a moment of your time."

"Never!"

"Hurry!" he grunted. "Come to Poppa before the storm hits!"

"I won't do it!"

"At least come back into the light so I can admire your pretty face and muscular chest before it's too late."

"No!" I shivered helplessly in the dark as the great storm approached. The lightbulb began to sway in a circular motion, like a rotating sun. It caused creepy images of Hitler to be cast against the walls and it had me going from dawn to dusk over and over again. The orbiting light gained momentum and brought scorching heat when at its closest point to my body, but there was bone-chilling cold when it went south on me like the passing of the seasons. Hot and cold! Hot and cold! Then, fire and ice. Round and round the rotating sun went, picking up speed as the storm approached. "I think I'm embracing death," I announced, as my burning flesh turned to frozen sweat and then back again. "I'm embracing death!" I proudly jumped for joy. "I'm embracing death!"

"Good for you," he snorted. "But what you do away from the table is your business and will not count toward passing my class. So, you'll just burn through a life you can't afford to waste, when an easy solution is at hand." He guffawed. "Yes… sometimes you have to compromise to get the job done, and so with that being said, I'll even allow you to pass my class with a hand job at this point!"

"Never!" I gritted my on and off again chattering teeth, which were starting to chip away. "I'm not coming anywhere near you! Not now, not ever!"

He squealed and his piercing eyes vanished up inside is head to where there was a blue glow coming out the hole in his temple. He stood erect and gave the Nazi salute with his free hand while the other frantically jerked back and forth down below the wood surface. "Heil Hitler!" he screamed, before collapsing on the table amid a cloud of dust. "Sadly," he pouted from his prone position, "I finished without you." He brought his date hand out of hiding and assumed the tripod position. "Now let's get back to business while there's a lull in the storm."

Without realizing it, the peace and quiet had returned during that heated moment. I took two awkward steps forward and was relieved to be back in the steady warmth, now that the lightbulb had stopped orbiting for the time being. "What about that opening where the piss came from," I inquired, while pointing in that direction, "can a person fit through there?"

"That will be covered in a future lesson," he replied. "If you had accepted my friendly advances, this would be a moot point right now because you would be free to go on to your next class."

"Sorry, but I'm into girls… not dirty old men like you."

"I like the ladies, too!" He smiled, dreamily. "Fitzhugh sends me female recruits some years. I had a beautiful fourteen-year-old princess a few years ago that I'll never forget. She was a budding Nordic beauty of fine pedigree with blonde hair and blue eyes. Her name was Astrid, and she looked like she belonged on the Alps. She came to me with only four lives, but her heart was full of pride and determination. She was so fine, I'm almost ashamed to admit I tricked her into having sex with me twice before I finally let her go." He guffawed yet again. "But she not only passed my class with honors, she even had the cunning and tenacity to survive the remainder of her hundred-day sentence!"

It was a relief to hear some positive news for a change. I wanted to celebrate her achievement, even if it had come at a hefty price. But the celebration was cut short when the rumbling resumed and began to shake the ground, as white concrete powder started to cascade down from cracks in the ceiling. "The storm is getting strong again!" I stated the obvious.

"This always reminds me of my last day on earth," he said, before sighing forlornly. "Russian troops were in Berlin and they were pounding my bunker relentlessly with artillery and all I had left to stop them were a few Hitler Youth with toy guns. That's when I decided to take matters into my own hands by popping a cyanide tablet into my mouth, then pulling the trigger on my gun." He glanced to the heavens. "I thought that would be the end of me, but no! As it turned out… it was just the beginning." He cocked his head to one side and the bones in his neck snapped, crackled, and even popped. "I can't tell you how many times I've died since I committed suicide, but the number is staggering!" he stated smugly. "So, who better than I to teach you how to embrace death?"

I heard the squeal of straining and bending steel up above. Pebbles began to fall from the ceiling. I was inclined to get under the table to protect my head, although I fought the urge to take shelter and stood tall. "I'm not afraid to die," I croaked. "I'm embracing death as we speak."

"That's the spirit!" he said, before using his date hand to point in the direction of the corner to my rear left. "But now you must return to the corner from which you've been originating from, before the storm gets any closer."

"What... why is that?" I asked, as something larger than a pebble glanced off my head, almost sending me reeling to the floor.

"It's safer for one thing," he replied. "But even more important than that... you will learn by watching your teacher embrace yet another horrible death from that vantage point, as the ceiling will collapse here in the middle of the bunker first, while that corner will be the last to go." He paused to clear the decay and concrete dust from his throat and his head whistled yet again. "Just don't forget about securing the two twelve inch rods of steel and the chunk of concrete you'll need to further your education, or you will have to repeat this part of the class over again."

I went to my corner and froze in the darkness, while observing Hitler calmly wipe the snow and pebbles off the surface of the table, as the lightbulb began to circle overhead once again. He then leaned forward and rested his head face down on the wood surface.

Between the lightning bolt strikes and the rumbling and the squealing of steel, I heard him snoring. His greasy salt and pepper hair began to take on powdery snow and so did the back of his tattered and worn brown coat, yet he seemed unfazed.

The angry storm continued to strengthen, until it sounded like a freight train gone wild. The bunker shook mightily. The lightbulb went crazy. It lost its orbit and bounced around every which way, flashing light across all four corners of the room to where I was able to catch glimpses of the opening in the ceiling in the X corner. I was excited to see that the pee hole looked big enough for me to fit inside, although it would require that I slide the massive oak table over to climb up into it.

With time no longer on my side, I vowed to make that the very first thing I did when I returned amongst the living again, rather than try and nail myself to the floor to please Hitler. Forget that!

Hitler was now covered in a mound of snow, as pebbles smacked the table with such frequency; it seemed like he was caught in a hailstorm. The ceiling began to sag in the middle of the room. The lightbulb lowered, until it was resting in the snow piled on Hitler's back. The subdued glow illuminated the once mighty fuehrer like a fallen angel.

The bunker moaned and groaned, then the lightbulb popped as the ceiling above Hitler suddenly collapsed with a mighty roar. Besides darkness, I was hit with a powerful shotgun blast of mud that was laced with wood chips from the exploding table along with tiny shards of steel and crushed stone and bone that sent me to the ground in agonizing pain.

I was busy pulling fragments from my body when an even louder roar was followed by a wave of mud that carried me up the wall, until I hit my head on what was left of the ceiling in that corner. Dazed, I sank into the chilly depths of the razor-sharp mud that filled the room. Breathless and blind, I hit bottom bleeding from every pore in my beaten body, as the weight of the world easily crushed the remaining life out of me. If nothing else, it was liberating to be free of my painful flesh and all of my broken bones. Liberating!

# Chapter Twenty-Four
### *Graduation Day*

Again, I didn't have to be told... I knew I was dead. Been there, done that five times and still there was no heaven that I could see. I floated in eternal darkness. Like before, the Green Fog came for me and I was born again into more darkness that was freezing cold.

But suddenly, there was light. It once again came from the center of the bunker where Hitler was beginning to stir with his face down on the table—and like the table, the bunker appeared whole again. I returned to the warmth of the light, while Hitler rose to a semi-erect position. "I see you've come up short on your school supplies," he razzed. "Did you at least enjoy your mud bath?"

I grimaced at the recollection. "It smelled like shit."

He nodded in agreement. "Ja, Ja, Fitzhugh is not above mixing in a little fertilizer now and then to help his recruits grow big and strong. Hopefully, the smell didn't overwhelm you?"

"It overwhelms me now!" I shook my woozy head, feeling groggy and hung-over. "Coming back from the dead is starting to kill me."

Hitler cleared the decay from his throat like he was about to lecture, and so he did... "Your soul is like a cat with nine lives, except that it has a chance to age like fine wine before you are brought back to life." He primped. "And so, Fitzhugh... in all his infinite wisdom, would like nothing more than to see all of his recruits survive their grueling sentences, but only by the skin of their teeth. This way he can send them out into the world with old souls in young bodies that will one day represent him well in his bid to not only control the earth, but the heavens above."

"If that were true, you'd think he'd have more recruits leaving out of this place alive, instead of ending up as lost souls in that black hallway."

"It's a weeding out process that begins with the first meal," he explained. "But Fitzhugh doesn't need many to survive his reform school to bring mankind to its knees. Besides… you've already been made aware of the incredible damage just one well-placed recruit can do." He used his thumb to point proudly at himself. "So, all he really needs are a few survivors and the shit will hit the fan!" he declared. "And when the trumpet finally sounds, Fitzhugh will empty his hallway of lost souls by releasing them on the angels in heaven above, while Marty is busy doing the job of the anti-Christ on the ground below. The extermination campaign could last months or maybe even years, but unless God enters into the equation with feet on the ground, all the hopes and prayers of the dwindling masses will not stop Fitzhugh from taking planet earth by storm!"

"Whoa… why are you telling me this?"

"Because it's subject-matter that's covered in my class. And since you've already paid the tuition with your life, it would be remiss of me not to give you the lesson on Fitzhugh before you drown again."

I pointed a shaky finger in the direction of the X corner. "I'll bet that opening in the ceiling is the way out of here."

Hitler seemed impressed. "Hmmm… perhaps you're a better student than I thought."

My confidence soared, and I grabbed the end of the table. "I hope you don't mind, but I need to borrow this for a moment."

"You can't do that," he soughed. "I need the table for support. I'll fall without it!"

"Sorry," I returned, apathetically. "I need something to stand on so I can get out of here."

"But there are still valuable lessons to learn!" he clamored. "And besides that, you don't have any clothes. They won't be waiting for you up top until you pass my class."

I shrugged, dismissively. "I don't care at this point. I just want out of here before the piss comes again." It began as a tug of war, although I quickly pulled one end of the heavy table away from Hitler, while he hurled one curse word after another my way. I stopped when he had run out of oak, wanting to see what was to become of the fully exposed fuehrer. First off, he looked hilarious standing nude from the waist down—especially considering his upper half was in formal military attire, albeit dusty and worn. He briefly maintained his shaky balance by flapping his arms this way and that, while still managing to curse me out. He then howled like a werewolf when his ankles tore from his feet and slid out from under him to where he fell backward with the back of his head taking the brunt of the fall. It hit the concrete with a mushy thud and then there was silence. Motionless. Eyes closed. Hitler lay spread-eagled with his ankles oozing blood, while his feet remained nailed in place, erupting in a volcano of puss. At first, I thought he was dead, until he twitched, then rolled over on his stomach and began crawling in the opposite direction of where I was looking to go. He soon disappeared into the darkness, leaving behind two trails of blood on the slimy floor. I then got behind the table and pushed with all my might toward corner X, hoping to beat the next Fitzhugh Flush and never see or hear from Adolph Hitler again.

I pushed my way into the freezing darkness, until I hit a wall. The sound of wood hitting stone reverberated throughout the bunker. I slid the table firmly into the corner and climbed aboard. Using a hand on the slimy wall for support, I got on my toes and raised my other hand up as high as it would reach and let my fingers run the ceiling, until I felt an opening. I pictured a corrugated tin pipe because that's what it felt like inside. I waved my hand around the perimeter of the hole and was pleased that it was in fact wide enough for me to escape from. *But how was I going to get up inside?* It was then that I bumped into the knotty end of a rope. Upon further inspection, I realized it was positioned so that it hung down from the middle of the hole. I fingered the big, slimy knot, then recoiled and jumped in an effort to grab hold, but I slid off. I got into jumping position to try again. This time I caught the rope above the knot and found it thick and just as slimy. I slid down to the knot, lost my grip on that and a foot later, my feet slammed back down on the table with a meaty smack that echoed in the bunker and the sound continued on up into the dark shaft above my head, before getting lost in space.

"Having problems?" Hitler snickered, as I gasped. His harrowing voice sounded way too close for comfort.

"Where are you?"

"I'm under the table."

I shrieked. "You keep away from me!"

"You have nothing to fear but fear itself." He guffawed. "Besides that… I don't have a foot to stand on at the moment, so I can't chase you down. And even if I could… my poor, little dick disappears in the freezing cold. How 'bout yours?"

I didn't bother answering the prick. Instead, I jumped for the rope and grabbed it, only to quickly lose my grip and land back on the table. Undeterred, I was ready to jump again when a drop of something cold and wet hit me on top of the head. I dabbed it with my finger and sure enough… it was piss. I wanted to break down and cry, but instead I reached deep and jumped again. I latched on to the rope and slid off. I tried again and again with the same result. "Surely there's an easier way up this hole," I wailed. "Tell me before it's too late!"

"It's already too late." He laughed. "You'll never make it to the top before you get blasted with piss."

"Make it to the top?" I pined. "I can't even get started!"

"The solution to your problem will be covered in Lesson Number Six," he informed. "But for now it would be wise of you to move away from the hole, unless you would like to be splattered all over the table from the force of the piss that will soon be rushing down that pipe."

"Sounds like a better way to go than drowning."

"There are those who would agree."

My antenna went up. "Others have tried this before?"

"But of course," he replied. "A good twenty percent of my students are able to spot the pee hole before it's mentioned in Lesson Number Five. And the big recruits move the table over just like you, thinking they can just climb their way out. And when they find that they can't, most just foolishly scamper down from the table and huddle under the warmth of the lightbulb while waiting to be flushed away. But then there are those few who think outside the box and act quickly enough to succeed where others have failed."

I mused, thinking more clearly than ever before. "So, am I correct in assuming I can embrace death this way?"

The second drop of piss hit me on top of the head before Hitler gave me his answer. "Yes," he finally replied to my relative delight. "If you are willing to stand under the pipe, until the Fitzhugh Flush blasts you to smithereens, I will give you full credit for embracing a horrible death."

I swallowed hard. "Okay… then I'll be free to go, right?"

Before he could answer, the third drop of piss hit, and I was blasted so hard that my soul immediately separated from my body and I became a spectator watching my death unfold like the witness to a tragic accident. I saw that the force of the piss hit my head and it nearly exploded before my body slammed down on the table. I then bounced off the oak surface and hit the ceiling with enough force to leave organs behind, before being carried away by a yellow wave. I floated on the surface of the rising pee. My arms and legs were mangled to where I could pass for a dead spider. I got caught in the current and bounced off the walls and spun circles around the room before sinking down to the bottom, where I came to a rest near Hitler's body under the table. The frayed wire sparked in the middle of the ceiling. It lit up the entire room for an instant, although that was long enough for me to notice what looked to be a folded ladder attached to the underside of the table. The lightbulb popped, and everything turned from amber to black.

Again, I floated in eternal darkness. I thought long and hard about that ladder and how I was going to use it to escape from hell, when I finally found heaven! I wanted to warn God about Fitzhugh, but the angels sent me away before I could speak to the Big Man. I was only there for what seemed like a precious few seconds, although from what I could see beyond the Pearly Gates, heaven looked far more inviting than any place on earth. It was truly an honor to be that close to paradise, except that I was intruding on a sacred place where not a soul was lost and therefore, I had no choice but to leave. I resumed floating aimlessly in eternal darkness, until the Green Fog came for me and I returned to hell. I was drawn to the light when it popped on, and the first thing I saw was Hitler back on his feet again while standing at the restored table, looking just as gnarly as ever.

"Congratulations," he bellowed. "Your next class awaits you!" He tapped the surface of the oak with a bony finger. "There's a ladder hidden under the table," he divulged, before I could beat him to the punch. "It's designed to slide out once you release the latch. Then you take it to the X corner, where you will extend it into the pipe. The bottom three feet of knotty rope is slimy to the touch, but it is bone dry above that point. This will make your climb to the top much easier, and your clothes will be waiting for you at the surface."

"So, that's it?" I probed, while returning to the warmth of the light after my latest death. "I'm free to go?"

"Yes… you have passed my class and are now free to go."

I looked underneath the table and found the latch and after a quick turn of the knob, the ladder easily slid out, as if on tracks. The wood ladder was sturdy, yet surprisingly light. "I'll be leaving now."

"Go ahead, unless you care to stick around for another lesson."

"No thanks," I snubbed. "I want out of here!"

"Suit yourself." He gave a halfhearted Nazi salute. "Say hello to everyone up in the world for me. Tell them I said, 'Heil Hitler!'"

Focused on bolting from that godforsaken place, I took the ladder and headed for the X corner. I extended the ladder and poked it around in the dark, until I found the hole in the ceiling and eagerly began my climb out of hell with goose bumps and a chill running down my spine from the anticipation of seeing the light of day. I climbed past the slimy portion of rope just as I was running out of ladder. As Hitler had said, the rope was dry at that point. Giddy with excitement, I left the ladder behind and continued my climb up the dark pipe, finding a dry knot every two feet up. The more I climbed, the more excited I got, until I was climbing at a feverish pace that seemed to go on forever.

I heard a distant rumble that alarmed me, and I climbed even faster, trying to beat the approaching storm. I was getting tired, yet I continued my torrid pace. Then I heard another rumble and moved as though I was shot out of a cannon. I was going balls-to-the-walls, until I heard a loud ping that made my ears ring. It took me a moment, then I realized the top of my head had just rammed into something extremely hard and I was seeing stars… lots and lots of stars. I teetered while trying to recover, but then I dropped down a knot, and then another. I hung by a thread, not wanting to let go, but then I lost my shaky grip on another knot and yet another, until the knots were belting me on the way down. Falling fast, I banged against the walls of the corrugated pipe time and again to where I began spinning like a speeding bullet. My soul didn't wait around for my death this time either. I saw myself crash through the ladder and explode in a million pieces on the concrete floor.

I spent what seemed like an eternity wondering what had gone wrong. I floated in the darkness, until the Green Fog came for me again. I still heard rumbling when I returned to life and saw Hitler wiping debris from the table. Feeling a little rickety from my latest death, I stumbled over to my side of the table and looked him warily in the eye. "What happened?"

"Lesson Number Seven!" he bellowed. "Upon graduating my class, you must initial the table to make it official, and take your place in history. And once you have done so," he pointed north, "it will trigger the release of the manhole cover at the top of the pipe."

"Is that what I ran into… a manhole cover?"

"Ja! Ja!" He then waved a bony finger around, as if it was going to help him make his point. "While patience may be a virtue, it seems the opposite is true for poor students like you, who are always quick to leave the classroom, when there are still valuable lessons to be learned that will not only increase your chances for survival, but also make your life a pleasure to live from one day to the next on the off chance you should somehow make it out of Kilborne alive."

"What am I supposed to write with?"

"You can carve your initials with a piece of steel from the ceiling after the next storm hits," he replied. "Although, a pencil will do just fine in a pinch."

"A pencil? Where am I supposed to get a pencil?"

He grinned, sheepishly. "Lucky for you… I happen to have one."

"Okay… can I borrow it for a second?"

"Absolutely!"

"Great… where is it?"

"Unfortunately, you will have to come over to my side of the table and kindly remove it from my crusty bottom, which by the way, hasn't been wiped in decades." He guffawed, while I cringed. "So, who the hell knows what nasty bit of business you might find lurking back there after all these many years," he snorted, and I wanted to puke. "But the good news is… I have a finely sharpened No. 2 pencil inside me that I'm sure will do the job quite nicely."

"You're even more disgusting than I thought!"

"Well, if you don't want to take advantage of my pencil offer, I suggest you get back to your corner of origin before the ceiling starts caving in here in the middle of the bunker again. But just know that this time you better come up with a piece of steel to carve with before you die, because you're down to just two remaining lives by my count and you still have a long ways to go."

Even though I could ill afford to lose another life, Hitler's pencil offer was just too much for me to accept. And so without hesitation, I scurried over to the corner to my rear left, as the rumblings grew closer and more frequent. The angry storm quickly increased in intensity. Once again it sounded like a freight train coming down upon us. The bunker shook mightily. The lightbulb went crazy and flashed light across the room.

"Good luck with the steel," Hitler said. "I think I'll take a nap." He lowered his face to the table and was soon covered in white powder, while being pelted with pebbles. The ceiling began to sag in the middle of the room. The lightbulb lowered, until it was once again resting on the pile of snow that had accumulated on his back.

I huddled in the freezing corner with my arms protecting my head for when the ceiling caved in. The rumblings and the squeal of steel nearly burst my eardrums, followed by a mighty roar that brought darkness to the room. I was again hit by a shotgun blast of mud that was laced with wood chips from the exploding table along with tiny shards of steel and crushed stone and bone. As before, an even louder roar was followed by a wave of mud that carried me up the wall, until I hit what was left of the ceiling in that corner. I then sank into the chilly depths, finding plenty of steel rods waiting for me when I hit bottom. I grabbed hold of one of the sharp objects and celebrated even while being crushed to death. I then celebrated again after being freed from the pain and suffering of the flesh. It then occurred to me that my decaying teacher had taught me well, although embracing death was becoming a habit I could live without.

I floated in eternal darkness thinking about my family and friends, when not wondering how I was going to survive the rest of my sentence when I couldn't afford to die again. I wondered about a lot of things while drifting along. My soul even became like a sponge, soaking up random bits of information that filtered in from the far reaches of the universe. It was a learning experience that was made even more surreal to feel empowered with knowledge that was lightyears beyond my comprehension, like pieces from a future puzzle yet to be solved. The Green Fog eventually got back around to me again and I returned to the living, although my old soul now felt like a senior citizen hiding inside my body. The light returned and I hobbled up to the table with steel in hand. "Where do I sign?" I asked Hitler, who was already awake and in tripod position.

"I see you won't be needing my pencil," he chortled, before running his hand across the surface of the table. "You can initial anywhere you like. There is plenty of open space yet to be filled in my classroom over the next thousand years."

I used the piece of steel to carve JB into the oak and when I was finished; I heard metal grinding up above. I lumbered to the X corner and looked up the pipe and was stoked after seeing nothing but blue sky waiting for me at the end of a long climb. I was cautiously optimistic when I returned to my side of the table. "Am I really free to go this time?"

"You are now down to one life, with ninety-four days left on your hundred-day sentence," he replied. "The good news is that your initials are now etched forevermore, so even if you fail to make it through your sentence, here is written proof that you once existed." He pointed, belatedly. "But even though you've now passed my class, your journey has just begun. You're still foolishly young at heart, although at least you now have an old soul to help guide you along through the trials and tribulations of your one remaining life."

"And you say my clothes are waiting for me on the surface?"

"Ja! Ja!" he nodded in the affirmative, then gave me the Nazi salute. "Don't forget to tell the world I said, 'Heil Hitler!'"

Without uttering another word, I went over and released the latch and slid the ladder out from under the table and moved it into position so that one end was inside the opening of the pipe.

I labored to carry my old soul up the ladder and onto the rope, but then my tired muscles grew stronger with each knot that I passed to where I felt young again in body, if not spirit by the time I reached the surface. Squinting, I stuck my head out of the hole and was blasted with warm sunshine that reminded me of the lightbulb in hell. I heard birds singing while my eyes adjusted to the sunlight. Meanwhile, my lungs feasted on invigorating air that was loaded with fresh pine and laced with the sweetness of honeysuckle. After all that I'd been through down below, the surface seemed like heaven on earth. Except instead of God, I saw Marty standing in the middle of an ocean of blue.

# Chapter Twenty-Five
*Great Escape*

With the rising sun at his back, Marty cast a large shadow as he stood on the shimmering sea. It was mesmerizing to behold. But then I realized he was standing in a small canoe that was about a hundred yards out from the boat dock, where I climbed out of the hole and got dressed with the Big House looming on the cliff behind me.

Obviously, the Great Lake had replaced the Tall Grass while I was busy suffering down below—and obviously, hell was a lot closer to home than I had thought. Marty still hadn't noticed me, although I could see him dancing away with fishing pole in hand, when he wasn't using the boat's paddle as a guitar. Meanwhile, I failed to notice that the manhole cover had quietly slid back into place—the fit so perfect, I'd never know there was an opening to hell in the middle of the dock. Just one of the many illusions here at the creepy Kilborne Academy. In any event, I was confident that I was finally done with Adolph Hitler, so I went to the water's edge and shouted out to Marty with my hands waving in the air.

As it was, I was down to craving the company of a sketchy guy with an evil eye. My old soul was not pleased, although I was desperate for someone familiar in my life, even if that someone was supposedly being groomed to be the anti-Christ.

The crystal-clear waters were as still as a millpond, until Marty began paddling my way. I saw whole schools of fish follow in his wake, and I thought out loud: "If they don't fear him, why should I?" It was a question I put to my wary soul, who then shuddered at the thought.

Marty waved to me as he got ready to dock. I saw that he was wearing his tee shirt around his neck like a long black necklace and that his exposed skin had reddened. I gave him a sweaty hand up and we hugged like superficial friends, then I followed his lead and we sat on the edge of the dock, looking out on the Big Lake.

"How many lives ya got left?" he asked.

"I'm down to one," I croaked. "How 'bout you?"

"I've got six," he replied, smugly. "So, I guess you won't be hitting the buffet again."

"Nope! I just wanna get out of here and warn the world about this crazy place before it's too late!"

"Not me, man. I'd give anything to go back ta McBride's," he said, dreamily. "I had a good thing going at that tavern, until the Green Fog came along and kicked my ass back to the barn, where nine months zipped on by and I saw Martha give birth to my kid." He grunted. "I was like a fly on the fricken wall, hanging out next ta all those colorful prick skins, as she spit the little sucker out, who she named, Nathan."

"Well… I guess congratulations are in order."

He rolled his evil eyes. "That was only the beginning, man. Sixteen years went by in a flash and Nathan was screwing Martha, who hadn't aged a day in all that time, and nine months later she spit out a kid they named, Jethrow. And then it went on and on from there, until Berton escaped from the farm and screwed a girl other than Martha, and they had a kid and a few generations later a guy named Randy had Keith, and Keith had me."

"You were there for all that?"

He nodded in the affirmative. "I can't believe I'm my own fricken relative, man! But there I was… watching myself squeeze out of my mamma's tight opening. She was a cheerleader named, Brenda. She and Keith had a fling one night after a high school football game and nine months later I was all shiny and new." He gritted his teeth. "I was crying for some cuddle time with my mamma, but this nurse with big titties took me to a room where I got to hang out with a bunch of other newborns. One by one the others got ta leave, except no one ever came for me. I hollered for my mamma, but the bitch never showed, and I never saw Keith again, neither."

"If this is too painful for you," I commiserated, "we can always talk about something else."

He shrugged like it was no big deal. "It's cool, man. Besides, it feels good ta finally get all this shit off my chest."

"Okay," I said, trying to remain sympathetic to his needs. "If it makes ya feel better."

"Anyway... I saw myself get put in a clinic after leaving the hospital and that's where I spent the first few years of my life. That was home for me. Luckily, I don't remember a thing about those days, but apparently that's how it went down. Then when I was about three, I got moved to a foster home. I saw that I used to walk around with crap in my diaper. Nobody gave a shit about me. By the time I was five I was being moved around from one foster home to another. I was like a sack of potatoes that nobody wanted for more than a few months at a time. Unfortunately, I had memories of those days, so it became like taking a bad trip down memory lane." He paused to clear his throat, then surprised me with a smile. "Then one day, when I was around nine or so, I finally landed a permanent home. I was living the dream with the Reece family in a small house out in the sticks. Things started out real cool there with Mr. Reece treating me like the son he never had and Mrs. Reece trying to be the mother I never had. Then there was Tammy. She was the cute, little sister I always wanted. And she treated me like I was her long, lost big brother from day one."

"Sounds like ya found yourself a home!"

"Yeah, man. It was all good at first. But then came the day when Dad came home drunker than a skunk. I remember tossing and turning in bed that night, replaying the sight of him pushing Mom around for no good reason, cussing and slurring his words, until he passed out on the couch." He sneered. "Yeah... Dad showed his true colors after the newness of my arrival had worn off like yesterday's news. And then it was back to business as usual at the Reece household. I came ta find out that Dad only pretended to be a good father and husband between binges. And the strange thing was Mom and Tammy seemed to be okay with that. I guess they were just used ta living like shit; walking on pins 'n' needles, wondering which Dad was gonna show up from one day ta the next." He paused to reflect, and I braced myself for more bad news. "School became my favorite place to hang out, cause I can't tell ya how many times I walked in on Dad abusing Mom, while Tammy and I stood by crying." He groaned in such a way that it sent a chill racing down my spine. "I was just a punk kid back then." He grimaced. "Couldn't do nothing but watch that shit go on and on and on. It wasn't until I got older and bigger that I started ta get in Dad's face when he was making a drunken fool of himself. And the more I grew, the bolder I got, until Dad and I were on a collision course that was bound to get ugly."

Marty now had me on the edge of my seat. "What happened next?"

"It was a Friday afternoon," he recalled, "and I was gearing up for the weekend when things were worse than expected at home. I walked in the front door and stumbled upon Dad tearing into Tammy on the living room couch, while Mom sat on her fat ass at the kitchen table with tears running down her sorry face. That's when I decided to take matters into my own hands. 'Get off her,' I shouted at the drunken asshole. 'Get off!'

"Dad yelled back: 'Get out-a-here, boy!'

"I went over and grabbed his flabby arm and tried to pull him off Tammy, but he shoved me back. I tried again and was shoved back again. Dad was a lot stronger than he looked, so I went into Tammy's room and came back with her softball bat and said, 'I'm telling ya for the last time to get off her!'

"'You don't have the balls ta hit me, boy!'

"I'm telling ya, Johnny… something in me snapped when he said that." Marty clasped his hands together like he was holding a bat. "Up until that point, Dad was right about me… I didn't have the balls to hit him. But all that changed with one swing of the bat!" He took a practice swing that took my breath away. "By then I'd been putting up with six long years of his bullshit, so I didn't see any reason ta hold back. I just let him have it with all my might!" he proclaimed, while I winced. "Dad went down to the floor in a fat heap, moaning and groaning and rolling around. I'd given him a solid shot across the back, but I still wasn't done with him. No… I swung again and got him in the neck. He was out cold, but I still wanted more. I wanted to finish him off once and for all, so I looked down at the back of his head and took aim." Marty took a moment to muse. "I don't know if it was Mom's screaming or if it was Tammy's crying, but something came over me and I let the asshole off the hook." He shook his head in disgust, although I felt relieved. "Mom apparently called the cops while I was chilling in my bedroom and she blamed me for everything!" He grumbled. "According to her… Dad was the one trying ta pull me out from between Tammy's hot virgin thighs and that's when I got her bat and unloaded on him for not letting me screw the crap out of his precious, little daughter."

"Hmmm… was she telling the truth?"

"Hell no!" he whined. "But that didn't stop the cops from hauling me off ta jail. I was then taken to the courthouse the following morning and given a hundred-day sentence by that creepy judge. The next thing I knew, the Three Little Bitches had me all chained up on a school bus and off we went, motoring halfway across the country, until we stopped to pick you up in New Jersey. And now here we are six days later," he crooned, "sittin' on the dock of some strange bay, wastin' time by the fricken century, while waitin' for the tide to roll away and return ta hay."

"Sounds like a hit song."

He whistled a note while playing his air-guitar. "Do ya think?"

"Not to change the subject," I snuffled, "but do ya know what horrible thing is planned for us next?"

"Not a clue, man. I came up from hell yesterday and found that canoe waiting for me at the dock and I've been out fishing ever since." He spit into the sparkling water and I noticed that his spit turned blood red on the way down to the sandy bottom.

It was then that my old soul waved the caution flag. I glanced back in the general direction of the manhole cover, thinking hell was way too close for comfort and so was Marty. "I don't know about you," I said, while getting to my feet, "but I'm ready to go check inside the Big House and see what's going on around here."

"Sure thing," he said, wobbling to his feet. "But after fishing all night, I may need ta take a little nap before our next adventure."

We went to the other end of the dock and made what looked to be a steep climb up the ladder, although we reached the balcony only five rungs later, where we found the backdoor to the Big House wide open. From there I could see that the front door was also wide open and beyond that, on the other side of the gate way out by the front of the property was my mother's white station wagon.

Stoked beyond belief, I took off running in that direction. I went in the backdoor. Zipped through the entry hall. Ran out the front door. I then followed the cobblestone driveway down to the locked gate with Marty in hot pursuit. "Mom! Dad!" I shouted at the Green Fog encased vehicle. I then shook the iron bars with all my might, but I couldn't get the gate to even budge.

"You can't leave," Marty twittered. "We haven't finished our fricken sentences yet."

"I don't care about that," I spat. "Help me get over the wall!"

"Okay… but it's your ass if ya get caught escaping, man."

"I'll take my chances," I returned. "I just want out of here!"

With adrenaline pumping wildly through my veins, I climbed Marty's back and reached the top of the slick stone wall and jumped down to the other side. "Mom! Dad!" I ran to my mother's car and opened the backdoor and was hit with a blast of Green Fog. My head began to spin to where I could hardly keep my balance and so I got in the car and locked the door behind me, although now I was lost in a forest of green cotton candy. I heard hissing and smelled honeysuckle. "Mom! Dad! Are you up there?" I wanted to feel around the front seat, except that I was suddenly frozen in place. "Mom! Dad! Say something! Let me know you're there!"

The sweet-smelling fog began to bubble. The cabin of the car was soon filled with large bubbles and tiny bubbles and scrubbing bubbles that began to cleanse my mind of Kilborne. It was a relief to have thoughts of that godforsaken place washed from my memory, although now that those thoughts were being slowly but surely taken away from me, I wanted to remember every last detail. I wanted to remember playing a deadly game of baseball and surviving a historic battle, and the strange times I spent with Marty, Martha and Willie, and worst of all… Hitler! I especially wanted to warn everyone about Fitzhugh and his Three Little Bitches, yet by the time the final bubble had burst; I was completely clueless of anything and everything that had to do with his reform school from hell.

The fizzing green bubbles were replaced by a long period of silent blackness where the previous six harrowing days had not only been wiped from my memory, they had been wiped from the calendar as well. I was resting in peace, until startled by the sound of a gavel being hammered that reverberated through my mind only to be followed by a crotchety old voice that bellowed: "Case dismissed!"

And then there was light. I found myself peering out the windshield at the stately courthouse that was parked directly in front of my mother's car. "Did we already see the judge?" I questioned my parents, who were sitting in the front seat.

"I told you it'd be a cakewalk," Dad replied. "We were in and out of there so fast that I can't even recall what the judge looked like anymore, although I could've sworn I saw a strange green mist filling the courtroom when we were in there."

"I remember smelling something incredibly sweet," Mom said, before checking her watch. "Hey, it's only 10:30. We were only in there a half-hour this morning!"

"It didn't even seem that long," I reflected.

Mom gave a sigh of relief. "Hopefully, it'll go this easy when we meet up with your principal, Johnny."

"Hopefully," I said with fingers crossed. And so it did, although pissy Mr. Campbell threatened to watch me like a hawk the rest of my years at Jefferson High School.

I was glad that my troubles at school and with the law were now safely behind me, and other than having a voracious appetite like I hadn't eaten in days, life was back to normal again. So normal that I tossed and turned in bed Sunday night, thinking about my return to school. Dreaded school!

But that was before my teacher grabbed my attention with her latest miniskirt offering and a pair of black leather boots that were definitely made for walking. "Class," Miss Willows purred, "get out your notes and let's start the morning session with a history quiz!"

As per usual, my history notes were nowhere to be found. But instead of shriveling in my chair like I was hiding out, I sat tall and patiently waited my turn, somehow confident that I had overcome far greater challenges before.

# Chapter Twenty-Six
Fast Forward

In spite of my best efforts, I still had to endure two weeks of summer school to pass Miss Willows' history class. But it wasn't all bad though; we actually got so close that we kissed during a private moment. Shocking as that was, we kissed again and again, until we were lost in each other's arms. Going to school had never been so much fun, although Miss Willows and I quietly went our separate ways after I passed her class—and not a word of this was ever mentioned again by me, until now that I'm telling the world my incredible life story, be it ever so strange and bizarre.

The seasons began to change quickly following the summer of 1969. I grew tired of playing sports during my junior year and shocked the football coach by not playing my senior year. And as for baseball… I felt like I'd been there and done that, so I quit that too and became just another student looking forward to graduation day.

Mitch and I piled into my rusty Pontiac Grand Prix one cold Saturday morning. We were heading north to check out Syracuse University. It wasn't all business though… Rudy was already a freshman at the school, and we were looking to party with him for the weekend, then scope out the campus between binges. Mitch and I smoked a joint to pass the time away on the long drive up, then another. "I have no idea where we are," I guffawed, "and we're getting low on fuel."

He snorted. "I guess one joint was all we needed."

I pulled off the highway and stumbled upon an old, rundown gas station in the middle of nowhere. "The place looks closed," I observed. "Not a soul in sight."

"The whole town's closed," he said, after pointing to a weathered plaque on a broken light pole that read: FITZHUGH FALLS. POPULATION ZERO.

I was drawn to a *No Trespassing* sign that sat at the end of the dead-end street we were on. I pointed straight ahead. "It's like that mountain down the street is calling my name."

"You're stoned, man," he twittered. "It's not any different than all the other mountains around here."

I shook my foggy head in the negative. "Somehow this one's different. Do ya wanna check it out?"

"That's not exactly a *welcome* sign out front," he snickered. "But I'm up for a little adventure, if you are?"

"Let's do it!" As if possessed with teenage balls of steel, I drove past the sign and headed up a winding gravel road, finding traces of snow on the ground and in the forest of trees the higher we went. We kept going around and around, until we passed through a thick layer of clouds near the top and cleared that just before reaching the peak of the mountain where everything was dark and gloomy with another layer of thick clouds up above. I brought the car to a stop in front of a thorny old gate that was parked in the middle of a crumbled stone wall. The gate sat below a rusted metal sign whose remaining letters spelled: KIL. I peered beyond the gate and crumbled wall at the charred remains of a building that sat on top of a snowy hill. "Not exactly what you'd call paradise," I quipped, trying to hang on to what was left of my high.

Mitch moaned. "Seems more like hell."

It was unsettling to see vultures hanging like eerie statues from dead trees. "This has got to be the creepiest place on earth," I said, before making sure my door was locked. "But it's like I've been here before."

"Yeah, maybe in a nightmare."

I took a deep breath and sighed. "No doubt."

"I don't know about you, man," he soughed, "but I'm not stoned enough to hang out here any longer."

My teenage balls of steel had long since shrunk to pea size and felt rusted at best. "Yeah, let's get out of here while we still can."

We left Fitzhugh Falls in the rearview mirror and found gas in a neighboring town. And after a bite to eat and another joint to ease our nerves, we eventually found Syracuse University. I liked the school, although it was a little too cold for me. I ended up going to sunny Arizona State University. I was hoping to earn a business degree, except I majored in tequila shots, beer bongs and ultra-tan sorority sisters in skimpy outfits instead. Needless to say, I was going to school for all the wrong reasons and didn't make it past my second year. Mom welcomed me back home with open arms, but Dad was determined to make a man out of me, and so he got me a job in construction working for the same firm he had been with for twenty plus years. I was a laborer. It was hard work. Certainly harder than going to school and not near as much fun. And the scenery wasn't as good, either. Instead of feasting my eyes on pretty girls, I was surrounded by gritty blue color men who always gave me shit because I was the youngest guy on the job. The hours were long, the pay was good, and I was able to save some money. But I really didn't want to spend the rest of my life following in Dad's footsteps, so I quit after six months.

Rather than return to school, I stumbled around from one low paying job to another for a year, always in search of a pot of gold at the end of a rainbow. And when I didn't find that pot of gold in New Jersey, I decided to continue my search out west in LA.

The busybody twins were still toiling away in the eighth grade when I left home against the wishes of my parents, leaving behind family and friends to venture off alone. It was a scary move on my part, but one I felt I had to make.

As far-fetched as it was, I secretly wanted to become a movie star, but so did just about everyone else in LA. It was a futile attempt on my part. The closest I got to the silver screen was installing cable TV. It wasn't a bad gig, except it did little to advance my tiny bank account, which was often hovering in the single digits when not overdrawn.

For fun I played the drums in a wannabe punk rock band, where we all wore black and had diamond studs in our ears and spiked hair streaked with purple fairy dust. Unfortunately, we looked better than we sounded and didn't last long, although we did go to see an old fortuneteller one lazy Saturday. She told me I'd be rich and marry an incredibly beautiful woman with blonde hair and that something ominous would happen one day when I was much older, but she was clueless as to what. I of course had my doubts, because I couldn't even afford to go out on a date, let alone get married. But then again, I had no problem believing her with regards to an ominous future. It seemed I was already living that lifestyle.

Although I didn't have the budget to afford a girlfriend, I managed to have my fair share of flings in my early twenties, but nothing serious. The serious women weren't interested in a guy who drove an old clunker and lived in a crappy apartment with lots of shitty roommates, when not flirting with homelessness.

I continued to stumble along by the skin of my teeth, until I landed a sales job in my mid-twenties. I was shocked that I could sell. It opened up a whole new world for me. I sold everything from office supplies to investments, but then I got my real estate license and was soon selling the crap out of Beverly Hills.

Every morning I would start my day by saying: *If I can't be a star, I can at least sell to the stars!* At the end of the day, I didn't care if the customer was a celebrity or not. If they had the cash, I treated them like a star and that made me a hit when it came to generating sales and getting referrals. I was making money hand over fist, playing the leading role in a rags to riches story right out of neighboring Hollywood.

I continued to plug away, day and night, and especially on weekends to where I hardly saw the sun except in passing, but the money was nonstop. I further advanced my fortunes by flipping houses before anyone even knew what flipping was. And when there weren't enough houses to flip, I began building the homes I sold. I then took that a step further and started developing the land for the houses I would build and then sell.

I was still a kid at heart, although when it came to business, it was like I was wise beyond my thirty years. Heck, I even invested in tech stocks long before it became the popular thing to do. And while I was indeed proud of my accomplishments, I never once allowed myself to forget the fact that had I not found my niche in life, I could've just as easily been a penniless bum on the street.

It was like a blur, but somewhere in that tumultuous timeframe I got rid of my shitty roommates and moved from my crappy apartment and bought a house in Malibu that overlooked the ocean. And my new Porsche was anything but an old clunker. In short, I had everything a man could want, and the serious women were taking notice. I didn't get much chance to ask many of them out, because they were usually beating me to the punch. It got so they were coming on to me in droves, but still there was no Ms. Right.

It was the Christmas of 1984 and as per usual, I flew home for the holidays. David picked me up at freezing cold Kennedy Airport and we headed to the house I used to call home. I gave him a playful jab to the shoulder along the way. "Well, brother… you're twenty-three now and still working a part-time job. What's up with that?"

David, who was tall, dark and still living at home, shrugged before saying, "I'm thinking of giving college another try."

"Really?" I acted surprised, although I had heard that before. "When?"

"I don't know. Maybe I'll take a few classes in the spring."

"Well… if you should change your mind, just know that you can always come out to California and work with me," I offered. "It's better than living off Mom and Dad for the rest of your life."

"Don't give me shit, Johnny. It's the holidays."

"Okay, fine."

Since we hardly saw each other outside of Christmas anymore, I decided to bite my tongue and enjoy the rest of the snowy ride into Jersey by employing elevator conversation to kill the time.

"Home, sweet, home!" I crowed, as David pulled the car in the driveway. I admired the Christmas lights covering the snowy ground, not to mention the ones that lined the icy rooftop. "I love coming home this time of year."

David laughed. "Compared to that mansion you got, I'm sure this place seems like a dump!"

"Home is where the heart is, David. But you're welcome to come stay at that *mansion* anytime you like."

"And then what?" he snubbed. "You'll put me to work?"

"Having a full-time job wouldn't kill you at your age."

"Yeah, easy for you to say… you make millions!"

I wanted to knock some sense into my lazy brother, but Mom was waiting to greet us at the front door. "Johnny!" She gave me a big hug and kissed my cheek, before stepping back to have a better look. "You're always so tan and healthy looking, but you're not getting any younger. When are you gonna get married?"

"When I find the right girl," I gave my standard reply. I saw that Mom was looking thinner and Dad, who had come in from the kitchen, was looking heavier, although they appeared to be happy and in good spirits. Emily was there at the house too. She was a blonde beauty that reminded me of how Mom used to look in her younger days. Her boyfriend, Mark, was also there. They shared an apartment and were planning on getting married in the spring.

It was good to be home, but business called and so I flew back to California the day after Christmas and celebrated New Years with a few married friends, with me bringing along a girl that I'd been dating on and off for a few months. I rang in 1985 with her like we were going to last, although we didn't even make it 'til dawn. No problem though, I continued to test the waters of the LA basin, looking for Ms. Right. And I found her time and again, if only for a night. Otherwise, I routinely worked my ass off, just to come home to a big empty house with a great ocean view and only the sound of crashing waves to keep me company at night.

# Chapter Twenty-Seven
## *Ms. Right*

Another year and change bit the dust and it was now the spring of 86. I had just landed at DFW Airport, looking to close on property for a subdivision project I was developing. Compared to pricey LA, land was comparably cheap in the Lone Star State and therefore hard to pass up, especially when Texas was about to go from a sleeping giant to one of the fastest growing, most dynamic places on the planet. But I didn't want to live there—just invest from afar.

I got a rental car and drove over to the Worth Title Company in what was scheduled to be a day trip. Besides not being a fan of hotel rooms, I was looking forward to sleeping in my own bed that night, before getting an early start on another ass-busting day in LA.

The receptionist met me after I walked through the office door of the title company. "Welcome to Texas, Mr. Bishop," she said with a pleasant southern twang, before pointing to a leather couch. "If you'd like to have a seat, I'll have our branch manager meet ya here in a moment."

I took a seat and killed time by thumbing through a local newspaper. No sooner had I turned a page when I heard heels clicking on a tile floor. They were moving with a purpose, getting louder with each step. I lowered the paper and saw a stunning blonde strutting toward me that nearly took my breath away.

"Good morning, Mr. Bishop," she said, greeting me with a confident smile that gave me goose bumps. She was in conservative attire, looking and sounding professional in every way. "My name's Leslie Henderson, and I'll be walking you through your closing documents today."

Dreamlike, I floated to my feet and locked in on her sparkling blue eyes and I began to melt. First impressions being what they were, I felt like I was standing in the presence of Ms. Right. She looked to be in her mid to late twenties and seemingly a perfect blend of mesmerizing beauty and sophisticated brains with all the bells and whistles a guy like me could possibly want. And best of all, there was no ring on her finger. Giddy, I was like a little schoolboy with a heart-pounding crush, and she was my teacher. In fact, she reminded me a lot of Ms. Willows back in the day.

"Hello… Mr. Bishop?"

"Oh, sorry. Just call me, Johnny."

"If you wouldn't mind coming back to my office, Johnny," she said, stoically, "I have the docs waiting for your signature."

Although suddenly parched, I was able to pull it together and make small talk during our walk down the hallway to her sunny corner office, which smelled of flowers and perfume.

"Would you like a soft drink before we get started?" she asked.

"Do you have bottled water?"

Leslie nodded affirmatively like she could deliver the goods, before steering me toward a chair that was part of a quartet at a small conference table. "If you'd like to have a seat," she said, "I'll be right back."

I steadied my nerves and primped as best I could while waiting for her return. In the world of business, you've got to be prepared for anything and everything, but I was not prepared for this encounter. No sir! I was thrust into a position of vulnerability and weakness for the first time in many a year, and it was thrilling!

Leslie soon returned with a stack of papers in one hand and a bottle of spring water in the other. She sat down next to me. Our knees touched and my heart skipped a beat. I tingled all over. She had my undivided attention when she went over the docs. I heard her every word, although my focus was on her. I noticed that her long blonde hair was thick and that it started to curl past her shoulders. And that her well-manicured nails were painted red like her full lips. She also had white teeth that shined brilliantly against skin that was tan and smooth. I did my best to try and humor her anyway I could, but she was all business. I signed where she told me to sign, then I handed her a cashier's check for two million dollars to seal the deal. We shook hands, then made more small talk on the way out to the main entrance, where she offered me her business card. "Here, Mr. Bishop… don't hesitate to contact me when you need title services in Texas again."

I pocketed her card like it was made of gold. "Thanks, Leslie. Any chance you're free for lunch?"

She smiled, politely. "I do appreciate the offer, but I'm booked solid through the afternoon."

"How about dinner?"

She was taken aback. "Don't you have a plane to catch?"

I shrugged. "I can always take a later flight."

Again, she smiled politely. "I'm sorry, but I have other plans this evening."

It's not that I believed her, but short of being rude, it seemed I had no place left to go, except out the door. "Okay then… I guess this is goodbye for now. Take care, Leslie."

"You too, Mr. Bishop. Have a safe flight home."

Halfway out, I stopped dead in my tracks. "Sure about dinner?"

Yet another polite smile ensued. "Maybe some other time, but right now I need to get back to work."

"Okay," I pouted. "I'll let you go."

Save for a copy of my closing documents, I left empty-handed, like I'd just walked out on Ms. Right—and it might be a year or two before I returned to Texas again. Surely, she'd be married by then!

With hours to kill, I returned to the airport with my tail between my legs and parked myself in a chair by my gate and people watched. I saw a myriad of faces come and go, although Leslie's was the one that stuck in my mind. I couldn't stop thinking about her. I held her business card up to my nose and smelled its flowery scent. I put the closing docs on my lap, but I wouldn't let go of her card. It was all I had left of her. Time and again I held it up to my nose to catch a whiff of the fading scent.

After hours of agonizing waiting, my flight left without me. I decided home could wait. I rushed over to a payphone and called her number, but she was gone for the day. I got another rental car and drove around for a couple of hours like a lovesick puppy, then got a hotel room near a highway. The passing cars sounded like crashing waves, which almost made me feel right at home—especially considering I was alone.

I thought of Leslie through every toss and turn of a seemingly endless night, before waking at the crack of dawn.  I got out of bed and took a shower and had no choice but to get back into the same clothes as the day before, which consisted of jeans and a maroon button-down that was now wrinkled. I put on my tan loafers and began pacing back and forth in my cramped hotel room until 9 am. I then took a seat on the edge of the bed with the phone in one hand and her business card shaking in the other and dialed her number. I got through the receptionist without a problem but hearing Leslie's voice come on the line was intimidating enough to make me go speechless.

"Hello, Mr. Bishop… are you there?"

Silent as the night, I needed a moment to gather myself. "Ah, yeah… I'm here," I finally managed. "Ah… just call me, Johnny."

"Is there something wrong with the docs, Johnny?"

"No… not that I'm aware of."

"Then what seems to be the problem?"

"No problem really." I trembled. "I was just wondering if you were free to meet me today?"

"You're still in town?"

"Ah, yeah… I missed my flight."

"Hmmm… is this a business meeting we're talking about here, or something else?"

I swallowed hard. It was the moment of truth and I wanted to tell it rather than start off on the wrong foot. "Something else."

The silence that followed was deafening. "That's very sweet of you, Johnny. I'm truly flattered, but I don't date customers. It's just not a good business practice to adopt."

I was shot down for sure, although I instinctively knew how to come back from the dead. "Then don't think of me as a customer," I suggested. "I'm just someone you met on the job and now we're talking about getting together for a harmless lunch."

She laughed. "You make it sound so simple."

"I promise not to bite."

After a brief pause, she sighed wistfully like she was about to step off the end of a diving board into shark infested waters. "There's a Red Lobster down the block from my office," she said with a hushed voice that made me quiver. "I'll meet you there at noon."

"Great! I'll see you then!" I hung up the phone and jumped for joy. I then checked my look in the mirror and headed for the Red Lobster. I was of course the first customer in the parking lot. I killed time by looking over the docs I blindly signed yesterday and was surprised to find a page missing. I checked again and the page was nowhere to be found in the thick stack.

Noon finally came around and my heart began pounding again when I saw Leslie, who was looking just as stunning as the day before. I got out of the car and wanted to plant a kiss on her painted lips, or at the very least give her tall, slender frame a big hug, but she offered me her delicate hand instead, which I gladly shook. "Hi, Leslie… glad you could make it."

"Johnny… I just want you to know right up front that I'm treating this as a business lunch."

"That's fine," I returned. "Because I noticed a page missing in the documents, so we still have some unfinished business."

She turned shamefully white. "Oh, I'm terribly sorry about that!"

"No problem… I just need to get a copy of it before returning to California."

"I can have it for you after lunch, if you like?"

"Works for me," I smiled, assuredly.

Matter resolved, we entered the restaurant and were seated at a tucked away table for two and Leslie was ready to order without even looking at the menu like she was in a hurry to leave.

"Do you come here often?" I asked, assuming she knew what was good at the eatery.

"I usually bring my lunch from home," she replied. "But sometimes we meet here after work for a drink."

"We?" I probed.

"Me and the girls," she divulged. "I don't have a boyfriend, if that's what you're wondering?"

I felt like fist-pumping the sky, although I limited the celebration to a slight grin. "I would think you had a bunch of guys lined up at your doorstep."

"I'm too picky for that."

"Yeah, it's good to be a little picky, but you don't want to get carried away and end up old and alone like me."

She smirked while giving me the once over. "You're old?"

"I'll be thirty-two this year."

She looked surprised. "Huh… I thought you were around my age."

"Oh, really? How…"

"—I'm twenty-six," she interjected. "But I still can't believe you're an old man."

"Must be the ocean air keeping me looking young."

She smiled, dreamily. "I love the beach."

I heard opportunity knocking. "You're welcomed to visit."

She snickered. "Let's see if we can make it through lunch first."

"Fair enough," I countered. "Because there's still a chance we might hate each other by the time dessert comes around."

"Speaking of which," she returned, "they have a great strawberry cheesecake here."

"I'll split one with you," I suggested, and she immediately nodded her approval. The conversation was engaging once the pretenses were finally out of the way. Barriers were broken over lobster and common ground was found with that mouthwatering cheesecake. Honestly, the food wasn't the greatest in the world, although being with Leslie made it the best meal I ever had. "So, what's for dinner?" I asked, while paying for lunch.

"How long are you planning on being in town?" she inquired.

I smiled, slyly. "As long as it takes."

She snorted. "Then you might need a change of clothes."

"Want to go shopping?"

"I've got to go back to work, Johnny."

"What about dinner?" I insisted more than asked.

After what seemed a lengthy delay, she reached into her purse and pulled out a pen and another business card and began writing on the back. "Here… this has my home number on it. I get off at five." She handed me the card. "But just so you know… I'm not about to get serious with a guy who is just passing through town. I want something meaningful and lasting in my life, or nothing at all."

"Fair enough."

She gave me a peck on the lips. "What about that missing page?"

"It's page number forty-five. I'll get it from you tonight."

I went back to my hotel room and made a few calls, letting people know that I hoped to be out of town for a few days—maybe longer, if I got lucky. I then found a mall and did a little shopping.

I gave Leslie a call shortly after five and she gave me the address to her place. I learned that she still lived at home with her parents and so I got directions and prepared to meet them, along with her younger brother and sister, who were both attending a local college.

I handed Leslie a dozen roses after she answered the front door of their nice suburban ranch style home. "Here, these are for you."

"Thank you, Johnny… that's very sweet of you!" she said, before attempting to hand me a piece of paper. "Sorry about the missing page."

I jokingly pulled away from the paper like it was a hot potato. "Maybe you should hold onto it for a few days."

"Are you really planning on staying that long?" she queried.

"Hopefully longer!"

We kissed; then ventured into the kitchen where I met the family. They were great, easygoing, down to earth people. Leslie and I decided to eat with them, rather than go out. We then played cards and watched TV, until almost midnight. I said my goodbyes to the family, then kissed Leslie a few times by the front door. "Thanks for inviting me over."

"It was my pleasure," she purred.

"Do you have to work tomorrow?"

She laughed. "Of course, Johnny. I can't just take off like you."

"Can I at least hang out in your office for part of the day?"

"No silly. Just call me after five and we'll get together then."

I did as told, and one date led to another and then another. The rest of the week became a blissful blur, until it was Sunday morning in bed. We'd just ordered room service while cuddling in my hotel room. I wanted the good times to last forever, but LA was calling. "So, how do you feel about California?" I asked with bated breath.

"I wouldn't mind visiting there from time to time, but my family and friends are all here in Texas."

I nodded, expecting her to say as much. "So… I guess it's a good thing you weren't planning on getting serious with me, because I've got to go back to LA tomorrow."

She sighed, forlornly. "I knew this day was coming and I promised myself not to cry."

I looked into her glassy blues and then moved in for a kiss, as I wiped a tear from her cheek. "Of course, I could always come right back after taking care of some business."

"Don't tease me, Johnny."

"I'm not." I nibbled on her ear. "In fact, I've given serious thought to managing the Texas project myself, rather than trying to run it remotely." I kissed her neck. "Besides, it makes more sense than to trust some local contractor that I've never worked with before."

"I suppose that does make sense," she agreed.

"But I'd still have to split time between here and LA."

"Works for me," she cooed.

"Well, if it works for you… than it most certainly works for me!"

Filled with joy, we made love until room service knocked on the door. We ate, then went at it again. Sex was never better! I kept waiting for the newness to wear off our relationship, but it never did. Every moment with Leslie was a moment well spent, even if we were doing nothing at all.

I was soon spending so much time in Texas that Leslie's friends became my friends and then six months later, her family became my family. It was a big Texas wedding held at the iconic Robert Carr Chapel in Ft. Worth. Our parents, siblings and close friends where all in attendance. Even some of my business associates and key employees where there on that cold winter day when I married Ms. Right. Luckily, there was enough big hair in the gathering to keep everyone warm.

After dancing most of the night away, Leslie and I left for Disney World the following morning and celebrated the first magical week of our honeymoon with Mickey and Minnie, before flying off to Maui for a week of fun in the sun. We then spent two weeks at my Malibu house before returning to Texas and moving into an apartment while our new house was being built in the subdivision I was developing.

We couldn't be happier. But that didn't stop me from worrying about that old fortuneteller now and then, because two of the three things she foretold had now come true—and the only thing missing was that she said something ominous would happen to me later in life.

# Chapter Twenty-Eight

*Déjà vu*

I still had plenty of business in LA that forced me to do a lot of going back and forth during the first few years of our marriage. When in LA, I shared my Malibu house with David, who was living there with his girlfriend, Sophie. My brother worked part-time for me when he wasn't busy surfing. Meanwhile, we were uncles again. Emily now had two girls with blonde curls—Meagan and now Muriel.

It was the fall of 89 when I finally fazed out of LA by selling off what was left of my company out there. I kept the Malibu house for a while, although it mostly sat empty after David and Sophie got married and bought a place of their own.

Leslie became pregnant, and Adam was born in 92. But we didn't stop there. Elizabeth was born two years later. They obviously weren't twins, although Adam and Elizabeth looked and acted like Leslie in many ways, which was a good thing. And speaking of twins, David and Sophie had them in 93. Boys named Cody and Glen.

Once an anal workaholic, I was down to being semi-retired by the time I hit forty. When I did work, I officed out of the house while others did the heavy lifting for me in the real world, because I was living in a champagne bubble. It got so ridiculous that I was only being bothered when there were major problems or big deals in the works. Otherwise, except for personal calls… my phone was silent.

Once we were out of the diaper stage, most evenings and weekends were spent doing things like coaching little league baseball for Adam, when not busy being a soccer mom for Elizabeth. We left Leslie in charge of the snacks and just about everything else for that matter. She pointed us in the right direction and kept the family focused and on track, which included going to church every Sunday morning, without fail.

We traveled as a family to many faraway places and did the tourist thing, when not venturing out into the unknown. We loved to ski, so we bought a place in Vail and vacationed there almost every winter and some summers too. Besides hitting the slopes, one of our favorite things to do in Colorado was to go on long horseback rides and camp out in the wilderness like the early settlers once did.

When we weren't in the mood to rough it, we also had a fancy boat that could sleep eight and a bunch of other really cool toys that we hardly ever used, although they were available for family and friends upon request.

That was my incredible life in a bubble. A champagne bubble! My only fear was that it would burst, because no matter how many years went by, it always seemed too good to be true. But rich or poor, tragedy eventually touches us all. Such was the case when Dad got sick. I was forty-five and crying like a baby after watching Brad Bishop take his final breath. He had succumbed to colon cancer at the age of seventy-two, and all the money in the world couldn't bring the teddy bear back for even one more day.

Another decade was about to pass like it had been shot out of a cannon. It was now Friday, May 22, 2009. I was scheduled to board a plane that morning from DFW Airport and head up to Jersey to help Emily and David move Mom into a nursing home, then spend the weekend getting her old house ready for the new owners before returning to Texas.

Leslie stopped the car at the departure terminal. "Have a good flight," she said. "Don't forget to call me tonight."

I gave her a hug and kiss, then grabbed my carry-on suitcase from the backseat. "See ya Sunday night. Love you!"

"Love you, too!" She blew me a kiss and drove off.

After a bumpy flight, I picked up a rental car at JFK Airport and off I went. A half-hour later I stopped in front of Mom's house and was quick to notice a red FOR SALE sign in the front yard. I knew one was supposed to be there, except it was like I'd seen that exact same sign before. The SOLD sticker at the bottom marked the end of an era that brought a tear to my eye.

I got out of the car and saw a swarm of kids running around and it brought back fond memories of my glory days with Rudy, Mitch and Billy. I had stayed in touch with those guys for a number of years after moving to California, although sadly, Rudy eventually disappeared and the last time I saw Mitch and Billy was many years ago at a class reunion.

Emily greeted me at the front door with a concerned look on her face. "Johnny... I'm so glad you're here!"

"Is something wrong with Mom?"

"No. But there was a stranger in her house!"

I stopped dead in my tracks. "What?"

Emily waved me into the living room and pointed to the empty couch against the far wall. "He's gone now, but he was sitting right there next to Mom when I walked in this morning."

"Where's Mom now?"

"She's upstairs in my old room putting back pictures that were scattered on the floor."

I rushed up the stairs and into Emily's old bedroom where I found Mom on her hands and knees looking at her old scrapbook. "Hi, Mom. Are you all right? I heard there was a stranger in the house."

She pointed to an old picture of me and smiled dreamily. "I was admiring this old photo of you from your teenage years, and then it dawned on me that you were the boy who was here this morning."

I shook my clueless head. "Sorry?"

She leaned forward, as if to keep it our little secret. "It all started when you visited me from the past last night."

I stifled a laugh. "Is that so?"

She frowned. "I know it sounds crazy, but I've never been clearer about anything in my life!" She reached into her pink housecoat pocket and pulled out a shiny coin. "You gave me this before leaving this morning when you were a teenager... and now I'm giving it back to you this afternoon, now that you're back to being an adult again."

It saddened me to hear what I thought was surreal gibberish coming from my Mother's mouth. I took the coin from her hand and saw that it was minted in 1776 and it looked brand new. "This could be worth thousands. And you're saying the kid just gave it to you?"

"You gave it to me, Johnny. It was you!"

I wanted to roll my eyes, but she was so sure of herself that I didn't want to insult her intelligence, or what remained of it. "Thanks, Mom," I said, posting a warm smile. I put the coin in my pants pocket and was ready to get back to reality. "Is David in town yet?"

Mom nodded affirmatively. "He and the boys flew in last night. In fact," she chuckled, "I thought you were either Cody or Glen when I first saw you last night, until I saw this teenage picture of you this afternoon and then everything made perfect sense to me."

Standing at the doorway, Emily had been quietly observing us, until now. "David's not coming, Johnny."

Surprised, I turned to face her. "What?"

"He called my cell last night to inform me that he couldn't get out of a prior engagement." She smirked. "My guess is he decided to go surfing for the weekend instead."

I groaned. "Bummer! I was counting on his help."

Emily rolled her eyes. "Huh! You of all people should know better than to count on David for anything."

"Emily," Mom snapped, "now you stop talking about your twin brother like that. He's a good boy!"

"You always did like David the best," Emily clamored. "You never stopped babying him and that's why he turned out like this."

"Let's not argue," I insisted. "We've got too much work to do."

We began by boxing up the pictures; then Mom went to her bedroom to get dressed for the day, while Emily and I hit the kitchen to finish packing up dishes. "As you can see," she said, "Mom has a loose grip on reality these days."

"Maybe so, but that coin she gave me is real. I'm just glad we're moving her out of harm's way today."

She gave me a hug. "Thanks to you, we can afford to send her to a place that offers special care. You'll like the facility when you see it. I wouldn't mind living there myself one day."

"Why… are you planning on getting Alzheimer's too?"

"Not if I can help it," she replied. "But I'm a lot like Mom."

"Except that you were always a little heavier," I ribbed.

"Asshole!" She kicked me in the shin. "Just for that you get to clean out the garage tomorrow. It's loaded to the gills with crap."

"Ouch! Aren't you gonna help?"

"Not after that remark."

"Come on, Emily… I was just kidding."

"Take Mark and I out for dinner tonight," she countered, "and I'll get him to help you with the garage tomorrow."

"Deal!" I declared. "What about Meagan and Muriel?"

"Both girls had plans tonight, but they'll stop by tomorrow and give us a hand."

"Sounds good."

Emily and I finished in the kitchen and packed Mom's suitcase and we met Mark at Mom's favorite Chinese restaurant. She enjoyed her meal out and then we moved her to the nursing home where she immediately made friends and was soon glad that she had made the move. We left her in good spirits, which was a relief for all concerned. She was in a safe spot and Emily was close enough to look in on her a few times a week.

I got in my rental car and followed Emily back to her house, which was only two towns over from where we had grown up. We hung out for a while in the living room; then she set me up on the basement couch before going back upstairs. I took a seat and called Leslie just before midnight.

"Hey, babe… what's going on?"

"Not much, honey. How was your flight?"

"Bumpy as can be. How are the kids?"

"Adam's still out on a date and Liz is having a sleepover upstairs in the game room," she replied. "How did your mother take the move?"

"Better than expected. She was in a heated game of spades when we left her."

"Oh, so she's already met people?"

"Yeah. It's all good, except that there was some teenager camping out in her house last night."

Leslie gasped. "What?"

"Mom probably left the front door unlocked again and the guy just walked in and made himself at home."

"Oh, my."

"But the strange thing is, he gave her a valuable coin before leaving this morning." I eyed the shiny relic as it sat on the end table.

"Gosh, Johnny… any idea who it was?"

"Mom seems to think it was me coming back to visit her from my teenage past." We groaned in unison. "Emily saw the kid, but her mind's gone blank on his face. I think she went into shock when all that happened, because she's confused on most of the details now."

"Well, it's a good thing your mother's out of that house."

"Yeah… that's what I'm thinking."

She sighed. "Oh well… how's the rest of the family?"

"Fine, except that David can't make it out here, so it's going to be a tougher weekend than I thought."

"Oh, so you could've used Adam's help after all?"

"I suppose. You were right again, as usual."

"I can always put him on a plane in the morning, if you like?"

"No, that's okay. Mark's going to help." My eyelids suddenly grew heavy. "Whoa… it's like I can't keep my eyes open anymore."

"Then I'll let you go so you can get some sleep."

"Wait, honey… don't say goodbye just yet."

"What?" she quizzed. "Is something wrong?"

"Ah, no… I guess not. But it's been a really strange day and I could sure use some cuddle time with you right now."

"Sorry, honey… you'll have to wait until Sunday night for that."

"I don't think I can make it that long."

"Are you sure you're okay? You don't sound right."

"Now that you mention it, my head's spinning."

"You just need a good night's sleep." She mothered. "Get some rest and call me when you get a chance tomorrow. Love ya!"

"Love you, too!" I put the phone down on the table next to the coin and shut the light. As expected, the room turned pitch black. But then I saw the coin was aglow in green. I blinked to clear my eyes and saw even more green. I then smelled something sweet that reminded me of honeysuckle, and I heard hissing that sounded like snakes. I wanted to turn the light back on to see what was happening, but I was helpless to do anything other than fall into a deep, immobilizing sleep. Everything faded to black and stayed that way for the longest time, until I was surprised by an enormous wave of green. It was light and airy like cotton candy, and sickeningly sweet.

When the green faded this time, I found myself sitting at a desk in the middle of an empty classroom. Everything looked so real, except that I assumed I was dreaming when I noticed a ghostly old man standing ten feet in front of me. He was dressed in morbid black and could've easily passed for a mortician, except that he already looked dead, himself.

"Good to see you again." The ghostly looking man surprised me with a hearty voice that suggested he was doing far better than he looked. "The last time we were together you were a pimple-faced kid," he snickered. "At least now we can talk intelligently as adults."

Short of waking up, I decided to amuse myself. "So, you're thinking we've met before?"

"Do you believe in God, Mr. Bishop?"

"I go to church every Sunday."

"Yes, but do you believe in God?"

"I've had an incredibly blessed life, so yes… I believe in God."

"Are you sure God's the one who's been blessing you?"

"Of course. Who else could it be?"

He grinned, smugly. "The name's Nathaniel Fitzhugh, and yes, Mr. Bishop… we've met before. In fact… we go back centuries!"

I had to laugh. "We do?"

"Being of the spirit world, I'm left with little choice but to live vicariously through those recruited for my reform school, and you are no exception. In fact, you impressed me so much by surviving your night in hell that I decided to throw you a bone!"

The laughter continued. "You did?"

"You were down to one life when I made easy your escape from the Kilborne Academy, rather than see you spend all eternity trapped in my black hallway like all those who had failed before you."

"Is that so?" I offered, incredulously.

"But freedom comes at a hefty price. You must now return to Kilborne and complete your sentence, plus serve additional time as penalty for leaving my establishment prematurely. You will be there for four thousand days learning wonderous things about the future, although it will seem like only minutes have passed before you are free to go. But then you'll return to the world and find yourself a forgotten man who is penniless and without family or friends to count on, and yet the ultimate challenge will still await you with the future of mankind hanging in the balance!"

"Wow… sounds like quite a fairytale you're spinning."

"More like a nightmare," he giggled all giddy-like. "Marty anxiously awaits your return to Kilborne, so he can get on with his life. Meanwhile, he remains stuck on sweet sixteen at the academy and he's seething mad that you've been living the good life all this time, while he has remained imprisoned for foolishly aiding in your great escape over my stone wall where I had your clueless parents waiting to return you back to civilization like you had never left."

"Marty?" I questioned, mindlessly. "Who's that?"

"Otherwise soon to be referred to as the anti-Christ, Marty has made excellent use of his time by acquiring the Wisdom of the Ages during his forty-year incarceration. Soon enough, unimagined evil combined with off-the-charts intelligence will be unleashed on an unsuspecting world to where even Hitler will seem like a hapless choirboy in comparison to the damage Marty will inflict!"

"If you're trying to scare me, it's not working."

"Have you read the bible, Mr. Bishop?"

"From cover to cover."

"Then you should know the end is coming," he preached. "I'm just doing my part to try and move things along at an accelerated pace to help free the planet of the corrupt species God has put on this earth. When the dust has finally settled on the flawed human race, I will attempt to start the world anew with my own version of Adam and Eve, with me serving as the one and only god, and the Kilborne Academy serving as heaven for future generations to come!"

"Still sounds like a fairytale to me."

"A fairytale that will not have a happy ending for those still alive when the trumpet blows," he sneered. "Really though... the way I see the future playing out here on earth... the only question that will remain is who amongst the living will be strong enough to serve as Adam, and who will be pretty enough to be my Eve?" he twittered. "I will then create the perfect world by repopulating the planet with a race of people that will be the absolute best mankind has to offer!"

"Look... I've had about enough of this..."

"While the Green Fog has kept you clueless of anything to do with the Kilborne Academy since your great escape long ago, it will soon restore your mind of the six harrowing days you spent there during your troubled teens. But I will completely rid you of any memory of our rather unsettling conversation here tonight so that you can have sweet dreams, until we meet again."

Before I could say another word, the arrogant ghost vanished into thin air and all that I could recall of our brief encounter was *sweet dreams*. The classroom then vanished, and I found myself sitting on a chair that was parked right next to the window in the bedroom I grew up sharing with brother, David. My *sweet dream* seemed more like a nightmare when I realized my body was frozen in place so that I couldn't so much as blink or turn my head or even move my lips to cry out for *help!*

# Chapter Twenty-Nine
*Bittersweet*

Helpless to do much else, I gazed dreamily out my once-upon-a-time bedroom window as a storm approached. The blue sky turned a dreary gunmetal gray and brought darkness to the empty street below. The bedroom was now dark enough to where a floor lamp standing in the left corner of the room lit up that side of my face. My image reflected off the glass in the window in front of me and strangely, I saw youth reflecting back. I appeared to be in my teens from the looks of things. Although in the shadows, the other half of my face remained the fifty-six-year old I saw when I looked in the mirror every day.

Compared to my younger counterpart, I'd aged like fine wine, I vainly concluded in a moment of levity. I even still had claim to most of my dark hair. And besides being pimple-free, there was hardly a wrinkle on my side of the face. But as far as differences went, it was like the tale of two cities when it came to expression. The mature man I had become had a look of deep concern, while the punk kid I once was had a clueless smirk that I wanted to wipe off my face, if only I could move.

A thunderclap lit the darkness. I looked past my image in the glass and saw green water balloons falling from the clouds. They glowed in the dark and splattered green upon contact with the ground. The green filled the street and it became a flowing river that glowed. I saw a fat kid in a striped shirt that reminded me of a bumblebee. He was splashing along down the middle of the road on a bike that reflected the glowing green and lit up his face. And then it dawned on me. It was Tom Ramsey. The kid Rudy and I had injured with a water balloon long ago. I saw my mother go swimming by next. She looked young and beautiful compared to the woman I had accompanied to the nursing home earlier in the evening. Next came Dad. The teddy bear was alive and well and even looked grizzly again! Tears of joy filled my eyes that I was helpless to wipe away.

Next came Emily and David. Although instead of being middle-aged adults, they were back to being the little busybody twins they once were.

I continued my strange trip down memory lane when other family members and friends swam by, followed by Leslie and our two kids. I then saw a couple of guys in a rowboat. One looked like a Boy Scout, the other a grungy rock 'n' roller. I didn't recognize either of them, but the rock 'n' roller looked pissed and angrily flipped me off as the two went rowing by. Then came a beautiful young woman doing the backstroke in a flowing white dress. She waved up at me and I tried to wave back, except I couldn't move an inch, save for the surprising erection that had suddenly and without warning sprouted up inside my pants. My heart even went pitter-patter at the sight of the unfamiliar girl with the long brown hair. Embarrassing as it was, my bizarre erection quickly went away when she disappeared down the road and then the water was empty.

I heard another thunderclap and there was a flash of white light followed by a tidal wave of green heading my way. I wanted to close my eyes and duck, although I had no choice but to watch the enormous green wave break through the window and flood the room. Besides being frozen in place, I was apparently anchored to a chair that was anchored to the floor. I was thinking I was about to drown, but then the water began to bubble like club soda. When the bubbles burst, my lungs were filled with oxygen that was honeysuckle sweet. Energized, I struggled to free myself from the chair only to wake up on my sister's basement floor after falling off her couch. "Wow! What a nightmare!" I muttered to myself.

I crawled around in the darkness, until I found the lamp. I turned the knob and the light shined down on the end table that held my cell phone. I picked it up and saw that it was 6 AM. I put it back down on the table and of course, there was the coin that had turned green on me during the night. Although hesitant at first, curiosity got the better of me and I picked up the silver relic and examined it front and back. Besides being cold to the touch, I found nothing out of the ordinary with the coin, so I returned it to the table.

Desperate for caffeine, I threw on some clothes and headed upstairs, where all was deathly quiet. Sister and hubby were still sound asleep. Rather than chance waking them by jostling around in the kitchen, I grabbed the keys to my rental and headed for the nearest Starbucks. I knew where it was; I'd been there before. I drove with a heavy foot, but instead of making a right into town toward the coffee shop, I inexplicably turned left and headed north on the turnpike—and that is where my incredibly bizarre story began eleven years ago—when I became a helpless passenger stuck behind the wheel of a runaway car.

"Turn around," I wailed. "Turn around!"

I was shocked to find myself like a puppet on a string. Against my will and better judgement, I put the pedal to the metal and continued to motor along—destination unknown—until my memory of all things Kilborne returned in a horrific flood on the way back to the reform school from hell, where teenage Marty proceeded to steal my wallet and the keys to my rental car while I sat frozen in place.

But that was yesterday's news and I'm now back in the present with nothing left to live for because I dread going through life without the love and support of my remarried wife and adult kids. And I dread having to start over from scratch at my advanced age and try and acclimate to a world that has already passed me by. A world where I was once a rich man with a thriving business and a mansion or two to live in, but now I have less than five hundred dollars to my name with no prospects for employment and no place to call home. It then occurs to me that I don't even have an old clunker to drive around anymore. In fact, things are so bad that not even Marty wants me working for him now that he has grown up to become a man of wealth and distinction with a company that is taking the world by storm. And so, I will soon begin a brave new day with my slate wiped completely clean and no earthly idea as to what I'm to do with the rest of my strange life. Heck, I guess that old fortuneteller was right. Something ominous happened after all. But she didn't warn me that the entire planet would be at risk!

I toss and turn, until an alarm jolts me out of my slumber, and I realize I'm at the Hotel California. The one in Beverly Hills! I don't know how I got here, but the accommodations are like paradise compared to the seedy hotel I checked into last night in Texas. Instead of roaches, there are mirrors on the ceiling and my empty bottle of booze has been replaced with pink champagne on ice. In search of answers, I go down to the front desk only to be startled when everyone in the lobby stops what they're doing to point my way, and mumble, "Hey, you're the battery man!"

I'm suddenly mobbed by masked marauders, having to sign one autograph after another, until the doorman adds to my surprise by handing me the keys to a Mercedes Benz. I gladly hop into the shiny black beast and the car drives off like it knows where it's going, making a precision left here and a methodical right there. I couldn't have driven the sophisticated machine any better had my hands remained busy on the steering wheel, instead of resting in my lap.

The surprise continues when a phone on the dashboard notifies me that Marty is waiting to greet me at his place of business with more good news. Apparently, he took matters into his own hands last night and paid my sister a handsome sum of money to remove her post and have her and her hubby forget they ever heard of Kilborne, thus paving the way for me to begin my new career at Marty Enterprises.

Relieved, I want to share the good news with Leslie and the kids, except that I dare not call until I get my story straight. Yes, I still have more questions than answers for a guy who's supposed to be wise beyond his years—though I do know more today than yesterday. And I assume I'll know more tomorrow and perhaps even much more the day after that now that I learn about the future while I sleep. I guess it could get scary after a while, because maybe ignorance really is bliss at some point—a point I'm sure to surpass now that I have a heart of gold that's designed to last an eternity.

The car stops in front of the iconic Capital Records building and I'm thinking Marty wasn't kidding about us making beautiful music together. But even Led Zeppelin can't make this the happy ending I was hoping for, although, it's seemingly a positive start for a man who was dead to the world. And to think… I wanted to drink myself into oblivion last night and never see the light of another day.

# Chapter Thirty

*Something Big this way Cometh*

I've found that time flies even when you're in the real world. At least it has for me. Twelve incredible months have now passed, and I've since moved into a cozy villa perched high in the Hollywood Hills with a panoramic view of the City of Angels that's to die for.

But I know life can be lonely in LA, although I've found making friends to be easy now that I'm famous. I've even reconnected with friends from the past, and my adult kids are already coming to visit me for the third time! Now if only I could win Leslie back from her new husband, everything would almost be normal again—except thanks to the stock options I was given by Marty, I'm already many times richer than the sum of all the years I spent working for myself put together.

So, instead of selling real estate for a living, I'm often jetting around the globe in that fancy 737 to promote the great battery I've been credited with inventing. And I see how it continues to improve life everywhere I go, because where there was once darkness, there is now light! *But with progress comes the inevitable growing pains*. At least that's what I tell myself when I see what's becoming of the oil industry. Our amazing batteries have even eclipsed the sun, as solar power has already become a thing of the past.

I try and remain politically correct through all the drastic changes caused by this new technology, because politics and business go hand and hand at the level I'm now operating at. I'm even wined and dined by the elite, because knowledge is power, and they want to be in on the next great invention before it becomes *Breaking News.*

Speaking of breaking news, it was just another fabulous day at the office, until I saw Marty without his blue contacts in. I looked past the pleasant smile on his handsome face and saw nothing but evil brewing in his brown eyes and my old soul was quick to warn me that there was trouble on the horizon. "Something big this way cometh!" is what it told me. "And only you can save the world!"

# Epilogue

Mr. Fitzhugh continues to manipulate our ever-changing planet in ways we cannot imagine. Our only real hope is that Johnny has what it takes to defeat Marty and then take on the evil spirit he unwittingly created, or we're all doomed to a fate worse than death.

# About the Author

Robert Bernardo is a retired businessman who has been writing fiction for over a decade. What started as a hobby, has blossomed into something much more. Mr. Bernardo is currently working on the sequel to *Wisdom of the Ages* and plans to have *Something Big* in the future. Inquiries can be made by contacting us at robertbernardobooks@gmail.com.